THE DAM KEEPER

A Jayne Robinson Thriller: Book 5

ANDREW TURPIN

The Write Direction Publishing

First published in the UK in 2023 by The Write Direction Publishing, St. Albans, UK.

The Dam Keeper paperback edition

ISBN: 978-1-78875-047-9

 Created with Vellum

WELCOME TO THE JAYNE ROBINSON SERIES!

Thank you for purchasing *The Dam Keeper* — I hope you enjoy it!

This is the fifth in the series of thrillers that feature **Jayne Robinson**. Jayne is formerly of the British Secret Intelligence Service (the SIS, or as it is often known, MI6) and is now an independent investigator. She has strong connections with both the CIA and MI6 and finds herself conducting deniable operations on behalf of both services.

The **Jayne Robinson** thriller series is my second series and so far comprises the following:

My first series, in which Jayne also appears regularly, features **Joe Johnson**, a former CIA officer and war crimes investigator. The Joe Johnson books so far comprise:

If you enjoy this book, I would like to keep in touch. This is not always easy, as I usually only publish a couple of books a year and there are many authors and books out there. So the best way is for you to be on my Readers Group email list. I can then send you updates on the next book, plus occasional special offers.

If you would like to join my Readers Group and receive the email updates, I will send you, **FREE** of charge, the ebook version of *The Afghan*. It forms a prequel to this series and to the Joe Johnson series and normally sells at $4.99/£3.99 (paperback $11.99/£9.99).

The Afghan is set in 1988 when Jayne was still with MI6 and Joe Johnson was still a CIA officer. Most of the action takes place in Pakistan, Afghanistan and Washington, DC.

To sign up for the Readers Group and get your free copy of *The Afghan*, go to the following web page:

https://bookhip.com/RJGFPAW

If you only like paperbacks, you can still just sign up for the email list at the above link to get news of my books and forthcoming new releases. A paperback version of *The Afghan* and all my books is for sale at my website, where you will find large discounts on bundles of my books. I can currently ship to the US and UK:

https://www.andrewturpin.com/shop/

Or if you live outside the US and UK you can buy them at Amazon.

Andrew Turpin, St. Albans, UK.

DEDICATION

To Jacqui, 1961-2022

"When I am dead, bury me
In my beloved Ukraine,
My tomb upon a grave mound high
Amid the spreading plain,
So that the fields, the boundless steppes,
The Dnipro's plunging shore
My eyes could see, my ears could hear
The mighty river roar.

When from Ukraine the Dnipro bears
Into the deep blue sea
The blood of foes, then will I leave
These hills and fertile fields —
I'll leave them all and fly away
To the abode of God,
And then I'll pray. But till that day
I nothing know of God.

Oh bury me, then rise ye up
And break your heavy chains
And water with the tyrants' blood
The freedom you have gained.
And in the great new family,
The family of the free,
With softly spoken, kindly word
Remember also me."

– "*My Testament,*" by **Taras Shevchenko**, one of Ukraine's
most famous poets.

PROLOGUE

Friday, June 9, 2017
Frankfurt

Aidan felt the woman's fingers lightly and briefly, but quite deliberately, graze the side of his thigh as they perched on their stools. In front of them, the bartender scooped peanut butter into the steel cocktail mixer on the wooden counter.

He glanced sideways at her, but her midnight-black eyes appeared to be focused entirely on the theatrical performance going on in front of them. This bartender, Heinrich, knew how to put on a show. Aidan had seen him in action a few times over recent months.

Next, Heinrich poured a generous volume of re-distilled bourbon into the mixer, followed by sugar, *blanco* tequila, pandan syrup, brine, and crystal-clear, clarified lime juice. He gave a running commentary on how the drink was put together.

This was the Himmel Bar's specialty, the King Clear cocktail, and Aidan knew that his companion, Irina, was going to love it.

Eventually, Heinrich poured the clear liquid into two glasses, placed a small decorative white flower in each, and pushed them over the bar toward Aidan with a wink. "This will make you the clear king of Frankfurt tonight," he quipped, inclining his head slightly toward Irina.

It was the same joke he had used last time, but Aidan laughed nonetheless.

Aidan handed one of the glasses to Irina, paid for the drinks, and indicated toward one of the vacant wooden tables at the rear of the subtly lit bar. "Shall we sit over there?"

She nodded, her curly, dark hair bobbing over her shoulders, and touched him lightly on the elbow as they made their way to the table, where they sat opposite each other. A single candle in a glass jar stood on the table, its flame flickering.

"*Prost!*" Irina said as she raised her glass, her tongue flicking lightly over her bottom lip. "Cheers, Aidan. That's what you Americans say, isn't it?"

Aidan grinned. "*Ja* . . . we can stick to the German. *Prost!*" He knew he wasn't going to screw up this date, their second, no matter what. It was a safe bet, as his friends back home in San Francisco would say.

Irina clinked her glass gently against his and they both took a sip of their drinks. The King Clear really had a unique taste. It was not a cocktail he had ever come across before.

He felt her knee brush against his beneath the table, then move away again. Her sheer, black lacy top showed off the shape of her breasts, a clear hint of a nipple pushing through.

Irina took another sip of the King Clear and looked up at him from beneath thick eyelashes. "Have you had a busy week?" she asked in her accented but fluent English. "You must be ready for a rest?" She gave a grin, her eyes flicking over his face.

Although she spoke fluent German and English, her accent was noticeably tinged with something else. It had made sense when she told Aidan, who spoke fluent Russian, that she was born in Georgia and had moved to Berlin with her parents at fourteen, around the time Georgia separated from the Soviet Union in 1991.

She was correct about the busy week, Aidan thought to himself. A series of fourteen-hour days during the past week had taken their toll. He hadn't told her he had spent the past six years working for the United States Army Corps of Engineers—the USACE—at their base in Wiesbaden, a forty-minute taxi ride away on the west side of Frankfurt. All he had said on their previous date was that he was a civil engineer for an American business. Neither had he told her his last name, and she hadn't asked.

"I need a drink, put it that way," he said as he raised his glass. "Busy is an understatement. But being here with you is helping."

She smiled. "What's been happening at work that's made it so busy?"

Aidan hesitated. "Oh, just a lot going on. It's far from easy. I have a lot of contractors to manage. They all want too much, give too little, and it's like herding cats. They all ask for more money, but don't follow instructions."

He glanced to his right at the wooden bar with its shelves full of spirits bottles, books, and framed prints. A scantily clad woman was perched on a barstool, talking to Heinrich as he mixed another cocktail. The Himmel Bar, a classic speakeasy-style place, was hidden in a basement behind an anonymous black door right in Elbestrasse in the center of Frankfurt's red-light district, near the main railway station.

The tables were rapidly filling up as the usual clientele of office workers, tourists, and a few seedier types filed down the wooden stairs. Aidan loved the general earthiness of the place.

He had been here alone several times over recent months, usually on a Friday or Saturday night when he needed to unwind. He hadn't sought out colleagues to go with him, although he had mentioned to one of them where he was going. It was easier to connect with women when he was by himself.

Despite conversations with several women, Aidan hadn't clicked with anyone until a month ago, when he found Irina on the barstool next to him and they began to talk. They had swapped phone numbers and agreed to meet again two weeks later, followed by another date tonight.

She drained her glass. "Another drink?" she asked. "I'll buy this time."

"Are you sure?" Aidan asked.

She nodded. "Of course."

"Okay, great. A bourbon on the rocks this time, please."

"Double?" She smiled.

Aidan nodded. "I guess so."

He watched as Irina walked to the bar. She was almost as tall as his five feet ten, and her slim legs and shaped bottom were neatly encased in stretch jeans. He guessed she was maybe five or six years older than his thirty-three, although he didn't like to ask. She had told him on their previous date that she worked as a personal assistant to the managing director of an Anglo-German telecoms equipment business in Frankfurt. She had gotten the job because she was bilingual and spent much of her day speaking to the London office.

Half an hour later, after a conversation that covered the latest films, their favorite wines, and Frankfurt's pizza restaurants, Aidan was feeling pleasantly drunk. What's more, Irina was pressing her calf against his beneath the table. Her perfume, while subtle, was quite heady, and he could feel himself beginning to stir.

She finished her drink, propped up her elbows on the table, and eyed him steadily. "Would you like to come back to my apartment for a nightcap?"

"How far is it?"

"A five-minute walk. It overlooks the river."

It had been two years since Aidan had parted company with his long-term girlfriend, a financial controller with the USACE, who had returned home to Miami. He had not had another relationship since, which was why he had begun venturing into Frankfurt.

He looked at her and a flash of trepidation ran through him.

Would I do this at home?

He knew the answer to that. No. Largely because of his family, and his father in particular, Aidan had spent his whole life avoiding any wild behavior that might bring unwelcome attention.

While his friends in college went out and partied every weekend, drinking in dorms and sneaking into bars before they were legally allowed, Aidan tended to choose low-key options that couldn't get him into trouble. Even when he turned twenty-one and started going to bars, he never got wasted or even that drunk. He was always too worried about what might happen.

He rarely lost his temper or behaved badly, not even in the raucous crowds at football games played by his favorite team, the San Francisco 49ers. He always chose long-term relationships with women over one-night stands.

But Aidan was a long way from home now. And Irina had become impossible to resist.

He nodded. "That would be great, actually. Let's go." He

stood, put on his jacket, and then held hers out so she could do the same. Then he followed her up the stairs to the exit.

They made their way past a couple of homeless people who were begging outside the hotel next door and dodged a couple of hustlers who were trying to usher tourists into the strip club across the street.

The apartment turned out to be a smart, minimally furnished place on the top floor of a modern three-story building that did indeed overlook the broad expanse of the Main River, which ran through the center of Frankfurt. It was right opposite the Holbeinsteg Bridge.

As soon as Irina closed the door, she removed her jacket, walked up to him, put her arms around his neck, and began to kiss him. Her warm tongue tasted good. Irresistibly good, in fact.

He tried to pull her closer, but she leaned back, unzipped his jacket and removed it, then began to unbutton his shirt. Her hands felt soft and warm across his chest and belly.

"Come this way," she said, taking him by the hand.

Her grip was surprisingly firm, and he didn't resist. She led him through the living room to a bedroom that contained an enormous bed with a plasma TV screen facing it on the wall. A row of mirrored fitted wardrobes ran down one side of the room, and a door led to an ensuite bathroom. Subtle lighting threw a pattern of illumination up and down the walls and across the ceiling. Irina clicked the bedroom door shut and walked up to Aidan, removing her top as she approached him.

Aidan pushed Irina slowly backward onto the bed and reached beneath her to unclip her black bra.

Very soon, they were making love.

After a few breathless minutes, Irina murmured into his ear. "Do you know what really turns me on?"

"Tell me."

So she did, kissing him at intervals as she whispered.

"Can I do it?" she asked.

He hesitated for a second, wondering where this was going, but decided to try to keep her happy. "Okay, sure. If it turns you on, it'll turn me on too."

She smiled. "It certainly will."

He rolled off her, and she reached over and opened a drawer in a bedside table, then removed two sets of handcuffs and some Velcro restraints. She also put on a black mask, of the type used at masked balls, which hid most of her features.

"A mask?" Aidan asked. "Why?"

"I like the feeling of mystery. Is that okay? Such a turn-on for me."

Aidan exhaled. This was getting more than a little weird, and he wasn't sure how to respond.

"All right, if you must," he said eventually.

Irina fastened Aidan's wrists to the top of the bed with the handcuffs and his ankles to the bottom with the Velcro so he couldn't move. She threw her thigh across his hips, climbed astride him, lowered her head, and kissed him deeply and slowly.

Then she began to make love to him again, this time with her doing all the work.

That was when it happened.

Through the brain haze caused by the pleasure chemicals that were rushing through him, not to mention the alcohol, Aidan gradually became aware that the lighting in the room had brightened a little and a humming noise was coming from somewhere. Then came a series of flashes, accompanied by faint clicks. Several spotlights in the ceiling flicked on.

Aidan tried to raise himself up but realized he couldn't move because of the restraints.

"What the hell . . .?" he began. "What's going on?" A shiver of alarm ran through him, and he sobered up instantly.

Irina continued to ride him, picking up the pace. "There's

nothing to worry about. You're on camera, that's all. I like to watch videos of me in action. It's a turn-on. Relax and enjoy it."

"*On camera?* What the hell do you mean, on camera?"

Aidan's mind raced.

Oh shit. She's filming us.

This can't be happening.

He'll never speak to me again.

Aidan again tried to sit up but failed to lift himself more than an inch or two, and Irina pushed him back down.

She remained on top of him for several more seconds, then eventually climbed off, picked up a key, and undid the handcuffs. Aidan immediately reached down and ripped off the restraints around his ankles.

He then leaped off the bed and grabbed his clothes, a sense of rage building inside him.

"This is unbelievable," Aidan said. "You've got no right to film and—"

But he was interrupted by the sound of the door clicking open. Aidan turned to see a heavily built bald man standing in the doorway, dressed in a black leather jacket.

"You can turn the cameras off now," Irina said to the man in a level, unemotional voice.

"You bitch. Who the hell are you?" Aidan hissed.

"You don't need to know who I am," Irina said, her manner businesslike. "But we know exactly who you are. And you've made a mistake. You work for us now."

PART ONE

CHAPTER ONE

Friday, June 9, 2017
   Langley, Virginia

The first thing that Jayne Robinson noticed as she filed into the seventh-floor office at the Central Intelligence Agency's head offices was that its occupant, Vic Walter, had changed his row of clocks.

Vic, the CIA's deputy director of operations, previously had five digital clocks with red-and-green LED displays on his wall for different key time zones across the world. He had inherited them from a previous occupant of the room, which sat on the top floor of the old Original Headquarters Building.

The five digital ones were gone, replaced by six old-style analog clocks mounted on elegant dark wooden bases. The label beneath the additional clock read KYIV.

The wooden clock bases matched Vic's wooden desk, which he had also recently acquired to replace his previous steel-and-glass model.

Vic noticed Jayne looking at the clocks. "Do you like them?"

"Yes, but why the need for Kyiv?" Jayne asked. "The time zone is the same as Moscow." Indeed, the Moscow clock was right next to it.

"It's symbolic," Vic said. "I don't need to tell you, of all people, that we'll be focused on Ukraine for years, given what Putin's planning there. I want a clock that underlines to everyone who comes in here what our priority is."

Vic glanced at Jayne, then at the other people in the room. "Take a seat. We have an operation to discuss," he said. He pointed to the meeting table near the window, which overlooked the CIA's extensive campus at Langley, a nine-mile drive northwest of Washington, DC.

He took a chair at the head of the table and waited for the others to sit down.

Jayne sat to Vic's left together with Neal Scales, Vic's number two in the Directorate of Operations, and the CIA's Kyiv chief of station, Abram Malevich, who had flown into Washington the previous evening.

To Vic's right sat two outside visitors, Lieutenant General Frank Merriden, who was commander of the US Army Corps of Engineers, and one of his senior subordinates, Colonel Anthony Richter, who was commander of the USACE's Europe District, based at Wiesbaden, near Frankfurt in Germany.

Merriden, who carried the title Chief of Engineers, was based at the Department of Defense's Pentagon headquarters building. He was an imposing character with a mane of silver hair, whom Jayne had never met in person before, although she had heard the occasional story about him from Vic and others.

The meeting had been convened at short notice. When Vic called her on a secure line the previous day, Jayne, a

British freelance intelligence operative who had previously worked for MI6, had been out walking near her adopted hometown of Portland, Maine, with her partner, Joe Johnson, a onetime CIA agent and now a private war crimes investigator.

It hadn't come as a surprise, though. Jayne's prior operation for Vic, several months earlier, had been focused on Ukraine, and he viewed her as a highly effective deniable operative on anything that involved Russia. So she had caught a plane to DC first thing that morning.

"So can you now tell us all exactly what this is about?" Jayne asked, looking at Vic.

Vic had explained on the phone that he, Scales, and Malevich had already had a series of highly confidential discussions with Merriden and Richter recently, and they now needed to bring Jayne into the circle. Vic had asked all of them to sign fresh secrecy and nondisclosure agreements before the meeting.

"Utilities—power, gas, water," said Vic, exchanging a glance with Merriden. "We believe that Putin may have a plan to target Ukraine's key utility services, but we don't know what. And we need to help Ukraine try to prevent and prepare defenses against that possibility. That's partly why the president's visiting Kyiv later this month, on the twenty-third—and he's pressuring me to find out more ahead of that trip. I'll be with him for the visit."

Vic had told Jayne prior to the meeting that President Stephen Ferguson had a top-secret, low-profile visit to Kyiv scheduled soon to meet with the Ukrainian president, Pavlo Doroshenko. The intention was to offer moral and practical support in the face of Russian hostility, including by escalating intelligence gathering—partly why Vic was due to go on the trip—and strategic and tactical military advice.

"If Putin's targeting utilities, what's the Moscow strategy?"

Jayne asked. "To make it look like an inside job, within Ukraine, and to make the president look like he can't control the country?" She knew Doroshenko was deeply concerned about pro-Russian minorities stirring up trouble inside his country.

"Probably, although that's what I need to find out," Vic said. "You're right. If there was an attack that looked like it was done by anti-government Ukrainian protesters, it might trigger social unrest and more anti-government feeling. People could argue Doroshenko can't keep law and order. That could give Putin the pretext he needs to invade and supposedly sort out the mess on behalf of the Russian minorities inside Ukraine. It would be straight out of his usual playbook."

To Jayne's left, she could see Malevich nodding. Vic always spoke highly of his Kyiv chief of station, whom he had promoted several times, although Jayne had had little contact with him until now. He hadn't been involved in her operation the previous year, which had uncovered an enormous and complex Russian plot to make Germany and other European countries dependent on Russian gas in order to deter their interference in a possible invasion of Ukraine. It had resulted in the dramatic resignation of the German chancellor, Erich Merck, who turned out to be on Moscow's payroll.

The audacity of that long-running Russian plot, and the clear threat against Ukraine that remained, meant Jayne had become more willing to take every opportunity possible to strike at Putin's regime and reduce his capacity to launch an attack on his smaller, less powerful neighbor. She believed it was her duty, and after eight months of relative inactivity, she felt ready for action once again.

"What do you want me to do?" Jayne asked.

Malevich cleared his throat. "We have a source within one of the Russian-aligned paramilitary groups in eastern Ukraine we would like you to meet," he said. "We've code-named him GRAY WOLF. Given that you've all been read into the files on need-to-know, I can tell you his real name is Aleksey Zhukov. He's Russian originally, and he lives in Donetsk, near the Russian border. He's second in command of the Donbas People's Militia and together with his boss, he works directly with the Kremlin and with the Russian army. But he's turned against the Moscow regime and has let it be known to me, via a third party in Kyiv, that he wants to meet us."

There was a short silence during which the only sound was that of Vic's new clocks, all ticking in sync.

Jayne was stunned. The Russian president, Vladimir Putin, had already seized the Crimean Peninsula from Ukraine in 2014. Since then, the Kremlin and Russian military had been covertly supporting a war in Ukraine's Donbas area, comprising the Donetsk and Luhansk regions, which was being run by pro-Russian forces trying to push those territories into Moscow's control. This sounded like a very important high-level source within those militias.

"GRAY WOLF has a lot to lose," she said.

"You could say that," Malevich said. "If it gets out that he's met us, he's dead. For that reason, he's wary of Ukrainian intelligence officers, because he believes, rightly, that the Russians have operatives all over Ukraine keeping them all under close surveillance. That's also why he doesn't want to meet anyone from our station in Kyiv—we're all under the microscope. He's terrified of being identified by anyone linked to Moscow. So he wants someone else—someone good, but more below the radar."

"And you think I'd be more below the radar?" Jayne asked with a thin smile. "Despite having exposed Russia's biggest asset in Western Europe only eight months ago?"

Vic pursed his lips. "I know what you're saying, Jayne, but—"

"I mean someone who's not on the daily track-and-follow roster for the GRU's and SVR's boys in Ukraine," Malevich interrupted. "You don't live in Kyiv, Jayne. You don't commute to work at the US embassy each day. They don't keep an eye on you every day."

"And apart from that," Vic said, "the Agency needs to be very careful in Ukraine. Between these four walls, we're already doing things we shouldn't be doing." He glanced at Malevich. "I want to keep Abram's people out of anything else we might do, if possible—I want to keep their profile low."

Malevich nodded.

Jayne knew the CIA was carrying out various covert operations in Ukraine to assist the country's military and the SZR, the Ukrainian intelligence service, in preparing for an increasingly likely Russian invasion.

The CIA activities ranged from training Ukrainian snipers to helping the military prepare for anti-tank warfare and surveillance evasion. In some cases it was deeply questionable whether existing US legal authorities for the CIA, termed "covert action findings," really covered what the Agency was doing.

"So isn't a trip by President Ferguson to Kyiv going to attract a lot of attention, just when you want a low profile in Ukraine, given all this covert assistance Langley is providing?" Jayne asked.

"Good question," Vic said. "But the plan is to turn Ferguson's visit into a double bluff. Nobody would think he'd go there if we're doing stuff that we shouldn't, right?"

Jayne felt less sure about that than Vic appeared to be, but that was his call, and the president's.

"Does Valentin Marchenko know what you're planning?" Jayne asked. She had built a good working relationship with Marchenko, the SZR's deputy director, during operations in recent years. He would need to be involved in this one, as it would be on his territory, not to mention that the SZR had access to a lot of information and resources that the CIA did not.

"He knows, Jayne," Malevich said. "We get along well with him—we're doing useful work that helps him out. You can meet with him when you're in Kyiv. He will no doubt give good advice."

"Neal will go with you," Vic said. "He's got a solid engineering background, and he's worked on power, gas, and water strategic issues in Afghanistan and Syria and elsewhere." He chuckled a little. "And, of course, he might be part of the senior management hierarchy here, but like me, he still likes to get his hands dirty."

Jayne glanced at Neal. "Does he have to?" she said, a wry grin on her face.

Vic guffawed, as did Neal.

"No, seriously, I'm glad you're letting him out of the office," she said. "It's been a while since we worked together on an operation."

She knew Neal did indeed have a good knowledge of such issues. She had known both him and Vic since the late 1980s, when they were all working in Pakistan and Afghanistan, Jayne for MI6 and the others for the CIA. It was at that time that she first met and had a brief initial relationship with Joe, who was then a CIA colleague of Vic and Neal. Like many members of the CIA's Directorate of Operations, both Vic and Neal found it hard to leave field operations completely behind once they were promoted to desk jobs. It was a running joke. Once an operative, always an operative.

"This GRAY WOLF," Jayne said. "What's his motivation for talking to us?"

Malevich pursed his lips. "Apparently, his brother's been sent to IK-2 near Moscow. It's one of the modern gulags, the so-called correctional colonies. The Russian government wanted to buy his business, but he refused—not a move that's going to help his life expectancy. They then dumped some trumped-up charges on him related to tax evasion. Complete bullshit. The guy says his brother's being tortured. He's turned against the Kremlin since that happened. We've checked it out. It's all true."

It sounded a familiar story in modern Russia.

"We've been tailing him twenty-four seven for the past three weeks," Malevich continued. "And we hacked his phone. We're certain he's kosher. He's done nothing and made no calls that raise red flags, met nobody that causes us concerns."

"Right," Jayne said.

"We'd need to get you a new legend," Vic said.

Jayne had several existing legends, or false identities, but she had used them all inside Russia and Eastern Europe, and they had become compromised and were therefore of little use now.

She looked at Vic through narrowed eyes. "I'd need that, would I? Is that because the job might involve going into Russia, by any chance?"

Vic pushed his metal-rimmed glasses up his nose. "Hopefully not. There's no need. It involves meeting GRAY WOLF on Ukrainian soil."

Jayne gave a slight sigh. "Sure, but as we all know, these types of operations have lives of their own."

Vic shook his head vigorously this time. "There's absolutely no intention of you going into Russia. But nevertheless, we think a new identity would be useful. Just covering our asses."

There was a pause that lasted a few seconds.

Jayne indicated toward Merriden and Richter. "And what exactly are these two gentlemen here for? Presumably they're playing some part in the operation?"

"Correct," Vic said. "You'll be working for them, theoretically. You need a cover story, because the Agency isn't technically working there. The story will be that you're with an engineering consulting firm that's helping the Ukrainian government prepare a strategy to deal with any natural disasters, floods, water supply problems, and so on." He glanced at Merriden.

"Yes, that's the plan," said Merriden in a bass voice that spoke of too many cigarettes. His silver mustache had a faint tinge of yellow nicotine. "We have a team of engineers that is helping the Ukrainians put together a crisis management strategy covering disasters of various kinds—how they would cope if, say, their water or power supplies were wiped out."

Richter, a cheerful-looking man with a chiseled chin and neatly groomed gray hair, wearing an army multi-camouflage uniform, leaned forward. "It's all quite legitimate, and we've done similar projects with other former Soviet satellite states. You and Neal would become members of that team. It's a very good cover. We're happy to help Vic with this—it's an important job."

Both Merriden and Richter had a down-to-earth air about them, as engineering types often did, and their brief explanations made sense.

"All right," she said, glancing at Neal. "We can discuss this further, if Neal's also happy."

Neal nodded. "I've already agreed. That's why we brought you in."

Jayne turned her attention back to Malevich. "What's the time frame for the meeting with GRAY WOLF?" she asked.

"As soon as possible," Malevich said. "He said his information is urgent. So I'd like to do it next week."

Vic nodded. "We can't afford to delay. I'll get the OTS working on the new legends immediately. You can both travel on Monday. Okay?"

The OTS was the CIA's Office of Technical Services, which supplied everything from false identities and documents to disguises and monitoring devices.

Jayne nodded. "I can do that."

"Fine with me," Neal said.

"That's good," Malevich said. "I'll get the meeting arranged for a week from today, next Friday. That will give us time to get ready, plan properly, and allow us time to meet with Valentin Marchenko too." He eyed Jayne, then Neal, an apologetic expression on his face. "You won't be able to fly straight into Kyiv for this operation, though. Too much scrutiny at the airport. You'll have to fly to Warsaw. Then we'll drive you."

"Drive from Warsaw?" Jayne knew the journey from the Polish capital was well over eight hundred kilometers. "How long?"

"Sorry. It's about eleven hours."

Jayne cursed.

Malevich held up his hands in apology. "I'm afraid there's more bad news. We won't be able to hold the meeting in Kyiv —GRAY WOLF won't be easily able to get there from Donetsk. He has suggested we do it near the nuclear power station at Zaporizhzhia, in the east. Unfortunately, that's another eight-hour drive from Kyiv."

Jayne pressed her lips together. "Hardly ideal, but I guess the important thing is making it as easy as possible for GRAY WOLF."

Malevich nodded. "The power plant, as you probably know, is on the Dnipro River, which still leaves him a four-hour journey from Donetsk, but he says that's much more doable than coming to Kyiv. He can travel there on the pretext of doing a solo surveillance trip as part of planning for a supposed rebel strike on the power plant."

Jayne raised an eyebrow. She knew the nuclear power

station was the largest of its type in Europe and was critical to Ukraine. "Good to know we're doing our bit to help them put a plan together to blow up the nuclear plant."

"He won't actually get anything useful," Malevich said. "And such a trip is far less likely to arouse suspicion among his militia group."

That made sense. Jayne nodded.

"And I'll get my special projects team in Kyiv prepared," Richter said. "They've been told to expect a couple of new arrivals. I have tasks in mind for you that will provide the cover you need for a meeting. I'll brief you when you're in Kyiv."

Vic placed both palms flat on the desk. "Good," he said in his trademark gravelly voice, looking at the two USACE men. "In that case, I can allow you both to depart and continue with your day. Thank you very much for coming, gentlemen. We know you are extremely busy. I need to continue the briefing here with Jayne, Neal, and Abram."

Vic stood to end the meeting, as did Merriden and Richter, and he led them to the office door, where they were escorted out by his red-headed executive assistant, Helen Lake.

"Right," said Vic as he returned to his chair. "Jayne, apart from meeting GRAY WOLF, there is another task I would like you to tackle since you're going to Eastern Europe that I couldn't discuss in front of our USACE friends. And I've promised Arthur you'll do this." He indicated with his thumb toward a connecting door that led to the neighboring office of the CIA's director, Arthur Veltman.

She knew exactly what he was going to say.

"Kira Suslova," she preempted.

"Indeed. Chess Queen of the Kremlin." He gave a half smile. "I think I'm correct in saying we still hold two billion of her dollars. I would like you to try to leverage that somewhat further, while we still can, and see what you can get from her. If nothing else, any useful information that we get from GRAY WOLF will need to be verified, and you might be able to use Suslova for that."

Jayne had a checkered history with Suslova.

The Russian was a special adviser to Putin and one of the true insiders at the top table of the Kremlin. Like Putin, she had worked as a spy for the KGB, Russia's foreign intelligence and security agency, in East Germany during the 1980s. She also happened to be an international chess grandmaster in her younger days and was now, on Putin's direction, running for the highly politicized role of president of the International Chess Federation, FIDE.

Eight months earlier, Suslova had ordered the killing of the CIA's then main asset inside Russian intelligence, Anastasia Shevchenko, whom Jayne had helped to recruit and had been responsible for.

But soon after that, Jayne had coerced Suslova into providing the key lead that uncovered the German chancellor, Merck, as a Russian mole by arranging for her bank account to be drained of $2 billion of the Kremlin's money. So far, it hadn't been returned and was still sitting in a CIA offshore account, although nobody at Langley would admit that.

It was indeed time for another meeting with Suslova, Jayne reflected. Vic was correct: the $2 billion was very good leverage indeed.

"I will see what I can do," she said. "But it will have to be outside Russia. I'm not going back there—they'll kill me next time for sure after what I've done. And I can't trust Suslova—she's dangerous."

CHAPTER TWO

Saturday, June 10, 2017
   Moscow

President Putin's relentless focus on Ukraine and his unstated yet clear intention to mount a full-scale invasion had given Kira Suslova some relief from his scrutiny. One of the other key advisers at the three-story Senate Palace building, Igor Ivanov, the so-called Black Bishop of the Kremlin—now sitting opposite her—was tasked with laying the foundations for that operation.

So far, Suslova had succeeded in escaping the blame for the loss a few months earlier of the Kremlin's biggest asset in Europe: the man she had played such a major part in recruiting back in 1988, Germany's now disgraced ex-chancellor Erich Merck.

The attention on Ukraine meant that Suslova had hardly been questioned in recent months about the progress of her global campaign to win the presidency of the International Chess Federation. That was just as well, because unknown to

Putin, the main funding for that particular campaign, a $2 billion package that the president had awarded her a year earlier, was no longer in her control.

Instead, the money was in the hands of her country's main enemy, the United States, and specifically the CIA, thanks to that devious British operative who was a contractor for them, Jayne Robinson.

Suslova knew she had to get that money back, but after months of brainstorming and strategizing, she had made no headway.

She glanced around the polished oak meeting table at one end of President Putin's ornate wood-paneled private office on the second floor of the palace, which stood just inside the walls of the Kremlin, overlooking Red Square.

It was a routine gathering of the president's closest advisers—all men, apart from her—whom he cajoled, pushed, and openly threatened to do his bidding. They were all waiting for the president, who was sitting at his dark oak desk a few meters away, tapping away at his laptop. Behind him, a Russian flag drooped from a pole.

Apart from herself and Ivanov, who had papers piled on the table in front of him, there was Maksim Kruglov, director of the SVR, Russia's foreign intelligence service, who sat immediately to her left.

To Kruglov's left, next to the president's seat, was Gennady Sidorenko, who was head of Kruglov's personal counterintelligence unit, which was separate from the rest of the SVR. He also acted as Putin's dedicated counterintelligence adviser and investigator and worked from the Kremlin three days a week. He was the president's chief witch hunter, responsible for tracking down the spies who were betraying the Motherland.

Across the table, next to Ivanov, sat the director of Russia's foreign military intelligence service, the GRU,

Colonel General Sergey Pliskin, and the director of the domestic security and intelligence service, the FSB, Nikolai Sheymov.

Such meetings still made Suslova nervous, even after years spent working in the Kremlin. She wondered which of her colleagues had secrets tucked away like her, that if known would at best terminate their careers, and at worst see them strung up like a piece of meat in a butcher's shop in one of the FSB's second basement torture chambers. It was impossible to say. Maybe she was the only one, but probably not. Few of them liked to make eye contact.

Finally, the president closed the lid of his laptop, pushed back his chair, and walked around to join his team. He sat at the head of the table and scrutinized each with a pair of laser-like blue eyes.

"I will make this a quick meeting," Putin said. He turned to Ivanov. "Igor, please update us on the water situation in Crimea. Any improvement?"

Suslova had been watching the Crimean water crisis with interest. After Russia's annexation of the Crimean Peninsula in 2014, the Ukrainians dammed the North Crimean Canal that ran south from the Dnipro River near Kakhovka into the Crimea and supplied 85 percent of the peninsula's water.

That had created a real crisis in Crimea, a naturally dry region at the northern end of the Black Sea. The 2.4 million residents were now forced to rely on collecting water in plastic containers from trucks that shipped it by road from the Russian mainland. It had made agriculture impossible, as there was not enough water for irrigation, and had driven farmers out of business.

Ivanov shook his head. "No, sir, no improvement. We have decided to make another large increase in the number of water trucks to help residents, but that won't assist farmers."

"And the court case?" Putin asked.

"The lawsuit goes tomorrow to the European Court of Human Rights, sir, as I promised. It will accuse Ukraine of genocide. But you can guarantee nothing will happen."

Putin sat in silence for a few seconds. Suslova knew the situation in Crimea was embarrassing him, not least because he had promised Crimeans a better life under Russian rule than they'd had under Ukraine. Options to improve things were limited. The charade of filing a lawsuit against Ukraine was a public relations stunt that had a zero chance of success.

"Igor, what about the operation we have discussed?" Putin asked, in a lower tone of voice, as he looked directly at Ivanov. "Are we in a position to share details with this team yet? I would like to involve more of them soon."

Suslova's ears pricked up.

What operation was this?

Ivanov leaned forward, pushing his elbows onto the desk, and shook his head, his forehead deeply creased. "Soon, sir. But there are details still being resolved, and we have elements we still need to put in place. I would like to ensure it remains strictly confidential until we are ready."

"Let's discuss it in private after this meeting," the president said. "You are going to need more high-level support. It is too big for you to handle it all yourself."

"Yes, sir." Ivanov visibly exhaled in relief. Suslova could tell he was irritated with Putin for even having mentioned the operation. It was clearly highly sensitive.

As Ivanov spoke, his left elbow slid forward and pushed against his files, shoving one of them forward out of alignment so that Suslova could see the previously hidden label on the top. Always adept at reading upside down, she deciphered it immediately, despite the small print.

Operation Noi, it read.

There was a white-and-blue sticker in the left-hand corner

of the file with a code number written on it in black marker pen: *170529 NOI S1*.

She instantly memorized all the details. Old habits died hard.

The colored sticker told Suslova that the file had come from the high-security GRU files archive, located in the basement of the GRU headquarters building, the monstrous nine-story gray steel-and-glass building that stood at number 3, Grizodubovoy Street, the two-lane highway in the Khoroshyovsky District of Moscow, seven kilometers northwest of the Kremlin.

The blue color and the S1 code signified that the file was kept under the highest level of security, and the 170529 number indicated that the file had been created very recently, on May 29.

This must be a new operation.

Was it the one that Putin had vaguely referred to a few minutes earlier?

Although most top-secret files within the Kremlin, Russian intelligence, and the military community were held electronically on encrypted servers that were almost impossible to break into, many of the senior leaders also preferred paper copies of documents that could be perused and written on in a more traditional manner. Those files were always kept securely within the various departmental archives when not in use and guarded around the clock.

Very quickly, Ivanov realized what he had done and straightened the files again so the label was once more out of sight.

Operation Noi.

As Ivanov adjusted the files, he looked up sharply. Suslova was a fraction of a second too late in averting her gaze, and he caught her eye.

Had he seen her looking at the file?

It was difficult to say.

That operation was unknown to Suslova. But she wasn't surprised. Putin liked to divide and rule, and his chief weapon in doing so was information. He was invariably selective in whom he included when providing details of his projects and operations, and this meeting was no exception. Half the time, unless one was directly involved, it was almost impossible to know precisely what he was referring to.

Even though she had an ongoing, intermittent physical relationship with the president when he demanded it—which, thankfully, was far less often these days than in the past—it made little difference in operational matters. Suslova felt that sometimes, if anything, he treated her more harshly than others.

The meeting continued for another twenty minutes, during which several important issues were discussed at a high level, including a planned increase in surveillance operations in the Black Sea. Putin then called an end to the meeting and told everyone to leave.

As Suslova was heading for the door, Putin beckoned to her.

"One minute," the president said. "Have you made any progress with the chess theme for my swimming pool?"

"I'm working on it still," Suslova said.

Because of her chess expertise, Putin had asked her to take charge of a small project, but one he viewed as important, to develop a chess-related decor for the indoor swimming pool at his palace on Russia's Black Sea coast at Cape Idokopas. The president was not really a chess enthusiast, nor was he a good player, as she knew well, having played a few games with him years earlier when they had both worked for the KGB in East Germany during the Cold War. But many of the guests at Cape Idokopas enjoyed chess, like most

Russians, and Putin was anxious to project the right patriotic image.

However, Suslova had been dragging her feet with the project. Her view was that it could be handled by somebody at a much lower level than her.

"What are you thinking of doing there?" Putin asked.

"I am thinking of a large chess set at one end of the pool, with pieces this size," Suslova said, putting her palm at thigh height to indicate the scale and trying to inject an enthusiasm into her voice that she did not feel. "It might be fun for people using the pool area to play."

Putin nodded his approval. "A good idea." He eyeballed Suslova. "I need you to make certain that the pieces are of the highest quality. And I want this done quickly."

It was typical of the president, a notorious micromanager, to make such a comment, even when he had so many much more important international crises on his hands. He had an unrelenting focus on matters both large and small.

"Of course," Suslova said. "Sculpted pieces depicting Russian war heroes might work well."

She had already pinpointed an internationally well-known company in Tbilisi, Georgia, that specialized in such chess sculptures and in fact had made a chess set for the garden in her own lavish dacha in the exclusive Rublevka area of Moscow. The company owner was a Russian, Nikolas Kamov, whom she had known from her time as a chess grandmaster, but who had immigrated to Georgia because, privately, he hated Putin. That didn't stop him from taking advantage if there was the possibility of a hugely lucrative contract, however. Money spoke louder than conscience.

Suslova had been talking to him about bringing his team to Cape Idokopas for meetings to measure the pool site and to design and plan the chess set installation.

"I like that," Putin said. "Get moving with it. But make sure you brief me before going ahead."

Suslova could see the president was growing impatient. She had better get this thing done for him.

She had often been to the Cape Idokopas palace with Putin during and after its construction over the course of their on-off affair, which had lasted more than twenty years. Although she didn't like it, she felt she had little choice, given that her career would immediately end if she spurned him. Thankfully, now that she was in her late fifties, these days he mostly turned his attention to younger alternatives.

Putin placed a hand on the small of Suslova's back and ushered her toward the door, indicating that the conversation was over.

As Suslova left the office, though, her mind was not on the president's chess set. Rather, she was thinking about how to find out what Operation Noi was, exactly.

CHAPTER THREE

Friday, June 16, 2017
Zaporizhzhia, Ukraine

Jayne adjusted the white US Army Corps of Engineers safety helmet she had been given and peered out the window of the yellow security checkpoint building on the approach road to the Zaporizhzhia nuclear power station.

There was still no sign of the blue Volvo she and the rest of the team were expecting.

The target time for the meeting with GRAY WOLF of 16:17 had already passed several minutes ago. However, they were giving him leeway since he had to drive for more than four hours from Donetsk on poorly maintained roads with high accident rates.

Jayne also knew he would need time to ensure that he was not being tailed before heading to the meeting site. He was unable to communicate with the meeting party, as a phone call or text message would be far too risky. So they would just have to sit and wait.

She glanced at her phone screen again. The time now read
16:26. She put the device back into her pocket, adjusted the
red USACE reflective vest she was wearing, and returned to
her seat at a meeting table positioned next to the window.

The position gave them a clear view eastward down
Promyslova Street, the long, straight approach road that led
to the power station, and of the concrete parking lot across
the other side of the street, where GRAY WOLF was to
leave his car. The street, home to a mess of industrial buildings and factories, was lined by a tangle of oil and gas pipe-
lines and high-voltage power cables.

Only 250 meters in the other direction, down the street
to the west next to the Dnipro River, stood six enormous
concrete structures, each topped with a cathedral-like red
dome. These were the pressurized light water nuclear reac-
tors that comprised the plant, each capable of generating
950 megawatts of electricity. Their combined output
amounted to roughly a fifth of Ukraine's total power
requirements.

On the opposite side of the square wooden table from
Jayne sat Neal Scales and Abram Malevich. Like Jayne, they
were both wearing white safety helmets and red USACE
reflective vests, complete with the organization's red-and-
white castle logo on the back and the breast. They all looked
every inch a civil engineer dressed for a site visit.

Standing at the window, leaning back against the sill, was
Valentin Marchenko, the deputy director of the SZR, also in
a USACE reflective vest. He tugged at his goatee, his trademark pack of Marlboro Reds tucked into his breast pocket.

They had asked Anthony Richter, the USACE Europe
District commander whom she had met a week earlier at
Langley, to remain in Kyiv with his Ukraine-based team.
Despite Richter's role in facilitating the meeting, including
arranging the USACE uniforms, they didn't want him over-

hearing what was likely to be an exchange of highly classified information.

A kilometer away from the site was the USACE Ford minibus Richter had provided to transport them from Kyiv, together with the driver, one of Marchenko's SZR operatives.

Jayne had been impressed with the planning that had gone into the operation so far. Marchenko had pulled a few strings with his contacts at Energoatom, the Ukrainian nuclear power plant operator. He had arranged for them to use a rear private meeting room at the security building for the rendezvous with GRAY WOLF.

All of them had traveled to Zaporizhzhia from Kyiv using the cover story that they were members of Richter's engineering consulting team that was working in Ukraine at the invitation of the government. The USACE had been asked to assess the state of Ukraine's seven hydroelectric dams, located at various points along the length of the Dnipro, Europe's fourth longest river, which wound its way through Ukraine en route from Russia to the Black Sea.

Although named after Zaporizhzhia, the eponymous nuclear plant was almost eighty kilometers downriver from the city. The plant had been included in the USACE project because of its dependence on water from the Dnipro River for cooling purposes.

The key to the operation's success, of course, lay in GRAY WOLF being undetected by any covert counterintelligence operatives from the Russian military, the GRU, the SVR, or the Donbas People's Militia of which he was deputy leader. Although unlikely, such surveillance could not be ruled out.

In an attempt to ensure GRAY WOLF was "black," or free of surveillance, Marchenko had deployed SZR operatives in unmarked vehicles at strategic points on the roads around the power plant. Their job was to sound the alarm if they saw anything that suggested he was being followed when he arrived, thus allowing Jayne and the team to abort the meeting.

Marchenko's phone beeped loudly and Jayne jumped a little, as did most of the others. The tension in the room was palpable.

The SZR chief jerked himself upright, picked up the phone, jabbed at the screen, and studied it carefully.

"GRAY WOLF is on his way in," Marchenko said. "He'll be in the parking lot in about five minutes, according to my officer stationed near the main highway. He says he appears to be clear of any tail, is driving normally, and seems unflustered."

Marchenko turned and looked out the window toward the parking lot.

Jayne also stood. "Good," she said as she walked to the window and joined him. Together, they scanned the street outside.

Neal, a tall, wiry man, pulled his safety helmet down over his blond hair, which he deliberately kept looking untidy. "This seems promising," he said.

Sure enough, a few minutes later, a tiny speck appeared at the far end of Promyslova Street and gradually drew nearer. It was the blue Volvo, moving at a steady pace.

When it reached the entrance to the parking lot, it turned right and pulled in about forty meters away at the end of a line of other parked cars, which belonged to employees at the power plant. Jayne could see the car was a little battered, with a large dent in the front passenger door. The car also had a variety of other scratches.

Several seconds later, the driver's door opened and out climbed a barrel-chested man with black hair and a heavy mustache, wearing a charcoal jacket.

This was Aleksey Zhukov, or GRAY WOLF.

He stood for a few seconds, ostensibly looking at his phone, but Jayne assumed he was checking the rest of the parking lot and his surroundings before making any further move.

Eventually, he slid his phone into his pocket, locked his car, and walked purposefully toward the security building.

Before GRAY WOLF reached the check-in desk window at the front of the building, Marchenko opened the side door that led directly into the meeting room, greeted the visitor in Russian, and beckoned him in before closing the door behind him.

Malevich briefly introduced himself and the others to GRAY WOLF, who shook hands with each of them, scrutinizing them with a pair of intelligent hazel eyes.

"Please, take a seat," Malevich said. "I hope you had a safe journey here?"

The subtext of his question was clear and was one that everyone wanted an answer to. Had GRAY WOLF avoided surveillance on the way in?

"I'm confident I'm black if that's what you mean," GRAY WOLF said. "Although my car's air conditioning doesn't work, and neither does the radio. So the journey could have been better." He sat down amid stifled laughter from the others, which broke the tension.

"First, we need to keep this meeting short," GRAY WOLF said. "Ten minutes, maximum. I can't stay any longer. Is that understood?"

"Of course. Understood," Malevich said. Jayne nodded, as did everyone else.

"Good," said GRAY WOLF. "Be assured, I took a lot of precautions to check for possible surveillance, which is why I am a little late, for which I apologize. But my colleagues and Russian counterintelligence are not especially likely to follow me here, unlike in Kyiv. It's too exposed here, with little cover. Normally it would be dangerous for me to carry out such a trip to a high-profile site like this, given my militia role, and unless my colleagues have a good reason, they wouldn't want to put themselves at risk too. They are probably happy for me to go solo."

That made sense to Jayne and was reassuring.

"Can we first arrange for a follow-up meeting to this one?" she asked. It was something she always preferred to do first, if possible, and was good tradecraft, in case the meeting was disrupted.

GRAY WOLF shook his head. "It's not possible to arrange far in advance. It's difficult to predict my situation. I will need to do so using the same channel of communication as for this meeting."

Jayne nodded.

"Fine," Neal said. "But do you have a direct way of communicating if we need to do so?"

GRAY WOLF hesitated. "I have a burner phone, which I change fairly frequently. But I keep that for absolute emergencies. I would rather not give you the number unless I have to."

That was understandable, Jayne thought.

"All right," Neal said. "We understand that your desire to meet us was partly due to your brother's situation."

GRAY WOLF nodded. "He is in deep trouble in the gulag, in IK-2. His health is poor and he is deteriorating. I fear he may not have a long time left. He has taken a lot of beatings. That is how those bastards operate." He paused and then continued, his voice now lowered. "They will take his business soon, and they will probably take his life with it. There will be a payback for that against the Kremlin."

There was steel in his voice, which Jayne noted.

He was likely telling the truth, in her view.

"The messages we received from our intermediary said

you had some very important information you wanted to pass on to us," said Malevich. "We thank you for taking the obvious risks involved in communicating this information to us. Does the information relate to future Russian activities in eastern Ukraine?"

GRAY WOLF leaned back in his chair and folded his arms. "My superior, the head of the Donbas People's Militia, and I have close contacts with very senior people within the Russian military, the GRU, and the Kremlin. They direct our activities closely. To do that, they need to confide in us, though not always in detail. I have acquired some very sensitive information this way."

Jayne folded her arms on the table in front of her and focused intently on what he was saying.

"I believe it is not just limited to eastern Ukraine," GRAY WOLF said. "I have learned from a contact of mine within the GRU the outline of a major operation that is underway to strike against dams and cause massive disruption to hydro-electric power and water supplies. I needed to be told because they needed to ensure it didn't clash with anything that our militia force was planning."

"Does this operation have a name?" Jayne asked.

"Operation Noi," GRAY WOLF said.

"Noi?" Jayne asked. "That's Russian for Noah. As in the flood."

"Yes," GRAY WOLF said, with a curt nod in Jayne's direction.

"So they plan to destroy dams, cause huge flooding, and take down Ukraine's power supply?" Malevich asked. "If so, that would be a massive expansion of the military activity we're seeing in the Donetsk and Luhansk border regions—the dams are in the main part of Ukraine, including Kyiv."

The enormity of this struck Jayne immediately.

The idea of Russia running a large-scale operation inside

Ukraine to destroy its dams and possibly strike at the country's capital city sent her mind into overdrive. She could see that Malevich and Marchenko both looked shocked.

GRAY WOLF nodded. "It would be huge. But my understanding is that it will be made to look like it is carried out by those inside Ukraine who oppose President Doroshenko's leadership."

Jayne leaned forward. "There are several hydroelectric dams along the Dnipro River. Do you know which are the targets? And who is going to do it and when and where? Is this a GRU operation?"

GRAY WOLF shook his head. "It will be a GRU Spetsnaz operation, I understand, but I don't know when and I don't know which dam or dams. Sorry."

"Or how this will be done? Bombs, explosives?" Malevich asked.

There was another shake of the head from GRAY WOLF. "I just don't know."

"What else do you have?" Jayne asked. "Like, who is running this operation at the Kremlin?"

"I don't know," GRAY WOLF said. "But I have learned that it does have an operational chief outside Russia. It's being masterminded by someone code-named Khranitel Plotiny."

"Khranitel Plotiny?" Malevich echoed.

GRAY WOLF nodded. "The DAM KEEPER."

"The DAM KEEPER," Jayne repeated. "A woman or man? A Russian or an agent outside Russia? I assume you don't have a proper name."

GRAY WOLF shrugged. "I don't know if it's a woman or a man. And no, of course I don't have a name. But I'm fairly certain I will find out quite soon, because I've been told there is going to be closer cooperation between our militia unit and the team run by this DAM KEEPER. They will need us. You will need to let me find out who it is when I can—and then I will inform you."

He looked at his watch. "I need to get moving. I've told you everything I know."

"Are there any developments with your militia operations in the Donbas?" Marchenko asked.

GRAY WOLF shook his head. "Just more of the same. Disruption, coercion and corruption of local officials, a buildup of forces. One new development: the Russian army is establishing a new army, the Eighth Guards Order of Lenin Combined Arms Army, based in Rostov-on-Don, which will control our separatist militia inside Donetsk and the one in Luhansk. It is a clear sign that Moscow is ramping up its presence—likely ahead of an upcoming invasion. I will get more details for you next time."

"Thank you," Marchenko said.

GRAY WOLF stood and looked at those around the table, who also rose. "I need to go. This has been an encouraging first meeting. I am putting a lot of trust in you all. I am sure it will be repaid."

"Thank you," Malevich said. "Be sure your trust will be rewarded. You are safe with us. I will be in contact via our intermediary." He paused. "Can I ask once again if you would give us your burner number, in case we need it?"

GRAY WOLF exhaled. "Okay. For absolute emergencies only." He recited a Ukrainian cell phone number, which Malevich tapped swiftly into his own phone.

"Thank you," Malevich said. "Hopefully, we will see you again soon."

He walked to the door and held it open while GRAY WOLF shook hands with the others.

As Jayne took her turn to say farewell, she felt impressed with GRAY WOLF. He appeared to have provided some top-class intelligence, albeit lacking in detail, with the promise of more. Of course, it would require rigorous verification to ensure he wasn't actually working for the Russians, but her gut feeling, honed over many decades in the intelligence-gathering business, was that he was genuine.

GRAY WOLF slipped out of the building. Jayne peered out the window and watched him walk across the street and into the parking lot. He opened his car door and climbed in.

A few seconds later, his car rolled toward the parking lot exit.

Neal flipped open his laptop and tapped out a brief note to Vic back at Langley to confirm the meeting had been completed successfully.

Meanwhile, Jayne walked through the door and stood outside, watching the Volvo as it turned into the street and began to drive slowly away from the power station. Malevich and Marchenko did likewise and stood next to her.

"He's an operator," Jayne said. "We'll need to look after him. Could be a top-class source for all of us."

"He already has been," Marchenko said, as he took his pack of Marlboros from his breast pocket, removed a cigarette, and lit up.

As she watched Marchenko take his first drag, Jayne became aware of a noise above them, a buzzing that was growing louder. She peered at the blue skies overhead but could see nothing.

The noise grew a little louder.

She raised a hand to shield her eyes from the glare of the sun.

Then she saw it.

It was a large commercial-type drone, a quadcopter with four propellers, coming from the direction of the power station and heading rapidly in their direction, flying directly above the street.

In a flash, Jayne realized that this was no normal surveillance drone.

It was too large, was moving at high speed, and had a silhouette that made it look like a hornet, as well as sounding like one, with a slim black body that she guessed must be nearly a meter long.

"Shit!" Jayne shouted. "Drone. And it's got a bloody huge missile slung underneath. Looks like an RPG."

Jayne knew that the rocket-propelled grenade, specifically the current RPG-7 variant, was a staple weapon for the Russian army and was made by a Russian company.

She could see in her peripheral vision that Marchenko and Malevich were also scanning the sky, heads tilted back, also shielding their eyes from the sun.

Alarm bells went off inside her mind as she realized what was happening.

The drone was heading directly down the street, pursuing GRAY WOLF's Volvo and gaining ground rapidly.

"The bastards are after GRAY WOLF," Jayne shouted. "Warn him."

Malevich swore violently as he whipped his phone out from his pocket and tapped furiously on the screen.

Jayne could hear the repeating beep, beep, beep noise.

"It's switched off," Malevich said. "Shit."

The drone was now several hundred meters down the street, gaining ground fast on the car. From the leisurely way in which he was driving, Jayne knew that GRAY WOLF was completely unaware of what was chasing him.

Seconds later, she saw the drone descend as it closed in on the car, but she lost sight of it against the dark background of the factory units behind as it dipped below the skyline.

Then came a huge blast, a deafening boom that reverberated right down the street.

GRAY WOLF's car erupted in a ball of orange flame that mushroomed upward.

Pieces of burning debris were thrown in all directions, and a cloud of black smoke shot skyward from the wreckage of the Volvo.

"Bloody hell," Jayne shouted. She spun around and faced Marchenko. "Call your van driver, now! Let's get out of here fast. We'll be next. We've been stitched up by someone."

CHAPTER FOUR

Friday, June 16, 2017
Zaporizhzhia, Ukraine

The van engine screamed in low gear as the SZR driver accelerated away from the nuclear power station. The driver then braked hard as he approached the burning wreckage of GRAY WOLF's Volvo, which was blocking the center of the street. He carefully steered around the debris, pieces of metal, plastic, and glass crunching beneath the van's tires as he did so.

There was no point in stopping to check on GRAY WOLF's condition.

His chances of survival were zero.

Indeed, the damage to his car was so great that nothing resembling a body could be seen.

The car's roof had been blown off, a car seat could be seen more than thirty meters down the street, and one wheel had rolled even farther into the entrance of a factory unit.

Flames had engulfed the rest of the vehicle, which was a burning, mangled jumble of bent and broken steel.

Once he had navigated around the wreck, the SZR driver accelerated again.

Jayne's entire body felt rigid. Her eyes scanned the street ahead of them, looking for any sign that whoever had destroyed GRAY WOLF was coming back for another try, this time with them as the target. She could see the others were equally on edge.

In the front passenger seat, Marchenko was on his phone, rapping out instructions to his SZR head office in Kyiv to ensure all border crossings into Russia were put on high alert in case whoever had carried out the hit on GRAY WOLF tried to get out of Ukraine. Jayne somehow doubted that was going to produce the drone operator, who in her mind almost certainly had to be a Russian GRU undercover operative based inside Ukraine.

Apart from Marchenko, nobody said a word until they were on the highway heading out of the industrial area where the nuclear power plant was located.

"How the hell did that go so badly wrong?" Malevich said eventually.

"Someone tipped them off," Jayne said. "But the tip-off must have come in late. Otherwise, surely they would have blown up the entire security building while we were all in it, not just GRAY WOLF's car after he left."

Neal nodded. "We'll need a thorough counterintelligence investigation into this—no stone unturned. Someone's leaked it. If GRAY WOLF wasn't under surveillance as he came into the meeting site, somebody must have informed them exactly where he was going. We'll go through everyone on the ops team who had access to the intel, CIA and USACE." He looked at Marchenko. "Valentin, I assume you'll do likewise?"

Marchenko turned around and shook his head slowly. "I

owe you all an apology," he said. "I have to accept the responsibility for this on behalf of my team. We had no idea, and you're all operating on our territory." He stared down at the floor of the van.

There was a pause.

"It's likely not your team's fault," Jayne said. She reached over and placed a hand on Marchenko's shoulder. "If it was, we'd likely all be dead. Like I said, they would have hit the security building."

"Well, let's make sure he hasn't died for nothing," Neal said. "He's given us a starting point—Operation Noi. And we have a code name for the head of the operation."

"The DAM KEEPER," Jayne said. "Who the hell's that?"

Nobody responded.

The scale of the task facing them was clear. With GRAY WOLF in place and able to feed more information, they had a way forward. Without him, their chances seemed slim.

It took more than two hours to drive back to Zaporizhzhia city. It was only when they had crossed the hydroelectric dam over the Dnipro River, and were back on the long divided highway heading west toward Kyiv that Jayne began to relax a little.

She tried to think through the options if they were to chase down the somewhat vague leads obtained. There seemed few options. In fact, Jayne could think of only one other avenue open to them, and that was Kira Suslova.

But there seemed little chance of getting close to her immediately. Even to set up a meeting so she could explain to Suslova what she wanted would be a huge undertaking.

Or was she just being naturally pessimistic, as she sometimes felt at the start of a difficult operation?

Jayne would have to remind herself that, as had often been the case in the past, she could proceed only one step at a time and trust she would make enough good decisions to get there, eventually. In the past she had done so, but sometimes the margins between success and failure were extremely fine. She worried constantly that as she got older, her judgment, her reflexes, or even simply her physical capabilities might one day let her down.

She turned her head to look out the window. Flat, golden Ukrainian wheat fields stretched out on both sides of the highway. This was the breadbasket of Europe, from where grain was shipped all over the continent and far beyond, including East Africa. She caught Neal's eye.

"What are you thinking?" he asked.

"About where to start," she said. She didn't want to confess her doubts and insecurities to Neal now.

"Our chess friend?"

"Can't think of any other options."

That was what she enjoyed about working with Vic and Neal, not to mention Joe Johnson. They all had such similar backgrounds in terms of their intelligence agency experience, dating back to Islamabad in 1988, that they were usually on the same wavelength. Their approaches sometimes differed a little, but their objectives were usually very aligned.

Neal, a father of two sons aged twenty-four and twenty, was now one of the longest-serving operators in the CIA, sometimes to the dismay of his wife, Marie. When Vic had been promoted to deputy director of operations three and a half years earlier, he didn't hesitate in immediately promoting Neal, too.

"We may not keep the leverage we've got for long," Jayne said. "Even if we keep her $2 billion, at some point, Putin is going to find out she's lost it and why, and if that happens, she'll be history and our source will be finished. We need to maximize it while we have it."

Neal nodded. "The only question is, what if she decides

she can write off the $2 billion and sees it as the price for knifing you in the back?"

"Thanks for cheering me up."

However, that was indeed the only question, Jayne thought to herself. Neal was right. It was a gamble.

CHAPTER FIVE

Friday, June 16, 2017
   Frankfurt

It was Aidan's second visit to the old warehouse since his traumatic encounter with Irina and her colleague in her apartment a week earlier. And, as on his first visit three days ago, the video of the entire sordid episode was playing on a six-foot projector screen fastened to the bare brick wall. It was just as horrific as last time, with him lying on his back and her straddling him. The soundtrack made it worse, with its moans and grunts.

Aidan had felt somehow compelled to watch it the last time. Now he couldn't bring himself to do so again and kept his eyes averted.

"Turn that off," Aidan said to Irina, who was standing near the screen. "You showed it to me on Tuesday. I don't need to see it again."

"Aw, watch it again," Irina urged him, a faint smile on her lips. "It's so hot."

She was obviously getting some kind of perverse pleasure from his intense discomfort. So too was her male colleague sitting at a wooden table, the same bald man who had helped Irina at the apartment. He was heavily muscled and looked like a military type.

"There are laws against that kind of thing," Aidan said. "You'll find out the hard way when you get chucked into some German prison. Which will happen, believe me."

"I don't think that's going to happen," Irina said as she dropped into a chair opposite the bald man. She flicked her dark, curly hair back over her shoulder. "As I've already warned you, if you tell anyone, or try to do anything stupid, or anything that we don't instruct you to do, or try to obstruct us or lie to us, I promise you it will go straight to every major TV news company and newspaper in the States. It will be all over social media and will go viral—I have access to click farms that will make sure of that. If I go down, I'll make sure you go down with me."

Aidan grimaced. It was the same threat she had made on Tuesday. Yet again, he felt as if he had just been punched hard in the stomach.

"Go screw yourself," Aidan said.

"I think I screwed you much better," Irina said, another slow grin crossing her face, which had a yellowish tinge from the fluorescent strip lights that hung from the high ceilings.

He glanced around the room, which contained only an old sofa, the wooden table and chairs at which they were seated, and a TV set. The sex video was coming from a mini-projector that stood on the end of the table, next to Irina. There was also a laptop and a Bluetooth speaker on the table. High on the wall above the projector screen, a metal grille was set into the wall, which Aidan assumed was for ventilation. The building was extremely old-fashioned and direly needed modernization. Aidan guessed it had been occupied by these people at short notice.

Irina tapped her fingers on the table. "I imagine our video would make your daddy back home very angry, and the rest of your family too, no doubt. Maybe they'll disown you. But apart from that, after word gets out that you leaked critical information, that you were a traitor, you'll without any doubt lose your job and will probably never work ever again for any American company or organization. You'll probably face charges and end up in prison."

Shit.

Another sharp spike of anxiety ran right through Aidan. She was almost certainly correct about the reaction back home if the video went viral. The consequences would be almost unbearable. He had spent his whole life trying to avoid situations that were far less embarrassing than this one. That was why he had felt compelled to meet Irina's demands —he could see no alternative.

At last, Irina tapped the space bar on her laptop and mercifully, the video stopped.

Aidan felt a surge of depression run right through him.

He looked down at the wooden floor. "What more do you want?" he asked, his voice flat. "Can't you just let me go and leave me alone now? I told you everything I know a few days ago."

"I need you to keep me up to date with everything your team is doing in Ukraine," Irina said. Now her accent sounded more threatening, and her voice a few notes lower. "Everything. Who they are meeting with, what is being discussed, and what they are being told. We know a lot already through other sources, so don't bullshit me. I'll know straightaway if you're lying, and you'll then feel the consequences."

Aidan folded his arms. "What did you do with the information I gave you on Tuesday?" he asked. "Something happened, I know that."

"Don't worry about that," Irina said, playing with her hair. "That's nothing to do with you. But I do need to know about your special projects team's links with the CIA and what they are planning, especially in the next week or two. I want to know exactly who is working on what, with whom, and when, and why. If you lie, I will know immediately. We have our sources with whom we can check."

Aidan felt his throat dry up. This had to stop.

Irina paused and glanced sideways at her colleague. "What's more, if you don't talk, my friend here will take whatever steps are needed to make sure that you do. You're not leaving until you tell us what we need to know. And then you'll come back again with more information in a few days."

Aidan sat and stared at Irina for several seconds. He couldn't get the image of her gyrating on top of him out of his mind.

She stared back, unblinking, her dark eyes focused on his.

"I've asked you before. I'll ask you again. Do you work for the Russians?" he said, his voice cracking. There could be no other logical reason this had happened.

"You don't need to know anything about us," Irina said. "Nothing." It was the same answer as before.

He had known as soon as things went wrong at the apartment a week earlier that this was a honey trap of the kind he had been warned about.

Idiot.

Aidan looked down at the floor and tried to think through his options. He could just refuse to talk anymore and call her bluff. Maybe she was bullshitting and the threats to send the video to newspapers and social media were hollow.

But something in her manner told him there was no bluff involved here. She had gone to a huge amount of effort to get him precisely where she wanted. She'd even screwed him. This had all been carefully planned, of that there was no doubt. She was a professional.

He was also well aware that he couldn't do anything to upset these people. If something went wrong and he failed to turn up for work in Wiesbaden on any particular day, alarm bells would start ringing in the office, the German police would probably be called, there would be an investigation, and the truth of what had happened would inevitably come out. The media would get hold of it. That would probably end up being just as bad as the threats Irina had made earlier.

He looked up. She was still staring at him.

"I know what you're thinking," she said. "But don't even think about it. Best to talk and don't make us angry."

Aidan swore softly under his breath.

"You whorehouse bitch," he whispered.

Across the table, the bald man stood and glanced at Irina. "I don't like the way he's speaking to you," he said, bunching fists that were roughly double the size of Aidan's. "Can I?" he asked, taking a pace toward Aidan.

She motioned for him to stop. "No, don't touch him," she said. "Not yet. If he tries anything, then you can. But I don't think he will. He's not that stupid. He'll calm down when he realizes he has no choice."

The bald man nodded and sat down again.

As he did so, Irina's phone rang. She glanced at the screen, then answered it and told the caller to wait.

She turned and signaled to the bald man. "Get this guy upstairs into the small waiting room," she said. "We both need to go on this conference call—in private. Come down and join the call when you've locked him in. We can bring him back down when we're finished and talk to him then."

The bald man grabbed Aidan by the forearm with a tight, muscular grip, and propelled him across the rough floor boards, through a swing door, along a short corridor, through another door, and up a flight of badly lit concrete stairs. Their footsteps echoed down the stairwell.

"Where are we going?" Aidan asked.

"Here," the man said as he stopped, kicked open a door, and pushed Aidan inside a small, windowless room. "You will wait until we've finished. I will come and get you."

He turned, exited the room, and pulled the door shut behind him. He locked it from the outside with a sharp click.

Aidan swore to himself.

The only furniture in the room was a circular metal table and two wooden chairs. The walls, like those of the much larger downstairs room, were of bare brick, and the ceilings were equally high. It had similar fluorescent strip lights as downstairs and a metal ventilation grille high on the wall, again like the downstairs room.

It felt just like a prison.

Now Aidan really felt he was in serious trouble and well out of his depth. The whole situation had escalated at high speed, and he felt completely out of control in a way that he had never experienced before.

Aidan sat on one of the chairs and tried to think through his options.

He just wanted to get out of this mess.

But he was struggling to see how he was going to do that.

He tipped his head back and stared up at the ceiling. His gut feeling was that he had already done some significant damage. He just wasn't sure what.

After the encounter with Irina at the Frankfurt apartment a week ago, he had subsequently received WhatsApp messages from her on Tuesday. They instructed him to take a taxi that would collect him that evening from his rented house in Wiesbaden after he had returned home from his work at the nearby USACE Europe headquarters.

The taxi delivered him to the same warehouse where he was now, only a kilometer from the apartment.

Irina had shown him the video and then threatened him, just as she had today. She had known precisely which team he worked for at the USACE, who his boss was, and the type of projects they were engaged with in Ukraine. She had claimed to have sources with whom she could cross-check everything he told her, and said the consequences of lying would be a thorough beating at the hands of her colleague.

He had therefore felt compelled, extremely reluctantly, to answer the questions thrown at him about the work being done by the USACE special projects team in Ukraine: who was involved, what their schedule was, and what meetings they were having.

Aidan's role as assistant director meant he worked closely with his boss, Anthony Richter, who ran the team. Therefore, he knew precisely what was happening within it. Richter had shared most of the detail with him.

Then, today, he had overheard Richter's personal assistant on a call with Richter discussing some major incident that had occurred during his meeting in Zaporizhzhia that day. The assistant had sounded shocked.

Aidan had mentioned the Zaporizhzhia meeting to Irina on Tuesday evening and told her who was attending, including the names of three external consultants who were Richter's guests.

Although from the call he didn't pick up any precise details about what had happened at the site, and didn't like to ask as Richter hadn't briefed him, it was obvious there was a connection.

Now, he found it difficult to believe he had been so stupid.

During his briefings several years earlier, prior to his posting at Wiesbaden, he had been warned about honey traps. The warnings had been repeated to all staff since then at intervals. But he had never dreamed it could actually happen to him.

At the time, and especially after a couple of cocktails at the Himmel Bar, he simply thought he'd got lucky with a beautiful woman.

He sat in silence for a few minutes, staring upward.

From somewhere in the building, he could hear the distant sound of voices.

It took him a few moments to notice the sound was coming from the metal grille, high on the wall.

One voice was female. Irina. Another was the bald man who had locked him in here. And there was another tinny male voice that sounded as though it was coming from either the laptop or the speaker Aidan had seen downstairs. That must be the caller who had phoned Irina.

Aidan realized that their conversation must be echoing up a ventilation shaft in the wall, via the grilles in each room.

The voices remained a little faint, so Aidan lifted the table to the wall and stood on it. Now his head was right next to the grille and the sounds were more distinct.

They were speaking Russian.

"*. . . So, Igor, the drone strike succeeded?*" he heard Irina ask. She continued to ask something else that was not clear.

"*Yes, Anke, he's dead,*" came the tinny male voice through the speaker.

That confused Aidan for a moment. Anke? That wasn't her name.

"*But the other targets—Robinson, Scales, Marchenko—are still alive,*" the man continued.

Aidan could hear the annoyance in the man's voice even through the ventilation shaft.

Irina swore loudly.

"*Second drone malfunctioned on takeoff, like many recently. The ongoing component problems,"* the man continued. *"It proved impossible to carry out a hit on the security building."*

The voices became a little quieter, and Aidan only caught scraps of the conversation that followed.

". . . you've known the DAM KEEPER longest, so can you brief him?"

"Yes, Anke, I'm already planning to talk to him . . ."

Aidan frowned. The guy kept calling her Anke. Was that her real name instead of Irina?

". . . I will accelerate our plans . . . activate Operation Noi, and increase stocks of ammonium nitrate if needed . . ."

". . . Our security remains tight. Nobody suspects anything, we believe . . ."

". . . Can DAM KEEPER find out from his colleagues what . . . "

None of it made any immediate sense to Aidan, but he continued to listen, now standing on tiptoe in order to get closer to the metal grille to hear better. He cupped his hand next to his left ear and applied it to the grille, which also helped.

". . . let me update you on Operation Noi . . ." That was the male caller's voice. *"DAM KEEPER has given me these high-level government details . . ."*

Aidan heard and understood enough of the conversation that followed to feel utterly shaken.

Surely that couldn't really be what these people were planning to do?

This had to be some kind of elaborate sting, in which he was playing a very unwilling part.

Or was it true?

He continued to listen for several minutes, his head buzzing in disbelief.

Then, from behind him, there came a sharp rattle and click of a key in a lock, a squeak, and the sound of the door opening quickly.

Aidan spun around, glimpsing the bald man in the doorway as he did so. But then he slipped on the table and fell backward onto it, causing it to collapse beneath him and depositing him in a heap on the floor. He banged his right hip and rib cage hard on the floor as he fell and gave an involuntary yelp of pain.

He lay on the floor and looked up.

The bald man was standing above him, staring down.

"What the hell were you doing up there on the table?" the man said. He glanced up at the ventilation grille and paused, his ear cocked. Sure enough, in the ensuing silence, the faint sound of Irina's voice—or was it Anke?—from downstairs could be heard emanating through the grille.

"You were listening," the man growled.

"No, I was just—"

The man didn't give Aidan a chance to finish. He bent down, grabbed him with both hands by the shirt collar, and yanked him up, ripping the back of his shirt as he did so.

"Get up, you fool. I'm taking you downstairs to talk about this."

CHAPTER SIX

Friday, June 16, 2017
Frankfurt

Anke Leonova turned around as the door behind her clanged open. In marched Gavrill Rezanov, sweat glistening on his bald head as he propelled their new asset, Aidan, by his shirt collar, which was now badly ripped.

She swiftly tapped the red button on her phone, ending the call.

"What *are* you doing?" Anke began, a note of anger in her voice. She had instructed Rezanov only to check that Aidan was still secure, not to drag him down here while she was still on the call.

"Wait. I've got a good reason for bringing him," Rezanov said. "When I got to the room, I found him standing on a table listening to you on the call, through the ventilation shaft. It's possible to hear from upstairs what we were saying down here." He let go of Aidan and pointed to the grille on the wall above the projector screen.

Anke's eyes shot to the grille. "What do you mean?"

"The sound from this room—it goes up through the ventilation shaft." Rezanov waved his arm upward to emphasize his point.

"*Sooksin*," she muttered. "Son of a bitch. Are you sure?"

"I heard you talking myself from up there. He's heard everything."

Anke bunched her fist and slammed it on the table. "Didn't you check all that kind of thing?" she asked. "I told you to make sure the room was secure. You had one job to do."

Rezanov threw up his hands. "It is secure. He was locked in. There are no windows. But—"

"But you didn't check the soundproofing? You fool."

Aidan shook his head. "I heard nothing. I wasn't listening. I just—"

Rezanov grabbed Aidan by the collar again and shook him. There was another ripping sound as his shirt seam tore even further. "You are a liar. You were up on a table listening until you fell off. I saw you."

Anke stared at the two men. Clearly, Rezanov was telling the truth.

"You were standing on a table, deliberately listening to our private conversation down here?" She pointed an accusatory finger at Aidan.

"No, I heard nothing."

"Bullshit," Rezanov spat. He turned to Anke. "We can take care of this. I can kill him."

"No," Anke said. "Let me think."

Anke rocked back on her chair and mentally ran through everything she and Rezanov had just discussed on the conference call with Igor Ivanov. They had gone into a lot of detail. He had used her real name too.

Shit. Just about everything.

Why didn't I check that soundproofing myself? Idiot.

This was the problem with acquiring and using buildings at very short notice for such operations. There was no time to get everything set up properly and check for anomalies such as soundproofing. This old redbrick warehouse, on Hanauer Landstrasse, in the industrial area adjacent to the Frankfurt East shipping container railway terminal, had been available on a short-term lease, but it was far from ideal.

Anke folded her arms and scrutinized Aidan, her mind now whirring.

Had he heard everything?

She had to assume he had.

She cursed loudly as she realized the implications.

What to do?

There was now no way she could let Aidan return home and go back to work—at least not until the entire operation was complete. The risk of him spilling the beans was just too high, even allowing for the hugely incriminating sex video she now possessed, which would undoubtedly cause him enormous embarrassment if it became public. He might just decide the price he would pay for it going viral was worth it, and he might then pass on what he had just heard.

Yet, at the same time, she couldn't hold Aidan here in this building for too long. His work colleagues, his friends, his family, and others would realize quickly that he was missing and would trigger a manhunt, likely involving German police.

If a huge police hunt began, her chances of avoiding discovery were low. There was too much CCTV covering most streets and properties in almost every city and town across the world these days. It was hard to cover one's tracks completely.

Furthermore, corrupting and blackmailing someone was one thing. Holding them captive on German soil was quite another. She would be thrown into a German prison if discovered, of that she was certain.

Anke had carried high hopes that her recruitment of Aidan would pay further dividends in the future. The information he had passed on so far had been high-carat gold and had earned her tremendous credit with Igor Ivanov. She imagined Ivanov might have mentioned her name at the Kremlin, maybe even in briefings with the president.

To have uncovered a meeting between CIA operatives and a traitor within the Donbas People's Militia, Aleksey Zhukov—someone who was trusted by the Kremlin and by the Russian army—was a serious success.

But more than that, Aidan had also given her the names of the CIA and SZR operatives involved in the meeting with Zhukov—Jayne Robinson, Neal Scales, and Valentin Marchenko.

The names meant little to Anke.

However, they clearly meant much more to Ivanov.

He had been even more delighted with that information than she had expected, although ultimately furious that the planned hits on all of them had taken down only Zhukov in the end.

The failure of the second drone had nothing to do with her. She had carried out her part of the operation flawlessly. That information she obtained, resulting in the partial success at Zaporizhzhia, had raised her hopes that she could squeeze much more high-quality confidential information from Aidan about what the USACE and other US agencies, including the military and intelligence services, were doing in Ukraine.

But those hopes had now gone out the window, she knew that.

Anke stood and walked over to Aidan, her arms tightly

folded. "You have just made a big mistake," she said, eyeballing him. "And it's going to cost you."

She turned to Rezanov. "Take him to the other secure room upstairs, at the back of the building. Lock him in there. Make sure there is no ventilation system screwup this time. If there is a grille, board it up."

Rezanov nodded, grabbed Aidan by the collar again, and frog-marched him out of the room. She could hear their footsteps clattering down the corridor.

Anke tried to think through what other steps she needed to take.

She decided to ask Rezanov to keep watch outside the building, where he could spot any approach by police, intelligence services, or anyone else. He could also help her plan the next step, which would have to involve getting Aidan Scarpa out of Frankfurt.

First, though, she needed to arrange surveillance of the Himmel Bar, as it seemed to her that was where any search for Aidan was most likely to start. She picked up her phone and found contact details for a local Frankfurt-based freelance operative who she knew had done surveillance work previously for the GRU in Germany, was skilled with a camera and zoom lenses, and very professional on the street.

Aidan had probably, at some point, told someone he was drinking at the Himmel, Anke assumed. If the freelance operative could spot any sign of an investigative team in or outside the bar, that would at least give them some warning about what was happening. Her instinct was that those who had narrowly escaped the strike in Zaporizhzhia—Robinson, Scales, and Marchenko—would almost certainly now be looking for the source of the leak that had killed Zhukov and placed them in jeopardy.

Given that Aidan could not now be allowed to return to his apartment or work, their answer would be obvious. And therefore, the Himmel Bar would likely be high on their list of places to check out.

She called the operative and explained quickly what she wanted. She then gave him precise instructions about how to send his updates and photographs by secure, encrypted email to her, to the GRU's headquarters in Moscow, where they could be properly analyzed, and to Igor Ivanov's office.

Anke's chief concern now was to ensure she evaded the CIA and the SZR, which might not be straightforward.

If this now went wrong, Igor Ivanov, rather than praising her at the Kremlin, would have her on toast.

He would have her sent to either Lefortovo or Butyrka, the two most notorious prisons in Moscow, where her fate in one of the basement torture rooms would have only one outcome.

Pizdets. Deep shit.

But she knew she couldn't just bury her head in the sand. She was going to have to explain everything to Ivanov and work out a solution. Better to do it now, before things escalated and the situation got any worse.

At thirty-nine, Anke had recruited many assets for the Motherland using similar methods to those used on Aidan. She had become immune to the emotional side of what she did for a living. They had taught her how to block all of that out at State School 4, the so-called sexpionage college at Kazan, about seven hundred kilometers east of Moscow.

Graduates from the college, nicknamed "swallows," were mostly deployed across the Soviet Union's and Russia's foreign intelligence agencies, the SVR and the GRU, during the Cold War and afterward. Anke graduated from the college at the age of twenty-two and subsequently joined the GRU, specializing in recruitment of high-level assets across Western Europe. She was fluent in English as well as several European languages, including German and French, and adept at mastering new identities, which she had done for this operation. The passport she was using was Georgian and identified her as Irina Nicoli, the name she had given to Aidan.

While with the GRU, she had worked for Ivanov, a former senior officer with the service. She also carried out occasional special assignments for him after he became deputy prime minister, including infiltrations of the United States and Canada. Then, when President Putin put Ivanov in charge of special operations inside the president's office, he handpicked her to join him.

Although Ivanov was an extremely tough, demanding boss, the financial rewards of her role were large. She had a luxurious four-bedroom apartment in the prestigious Khamovniki district of central Moscow, on the sixth floor of a building that overlooked the Bolshoy Kamenny Bridge, spanning the Moskva River. From her living room, she had a clear view of the red Kremlin walls across the river and the imposing Senate Palace building within.

Her bank accounts already contained more than enough to fund a very comfortable retirement when she was too old to continue doing this for a living, which she figured would be the case within five or six years.

She had told Aidan that she had been born in Georgia and had moved to Berlin with her parents when Georgia separated from the Soviet Union in 1991. A little of that was kind of true, but the family's move in 1991 had actually been to Moscow, not Berlin.

Anke paced up and down the room, thinking about what to do next and what precisely she should tell Ivanov. It was tricky.

Eventually, she sat at the table, took out her phone, and dialed Ivanov's number, using the usual end-to-end secure encrypted service that she always used for their conversations. This time, she left the conference call speaker switched off. Rezanov didn't need to be included in this conversation.

Ivanov listened without speaking as she told him what had happened and outlined the steps she had already taken to detect attempts by Western intelligence to locate Aidan Scarpa.

When she finished, Ivanov swore violently at her, shouting so loudly it forced her to hold the phone away from her ear—which was more or less what she had expected.

It had happened before, and she knew she just had to ride it out.

Eventually, Ivanov calmed down a little and his voice dropped.

"This is what you will do," he said. "You'll follow EAST SNAKE TWO protocols. And I don't want any stupid mistakes this time; otherwise it's the end of the road for you. Understood?"

"Yes, sir."

She listened carefully as he went through a lengthy series of instructions.

CHAPTER SEVEN

Saturday, June 17, 2017
    Washington, DC

It had been at least six months since Vic Walter had seen the defense secretary, Philip Monterey, for a one-to-one meeting, and years since he had been summoned to the enormous concentric Pentagon building for such an encounter on a Saturday.

Normally, it was Vic's boss, Director of Central Intelligence Arthur Veltman, who conducted such meetings. But Veltman was currently in Berlin for discussions about Russia and Ukraine with his counterpart at the German foreign intelligence service, the BND.

An hour and a half earlier, Vic had been taking the rare opportunity to sit and drink a coffee with his wife, Eleanor, in the garden of their redbrick house on the corner of Sherier Place NW and Manning Place NW, in the Palisades suburb of DC. She had spent most of the time updating him on her plans to prune and move shrubs and plants in the garden, all of which he had approved of. It was easier to leave it to her.

But then his phone rang. Now he was entering Room 3E880, Monterey's luxurious office complex on the third floor of the Pentagon.

Monterey, a bespectacled man in his mid-fifties, with a fleshy face and slicked-back dark hair, stood as Vic walked in and shook hands with him.

"I'm sorry to drag you in here on a weekend," Monterey began. "But there's no alternative, believe me. I couldn't brief you on the phone. Would you like a coffee?"

"I was halfway through one at home when your assistant called," Vic said. "So yes, I could do with one."

Monterey pulled out a seat for Vic at the circular meeting table near his window, then walked to the door and gave his coffee order to his assistant, sitting just outside.

The office was on the northeast corner of the outer ring of the building's five-ring structure. Looking eastward, Vic could see the Potomac River and Columbia Island. In the other direction, to the west, was the green expanse of Arlington National Cemetery, the military cemetery maintained by the US Army.

A few minutes later, after a short discussion about the previous night's victory by Monterey's beloved Washington Nationals against New York Mets, the coffee arrived.

"Anyway, enough of baseball," Monterey said as his assistant exited the room. "We have a situation."

"I assumed that, Philip," Vic said, as dryly as he could.

"I had a call earlier today from my USACE commander, Frank Merriden," Monterey said, as he took a sip of his coffee. "I know you met him at Langley recently, together with Colonel Anthony Richter."

Vic nodded. "I did. I assume you know that their special projects team has been helping provide us with cover for an operation in Ukraine, which took place yesterday. It didn't quite go as planned."

"Frank has briefed me on what happened to your operation and your source," Monterey said. "And the situation I'm referring to concerns an assistant director in that special projects team, who is based at the USACE Europe headquarters in Wiesbaden."

Monterey raised an eyebrow, clearly testing to see whether Vic knew whom he was talking about. He didn't.

Vic pushed his glasses back up his nose. "Go on."

"This guy was helping coordinate the Ukraine-based USACE people who were supporting your team on the ground. He's been an insider with significant access to the details of who, what, where, and when."

Now Vic was feeling somewhat impatient. Monterey almost seemed to be enjoying having a piece of intel that Vic didn't.

"Come on, then. Tell me who."

"Guy named Aidan Scarpa. He went missing last night and failed to show up for work at the Wiesbaden offices this morning. The team, of course, was called in for an inquest after what happened at Zaporizhzhia, although they wouldn't normally work Saturdays. Seems that Scarpa went off by himself for a bit of Friday evening refreshment in Frankfurt and never returned. He wasn't at his apartment this morning when we sent people round to check."

"Aidan Scarpa?" Vic repeated. An alarm was going off somewhere in the recesses of his mind. Had he heard the name a few years earlier?

"That's him."

Vic hesitated. "This rings a bell. Who is this guy?"

Monterey pressed his lips together in a straight line. "It's the president's estranged son."

Vic felt as though an electric current had shot through him. "Holy shit."

Now he remembered.

Monterey's face remained impassive. "Only child from the president's first marriage," he said. "He's thirty-three now. They don't speak, or hardly. Haven't for twenty-five years at least. The president split up with the mother, Molly Scarpa, on bad terms. The boy then switched to his mother's maiden name—or rather, she switched it for him."

"Yes, of course." President Ferguson was currently on his second marriage. Vic had been told a few years earlier by someone inside the Pentagon that Aidan Scarpa was working for the USACE in Europe.

"But I didn't know he was on this team," Vic said as he drained his coffee. "Didn't know he was in Frankfurt. General Merriden never mentioned him when we had a planning meeting at Langley just over a week ago. Neither did Richter. I hadn't seen the access list for the operation. That was in the hands of two of my senior team, Neal Scales and Abram Malevich, who—"

"Who may not be aware he was the president's son," Monterey interrupted.

"I am completely certain they would have flagged it for me if they knew."

"Not many people do know, even inside the USACE and the Pentagon. That's on the president's orders. He wants the guy kept low-key. That would be why Frank didn't mention it —our senior team is under orders to disclose it only when absolutely necessary. We trusted Scarpa and still do trust him, until we receive evidence that convinces us otherwise. So Frank probably didn't see the need to inform you. But in any case, it might have been that Scarpa wasn't confirmed on the team at that stage. The operation was put together quickly."

Vic threw up his hands. "That's fine until things go wrong.

Surely it's something he should have mentioned—especially given that the president is due to visit Kyiv on the twenty-third." Vic could feel the anger building inside him. "What's this Aidan Scarpa's profile like? Hasn't there been any media coverage about him?"

"The media hasn't seemed interested in him," Monterey said. "There's been the odd piece, but they seem to think Scarpa is just a boring engineer. Which he is. He's had a good track record in his job."

Vic leaned back in his chair. "What's your gut feeling about him, from what you know? Does he sound like someone who would leak details of an operation and cause the death of an agent who was trying to help us against Russia?"

"I don't know enough to say," Monterey said. "And we don't know yet if he caused the problem with your operation, do we? But he is missing. And that's worrisome."

"So he was by himself when he went out last night?" Vic asked.

Monterey shrugged. "It seems so."

"And nobody knows where he went?" Vic asked.

"No."

"What a screwup. Surely, someone must have been keeping him on a tight leash while the operation was going on. I'm surprised he was allowed out at all last night after what went down in Zaporizhzhia."

Monterey shook his head. "The USACE isn't a prison camp. We'll have to get to the bottom of it."

"Does the president know?" Vic asked.

"Not yet. We're informing Phil Anstee as we speak, and the president will be told later this evening."

Phil Anstee was the president's national security advisor, a tall, dark-haired man whom Vic knew reasonably well.

"Maybe Scarpa just got lucky with some girl on his night out and hasn't come back yet," Vic said. "Is he single?"

"He is. But the team in Wiesbaden thinks that unlikely. He knew he had to be at the office this morning and has never failed to show up for work before, I'm told."

Vic gazed out of the panoramic office window, across the Potomac, and toward the Washington Monument beyond. He sometimes wished he had a view like that from his own office.

"What's being done to locate Scarpa?" Vic asked.

"The USACE security team is on it," Monterey said. "We are discussing our next steps and whether to involve German police now or wait and see if Scarpa shows up. But this could be serious, and so I would like to ask for your help. We will probably need the NSA too. That's why I've called you in here."

The National Security Agency, based at Fort Meade, northeast of Washington, was the United States' specialist signals intelligence service, focused on tapping into and monitoring phone, internet, and email traffic globally. Vic's teams at the CIA worked regularly with them.

Vic leaned forward and looked Monterey in the eye.

The defense secretary was clearly in a tight spot. If it emerged that one of his USACE team had been leaking highly classified information to the Russians, costing the life of a potentially highly valuable CIA asset, and that team member was the US president's son, this could be a resignation matter.

But it wasn't just Monterey who could be in trouble here. Vic would likely be in the firing line too, given that Scarpa had been allowed to work on the CIA operation without, it seemed, proper vetting of his background or full disclosure.

Vic knew he had no choice but to try to come to Monterey's

rescue. If he played his cards right, and if things went his way, he could earn a lot of credit with the defense secretary. That could potentially help him strengthen his position in the shark-infested political waters surrounding both the Pentagon and Langley.

Of course, if it all went south, the converse was true.

There immediately seemed to be a great deal at stake.

"Don't worry, Philip," Vic said. "We'll do all we can to find him. But I suggest for the time being you don't involve the German police. That would guarantee wall-to-wall media coverage, which may not be what we want right now. Tell the president that we're on it immediately and that we're being extremely discreet. I'll get our team in Kyiv for the GRAY WOLF meeting to work on this straightaway given the link-age. I want to keep it as tight as possible and minimize the potential for leaks."

CHAPTER EIGHT

Monday, June 19, 2017
  Frankfurt

It had been many years since Jayne had been in the sprawling Frankfurt CIA station, on the sixth and highest floor of one of the slate-roofed buildings at the fortified American consulate building in Giessener Strasse. The station, one of the CIA's busiest in Europe, was now home to the Agency's massive Center for Cyber Intelligence Europe unit, an espionage operation that covered the entire continent and beyond.

Jayne's previous spells in the city had been during her long career with MI6, Britain's foreign intelligence service. Her fluency in German, among other languages, meant she was often deployed on operations in Frankfurt, Berlin, and other major centers.

She and Neal walked along a cream-colored corridor, past the steel security doors for the cyber unit, and into a secure room they had been allocated near the office of the Frankfurt chief of station, the highly experienced Hazel Foster. Jayne had come across Foster during her time at MI6, although not since she had become a freelance operative and begun carrying out jobs for Vic.

They had arrived in Frankfurt the previous evening from Kyiv on an unmarked CIA twin-engine Gulfstream V jet. The aircraft had been allocated to them by Vic, who had given them both an urgent briefing about the Aidan Scarpa development on a secure conference call. He had also sent a secure email containing file photographs of Scarpa and a background dossier.

Like Vic, both Jayne and Neal were irritated that Scarpa's status and connection to the president had not been flagged to them by the USACE before the operation in Zaporizhzhia. Never mind that Scarpa's relationship with the president seemed almost nonexistent. It seemed like a basic error of judgment, as well as discourteous, in Jayne's opinion, and amounted to incompetence on the USACE's part.

However, that had to be put to one side. Now Jayne and Neal were focused on starting their operation.

First, as a priority, Jayne needed to establish contact with and somehow meet Kira Suslova to try to build a line of inquiry inside Moscow to flesh out the intelligence obtained from GRAY WOLF about the DAM KEEPER and Operation Noi. Who and what were they?

During the operation eight months earlier, when Jayne had coerced and recruited Suslova by having a Ukrainian hacker drain her bank account, she had obtained a burner phone number from the Russian. So far, Jayne had not used it, but now was the time.

There was an obvious risk attached to doing so, given that Jayne had no idea whether Suslova's burner had been compromised since their meeting, was being monitored by Russian counterintelligence, or was even still in use. But there was no other option. She had to hope Suslova took all the appropriate precautions to maintain the phone's security.

Jayne sat at one of the three workstations in the room and took out a new cell phone with a fresh prepaid German SIM card, sourced by the CIA station. She loaded up the Signal encrypted messaging app, signed into her anonymous account, and found Suslova's account using the number the Russian had given her. Then she tapped out a short message.

Apologies for checkmating you last October—nothing personal. Need to arrange another chess match very soon—play for money this time? Let me know when and where.

There was no way Jayne was going to sign the message, but Suslova would know what that meant and who had sent it, Jayne hoped.

She pressed the green send button, a vaguely pessimistic feeling descending over her as she did so. Would the Russian be expecting such an approach and have a response ready that would turn the tables on Jayne?

Jayne reprimanded herself for catastrophizing, one of her bad habits. There was no way Suslova could get her money back without cooperating.

She switched the new cell phone off and placed it in her spare Faraday pouch, a small lead-lined bag designed to prevent the phone from being traced or monitored, then slipped it into her pocket.

The second urgent task they had was to locate the missing Aidan Scarpa to either confirm or rule out his culpability in the death of GRAY WOLF.

To that end, the USACE special projects chief, Anthony Richter, had flown back to Frankfurt from Kyiv and was now waiting for Jayne and Neal at the USACE Europe headquarters in Wiesbaden, a forty-kilometer drive west of Frankfurt.

Jayne glanced across at Neal, who was seated at a neighboring desk. "We'd better get moving."

The CIA station driver who took them to Wiesbaden navigated a very professional surveillance detection route, turning a thirty-five minute journey into one that lasted an hour and twenty minutes, mainly through the back streets and industrial areas of Frankfurt. It was better to be safe, given that it was impossible to know who they were up against.

The USACE Europe headquarters was in a modern pink nine-story office building on Konrad Adenauer Ring. As Colonel Richter, again dressed in his multi-camouflage uniform, escorted them into his third-floor office, he explained that the building was named for Amelia Earhart, who had been the first woman to fly non-stop across the Atlantic in 1932.

"We may need some Earhart-style grit to get to the bottom of what happened in Zaporizhzhia," Richter said, as he showed Jayne and Neal to a conference table in front of his desk. "But my sources in DC tell me you've got plenty of that," he added, looking at Jayne.

"We try," Jayne said.

"Well, I've got the special projects team members who worked on the Ukraine operation on standby downstairs, ready to interview. There are only two, apart from me and our missing man, Aidan Scarpa, who had access to what was happening. Otherwise, it was tightly confined. We can get started if you like. I suspect you have no time to waste."

Jayne studied Richter. "That would be a good idea. But can we start with you?"

Richter, who was holding a yellow folder with Aidan Scarpa's name on the front, looked slightly taken aback but recovered quickly. "Okay. Sure."

"It makes sense to start with the man in charge," Jayne said in an even tone. "Apologies if I'm being a little abrupt."

Richter stood facing her and Neal. "It makes sense. And I

would like to apologize for the lack of communication of Scarpa's involvement and links to the president. I imagined that my superior, General Merriden, would share that information if he thought it relevant. Lessons have been learned."

Jayne inclined her head in acknowledgment. "Mistakes happen. Apology accepted."

"I had planned to raise the issue, but you preempted me with the apology," Neal said, a distinct note of sarcasm in his voice. "Thank you."

Jayne was reassured by Richter's humility. There was no point dwelling on the mistake; it was time to move on. It may not have made any difference to what had happened, even if the Agency had been informed.

"So, what's your gut instinct about what happened to Scarpa?" Jayne asked as they sat at the meeting table.

"I wish I knew," Richter said. "I don't know him very well. Spoken to him a handful of times. We don't treat him any different because of his father, and he apparently never speaks about the president, so I wouldn't single him out for attention."

"What's his career path been?" Neal asked. "Any sign that he might cause a problem?"

Richter shook his head, opened the file that was in front of him on the table, and scanned it. "Aged thirty-three. Professional civil and structural engineer, joined USACE ten years ago. He's been working in our Europe special projects section for the past seven years. Done a very good job in places like East Africa, the Balkans, as well as Kosovo and Georgia. He's worked on a lot of humanitarian projects as well as military. No issues at all career-wise."

"How trustworthy is he, would you say?" Neal asked.

"Very trustworthy, delivers the goods," Richter said. "Look, our job at Europe District is to be an enabler of US foreign policy in both Europe and Africa. Like the rest of us, he seems to take that responsibility seriously. He'd signed all the usual classified information nondisclosure agreements, and there has been not the slightest hint he would ignore that. Quietly efficient, I'd say."

"Personal life?" Jayne asked.

Richter shrugged. "I believe, having spoken to his colleagues, he was in a relationship with another USACE employee which finished a couple of years ago when she returned to the US. I've not heard he had anyone since, but who knows what people do once they leave the office."

"Did he take his car?" Jayne asked.

Richter shook his head. "Still parked outside his rental house. A neighbor says he left in a taxi. We're trying to find out which taxi firm and where it took him."

"What about his cell phone?" Jayne asked. "Do you have the number?"

Richter consulted his notebook and read out the number, which Jayne tapped into her phone. "Stupid question, but have you tried calling it?" she asked.

"Of course. It's dead. Goes straight to voicemail."

Neal and Jayne continued the questioning for another twenty minutes, but it became rapidly clear that Scarpa, despite his father's position, had a solid but unremarkable profile at work and didn't seem out of the ordinary outside of work either.

"Thank you, Colonel," Neal said eventually. "Shall we call in one of the other two?"

Richter picked up his phone and summoned the first of the duo, the special projects section chief, David Gatwick.

Gatwick first gave a brief outline of the USACE's genuine project in Ukraine, which was to survey all seven hydroelectric dams and make recommendations for improvements and necessary repairs and upgrades, including the adjacent locks for ships and boats.

Then Jayne and Neal ran through a lengthy set of questions about the covert project with the CIA, Scarpa's role within that, and then a few more personal questions about the president's son, while Richter sat silently and listened.

But Gatwick turned out to have no more information about Scarpa than Richter, despite being his immediate boss. He confirmed Scarpa's previous relationship with a colleague and added that, to the best of his knowledge, he had not had a girlfriend since.

"There's not much more I can say," Gatwick summed up. "He played a good part in setting up the Zaporizhzhia operation. Seemed committed to getting the job done, as usual. Nice guy, very professional. I have no idea where he could have gone, and he's not the type I could imagine would deliberately betray anyone, let alone to the Russians. He's worked on many highly sensitive projects before, which is why we trust him. I like working with him."

Jayne leaned back in her chair and scrutinized Gatwick, a tall man with a crew cut. They were drawing a blank here. Should these senior guys have been keeping a closer eye on this particular employee, especially given the presidential connection? It would seem so.

She glanced at Neal and received a nod to indicate he thought there was no more they could obtain from Gatwick. The exchange was caught by Richter, who sent Gatwick on his way and summoned the final member of the USACE special projects team, Ian Burstein.

Burstein, with tightly cropped blond hair and a pair of broad swimmer's shoulders, was a peer of Scarpa, was at the same level, and was a year younger. He repeated much of what Gatwick had said about Scarpa's trustworthiness and likability and professional capabilities. He too confirmed that Scarpa's relationship with his girlfriend had ended two years earlier.

"Did he have any other, more recent relationships of any kind?" Jayne asked. She was keen to obtain a clear answer, because neither Richter nor Gatwick had been able to provide that, and in cases where people were compromised, it often happened through their relationships.

Burstein shook his head. "As far as I know, he didn't have a girlfriend, although I got the feeling he was ready for another relationship. It had been some time since the last one. He occasionally went out by himself for a drink, as you might do if you were looking."

Jayne leaned forward. "Where did he go? And when was this?"

"Into Frankfurt, mostly, I think. And it was over the past few months."

"But he didn't appear to have found anyone?" she asked.

Burstein paused for a beat. "No, he never hinted at dating anyone."

"What about his friends?" Jayne asked. "Who did he hang out with?"

"At work, I've probably been closest to him. We often go for a coffee or sometimes a beer after work. Outside of work, I got the impression he didn't really have a great circle of friends. He had been close to his former girlfriend. When she left, he seemed a bit lonely. I never got to know any of his other non-work friends, but I don't think there were many."

Jayne exchanged glances with Neal, who gave a slight shrug, as if to say that he, like her, thought they were making little progress.

"Thank you," Neal said. "We may need to talk to you again. We'll be in touch if so."

"And let us know if you think of anything else that comes to mind that might be helpful," Jayne said. "Even if it seems insignificant to you."

Burstein stood, shook hands with Jayne and Neal, and nodded at Richter.

He was halfway out the door when he turned and looked at Jayne. "There is something."

Jayne lifted her head. "What's that?" she asked.

"You asked if he had met anyone when he went out drinking by himself."

"Yes, I did," Jayne replied.

"Well, as I said, he wasn't dating anyone, as far as I know. But there was someone he mentioned in passing—someone he'd met and was going to have another drink with. That must have been at least three weeks ago, though, maybe four."

"Go on," Jayne said. "In Frankfurt?"

Burstein nodded. "He mentioned a cocktail bar. The Himmel, from memory. Said it was good. That was the conversation. He never said any more."

"Do you know where that is?"

"Not sure. Bahnhofsviertel, around the station, I think he said."

Jayne knew the area he was referring to from previous visits to Frankfurt. "The red-light area, you mean?"

Burstein looked down at the floor. "Well, it is around that area, I guess."

Jayne hesitated. She was going to have to ask the question. "You're not trying to tell me he was using a hooker, are you?"

Burstein looked embarrassed. "I don't know. He didn't say that, no. But that was where he met her."

"Did he mention a name?"

"No," Burstein said.

"And did he say how the date had gone? Did he tell you if he had arranged another?" Jayne asked.

"Yes, he said briefly that he'd enjoyed it and was fixing another one, but I don't know if that happened or when."

Despite further questioning, Burstein had nothing else of use to offer.

When he had finally gone, Jayne stood and walked over to the window. She turned and faced Richter and Neal. "We'll need to find out as fast as possible who Scarpa met at that bar and where she is. My gut tells me she could well be involved in his disappearance."

"CCTV's going to be the quickest option," Neal said. "We can't use official channels—police and search warrants. We'll need to hack into that bar's system and see if any of the footage is still stored. After a few weeks, it may well not be. I'll get on the phone with the NSA—Alex will help us out."

Alex Goode was one of Vic's and Neal's key contacts at the National Security Agency at Fort Meade, Maryland, and who Jayne knew quite well, having worked with him on operations in the past.

Richter tapped his fingers on the table. "If you want the NSA, you're in the right place. And you won't need to get Fort Meade involved."

"What do you mean?" Neal asked.

"Well, there's the Consolidated Intelligence Center, which is at the Clay Barracks complex, the army base. Clay Kaserne, they call it in German. It's eight kilometers from here on the east side of Wiesbaden, next to the army airfield," Richter said. "There's a big NSA facility there and a big US Army base, but I assume you knew that."

Jayne remembered being told about the new intelligence center at Wiesbaden, but hadn't realized there was an NSA facility there too. It was incredible how embedded the United States military was in this area of Germany.

"I know the NSA chief there," Richter said. "And I also know the commander of the 1st Battalion, 214th Aviation

Regiment, that's based at the site. I can ask if they can help with this."

This seemed odd to Jayne. "How do you know these people?" she asked.

"We built facilities there for the NSA only a couple of years ago," Richter said. "Cost them 160 million bucks. So I know the boss. I went the extra mile to give him the specifications he wanted. I've also built facilities for the regiment commander. Maybe it's time to call in some favors."

Jayne nodded. "Thank you. Please do call in the favors." She turned to Neal. "In the meantime, we need to visit the Himmel Bar—now."

CHAPTER NINE

Monday, June 19, 2017
   Frankfurt

The items of disguise that Jayne often took with her on trips included a shoulder-length straight blonde wig, a pair of plain black-rimmed glasses, and a reversible blue-and-beige lightweight jacket with plenty of pockets. They were basic accessories, but they were highly effective in engineering a rapid change of appearance when needed.

In the absence of anything more sophisticated, she deployed all three for the visit she and Neal made to the Himmel Bar. They had also obtained handguns and spare magazines from the weapons locker at Hazel Foster's CIA station, a Beretta for Neal and a Walther PPS for Jayne—always her weapon of choice—which was now tucked into her inside raincoat pocket.

The handguns and disguises seemed sensible precautions, although probably unnecessary. If Russian intelligence operatives really had used the bar as a recruiting ground, it was unlikely they would remain anywhere near it any longer than needed.

Although Neal had done little fieldwork in recent years, it was certain his details would be on all Russian intelligence databases. So he too deployed two simple disguise items. A tall, slim man of fifty-seven, with tousled blond hair, albeit now with more than a hint of gray, he donned a neat iron-gray wig and a pair of tortoiseshell glasses.

The pair of them also ensured their CIA driver carried out a thorough surveillance detection route on their way to the bar, which was on Elbestrasse, two blocks from the station and, as Jayne had recalled, in the center of the red-light district.

The driver dropped them three hundred meters from the bar, and they walked the remaining distance along Elbestrasse, keeping a careful check for any sign of surveillance.

The street was lined with a variety of sex shops, table-dancing clubs, cafés, budget hotels, and fast-food outlets. Cars and vans were densely parked on both sides of Elbestrasse, which was busy with tourists, office workers who had presumably finished early for the day, and local residents carrying shopping bags full of groceries.

It took Jayne and Neal a few minutes to find the entrance to the Himmel Bar, a black door hidden in an alcove next to a hotel. It was marked by a tiny sign next to a doorbell, which Neal rang. A few seconds later, a man opened it and let them in.

They went down a flight of wooden stairs and found themselves in a dimly lit, classic cocktail bar, with vaulted ceilings, olive-green walls, wooden floors, and candlelit tables. A bearded man was busy mixing drinks behind a bar laden with equipment that looked as though it belonged in a chemist's laboratory. Behind him on the shelves was an Aladdin's cave-style selection of bourbons, obscure whiskeys, infused gins, and just about every other spirit imaginable.

"Let's sit at the bar, then chat with the barman," Jayne suggested.

They sat on stools and perused the menu. Jayne ordered a Kaya Colada, the ingredients of which included Bacardi rum, milk syrup, and pineapple, and Neal an Elmo, with gin, rooibos tea, and lemon.

"Are you enjoying your drinks?" the barman asked in good English with a heavy German accent. He introduced himself as Heinrich.

It provided Jayne with an opening to engage him in a conversation about the cocktail-making process and the bar's history.

While she was doing so, she glanced around carefully, looking for hidden CCTV cameras. Most bars in Germany still didn't have CCTV in her experience, given the country's fairly strict privacy laws. This was partly a legacy of the backlash against overbearing surveillance by the Stasi state security service during the Cold War in East Germany. That said, the number of cameras was definitely on the increase, and the laws were being eased following terrorist attacks.

It took her a while, but eventually Jayne spotted cameras that were concealed between bottles behind the bar, above an air-conditioning unit, and in light fixtures.

"So, what are you guys here for?" Heinrich asked eventually. "Vacation or work?"

"A bit of both," Jayne replied. "We're here to meet up with a friend who sometimes uses this bar, but he's very late." She glanced at her watch. "He should have been here an hour ago, and we arrived later than we expected. I hope we haven't missed him. It'll be the second time if so. I was also intending to meet him here the week before last, on the Friday, but got held up through work and missed him then, too."

"What's his name?" Heinrich asked. "I've been here all afternoon. I might have seen him."

Jayne certainly wasn't going to give Aidan Scarpa's real name and she figured the barman probably didn't know him personally anyway. But she decided to take a gamble.

"Philip," Jayne said. "Hang on, I've got a photo on my phone."

She took out her phone and scrolled through her photos until she found the ones that Vic had sent.

"That's him," Jayne said, holding out the device. "Have you seen him today?"

Heinrich studied the photo. "Not today. But I recall him from maybe a couple of weeks ago. I remember a lot of our customers. He was in here with his girlfriend—a pretty girl. They were very into each other. I remember them because they both ordered our signature cocktail—the King Clear. We had quite a chat about how it's made."

"So he's definitely not been in here today?" Neal asked.

Heinrich shook his head.

"That's odd," Jayne said as she took a sip of her cocktail. "We arranged to meet." She creased her forehead, attempting to look puzzled. "Have you seen him at all since he was here with his girlfriend, then?"

"No. Sorry."

"No problem, thanks," Jayne said. "I'll give him another call."

Heinrich nodded to both of them, then turned to a waiting customer, a broad smile of greeting on his face. That was the end of the conversation, Jayne assumed.

Jayne and Neal moved to a table and spent another ten minutes in the bar finishing their drinks before leaving.

As they exited the door, Jayne carefully scrutinized the street in both directions. There were still a lot of tourists in the area, some of them staring into the sex shop windows or joking with the hustlers who were trying to entice them to see a live show.

A handful of bystanders were taking photographs of the street scene. A man with a professional-looking camera equipped with a flash gun was taking pictures of a pretty girl. A lady with a point-and-shoot was taking photographs of the hotel next door to the Himmel Bar. A man across the street, using an SLR camera with a zoom lens, appeared to be pointing it at a vintage open-top BMW parked nearby.

Jayne checked all of them carefully.

None of them were behaving suspiciously, although she gave the man with the SLR a careful second glance. His entire attention appeared to be focused on the BMW, however.

"Let's go," Jayne said. "Looks like we're going to have to rely on the NSA to hack into the bar's security system. There were several cameras in there."

Neal inclined his head. "Just have to hope they keep the video footage."

* * *

Monday, June 19, 2017
   Wiesbaden

Jayne got out of the unmarked CIA Audi A4 and stood looking at the white-and-gray concrete facade of the Consolidated Intelligence Center at the Clay Kaserne, the army barracks complex. It stood in contrast to the more traditional red- or gray-tiled buildings and military housing across the campus, which she guessed must be at least two kilometers long, including the airfield.

Although it was now five thirty in the afternoon, the parking lot was packed with vehicles. Around fifteen thousand US citizens were based in Wiesbaden, Richter had told her, most of them military and the majority housed on this campus.

Richter had arranged the visit directly with the head of the center, who had indeed returned the favors done for him during the construction of the facility.

Now Richter guided Jayne and Neal to a reception area where an armed guard took them through a lengthy security process, including passport checks, fingerprinting, and retinal scanning.

Jayne was already on the retinal recognition system thanks to a visit to the NSA's Fort Meade headquarters during a previous operation. Neal was also on the register, as was Richter. Despite that, the security process took more than twenty minutes.

Once the checks were complete, the guard took them along a corridor to a large steel door where he tapped a code into a keypad on the wall, then asked Jayne, Neal, and Richter to step in front of another retinal scanning device. Only then did the door slide open.

On the other side of the door stood a woman with a blonde bob and dressed in a white blouse whom Jayne vaguely recognized.

The woman stepped toward Jayne, a slight smile on her face. "Anna Falkenstein. I met you at Fort Meade three years ago. Remember? The oil refinery?"

Jayne did. "Anna. Yes, of course. What brings you here?" On their previous encounter, Anna had hacked into the email system of an oligarch's oil refinery on the Black Sea, obtaining critical information for Jayne and her partner, Joe Johnson.

"Promotion," Anna said, pushing a pair of thick black glasses up her nose. "I'm running the unit here now. I moved last year. My father was German, so I'm bilingual."

"I didn't realize you two would know each other," Richter said.

Anna, who looked to be in her late thirties, smiled. "Come this way. I'm assuming this is urgent?"

"You could say that," Jayne said as they headed to the elevator. "We're trying to find out what's been going on in a bar in Frankfurt's red-light district."

Anna raised an eyebrow. "We don't do seedy here," she said, with a wry half-smile.

"I'm hoping it's not seedy," Jayne said. "But it may be dirty in a different way."

A few minutes later, they were all seated in a sound-proofed room two floors higher up the building with a twenty-something technician who was hunched over a keyboard and twin monitor screens on a desk. Anna introduced him only by his first name, Sean.

Working on details about the Himmel Bar from Jayne and Neal, Sean tapped away, periodically swearing under his breath. Most of the time, his screen was full of code that made no sense to Jayne.

Finally, he tapped in another line, and the screen momentarily went blue. Then a grid of nine different video images appeared. In a narrow black band at the top in small capitals were the words *HIMMEL BAR MONITORING*. To the right was a short menu.

Sean turned his head. "I'm in the security system. These are live images—the same as the security team there is seeing if they're watching their monitors. The good news is they have an archive." He pointed to one of the lines on the on-screen menu. "However, I don't know how far back it goes. Who exactly are we looking for?"

Without revealing details of the connection to President Ferguson, Jayne told him about Scarpa. "I'd like to go back over the past month's video."

"Do you have an image?" Sean asked. "I have facial recognition software that will massively speed up the search."

Richter leaned forward. "I have a set of headshots from all angles of him on my iPhone."

"Show me the images," Sean said.

Richter did so, and Sean plugged a cable into the device, through which he downloaded the photos of Scarpa. They were the same ones that Vic had sent to Jayne and Neal.

Sean then dragged the images into a software app on his laptop, connected the hacked Himmel Bar security feed to the app as well, then clicked on the archive.

"Crap," he said. "The archive only goes back twelve days. I'll cover all of that period."

Jayne cursed inwardly.

Sean pressed the start button, and the video spun through at a blur. He explained that his software could operate at high playback speeds, analyzing each frame as it went. "It's still going to take some time, though, given there are nine camera feeds."

"Good work, Sean," Anna said. "I suggest we grab a coffee. It should be done by the time we return."

Indeed, when they returned to the room from the coffee shop on the ground floor, the analysis had been completed. A message on screen stated *Four Matches*.

Sean clicked on the link. All four matches were of the same person on the same evening, Friday, June 9.

"Exactly a week before the GRAY WOLF disaster," Jayne murmured to Neal. "Plenty of time to prepare a hit."

Each image showed a man who was unmistakably Aidan Scarpa. In the first he was sitting on a barstool in the Himmel Bar, being handed a cocktail by Heinrich, the barman. The next two, filmed by different cameras, showed him sitting at a candlelit table in a different area of the bar. In all of them, he was accompanied by a slim, attractive woman with shoulder-length curly dark hair and a low-cut, lacy black top. The final image showed the pair of them at the exit, leaving the bar, now wearing jackets.

"Can you run the video segments, please?" Jayne asked.

Sean did as requested. Each clip lasted about a minute. Although there was no sound, the pair appeared to be in deep and sometimes animated conversation for most of the time, smiling at each other and undoubtedly getting on well. In the video of them leaving the bar, they were close together and glancing at each other.

"There's no hint of any problem or conflict between them, or coercion," Neal said. "Quite the opposite."

Jayne nodded. "Can't argue with that. Can you get some good-quality still images of the woman? I'd like to run them through the CIA database to see if we can get a match."

Sean made a series of keystrokes and within a couple of minutes had three clear still images on his screen. He sent them to Jayne using an NSA secure file transfer system.

"Thank you," Jayne said. "I'm sending these to Langley. That might help us find out if this is just a case of Scarpa getting lucky in a bar with a beautiful woman or whether there's more to it than that."

CHAPTER TEN

Monday, June 19, 2017
  Moscow

Kira Suslova settled down with her first coffee of the morning, picked up a black knight from the carved ivory chess set and board that stood on one end of her desk, and held it tight in her palm.

The chess set had been manufactured from a souvenir she had brought home from a hunting trip in Zimbabwe—the tusks of a large bull elephant that she had shot dead.

There came a knock at the door of her second-floor office door. Before she could respond, it opened and in walked Igor Ivanov, holding a folder in his hand.

Suslova felt a flash of irritation. It wasn't yet eight o'clock, and it was typical of Ivanov, whose office was along the corridor from hers in the Kremlin's Senate Palace building, that he would walk in uninvited.

"I need your help with something," Ivanov said without

preamble. He walked to the chair in front of her desk and sat down.

She replaced the knight on her chessboard. It was ironic. This idiot might be known as the Black Bishop of the Kremlin, but like the president, he couldn't play chess. She had wiped the floor with him on the one occasion they'd had a game, many years earlier. He had never asked for another match.

"What's the problem?" she asked, looking at Ivanov from beneath furrowed eyebrows.

"The problem is in Germany," he said. He opened the folder, removed two photographs, and laid them on the desk in front of Suslova.

"Do you recognize these people?" Ivanov asked. "The pictures were taken in Frankfurt earlier today by one of our local freelance operatives."

Suslova studied the A4-sized color photographs. They both showed a woman and a man walking along a street. The woman had straight, shoulder-length blonde hair, black glasses, and a beige raincoat. The man was tall, with steel-gray hair and tortoiseshell glasses.

Neither of them rang any bells with Suslova. "No, I don't."

Ivanov jabbed a stubby, hairy finger at the woman. "That is someone you have come across before."

"Really?" Suslova studied the photograph more closely. The woman was slim, quite tall, and athletic-looking, but the bespectacled face and hair told her nothing.

She shook her head. "You'll have to tell me."

"Jayne Robinson."

Suslova fought hard to keep her face expressionless as she examined the photograph again. "Is it?"

"Facial recognition told us so," Ivanov said. "Removing variables such as hair, glasses, and so on. And the guy is Neal

Scales, deputy in charge of the CIA's department of operations."

Suslova leaned back in her chair, trying to appear unconcerned. "So what are Jayne Robinson and Neal Scales doing in Frankfurt?"

"She seems to be on the trail of one of our recently recruited assets who gave us a very valuable lead. We took out a traitor as a result, Aleksey Zhukov, the deputy leader of the Donbas People's Militia."

"Ah, yes. I know of him," Suslova said.

"I thought you might. He was someone I worked with directly and previously trusted. But he was stabbing us in the back when we weren't looking by supplying information to the CIA—including Robinson."

"Good work to stop that," Suslova said. "Who did the hit on Zhukov?"

"Boris Volkoff."

"A top-class operator." She knew Volkoff well and had used him herself on a few operations in the Caucasus, particularly in Georgia.

"Who's the asset who provided the intel?" Suslova continued. "And what's the problem?"

"I'm coming to that. The asset is someone inside the US Army Corps of Engineers, their civil engineering operation. But he unfortunately heard too much when meeting his handler in Frankfurt."

"Heard too much?"

Ivanov nodded. "Don't ask me how. But yes. He overheard operational details."

Now Suslova's mind was in overdrive. "That sounds like a major *khrenoten*. A real screwup. Who's handling this guy?" She knew better than to ask directly who the asset was or what he had overheard. But she wondered if it had anything to do with the sensitive operation that Putin had mentioned briefly in the meeting she and Ivanov had attended recently.

Ivanov nodded. "A *khrenoten* describes it exactly. Anke Leonova is handling him and is now trying to limit the damage. I have already told her what to do."

Suslova knew Leonova, with whom she had worked on a couple of occasions. She was a highly skilled swallow, a graduate of State School 4, and had reeled in several high-value assets across Western Europe through successful honey traps. The two women had a high regard for each other.

"How is she limiting the damage?" Suslova asked. "And how much did this asset overhear?"

"Far too much."

"Operational details?"

"Yes," Ivanov snapped, irritation written across his face. "I can't tell you everything—not yet, anyway. But he apparently knows enough that Leonova now can't allow him to return to his office or his home until the operation in question is completed."

"Can't allow him to return? So he's effectively kidnapped?"

Ivanov inclined his head in acknowledgment of her point. "It's a disaster. He should have been a good asset for us long into the future, but she and her colleague have properly screwed it up."

Suslova shook her head. This sounded like real incompetence, and quite unlike Leonova to have allowed it to happen. But there had been far too many such calamities involving the GRU in recent years, including bungled poisonings in the UK and in mainland Europe.

"What's his name? And his background?" Suslova asked.

"I can't tell you that right now, either."

"So, what's she doing with him?" Suslova asked. "Presumably she can't keep him in Frankfurt, or even in Germany very easily. There'll be a huge manhunt once the Americans realize he's missing."

"That's the problem." Ivanov paused. "We're having to move him out."

"How is she getting him out?" Suslova asked.

Ivanov folded his arms. "I can't tell you that."

"So you can't tell me much. What exactly do you want from me?" Suslova asked. Ivanov wasn't telling her everything, but he clearly hadn't just come to her office just to pass the time of day.

Ivanov eyed her steadily across the table. "I thought you might have some insights into how this Jayne Robinson operates," he said, slowly. Was there a note of sarcasm in his voice? Did he know? But he continued before Suslova could speak. "I've had dealings with her myself in the past, and she is damn good. But Leonova has one of our top operators with her."

"Who?"

Ivanov paused, visibly weighing up whether he should give the name. "Gavrill Rezanov."

Suslova nodded. She also knew Rezanov. He was one of the GRU Spetsnaz's top-ranking covert killers.

"And what's the plan?" Suslova asked.

"All you need to know is that I'm instructing Leonova to have Rezanov take Robinson out as quickly as possible. And we'll need all the help we can get to achieve that. So I'm hoping you can give me a few insights into what Robinson might do or how we might run her down."

A shiver of panic ran right through Suslova. What would happen if Robinson was killed by a hotshot Spetsnaz operator? Well, one thing was for sure, Suslova could permanently kiss goodbye the $2 billion that Robinson had so deftly siphoned out of her Shakhmaty Schet—her chess account—held offshore in Moskva Bank's branch in Cyprus. It was money Putin had allocated to her for bribes and payoffs to help her secure the presidency of FIDE, the International Chess Federation.

If she didn't get that money back, it was inevitable that Putin would eventually find out. In fact, it was nothing short of a miracle that he hadn't discovered the loss already during the past eight months.

Suslova knew that she was going to have to take a major risk and find a way to arrange a trade with the Americans. And to trade, at the very minimum, she needed to find out exactly who Leonova's asset was, where he was being taken and how, and details of Operation Noi. She would also need to find out how Rezanov was planning to get to Robinson.

That information might then give her at least a chance to bargain with Robinson and her CIA colleagues in order to get her money back.

But Ivanov wasn't going to tell her all that. To get it, she would either need to be on the inside or obtain the information from someone who was. She thought swiftly through her options.

"In my experience with Robinson, you'll need to expect the unexpected," Suslova said. "She's a sharp operator. Of course, I will try to help you. But it's difficult to do that from a distance. I am happy to offer advice, but I can't operate in the dark. You'll need to involve me more in what's going on, although I fully appreciate there are sensitivities and tightly held operations ongoing."

Ivanov stood. "I'll think about it." He took a couple of steps toward the door. "I will get back to you."

As the door closed, Suslova sank back into her chair.

Was Ivanov for real, or was this a trap? It was always impossible to know with him.

But either way, maybe there might be an opportunity here for a *dvoynoy krest* of Robinson—a double cross. To get her money back and knife the British woman in the back at the same time.

* * *

Monday, June 19, 2017
    Vienna, Austria

Not far from Vienna's magnificent old town center on the southern bank of the River Danube, Gavrill Rezanov lashed the mooring rope from the Sheerline 955 cruiser—the *Joy of Vilshofen*—around a fastening point on the marina's walkway and pulled it tight.

The journey had so far gone more smoothly than he and Anke Leonova had expected. After leaving Frankfurt, they had driven southeast for five hours in the black Jeep to Vilshofen, an old town on the Danube, where they had switched to the cruiser waiting for them at a marina.

They had then sailed east, traveling at a steady ten knots, downriver to Vienna, a journey that took more than twenty-four hours, including a frustratingly large number of stops to navigate locks.

Now they were at the Marina Wien, a new facility with two hundred moorings and a building that housed a restaurant, bar, and an outdoor patio overlooking the river.

Rezanov glanced around the marina, a low-level structure built from concrete and steel in the shadow of the riverside Donaumarina railway station.

Their boat was moored in the smaller of the two rectangular areas of water that formed the marina. Both were narrow and ran parallel to the huge river alongside. There were only two other boats moored there, which suited

Rezanov. The last thing he and Anke wanted were prying eyes.

A short distance away, in a small parking lot near the marina building, stood a blue Toyota Land Cruiser, into which they had already placed most of their few belongings. The Toyota, like their boat, had been arranged by one of the GRU's local agents in Germany.

Rezanov jumped back onto the deck of the *Joy of Vilshofen* and put his head around the door of the cabin.

"All quiet?" he asked Anke, who was seated at a table studying her phone.

She looked up. "Unfortunately not. I've just had a call from Igor Ivanov. Our photographer friend in Frankfurt has sent several pictures through to Moscow of visitors to the Himmel Bar. The GRU has identified some of them using facial recognition. Guess who?"

"Robinson?" Rezanov muttered.

Anke nodded.

"Bitch," Rezanov said. "That didn't take long."

"This is what I feared," Anke said. "That before long they would be chasing our asses. My guess is they'll be in Vienna soon."

"I don't think it's a huge problem," Rezanov said in a firm tone. "We just need to keep well ahead of them and ensure they are either knocked completely off track or delayed."

He pointed to a large black plastic box beneath the seat. "If we use that, it should delay the bastards permanently."

"I hope you're right," Anke said. "Otherwise you know what Ivanov will do."

Rezanov felt irritated at her tone, but said nothing.

He glanced over to the corner of the cabin, where the reason for this operation down the Danube, Aidan Scarpa, was lying on a mattress on the deck, a gag taped to his mouth, his hands bound behind his back, and his ankles taped firmly together.

"Let's get him into the car," Rezanov said. "The quicker we get on the road, the more chance we've got. Even if they work out we traveled by river, it'll take some time to find this boat. And then they won't expect us to switch back to the highway again."

Anke nodded and pocketed her phone. "Cover me while we get him into the Toyota." She walked over to Aidan, removed his bindings and gag, and ordered him to his feet.

"You'll walk next to us and remain completely silent," she told Aidan. "We're going to get in a car. My friend will be a couple of paces behind, with a handgun in one pocket and a knife in the other. One false move and you'll get either a couple of rounds or a length of steel in your back. I also have a gun in my belt, and I won't hesitate to use it. Understood?"

There was a slight pause. Rezanov had no doubt Aidan would comply. He didn't look like a martyr.

Aidan nodded and stared at Anke. "Where are you taking me?"

"Move," Anke ordered Aidan, ignoring his question.

They marched him off the boat, onto the walkway that ran the length of the marina, and into the parking lot, where Rezanov unlocked the Land Cruiser and instructed Aidan to get into the rear passenger side seat.

He then re-bound Aidan's wrists and refastened his ankles. Anke sat next to Aidan in the other rear seat, holding her gun.

"You set everything up," Anke said to Rezanov. "I'll keep an eye on him. Quick as you can."

Rezanov turned as she shut the door and hurried back to the boat.

A thirty-six-year-old operative in the Spetsnaz GRU's notorious Unit 29155, Rezanov had worked in mainland

Europe for most of the past six years and, unlike many of his colleagues, was fluent in both German and French.

But although extremely useful, languages were not his main expertise.

That was killing.

Rezanov had been trained to a very high standard at the unit's base, which was located behind tall concrete walls in eastern Moscow. He was a skilled operative with a variety of weapons, ranging from sniper rifles to handguns, combat knives, and RPG launchers. But he also had a deep knowledge of explosives and how to deploy them.

Now, on the boat, Rezanov opened the black box beneath the seat in the cabin and took out a reel of thin ballistic trip wire, made from high-strength twelve-strand polyethylene. It was his trip wire of choice, given its extreme toughness, its difficulty to spot due to its nonreflective qualities, even when viewed with night-vision equipment, and because it didn't stretch.

He then took out three empty tin cans of the type normally used to hold supermarket baked beans and, finally, three hand grenades.

Rezanov then used his Swiss Army Knife to cut three lengths of trip wire. These he fastened to a metal bracket that was about halfway up the boat's port side gunwale, at around knee height. He pushed the three grenades, base first, into the three cans so that the sides of the cans kept the safety levers in the safe position.

Next, he tied the other end of the trip wires to the hand grenades and stretched the wires across the back of the boat's deck at about shin height. He hid the cans holding the grenades behind three orange life jackets that he stacked up beneath the triangular table fixed next to the padded seating on the starboard side of the deck. Finally, he removed the safety pins from the grenades.

Anyone who inadvertently gave a slight tug on the trip wires—and it wouldn't take much pressure—would pull the grenades from the cans, thus releasing the safety levers and triggering the devices.

It was a simple and effective boobytrap that he had deployed successfully many times before. Anyone walking across the deck, unless they were incredibly eagle-eyed, would almost certainly set off at least one grenade, if not all three.

Once he had laid his trap, Rezanov walked back to the Land Cruiser and climbed into the driver's seat.

"All done," he said. "Let's go."

"Good job," Anke said from behind him.

Rezanov started the engine, slipped the gear selector into drive, and pushed down on the gas pedal.

CHAPTER ELEVEN

Tuesday, June 20, 2017
Frankfurt

It hadn't taken Vic's facial recognition team at Langley long to come up with an answer. Just as Jayne was arriving at the CIA station in Frankfurt, her phone beeped as an urgent message arrived on the secure app she normally used to communicate with Vic.

Have match to images. Also file on record. Connect with me on this link ASAP from Foster's office.

Vic had shared a link that he said would connect her to a proprietary teleconference device, the Cisco TelePresence System EX90. That seemed unusual to Jayne, although she knew the system was used within the US government and could be protected against electronic signal leakage to TEMPEST standards, a National Security Agency specification. Normally, he simply called her directly using his secure phone app.

Five minutes later, she was sitting in the top-floor office of

Hazel Foster, the chief of station, a slim woman with short reddish-brown hair and intelligent eyes. There were files piled up on Foster's desk and a half-drunk coffee in a mug bearing an image of the Kremlin, a legacy of a previous posting several years ago. Foster knew a lot about Russia.

Once Hazel had switched on her video system, Jayne connected using the link Vic had provided.

Several seconds later, on a monitor screen on the wall, Vic's somewhat ghostly image appeared. He didn't appear to be in his Langley office, and his pallor suggested he hadn't slept much. There was a loud beep as the sound on the secure conference call activated.

"Jayne, Hazel, are you alone?" Vic asked, without bothering to make any introductory pleasantries.

Jayne paused. What was going on? This wasn't Vic's usual conversational style.

"Yes, we are secure and alone," Jayne said. "What is—"

"Two things. First, I have an update for you. We've had a hit on the CCTV images of the woman with Aidan Scarpa," Vic continued. "She's a GRU whore."

"A GRU whore?" Jayne asked, sitting up in her chair.

"A swallow. Honey-trap specialist. Name is Anke Leonova. We have a file on her here, quite a thick one. She's got quite a track record of recruitment across Western Europe, and we're certain she's infiltrated the US and Canada, too. Learned her skills at State School 4. Speaks fluent English."

Jayne had never previously had dealings with any graduates of State School 4, an institution known to Western intelligence, which until its closure was a training ground for female honey-trap operatives, mainly from the KGB, GRU, and SVR. However, two of her former MI6 colleagues had fallen victim several years earlier to the charms of girls who had come through that establishment and had suffered significant hits to their career prospects.

"What name is she operating under?" Jayne asked.

"We think it's Irina Nicoli, from the airline and train manifests we've gone through. Traveling under a Georgian passport."

Jayne grimaced. "So our Aidan has fallen for the oldest trick in the book."

"Looks that way," Vic said. "I suggest you head straight to the NSA's unit in Wiesbaden again. Hopefully, they can quietly get into the CCTV networks around Frankfurt. They'll need to work out where Leonova is—and Scarpa."

Jayne folded her arms. "Yes, can do."

"And there's another thing," Vic cut in, glancing sideways. "Hang on. I just need to fetch someone."

He disappeared out of camera view, leaving Jayne and Hazel looking at each other. Hazel shrugged but said nothing.

A few moments later, Vic reappeared. "As you may have guessed, I'm not at Langley," he said. "I'm in the White House Situation Room. I have someone with me who would like to speak with both of you. It's the president."

Jayne exhaled as Vic moved his chair to one side and the unmistakable figure of Stephen Ferguson, the reelected president, slid into view.

"Hello, Jayne," the president said. "Good to see you again. It's been a while. And good to see you too, Ms. Foster. I don't think we've met previously."

"Mr. President, pleased to meet you," Hazel said, her eyes widening a fraction.

"This is a surprise, Mr. President," Jayne said. "Although I think we know why you'd like to speak with us."

Ferguson cleared his throat. "I have been briefed by Vic on the latest developments with my son and the identity of the woman who appears to have reeled him in. Believe me, I'm as surprised by what seems to have happened as you people. This is the last situation I thought I would find myself in. No doubt Aidan feels the same. But it is what it is, and I can see I'll be leaning heavily on you and your team in Frankfurt to resolve it."

"We'll do our best, sir," Jayne said. "As Vic has already doubtless told you, we've made a start, but it's very early days."

The president ran a hand through his neatly coiffured iron-gray hair. "There's little I can say that will help you very much on the ground as you get this underway. But I would like to stress that even though I see little of Aidan due to circumstances beyond my control, I still love him, and I'd give anything to ensure his safety. You have my authority to do whatever you need to do. Understood?"

Jayne glanced at Hazel, who nodded. "We completely get that, Mr. President," she said.

The president took a sip from a glass of water. "I've been debating whether to go directly to the new German chancellor to get this resolved. But doing so would raise Aidan's profile, and his and my history and the current situation would become front-page news—the story of the president's forgotten son. They might link him to the unfortunate incident in Zaporizhzhia with your Russian source, which I gather is deeply regrettable. All that kind of thing could fuel a media frenzy. It would not help your operation. It would also not help with my upcoming visit to Kyiv to meet with President Doroshenko. I don't want any distractions around that. Therefore, it's better for you people to try to get Aidan back behind the scenes, and hopefully to find out why the Russians are holding him."

"We will do all we can, sir," Vic said.

Jayne couldn't help but see the irony in the situation. The last time she had seen Ferguson was in Berlin, eight months earlier, prior to his November election for a second term in the White House. He had used the damning information she had unearthed to force the previous German chancellor, Erich Merck, to resign for acting as a Russian agent—the Kremlin's highest-placed asset for a very long time. The credit he earned had played some part in helping him to win the White House again.

Now they were back in Germany, hunting for Ferguson's son.

"I have to ask you all," Ferguson said, as if reading her mind. "Do you think this is simply a case of Russian revenge for what happened last year?" He turned toward Vic.

Vic inclined his head. "It is very possible, sir. But it is equally possible there is some other reason behind it."

Ferguson nodded. "I will leave it in your capable hands. But I would ask you all to do everything you can and more, to go the extra mile for me. It will mean a tremendous amount to me to get my son back."

There was a short silence.

"Sir, you have my word," Jayne said. "We will give this all we've got."

"And mine," Vic added. "We'll give this our best shot."

"Thank you," Ferguson said. "I'll leave you to it. I need to go to a meeting with the national security advisor to discuss this further. I'll be in close contact."

The president paused, his head down and jowls hanging a little over his collar. "Just remember," he continued, "we have a lot of military expertise and resources across Germany and Europe. If you need it, use it. You've got a green light from me. I'm sure Hazel can help you."

"Of course, sir," Hazel said.

With that, Ferguson raised a hand in acknowledgment and slid out of the picture.

Vic moved closer to the camera again. He glanced in the direction Ferguson had gone, and there was an audible click as a door closed.

"He's gone now," Vic said. "Thank you for that."

Jayne nodded. "It's the least we could do. But we're committed now, that's for sure."

"Indeed, we are," Vic said.

"All this raises questions, doesn't it?" Jayne said.

"What's that?"

"If Aidan was recruited as an asset recently by the GRU, just tell me one thing, Vic. Surely in his position, and with his background, they would want to run him as an asset for as long as possible and milk him for all the information they can get about what the USACE is doing in Ukraine and else-where. They would want him to remain in his work position."

Vic nodded. "But instead, he's disappeared."

"Why?" Jayne asked, leaning forward. "We have to assume it's because they're holding him—they're keeping him captive. And why is that? The answer has to be he knows something —knows too much. And they now can't afford to let him go. Otherwise, none of this makes any sense."

Jayne looked up at the video screen. There was a short silence.

Vic could be seen placing his hands behind his head and leaning back in his chair in the Situation Room, four thou-sand miles away.

"You're right Jayne. And that's what I, and President Ferguson, would like you to find out."

PART TWO

CHAPTER TWELVE

Wednesday, June 21, 2017
   Moscow

The Samsung Galaxy phone had been lying hidden under the insulation in the roof space of Kira Suslova's dacha in Rublevka. The data-only prepaid SIM card was next to it in a plastic bag, and the removable battery was downstairs where she could keep it charged in another phone.

Suslova had only used the phone once to send a message via Signal, the encrypted messaging app, which was the only app she had installed on the device and the only one she had activated.

That message had gone several months ago to the only person who had the number—Jayne Robinson—to tell her that she, Suslova, had been cleared in an internal Kremlin investigation of any involvement in the exposure of former German chancellor Erich Merck as a Russian agent the previous October.

Since then, she had periodically checked the phone for messages from Robinson. There had been none.

To use a phone securely in Russia was a significant challenge. All communications were likely to be monitored by the domestic security service, the FSB, whose tentacles reached everywhere. In her position, Suslova assumed she was under permanent and intense scrutiny and that her car, house, office, and all her government-supplied electronic devices were bugged.

Therefore, each time she powered up the phone, she went to great lengths to minimize the chances of it being detected amid the intense monitoring and recording of any personal communications inside Russia, especially Moscow.

In the area around her home in the exclusive, heavily guarded Parkville complex in Rublevka, eleven kilometers west of Moscow and next to the Moskva River, the population density was relatively low. That made it easier for the FSB to pinpoint the ownership of each phone that connected to one of the cell phone towers in the area and who they were talking to. All the towers were heavily monitored, she knew that.

But now, after pondering her next move after Ivanov visited her office, Suslova knew she had no choice.

She had to contact Robinson again and arrange a meeting somewhere outside Russia.

Even though the phone was partially dismantled, Suslova placed the device, its battery, and its SIM in a lead-lined Faraday case to block all signals and prevent it from being traced. She switched her regular phone off and put it in a separate Faraday bag to avoid it being associated with the Samsung by proximity.

She then drove the forty minutes to one of her regular haunts, the enormous Aviapark shopping center, northeast of the city, with its five hundred shops spread across six stories.

It was early evening and Aviapark, open until ten o'clock, was busy with shoppers and diners. Suslova carried out a lengthy surveillance detection routine that involved a tour of several shops, visits to cafés, and a stop at the cinema, which she left half an hour into the film. Then, when she was as sure as she could be that she wasn't being followed, she found a private toilet for disabled people and locked herself in.

After carefully checking for surveillance cameras, she swiftly assembled the phone, battery, and SIM and switched the device on. She had previously disabled Bluetooth and Wi-Fi on the phone to help reduce the likelihood of it being compromised.

There were hundreds, maybe thousands, of shoppers at the Aviapark, nearly all of them carrying active phones. That meant that her cell phone activity here would stand a much greater chance of going unnoticed because of the sheer volume of other devices connecting to nearby cell phone towers.

Suslova opened her Signal secure messaging app and was about to tap out a message when the device vibrated in her hand, making her jump a little.

A new message appeared in the list of chats.

Apologies for checkmating you last October—nothing personal. Need to arrange another chess match very soon—play for money this time? Let me know when and where.

Suslova stared at the screen for a moment, then exhaled. The account it was from was anonymous, and she didn't recognize the number, which had a German prefix. But clearly, the sender was Jayne Robinson, using a burner phone.

Given what Ivanov had told her, it was not surprising that she had received a message from Robinson.

But, my God. This British woman was an arrogant bitch. There was more than an element of rubbing salt into an already very sore wound.

She reread the message.

There was a definite note of urgency about it.

The timing could be no coincidence. It confirmed, in Suslova's mind, that Robinson was on the trail of the missing US Army engineer, as Ivanov had indicated.

Presumably, she wanted help in finding him—hence the message.

Well, if that was the case, Suslova knew it improved her own bargaining position up to a point. On the other hand, she couldn't allow anything to happen to Robinson before the $2 billion had been safely returned. After that, of course, the gloves were off.

This was going to be a tricky balancing act.

Suslova lowered the toilet seat, sat down, and thought through her options quickly. She had a few visits planned to other countries to carry out lobbying work for her campaign to win the FIDE presidency. Maybe she could bring one of them forward and then arrange a covert meeting with Robinson at the same time.

Mentally, she ran through the list of upcoming visits: Helsinki, Istanbul, Athens, and Rome, all of them to meet with presidents of national chess federations to secure their votes.

In truth, none of the locations were ideal for a covert meeting with a high-level contact. Rome wasn't due to happen for another three weeks, so she discounted that one. And the other three were all busy centers of activity for the Russian foreign intelligence service, the SVR. Helsinki was crawling with Russian spies, as was Istanbul. Athens wasn't much better, given Putin's focus on Greece as its relationship with the European Union worsened.

That inevitably meant the risk of surveillance by SVR teams was high in all the cities.

Of the three possibilities, Athens, which she was due to

visit in two days, was perhaps slightly less risky than the others. Suslova had been there often and liked the feel of the city, with its labyrinthine maze of narrow alleyways in some areas, its hills, and its crowds, which could make evading surveillance easier. Also, she was due to be there for three days, longer than the other visits, which might yield more opportunities for a rendezvous.

Suslova looked back at her phone, tapped on Robinson's Signal message, and typed a reply.

Agree a rematch would be good idea. Athens this Friday-Sunday? Can fix location once time/date agreed.

That was enough detail. She pressed send, double checked the message had gone through, then immediately switched off the Samsung, removed the back, and took out the battery and SIM card.

She then replaced all the components in the Faraday case, shoved it into her bag, flushed the toilet in case anyone was outside listening, and headed out the door.

Hopefully, Robinson could make the Athens location, as they might not get another opportunity to meet.

CHAPTER THIRTEEN

Wednesday, June 21, 2017
Frankfurt

"Is there any video of them outside the bar?" Jayne asked. "I'd like to see where they went after leaving, and if they did so by car, by cab, or on foot."

Jayne and Neal had returned, with Richter, to the Consolidated Intelligence Center in Wiesbaden for another meeting with the local NSA unit chief Anna Falkenstein and her colleague Sean. It was the obvious place to start to track Aidan Scarpa and Anke Leonova.

Anna turned toward Sean, seated at his terminal, who shook his head.

"We checked before," Sean said. "There is no camera outside."

"That figures," Anna said. "Most businesses here wouldn't have that if it captured images of passersby in the street. Privacy laws are tight in Germany."

Jayne held back a sigh. "So how do we work out where

Aidan disappeared to? It was four days ago. He left home in Wiesbaden in a taxi. We need to track where it went, and if we can't work with the police, how are we going to do that?"

Anna pursed her lips. "There is one possibility. We at the NSA have what you might call an arrangement with the BND."

"With the BND?" Jayne asked. She raised an eyebrow. The BND, or Bundesnachrichtendienst, was Germany's foreign intelligence service, the equivalent of the CIA or MI6 in the UK. "What arrangement?"

"The BND collects intelligence for us. Taps phones. Emails. Messages. If we ask, they'll do it, usually. It's meant to be for surveillance of US citizens only, but . . ."

"But not always just US citizens?" Jayne said, sitting up in her seat.

Anna shrugged.

The implications of what Anna was saying hit Jayne immediately. Germany's citizens were notoriously among the world's most vocal in opposing mass surveillance. It was likely to cause an enormous uproar if such cooperation between the BND and the NSA became known.

"You mean you tap German citizens' phones too?" Jayne asked. "Don't tell me. Including the chancellor?"

"No comment," Anna said.

That would be a yes, then, Jayne assumed.

However, the question of whether the BND was tapping their own chancellor's phone on behalf of the NSA was the least of Jayne's concerns now. "Could we get the BND to find out where that taxi carrying Scarpa went?" she asked. "He must have called the company or emailed them or logged in online to book it."

Anna gave a half smile. "We can try."

Jayne pulled out her phone, located the number she had

logged for Aidan Scarpa, and read it to Anna, who wrote it down.

"See what you can do," Jayne said.

Anna stood and made for the door. She turned to Sean. "Can you get these guys coffees and cookies," she said as she exited, indicating toward Jayne, Neal, and Richter. "I may be a little while."

After she had gone, Jayne stared out the window northward toward the military airfield a short distance away. A row of seven US Army helicopters stood on the apron. Only fifty meters to the east was a new army sports and fitness center.

She turned to Sean and Richter, who were standing to her right. "Are those all Black Hawks?" she asked, pointing at the helicopters.

Richter nodded. "All UH-60M variants. Remember, I told you the 1st Battalion of the 214th Aviation Regiment is based here—the commander's a good friend of mine. They use the choppers."

They were on to their second coffee by the time Anna returned, carrying a cardboard folder.

"Look at these," Anna said as she took two sheets of paper from the folder and placed them on the meeting table. "They're photos of an old warehouse in Hanauer Landstrasse, a street near the Frankfurt East shipping container railway terminal."

Jayne and Neal leaned over to look at the photographs. The prints were quite sharp, despite having been taken from video footage. A time and date stamp showed the previous Friday, June 16.

Both of the images showed one of Frankfurt's ubiquitous cream-colored Mercedes taxis with a large yellow sticker bearing the company's phone number. In the first, taken in front of a redbrick warehouse, Aidan Scarpa could be seen climbing out of the rear door. Standing nearby was the same woman whom he had been with at the Himmel Bar, Anke Leonova, also known as Irina Nicoli. Next to her was a tall, barrel-chested bald man with a military bearing. In the second image, the three of them were walking into the warehouse building. Parked near the entrance was a black Jeep.

"You're lucky with these," Anna said. "My BND guy found the taxi's license plate from Aidan's phone records. The company had texted the plate number to him so he knew to look out for it. The more unpredictable bit was whether we could track where the taxi went, but thankfully the driver had texted the destination to his controller in the taxi company's office. And while Hesse, this region Frankfurt's in, does allow surveillance in public areas, CCTV is still quite sporadic across the city, like most places in Germany. But this area near the rail freight terminal has been heavily affected by crime, so there are more cameras. That's how we got the images from the BND. They logged into police footage."

Jayne tapped on the image of the big bald man. "Do we know who this guy is?"

Anna nodded. "It's a Spetsnaz GRU operative, Gavrill Rezanov. We got a match from facial recognition."

"Bloody hell. They've got Spetsnaz operatives working on this?" Jayne said.

"No doubt about it," Anna said.

Jayne frowned. "We'd better get down to the warehouse."

"No point," Anna said. She removed another two photographs from her folder and placed them on the table. "The birds have flown the nest."

The first photograph showed Aidan Scarpa leaving the warehouse building, flanked by Leonova and Rezanov. The second showed them bundling him into the black Jeep.

"Shit," Jayne said. "Where did they take him?"

Anna shrugged. "That's what we're trying to find out. The BND found video of them driving away from the warehouse and into the next street. But that's it. There's no more. Like I said, CCTV coverage is sporadic."

Jayne cursed under her breath and glanced at Anna and Sean. "Are there any other tracking options you can use?"

"Maybe satellite imaging," Sean said. "You'd need to talk to the NRO about that."

Jayne turned to Neal. She knew he sometimes worked closely with Frank Baker, the director of the National Reconnaissance Office, the United States' spy satellite intelligence agency, based at Chantilly, Virginia, only half an hour from Langley.

"I'll talk to Frank," Neal said. "He'll get his team on this. Their satellites will be able to pick out the Jeep and track it."

That was the obvious option, Jayne thought. She had met Baker on a couple of occasions previously and knew his team could draw on imagery from a whole array of surveillance satellites globally. Baker had told her that the satellite camera images usually had sharp-enough definition to pick out cars and larger objects, although it struggled with individual people.

"Anything else?" Jayne asked.

"Maybe open-source information—we have a small team that analyzes that, including social media and other online information people have uploaded. We can explore those options."

"Yes, please," Jayne said. "Give it a try."

Sean nodded. "We can use the Jeep's license plate as the basis for a search—we have the tools to do that."

As he spoke, Jayne's German burner phone vibrated in her pocket. She took it out to find a Signal notification. She stood and took a few steps away from the others, then opened the app.

It was an encrypted response to her message to Suslova.

Agree a rematch would be good idea. Athens this Friday-Sunday? Can fix location once time/date agreed.

Jayne stared at the screen. Well, that was good news on the face of it. She hadn't really expected Suslova to respond so swiftly, despite her missing $2 billion.

She beckoned Neal over and showed him the message.

"What do you think?" she said. "Too good to be true?"

Neal inclined his head and lowered his voice to no more than a murmur. "Maybe. But do you have any other option right now for finding out what happened to Aidan? She's our only high-level source in Moscow. We can put a good backup plan together."

Jayne knew he was right. Suslova was the only option.

She tapped out a short reply.

Athens is good for me. Send more details asap.

CHAPTER FOURTEEN

Thursday, June 22, 2017
    Moscow

It was late into the evening as Kira Suslova stood at the window of her second-floor office in the Kremlin's Senate Palace building, looking out over Red Square.

The moon was rising low over the nine brightly colored domes of Saint Basil's Cathedral, their swirling green, blue, orange, and yellow hues all highlighted by floodlights against the night sky.

The cathedral, built on the orders of Ivan the Terrible in the 1550s, always reminded her of the flames of a fire at this time of night, the domes appearing to leap skyward against the blackness behind.

Sometimes she would stand and stare at the cathedral at the southern end of the square and the elegant State Historical Museum at the northern end and marvel at how she had arrived in this job, working down the corridor from the president.

However, tonight, her mind was elsewhere.

Suslova walked back to her desk, sat in front of her laptop, and toggled to her email inbox. It might be a good idea to make a final check before heading home for some late dinner.

She scrolled down her secure emails. There were several that had arrived during the past ten minutes. It was typical of the senior leadership team at the Kremlin and within the various intelligence agencies to send their most important emails late in the evening. They were always trying to create the impression that they worked longer hours, and harder, than everyone else. It was mostly for the benefit of the top man, the president, who ironically would likely be home nursing a glass of vintage wine from his cellar by now.

The fourth email was from Igor Ivanov. She clicked on it and tapped in her PIN, followed by a password to unlock the classified contents. The subject line read, "Meeting postponed." Apart from Suslova, it had been sent to the president and his personal assistant, plus the president's counterintelligence chief Gennady Sidorenko, the director of the SVR Maksim Kruglov, the GRU director Colonel General Sergey Pliskin, and the FSB director Nikolai Sheymov.

Suslova's heart sank even before she scrolled down to read the text.

I need to postpone tomorrow morning's briefing on GRU's Operation Noi. I know most of you have not yet been read into the Noi files. I intended to do that tomorrow. However, I now need to travel in the morning to Crimea for an urgent operational planning meeting. I also planned to give an update on the GRU operation involving the US source who provided us with ID on Aleksey Zhukov. As some of you are aware, we have been forced to take the source into custody for intelligence security reasons. I will update you all on these matters next week, or will send more details via this channel if appropriate.

Suslova swore to herself.

She had been relying on obtaining information on both operations, Noi and the US source, before traveling to Athens to brief Jayne Robinson. Now she could only give outline details. This was a major blow.

And what was the operation for which Ivanov was now going to the Crimea so urgently? That too was something he had not briefed the leadership team about. But presumably the president knew about it, and possibly others on the team; otherwise, he would not have referenced it.

Suslova leaned back in her chair.

Dermo. Shit. There was too much going on that she wasn't privy to.

Was there an alternative method of finding out?

She asked herself the question she often posed to herself in difficult situations. What would Josef Stalin, the ruthless dictator who once occupied the neighboring office, have done?

Certainly there were no options involving either the president or Ivanov, or the GRU director Pliskin, who was clearly being sidelined for both operations, even though both of them involved his service. That was typical of the way Ivanov worked.

What about others?

If Ivanov had prepared briefings, there was a faint chance he might have lodged physical files within the fiercely guarded archives of the GRU. The president, Ivanov himself, and most of the others in the group were old-school operators who preferred to read on paper, not screen.

Suslova wouldn't hold her breath over that, given the confidentiality of these operations, but maybe it was worth a try.

For years she had cultivated, flirted with, and given very generous gifts to the heads of the archives in all the main services—GRU, SVR, and FSB—in the certain knowledge that occasionally she would need their goodwill to lay her hands on some important documents at short notice. She knew exactly which French and Italian wines their wives liked and which electronic gadgets their children coveted.

That was her only chance. On her way home, she would take a detour ten kilometers northwest to the GRU's headquarters. That was one of the advantages of her elevated position as a chief adviser to Putin. She had access almost everywhere she wanted to go. The head archivist, Dmitry Govorov, she knew, would be at his desk until ten o'clock, maybe later. That gave her almost an hour.

Quickly, she switched off her laptop, packed her bag, and headed out the door.

Twenty-five minutes later, she walked into the GRU building, showed her pass to the guards at the front desk, and made her way down two flights of echoing concrete stairs to the second basement, where there were two more guards.

Govorov's office was through a set of double steel sliding doors that she activated with her GRU pass.

Suslova went through and saw immediately that apart from the night-duty officer, the head archivist was the only staff member still there. That was normal. All the strip lights across the open-plan office were out, apart from a glow coming from behind the closed blinds of Govorov's office at the far end.

She walked across and knocked firmly on his door. Only a second later, it swung sharply open. Govorov was standing there with his coat on, briefcase in hand. Just in time. He was obviously on his way home.

"Dmitry, I'm glad I caught you. And I apologize for the late visit."

Govorov gave a hint of a smile. "I was about to leave, but I assume this is urgent?"

Suslova had only recently given him an iPhone for his

eighteen-year-old daughter. He obviously had that in the front of his mind, and he knew she had the president's ear. She quickly told him what she needed: the files on Operation Noi and another unnamed operation relating to a US asset, both of which would have come from Igor Ivanov, not from Pliskin.

Govorov shook his head immediately. "There is a file on Operation Noi, but Ivanov has it, and he informed me he will keep it for the foreseeable future. And I haven't seen a file on the other matter you mention. Are they very new operations?"

"They are, yes. Well, do you know who is running Operation Noi for Ivanov?"

"I only know the code name." Govorov shrugged. "Sorry. You've had a wasted journey."

"Never wasted if I can catch up with you, Dmitry." She flashed him a smile, doing her best to make it as sultry as possible.

He laughed. "Come again when you can."

"Soon, I hope." She winked at him, turned, and made her way across the office and back out the steel sliding doors.

As she emerged onto the basement stairwell, she heard footsteps clattering down the concrete stairs above her. A second later, the paunchy figure of Gennady Sidorenko appeared on the landing above and stopped still, staring at her.

What was he doing here? She'd never before seen him in the building, and certainly not in the archives.

"Kira, nice to see you. So late too. What a surprise," Sidorenko said. He walked slowly down the stairs toward her. "What are you doing here at this hour?"

"Nice to see you too, Gennady," Suslova said. She always had the ability to remain cool in such situations, although her mind was now churning. "You too are working late. In my case, a Ukraine-related matter. And you?"

"Never mind. The usual rubbish." Sidorenko paused and scrutinized her again, his blue eyes protruding slightly. "Is our friend Govorov still in his office?"

Shit. The last thing she wanted was for Sidorenko, a notorious and extremely dogged hunter of traitors in some of the darkest corners of Moscow, to see Govorov now. He was bound to quiz the head of archives on what Suslova had been doing there. She'd have to hope he'd keep his counsel.

"Yes, he's still there, but I think about to leave," Suslova said as casually as she could.

"Good. I need to speak to him," Sidorenko said. There was a distinctly meaningful tone to his voice. He walked down the remaining few steps and disappeared through the doors to Govorov's empire.

Had he followed her from the Kremlin? she wondered.

CHAPTER FIFTEEN

Thursday, June 22, 2017
Vienna

The Black Hawk helicopter, its engines clattering, descended in a controlled manner toward the white cross on the rooftop concrete helipad next to Vienna General Hospital, near the city's famous old town.

Jayne looked out the port-side window of the chopper toward the hospital's main building, which rose twelve stories above them into a blue sky.

The cabin had been configured with nine seats, only four of which were occupied, while a pilot and copilot sat up front in the cockpit. To Jayne's right sat Neal, Hazel Foster, and the commander of the 1st Battalion, 214th Aviation Regiment, Lieutenant Colonel Richard Weaver, whose unit at the Clay Barracks in Wiesbaden operated the chopper and who had arranged the flight that morning at the urging of Colonel Richter.

Eventually, the aircraft settled with a slight bump onto the landing surface above a wing of the enormous hospital site, the fifth largest in Europe.

As soon as the pilot cut the engines, Weaver slid open the rear door on the port side and, with the ease of years of practice, jumped out onto the helipad. Jayne stood, straightened her shorts, and followed him out of the chopper, as did Neal.

It was their second stop in the Black Hawk that day. The first had been the quaint old town of Vilshofen on the River Danube, 390 kilometers southeast of Frankfurt, after the National Reconnaissance Office had tracked the black Jeep to a riverside marina there. The vehicle was still parked at the site.

A boat owner at Vilshofen had informed them that a pair matching the descriptions of Anke Leonova and Aidan Scarpa, accompanied by a bald man, had arrived in the Jeep four days earlier and had headed downriver in a white Sheerline 955 cruiser that had been moored at the marina.

Jayne and the pursuit party had then immediately taken off again in the Black Hawk, following the Danube to the east.

As soon as they were in the air, Neal had called on Anna Falkenstein at Wiesbaden for help in identifying the cruiser. Her team quickly established, by hacking into the Vilshofen marina's booking system, that the cruiser was called the *Joy of Vilshofen* and had been rented from a company in Passau.

Using that information, Frank Baker and his team at NRO headquarters in Chantilly had used their proprietary satellite tracking technology to locate the cruiser farther downriver toward Vienna, about 240 kilometers farther southeast as the crow flies. Apparently, it was now moored at Marina Wien, a new marina alongside the Danube.

Weaver's team had also obtained permission from the Vienna General Hospital's helicopter management department for the Black Hawk to land at the hospital helipad, which was only six kilometers west of the marina.

"Right, let's go find our car," Weaver said.

The three of them moved swiftly down a staircase from the first-floor helipad to ground level, where a rented Ford Galaxy MPV, also ordered by Weaver's team, was waiting for them.

Foster remained on the helicopter, as agreed. If things went wrong, they might need someone senior and highly experienced who had connections in the German diplomatic and intelligence communities to get them out of trouble.

A few minutes later, Jayne and Neal were being whisked along the south bank of the Danube by Weaver, who had taken the wheel.

As they passed the Hilton hotel on the riverside, Weaver cut off the main highway onto a narrow side street that ran parallel to the river, a few meters from the water. A few seconds later, the marina came into view, a strip of water between the road and the river equipped with scores of mooring points and floating walkways. Most of the mooring points were deserted, with just the odd yacht or cruiser tied up. None of them were the *Joy of Vilshofen*.

Halfway along the marina was a boat rental yard and a large two-story building that housed the marina offices, as well as a restaurant, bar, and patio area.

Jayne pointed to a small parking lot next to the marina building. "Can you pull in there? We should check this place out on foot."

Weaver drove through the open gate into the lot and braked to a halt. A couple of trees provided them with some cover as they climbed out of the car. It was only then that it became apparent there was a second, smaller mooring area on the other side of the marina building, beyond a hedge.

Only three boats were moored there, all at the far end,

of which only one was white. Its stern was tied to a mooring point next to the shore, and its port side faced them.

"The white one has to be our baby," Jayne said.

Jayne examined the boat. From a distance of almost two hundred meters, it looked deserted, as did the other two boats.

"No sign of Aidan or any Russians here," Weaver said. "Unless they're hiding belowdecks."

Jayne looked around. There was a man in brown coveralls behind them, outside the marina building, who was sweeping up around the outdoor tables and emptying trash cans into a black bag.

"Think we're too late yet again," Neal said. "We're making a habit of this."

Jayne said nothing, although he was not wrong.

Neal pointed toward the janitor. "Richard, how about if you go chat with him? He might have seen the boat arrive, or where they went to. I can go with Jayne and check out the boat."

Weaver nodded. "Sure."

As Weaver headed to the marina building, Jayne and Neal walked to the end of the parking lot and through an open gate that took them onto the floating walkway to which the boats were moored.

"Guns?" Neal asked.

"Yup," Jayne replied.

She removed the Walther from her belt, flicked off the safety, and racked the slide. Neal did likewise with his Beretta.

It seemed highly unlikely that they were going to need weapons, as there was still no sign of movement on the boat. But it was better to be prepared.

Her senses now raised to full alert, Jayne walked slowly

along the walkway toward the vessel. Now she could make out the nameplate.

She glanced sideways at Neal. "The *Joy of Vilshofen*," she said.

"Good to know the NRO got it right," Neal said.

The boat looked about ten meters long and was quite new, with a white fiberglass hull and stainless steel fittings. There was an integrated bathing deck at the stern with a waist-high door, level with the boat's gunwale, that led onto the main afterdeck. The raised helm, with a black wheel, was halfway along the boat on the port side and was covered by a large plastic canopy to give protection from the weather. Next to it was a closed black glass hatch that Jayne assumed led down into the cabin.

Jayne paused and turned to check out what Weaver was doing. He was facing them and was talking to the janitor, who was gesticulating toward the cruiser.

Now they were about twenty meters from the cruiser.

"I can go check the boat if you give me some cover," Jayne suggested.

"If you like. Or I can go?"

"I'll do it," she said. Although they treated each other as equals on operations, Jayne always had a subconscious awareness of seniority, stemming from years of working in the hierarchical structure at MI6. Despite his liking for hands-on work, Neal was, after all, deputy in charge of the CIA's Directorate of Operations. She didn't want to put him in unnecessary jeopardy.

"Okay, I'll cover you," Neal said. He crouched on the metal walkway, just above the water, as Jayne continued toward the boat, now holding her gun ready in front of her.

She half expected some Russian to emerge from the cabin door and open fire.

But nothing happened.

Jayne padded slowly forward.

When she reached the stern of the boat, she paused. Should she go onto the cruiser and take a closer look? She knew she would have to.

Jayne stepped off the walkway onto the bathing deck at the stern and grasped the waist-high gunwale, her eyes sweeping the afterdeck ahead of her. The only items left on the deck were three orange life jackets stacked beneath the table on the starboard side, next to the padded seats.

The boat shifted fractionally beneath her weight as she stepped over to the door that led from the small bathing deck to the main part of the afterdeck.

Instinctively, she checked the door latch and the area behind the small door before clicking it open. There was nothing that gave her any concern.

Then Jayne stepped through the door onto the main deck area, the table to her right.

As she stepped forward, she suddenly felt something brush against her bare knee.

Reactively, she looked down, and as she did so, in her peripheral vision, she saw the pile of life jackets move.

There was a metallic rattle.

Years of training, instinct, and self-preservation took over.

"Shit," Jayne screamed.

She turned and flung herself headfirst over the gunwale just as a deafening explosion erupted behind her. A split second later, there came another.

CHAPTER SIXTEEN

Thursday, June 22, 2017
  Vienna

The instant Neal heard Jayne scream and watched her dive off the boat, his operational instincts kicked in.

He knew what was coming.

Neal threw himself flat to the floor of the steel walkway, his forearms covering his head, just as a massive blast ripped through the back of the boat, only twenty-five yards away. Almost instantaneously, there came another identical explosion.

It felt as though the walkway kicked up viciously beneath him into his chest. A surge of water splashed into his face, something hit him hard on the forehead, and his entire body was sharply jolted and shaken, knocking the breath right out of him.

Bits of debris splashed into the water near him and clattered onto the walkway.

It took him several seconds to get his wind back. He put

his hand to his forehead and felt wetness. When he lowered it, he could see it was covered in blood.

Nevertheless, he hauled himself up onto his hands and knees, a feeling of dizziness now threatening to overwhelm him.

Jayne.

Shit. Where was she?

He lifted his head and scanned the area ahead of him. His view of the boat was partly obscured by a cloud of dark smoke and dust, but through it he could just make out the entire back of the boat in ruins, with orange flames shooting skyward. The stern was a ragged mess of smashed fiberglass and steel, and there were gaping holes in what had been the gunwale. The canopy over the helm had been completely ripped off, and there was no sign of the boat's helm or the pilot's seat.

Neal scanned left of the boat, desperately searching for any sign of Jayne.

He saw nothing.

The fire on the boat was rapidly gaining a grip, and the flames were shooting higher almost by the second.

There was no sign of Jayne.

What the hell had happened to her?

Then, out of the corner of his eye, he saw a movement several yards away toward the center of the marina. A series of splashes and the thrashing of arms.

God, is she drowning?

Neal hauled himself to his feet. He removed his phone and wallet from his pockets and placed them with his Beretta on the walkway. Still fully clothed, he dived into the water toward the splashing. As he did so, pain spiked through his right hip, but he kept going and broke into a front crawl.

As he drew near to Jayne, he realized she was trying to swim toward him but was making no progress.

Eventually, he reached her and his teenage lifesaving training kicked in.

Without speaking, he flipped onto his back, wrapped an arm around Jayne's chest, and pulled her close to him, so her back was pressed against his chest, her head out of the water.

Neal then swam backward, using his left arm and his legs to do so, while continuing to hold Jayne firmly to him with his right arm.

Eventually, he reached the walkway just as Weaver arrived.

"Thank God," Weaver said as he grabbed Jayne beneath the armpits and hauled her out of the water. He laid her gently on the walkway, facing upward.

Neal grasped the edge of the walkway and heaved himself up onto it. He then sat there, blood and water dripping down from his chin onto his chest, feet dangling in the water, and exhaled long and hard in sheer relief.

He could see Jayne flat on her back, gasping for air. She was physically shaking. Blood was dribbling steadily from a large, deep graze that ran down most of her left shin, which he assumed must have happened as she dived over the side of the boat.

There was a loud bang from the blazing boat as something exploded inside the cabin, and the flames soared higher.

Neal leaned over and grasped Jayne's hand. "Are you all right?"

She turned her head, looked at him, and coughed hard. "I think I will be. Give me a few minutes."

Although she was still trembling, at least Jayne was showing no sign of any serious physical injury apart from her shin.

Neal looked up to see Weaver staring down at him. "You've got a big cut on top of your forehead. We'll need to get that patched up."

"Something hit me," Neal said.

"It'll be okay," Weaver said. "Listen, we don't have a few minutes—we need to get out of here, quick. Or else we're going to be in a world of trouble if the Austrian police get here. Are you both able to walk?"

Neal nodded. He knew Weaver was right. An unauthorized operation on Austrian soil involving senior intelligence and army officers working for the US would inevitably cause major problems if it became known, even if they had ended up on the wrong end of a bombing by a Russian military intelligence unit.

Furthermore, it would likely lead to the entire operation being blown and hampered by the Austrian authorities. The Russians holding Aidan Scarpa would not be found, and President Ferguson would hold them accountable.

Jayne sat up. "You're right. We've got to go," she said. "We can't afford to get caught up in this. The bastards boobytrapped the boat. I felt my knee catch on the trip wire. Never saw it until then. Good thing I was wearing shorts—probably wouldn't have felt it otherwise."

"Grenades?" Neal asked.

"Must have been," Jayne said. "At least two. I heard a bit of a rattle. Saw some life jackets move when I bumped into the wire. They must have hidden the grenades behind them. When I realized, I dived." She patted her shorts pockets. "My phones and wallet are soaked. And I've lost my gun in the water."

Neal knew that he'd been saved from injury by the boat's waist-high gunwale absorbing most of the blasts and by him having the presence of mind to drop to the floor when he saw Jayne dive.

Jayne, too, had been fortunate that her dive had been just in the nick of time, and she had also been protected by the gunwale as she hit the water.

"Give me your hand," Weaver said to Jayne. "Let's try to

get back to the car. It's got a first-aid kit, so we can at least stop that bleeding."

He reached down, grasped her hands, and dragged her up, then wrapped one arm around her waist.

Neal picked up his phone, wallet, and gun, which he shoved into his belt and covered with his soaking shirt. He then took Jayne's other arm. Between them, water and blood dripping from their clothes, they walked her back to the parking lot where the janitor was standing near the Ford Galaxy, an expression of utter shock on his face. He must have witnessed the entire saga.

"Shall I call for an ambulance?" the janitor stuttered in German. "I can get a doctor. I'll get the police. You all need help. This is terrible. How did that happen? Was it a bomb? What went—"

"Don't worry," Weaver interrupted. "I am going to drive them to the Vienna General Hospital. I know where it is. Not far. It'll be quicker than waiting for an ambulance."

The janitor looked uncertain. "Are you sure?"

"Absolutely sure," Neal said. "The hospital will fix everything. We'll call the police, too. You don't need to do that. Thank you."

They eased Jayne into the rear seat of the car. Neal climbed into the front passenger seat, Weaver into the driver's seat, and they set off. As they pulled out of the marina and followed the signs for the main highway southeast to the airport and Budapest, the sound of sirens could be heard in the distance.

"I think we'd better get over the border by car," Weaver said. "Forget the chopper. I'll get the pilot to fly to Pápa. Can Hazel go with it?"

Neal nodded as he reached for the first-aid kit in the glove compartment. "Makes sense. We can meet her at Pápa."

He pulled out some antiseptic, gauze, and tape, twisted in his seat, and began cleaning Jayne's leg.

"Good," Weaver said. "I've got friends there. They'll have medics who can clean you two up, and we'll get a hotel fixed up too."

Pápa Air Base was a Hungarian airfield roughly halfway between Vienna and Budapest and had strong links with both the United States and British military, including special operations forces. Neal had once run a CIA operation that was headquartered out of Pápa, which was operated by the Hungarian Air Force but also acted as a reserve airbase for NATO forces when required. It was well equipped to handle helicopters, as a search and rescue unit was based there.

That seemed sensible to Neal. "I'll get the CIA Gulfstream down to Pápa too."

He knew that Jayne would need it to get to Athens for the rendezvous with Suslova. Pápa had a long runway that could handle the Gulfstream.

Nobody spoke for a few seconds. Neal finished bandaging Jayne's leg, turned around, and used the visor mirror to clean his forehead. The sound of sirens was getting louder.

"Shit," muttered Jayne eventually. "I screwed that up, really bad. And I checked for booby traps too. Saw nothing."

"Not your fault," Neal said. He could see she was still shaking.

Jayne shook her head. "And we're back to square one," she said. "We don't have a bloody clue where they've taken Aidan. The president will kill us when he finds out what happened."

Neal said nothing this time. He couldn't argue with that.

Two silver police cars with their trademark red-and-blue stripes screamed past them in the other direction toward the marina, their sirens blaring and blue roof lights flashing.

"We do have a clue how they're traveling, though," Weaver said. "The janitor was being helpful until that grenade went off. He said there were three of them who arrived in the boat. Two men and a woman. They left in a blue Land Cruiser, he said. About a couple of hours ago. Said there was something not quite right about them. They seemed to be arguing."

"Good work," Neal said. He tapped his phone screen to activate it. "I'll call Hazel first, then the NRO. Maybe they can trace the Land Cruiser."

CHAPTER SEVENTEEN

Thursday, June 22, 2017
  Budapest, Hungary

Jayne glanced at her watch as Lieutenant Colonel Richard Weaver steered the Ford Galaxy off the 8305 highway and through gate number one at Pápa Air Base. He braked to a halt in front of a double set of security barriers.

It was now evening, and the journey from Vienna had taken them just over two hours.

Thankfully, they had not been stopped en route by Austrian police before crossing the border into Hungary. Presumably, the janitor at the Wien Marina had been so shocked by what he had witnessed that he had failed to take a note of the car's license plate.

Jayne felt grateful for that, but far more that she was still alive. She was only too aware that if her reflexes had not been so razor sharp, the grenades would have blasted her far into the Danube.

The injury to her shin was messy, but far from dangerous.

Blood had seeped through the dressing, coloring it and her white sock red, but most of it had congealed.

What Jayne now needed most was a shower, a fresh wound dressing, and a change of clothing, as did Neal, who had a red-stained patch on his forehead.

While they were driving, Weaver had phoned ahead to the senior US Air Force commander at Pápa, Simon Grabowski, whom he knew quite well, to arrange for secure accommodation for them that evening and for medical care to check Jayne's and Neal's wounds.

Weaver also arranged for the Black Hawk, with Hazel Foster on board, to be flown to Pápa from Vienna before Austrian authorities made any connection between it and the explosion at Wien Marina. He also confirmed permission from Grabowski for the Black Hawk to use the airfield.

To Jayne's relief, Neal had also completed arrangements for the CIA's Gulfstream V to be brought to Pápa from Frankfurt. That meant she could use it to get to Athens the following day, and that gave her the confidence to arrange a meeting place there with Kira Suslova.

To Jayne's surprise, her main iPhone, which initially seemed dead following its immersion in the marina, had come back to life after she placed it above the air vent on the car's dashboard to dry it out. The phones these days seemed to be a lot more resilient than in previous years. Although she had a secure CIA online backup for the phone, and Neal could have obtained a new device from the Frankfurt CIA station, it would have taken some time to reinstate all the data and apps.

However, the phone containing the German SIM card could not be revived. Jayne removed the SIM and borrowed the spare phone that Weaver was carrying. Once she had inserted the German SIM, she sent a message to Suslova's burner suggesting they meet the following day, Friday, at 11:51

p.m. at a place Jayne had used before, which she now code-named BROWN SITE 3 for the purposes of this rendezvous. She sent precise coordinates so there could be no mistake.

BROWN SITE 3 was in the Vathi neighborhood of Athens, a couple of kilometers north of the Acropolis. It was on the corner of Filis and Smirnis, two narrow residential streets lined with apartment buildings and offices. It was located three blocks west of the enormous Field of Ares public park, built to honor the heroes of the Greek Revolution of 1821. The site was quiet, partly pedestrianized, and had a wealth of recessed doorways in which they could talk.

After a short delay, Grabowski, accompanied by Foster, met them at the security office next to the Pápa entrance gate and escorted them to the medical center, where a nurse cleaned, disinfected, and dressed Jayne's and Neal's wounds. They also used the medical center's showers and changed into clean clothing.

It was only then that they could hold a proper private debriefing with Foster in a secure meeting room at the air base. Vic, who was already at the CIA's Kyiv station ahead of President Ferguson's meeting with his Ukrainian counterpart, Doroshenko, the following day, joined them via a secure video link.

Pápa Air Base was a small, purely functional site mainly comprising prefabricated buildings, with no on-site accommodation. But Grabowski, a short, energetic man with a crew cut and wearing a brown leather flight jacket, had arranged rooms for them at the Villa Classica Hotel, five kilometers away in Pápa town.

The hotel, in the center of town, was better than Jayne had expected. She had never been as grateful for a soft bed. Sleep had been scarce over the past couple of weeks.

After a pasta dinner, she decided to give Joe, back home in Portland, Maine, a call to update him on developments.

He was out walking his dog, Cocoa, when she called using the usual secure end-to-end encrypted service they always used. Joe listened in silence as she described the blast at the marina. It wasn't the first time she had needed to describe a close brush with death to him, and it never got any easier.

"Thank God you're okay," Joe said when she had finished. "And whatever you do, don't give Suslova her money back until you've got Aidan safely home and you know why they are holding him. There's got to be some critical reason they're going to all this trouble, putting themselves at great risk. Any thoughts on why?"

"We have no clue," Jayne said. "But my gut says it must be something he knows. This Anke Leonova appears to have gone to quite some effort to recruit, or should I say, coerce Aidan as an asset. Now he's useless to Russia. So she must have a damn good reason for holding him."

"I'd say she must have had no choice," Joe said.

"Looks that way," Jayne said. Joe's instincts were usually spot-on.

"Sounds like they're quite desperate," Joe continued. "I want you back, Jayne, and my kids want you back. We don't want you to be another notch on a Russian assassin's rifle butt."

As was often the case, it took someone to forcefully ram the point home about her personal safety before she really grasped the impact her actions sometimes had on those who loved her. Her parents, when they were alive, had occasionally pointed that out to her, too.

"Don't worry, I'm being careful," Jayne said, trying to inject more conviction into her voice than she was feeling. "I've still got some reflexes and wits about me. I'm not doing badly for fifty-five."

The reality was, she knew she had been lucky at the Vienna marina.

For once, Joe didn't laugh at her self-deprecating joke.

Jayne was about to ask how Joe's kids were doing when there came a knock at her hotel room door. She walked over and looked through the peephole to find Neal, Weaver, and Foster standing outside. She opened the door.

"Sorry, Joe. I've got to go," she said into the phone. "I've got Neal and company at the door. I'll get back to you as soon as I can."

"All right. Be careful in Athens," Joe said. "I love you. Let me know if I can help."

"Will do. Love you, too." Jayne ended the call.

"Come in. What's happening?" she asked Neal, feeling slightly irritated that her call had been interrupted.

The three visitors walked in and closed the door behind them.

"I've had a call from Frank at the NRO," Neal said. The fresh white bandage on his forehead left him looking faintly ridiculous. "They've drawn a blank on the Land Cruiser in which the Russians left Vienna. No sign of it so far on the satellite images, and they won't be able to do anything overnight. So it's a question of restarting tomorrow morning when it's light here."

"By then, they could be a thousand kilometers away," Jayne said. She swore under her breath. Had Neal interrupted her call with Joe just to give her this bad news? "I'm thinking now might be the time to get the Austrian police involved."

Neal inclined his head. "Personally, I agree. But Vic says he's had another chat with the White House, and the president wants us to continue the way we have been." He shrugged. "It's sensitive for him, not least because he's heading to Kyiv for tomorrow's meeting with Doroshenko. He still doesn't want a stack of media coverage about his missing son overshadowing that. I might have taken a different view if it was my son. I'd just want him safe. But he's the boss—he's a politician, and he's got different priorities."

Jayne snorted but said nothing. She also disagreed with the president's stance. It seemed likely to her that all the details would emerge into the public domain at some stage.

"Anyway," Neal continued, "we think it would be best if Richard and Hazel stay here so they're positioned to get after the Land Cruiser once it's been located. Both of them know this region well. That would mean just you and I heading to Athens in the morning. I would have asked Abram Malevich to come over here from Kyiv, but he needs to be at the station there to prepare for the president's visit."

Jayne folded her arms. She was pleased that Neal could help her out in Athens.

"As long as we get some good backup from Athens station," she said.

"I'm sure we'll get that," Neal said. "Don't worry."

CHAPTER EIGHTEEN

Friday, June 23, 2017
Athens

The piercing Greek sun wàs slowly climbing into the sky as Jayne and Neal climbed out of the battered old Fiat CIA car sent to meet them at Athens International Airport. The sheer brightness of the light in Greece was always something that Jayne took a while to get used to, and she was feeling especially bleary-eyed after an early flight from Pápa Air Base.

The driver, having parked the Fiat on the side of Zoodochou Pigis street, handed Neal the car key and Jayne a package containing a Walther PPS from the weapons locker at the Athens CIA station to replace the one she had lost at the Vienna marina. The driver then climbed into the front passenger seat of a second CIA car that had followed them.

As the second car moved away down the street, they walked to the door of the narrow five-story apartment building that housed the CIA safe house designated to them by Athens station.

Neal carefully tapped the code into the security device at the door, opened it, and they made their way up a steep set of stairs to the third-floor apartment.

Just as they were entering the apartment, Jayne's replacement burner phone, obtained from the air base and loaded with her German SIM, vibrated in her pocket. It was an alert from her secure encrypted message service, Signal. She logged on to find a short note from Kira Suslova.

Confirm ok for BROWN SITE 3 11.51 p.m.

The meeting was on. That was a great relief.

The safe house was a two-bedroom apartment with linoleum floors, cheap wooden furniture, and a noisy air-conditioning system that made only a minimal impact on the stifling heat. The Agency was never willing to spend money on upgrading these safe houses.

Jayne accepted Neal's offer of the larger bedroom, while he took the smaller one. After moving her bags into the room, she sent a short confirmation on Signal to Suslova to acknowledge the meeting at 11.51 p.m.

She and Neal had decided to avoid visiting the CIA station, which was on the top floor of the US embassy on Vasilisis Sophias Avenue, a kilometer and a half to the east on the other side of Mount Lycabettus, the limestone hill that dominated that quarter of Athens.

Raising their heads above the parapet at the embassy was potentially too risky. She knew from previous visits to Athens and from a briefing note supplied by the CIA's chief of station that the SVR was running a high level of surveillance out of their *rezidentura* at the modern-looking Russian embassy on Nikiforou Litra street. The last thing they wanted was for a tail to be put on them, given the importance of the meeting with Suslova.

The decor in the safe house might have been tired, but the fridge had been well stocked, and there was a good supply of coffee. After a late breakfast, Jayne settled down to start work on a thorough SDR—the usual Agency shorthand for a surveillance detection route—and a backup plan in case there were problems.

She was mulling over a large-scale map of Athens when Neal walked into the room holding his laptop. On the screen, Jayne could see Vic sitting at a desk.

"Vic wants to talk to us both," Neal said, holding the laptop so Jayne could see the screen. "He's at Kyiv station, getting ready for Ferguson's visit."

Neal put the laptop down on the table where Jayne was working and pulled up a chair.

"Jayne, sorry to interrupt your preparations," Vic said over the video link. "I just want to check you're both ready for Suslova and to update you on things at this end."

"We'll be ready," Jayne said. "SDR preparation is underway, and I'll probably improve my looks when I get the blonde wig and glasses on."

"I prefer brunettes myself," Vic said, a faint grin on his face. "Look, I'll be leaving the embassy here soon for the walking tour and speeches."

"Walking tour?" Jayne asked. "I thought they'd be meeting at Bankova Street?"

Bankova Street was the common term for the Presidential Office Building in the center of Kyiv, where President Doroshenko was based. She had met him there the previous year.

"They've had a meeting there already, but they're currently en route to the hydroelectric plant offices in Kyiv, about half an hour's drive north of the city. The offices are on the dam over the river, next to the road. They're doing a short walking tour of the plant and speeches there."

Jayne felt surprised. "Why there?"

"They want to make a statement," Vic said. "It's a photo opportunity on the dam. They want the TV cameras there. The usual PR-driven approach. The two of them agreed to it on a phone call yesterday. They want to ram the message home to Moscow that the US is supporting Ukraine and particularly its dams and hydropower facilities. The strong subtext is that it's a warning to Moscow to leave their military at home and to back off Ukraine altogether. Ferguson is also, of course, eager to show that he will not be intimidated by the Russians grabbing his son—although he's obviously not going to refer to that."

"That should all go down well at the Kremlin," Jayne said, injecting a note of sarcasm into her voice. "They won't like the dams reference given the Ukrainians have blocked off the water supply to Crimea. And I still don't know how Ferguson can go through with all this while his son's in danger."

Vic shrugged. "Me neither. But you know what Ferguson's like. He seems to have some kind of capacity to keep his personal life completely separate from his job. Mentally very strong. Both he and Doroshenko are planning to make speeches saying the Russians need to get out of Crimea, they're occupying it illegally, and it's up to the invaders to provide water if they've taken land that isn't theirs. It's Ukraine's water, not Russia's."

Jayne nodded. It was a point that needed to be made.

"What have Ferguson's travel and security arrangements been like?" Neal asked.

It was a good question. Vic had so far kept the details of the president's route into Ukraine watertight and declined to brief them on how the president would get to Kyiv, which was fair enough in Jayne's view. Neither she nor Neal had any need to know.

"I'm happy to tell you now he's arrived," Vic said. "He flew into Rzeszów Airport in Poland last night, then his motorcade took him to Przemyśl Główny train station near the Ukraine border this morning. He came into Kyiv overnight by special sleeper train, Secret Service and guards all over it. Took ten hours to get here, and they picked up extra Ukrainian security people once over the border, I gather. Now they're driving him up to the dam in an armored motorcade—the usual SUVs, minivans, sedans. The USACE people have been helpful with the planning, as they know the dam. I've spoken to Charles Deacon this morning, and he tells me the president got some sleep on the train and is happy with everything and pleased to be back in Kyiv. He'll return the same way afterward."

Deacon was President Ferguson's personal aide. Jayne had dealt with him many times and liked his dry sense of humor. A bespectacled man with a hook nose, he dealt admirably with the multitude of hangers-on and political aspirants who tried to get access to his boss, while remaining a good source of advice and counsel to Vic and Arthur Veltman at Langley.

"If Deacon's happy, it must be going smoothly," Jayne said. He was renowned for his attention to detail and his high standards.

"That's true, as I know all too well," Vic said with the hint of a smile. "The media here, including the US correspondents, have only just been informed that Ferguson's in town. The journos and TV crews will be tripping over themselves in a race to get to the hydro plant. I suspect it will have Putin spluttering over his lunch, somehow."

Jayne gave a short laugh. "Let's hope so."

She saw Vic glancing at his watch.

"I need to go now," he said. "I've got a car waiting to take me up to the dam."

"Thanks," Jayne said.

Vic gave a brief wave and cut the connection from Kyiv.

Once he had gone, Jayne turned her attention back to planning her SDR.

BROWN SITE 3 was little more than a kilometer from the safe house as the crow flew.

But Jayne had no intention of taking anything like a direct route between the two points in the run-up to the meeting. Much of Athens was a rabbit warren of narrow streets and alleys, punctuated with a few squares, public gardens, and open spaces. Jayne planned to make good use of all the different types of terrain, as well as her naturally excellent feel for the street, to flush out any surveillance. She also aimed to use a good mix of the metro network, buses, trams, and taxis.

First, Jayne and Neal headed out in the Fiat for a drive around BROWN SITE 3 to familiarize themselves with the street scene. They pinpointed a spot outside a cell phone store one block west of the rendezvous point, in the wider and busier Acharnon street and agreed that Neal would park the car as near as possible to it. He could then act as either a backup in case of trouble or offer a swift getaway if required. Jayne hoped neither would be necessary.

After returning to the safe house, Jayne put together a rough plan. It would need to be flexible so she could change it depending on circumstances—for example, if she spotted a recurring face or vehicle, or anyone who looked out of place in their surroundings.

One of Jayne's skills was memorizing map routes accurately so that she wouldn't need to carry around a paper copy or keep continually referring to her phone once out on the street. That ability had come through years of practice, but was also partially inherent. It certainly helped to make her blend in with the local foot traffic and look more natural.

Once the SDR was decided, Jayne outlined the conversation she needed to have with Suslova. For security reasons, she wanted to spend no longer than the usual six minutes she allocated to such meetings.

It was typically long enough to say what needed to be said, provided she followed a tight script to use the time effectively.

After a light dinner of a salad with chicken, Jayne took out her blonde wig, her glasses, and her reversible lightweight jacket and set about transforming her appearance for the SDR.

She had almost finished dressing when a message arrived on her secure app from Vic, sent to both her and Hazel Foster. It said that Frank Baker and his team at the National Reconnaissance Office had located the blue Toyota Land Cruiser. It was now in Galati, a city on the Danube in Romania, at least a thirteen-hour drive from Vienna. The car appeared to be parked at a marina on the river.

Jayne sat back in her chair, stunned.

Romania?

What were the Russians going to do with Aidan Scarpa there?

* * *

Friday, June 23, 2017
    Athens

Gut instinct and a leopard-like ability to hunt in the darkest places and bide his time before striking were the cornerstones on which Gennady Sidorenko had built his entire career over thirty-five years within the SVR and the Kremlin.

Now into his mid-fifties, Sidorenko's belly had grown

almost in direct correlation with his seniority and standing as a counterintelligence wizard. He specialized in rooting out those who were traitors to the Motherland and extracting confessions from uncooperative suspects.

Most of his career had been spent within the KGB, and its successor, the SVR, Russia's foreign intelligence service, where lately he had headed up the small specialist DX unit within the director's office. His successes had brought him to the attention of the president, who had co-opted him for the Kremlin when there were counterintelligence issues that required resolving.

Never a team player, he often worked alone and on his own initiative and hunches.

One of those recent hunches had brought him to Athens, where he was now occupying an office on the top floor of the *rezidentura*, the SVR's base within the Russian embassy, two miles north of the US embassy.

In another office in the embassy, almost directly below him, was the object of his attention: none other than one of the president's key advisers, Kira Suslova, who had flown from Moscow's Vnukovo Airport on a Cessna Citation from the Kremlin's fleet the previous evening.

Sidorenko had followed alone, apart from the pilot and crew, half an hour later in a similar aircraft, also from Vnukovo. He had told nobody inside either the Kremlin or the SVR where he was going, besides the head of the aviation team through whom he had booked the jet.

Over the past eight months, something had been gnawing away at him, ever since the Kremlin's highly valuable principal asset in Western Europe, the now-imprisoned German chancellor Erich Merck, had been unmasked and forced to resign.

In the wake of that disaster, Sidorenko had devoted a

considerable slice of his waking hours to trying to figure out how Merck could have been detected after two and a half decades of operating successfully, including eleven years as chancellor. Had there been a mole inside the Moscow machine who had leaked it? Or had it been, as *The Washington Post* and other Western media reported, due to a diligent piece of research by a war crimes investigator, Joe Johnson, in the Stasi files in Berlin?

Sidorenko knew that Suslova had recruited Merck in the first place during her time with the KGB in East Germany, long before he had entered politics. She had continued to keep a close watch on him through Merck's handler, also now disgraced, the former president of the German chess federation, Wolfgang Paulsen.

He suspected that Suslova might have had something to do with the leak, but he had found no evidence or any motive for her doing so.

In any case, he had to proceed with extreme caution because he also knew that Suslova and President Putin had been conducting an on-off affair for many years at the president's whim. If he made one false step and wrongly accused Suslova of anything for which he did not have cast-iron proof, it would likely amount to signing his own death warrant. Suslova was also quite close to Igor Ivanov, another reason to be careful.

Still, Sidorenko found himself unable to let it go.

Professional pride and an arrogant belief in his own capabilities dictated that.

Hence his continued monitoring of Suslova.

When he found her leaving the archives in the basement of the GRU headquarters, and it then emerged she had been there to request the files for Operation Noi, his suspicions mounted sharply yet again.

Why did she want that file—which was permanently in Ivanov's possession?

Very few people even knew what Operation Noi was.

Now Suslova had come to Athens, ostensibly to conduct lobbying work with the Greek Chess Federation as part of her quest to become president of FIDE, which was another of Putin's pet projects.

But Sidorenko had a gut feeling that more was going on.

Was Suslova using the FIDE lobbying as cover for other, darker objectives?

Did someone inside Western intelligence have a hold over her?

If so, what?

He knew from his checks in the SVR files that former MI6 operative Jayne Robinson, who now worked mainly for the CIA, was Joe Johnson's partner and that she had been involved in Merck's unmasking. But he was still unable to pinpoint exactly what her role had been. Could she have somehow turned Suslova into a CIA asset, or found some blackmail material or other device to force her into disclosing information? It was difficult to say.

Sidorenko knew one thing, though: in this game, it was wise to rule nothing in and nothing out.

He had now co-opted two of the embassy's security guards on Suslova's floor to keep a watch on her office and to inform him immediately when she left the building. They would get a significant payment in return for their assistance and for keeping quiet about it.

Sidorenko now had a Makarov handgun tucked inside his jacket and had also obtained an old but well-maintained Citroën sedan from the SVR's garage at the embassy, which he planned to use if required.

When Suslova did leave, he planned to follow her himself. Although she was extremely adept at looking after herself in hostile environments and had excellent and intuitive survival skills, it had been some time since she'd worked on the street as an intelligence operative. Sidorenko was confident that his street craft was at least as good as hers. She wouldn't spot him, of that he was certain.

CHAPTER NINETEEN

Friday, June 23, 2017
    Kyiv

The sight of Secret Service officers patrolling both ends of the P69 highway that ran across the dam reassured Vic Walter as he stood at the entrance to the bland Soviet-era four-story office building on the western side of the hydro-electric power plant. The highway had been closed to traffic, and two military helicopters also hovered overhead, monitoring the situation below.

Alongside the Secret Service officers, Vic counted at least forty uniformed Ukrainian soldiers and another twenty-six police officers. There were four Spartan armored personnel carriers and two batteries of KPV heavy machine guns mounted on the back of trucks, one on either side of the center section of the dam.

President Ferguson's motorcade, from which he had alighted five minutes earlier, was parked directly outside the rectangular building. He was currently with Ukraine's president Pavlo Doroshenko, having a quick guided tour of the plant. The visit had been deliberately timed for late afternoon so that Ferguson's return by train to Poland could be conducted under cover of darkness again.

Vic was waiting with the CIA's Kyiv chief of station, Abram Malevich, the SZR's Valentin Marchenko, and the deputy hydroelectric plant manager, Danylo Korduba, who understandably seemed quite starstruck to have two presidents in his facility.

The BMW 4x4 that had brought Vic and Malevich from the CIA station was parked farther along the dam, away from the office and the president's motorcade.

President Ferguson's schedule had been tight, meaning that Vic had not yet had a chance to brief him on the latest update from Frank Baker at the National Reconnaissance Office about the location of the Toyota Land Cruiser that had carried his son out of Vienna. The vehicle was now in Galati, Romania, according to Baker, information that Vic had swiftly passed on to Jayne and Hazel Foster.

In a small parking area next to the office building stood three television crews and a select group of eight journalists, three of them from local Ukrainian publications and the others from the international cohort based in Kyiv. Ferguson and Doroshenko were both due to make short speeches to the media after the tour.

As they waited, Korduba explained to Vic how the hydroelectric plant functioned. Built in the 1960s, it consisted of twenty turbines in a 300-meter-wide concrete structure that formed the center section of the dam on the Dnipro River. Korduba pointed out that each huge turbine had its own waterway and was driven by water from the lake flowing through the dam into the river that continued through Ukraine toward the Black Sea.

Farther down the river in different parts of Ukraine were

six other dams and associated hydroelectric power plants, which together produced about 10 percent of the country's power, Korduba said.

He had just finished his short explanation when two Secret Service officers emerged from a set of double doors inside the building, followed by two Ukrainian soldiers in battle fatigues, then President Ferguson and President Doroshenko.

The two presidents made their way out onto a small area covered by a long white canopy designed to protect visitors from the weather. A lectern with microphones and speakers had been set up so the two men could address the media, gathered only twenty meters away.

Doroshenko moved to the lectern first and spoke in fluent, albeit heavily accented English with no notes, turning to Ferguson as he began.

"Mr. President, we are honored to receive you as our guest here today at just one of the hydroelectric dams that serve our country," Doroshenko said. "We are thankful for your support when we have an enemy at the gates—indeed, one who has already stolen a large portion of our territory in Crimea and appears to be trying to do the same in the Luhansk and Donetsk regions. Our message to Moscow is to back off and get out. We are stronger than you can ever imagine."

Vic listened carefully as Doroshenko continued for about five minutes. He never referred directly to the help Ukraine was receiving from the US, sensibly so, given the covert nature of most of it. But Doroshenko nevertheless made clear that the two countries and presidents were closely aligned. He then handed over to Ferguson, who stepped to the lectern.

"Thank you, Mr. President," Ferguson said. "I am glad to be here today to highlight the support we in the United

States offer to you and the people of Ukraine, a sovereign country under threat. It is a difficult time for you individually, for your government, and for your people—and indeed for us, and me personally. That said, we are determined to resist the illegal actions of a Russian government to annex Crimea and to threaten southern and eastern Ukraine, as well as the other moves Moscow is making that will inevitably escalate tensions between our countries. I can announce today further sanctions on Russia, both on individuals and organizations. I am referring to oligarchs, banks, businesses, and a wider group of the Russian leadership that surrounds the president of Russia. We will not hesitate to take further action if the Russian leadership escalates the situation."

Vic's ears pricked up at Ferguson's mention of his own personal difficulties, oblique as it was, and the reference to "other moves" and to further escalation. He never specifically mentioned his son, but for those in the know, this was a meaningful subtext.

Ferguson continued with his speech. "We will provide further assistance to the government and people of Ukraine," he said. "And what's more, we will—"

But President Ferguson got no further. From behind him, there erupted a deafening *rat-a-tat-tat* of machine gun fire as one of the batteries of guns on top of the dam opened fire, and an ear-splitting siren began to wail.

Vic jumped.

What the hell?

As the gunfire continued, four Secret Service officers rushed toward President Ferguson and bundled him toward the armored Cadillac in which he had arrived. Security guards also ushered President Doroshenko toward his black presidential car, parked near Ferguson's.

Several journalists in the media group began to shout and scream as they dived for cover.

Instinctively, Vic ran from his position, away from the building and past the president's motorcade. Out of the corner of his eye, he could see Marchenko, Malevich, and Korduba following close behind him.

"Drones," one of the Secret Service men shouted over his shoulder. "Coming at us down the lake."

As Vic ran, there came a massive explosion from the office building behind him. He glanced back and saw that all the windows facing the highway over the dam had blown out, scattering glass, bits of plastic, metal, and other debris across the road behind him. A piece of what looked like a plastic window frame landed to his left and skittered across the ground.

He could see the gunfire from the machine gun unit was directed outward, across the lake behind the dam. He immediately realized the gunners were trying to shoot down drones that were heading toward them.

Shit.

Was this the strike on Ukrainian dams that GRAY WOLF had warned Jayne and Neal Scales about in Zaporizhzhia? Was this Operation Noi?

Vic jumped over the knee-high traffic safety barrier and then dived to the ground on a narrow pedestrian walkway that ran between the barrier and a higher protective concrete wall topped with razor wire that ran along the edge of the dam. As he did so, he banged his right knee hard on the ground, sending a spike of pain up his leg.

Malevich landed just behind him, letting out a loud curse. Vic didn't see where Korduba and Marchenko ended up and wasn't going to look up to find out.

He covered his head with his hands and forearms, face right down against the base of the wall.

Meanwhile, the machine gun fire continued unabated for

at least another twenty seconds. Vic remained where he was but heard no further explosions.

Eventually, the gunfire stopped, and Vic lifted his head just as the president's motorcade sped off along the dam toward Kyiv, car tires crunching over the broken glass and other detritus.

Was that the end of the attack, or was it just the opening salvo?

"Are you okay?" Malevich asked.

Vic hauled himself up into a sitting position. He could see Korduba and Marchenko, who was bellowing into his phone, also sitting on the road a short distance away. Both were thankfully intact but looked predictably shell-shocked.

"Not really," Vic said, keeping his voice low. "Bastards. It's unbelievable. And what the hell are the Ukrainians doing? How did they let this happen? I hope the president's not hurt. He's lucky if so."

A uniformed Ukrainian army officer came running over from the direction of the machine gun truck nearest to them, dodging around the bits of debris on the highway. "Are you all right?" he asked, looking first at Vic, then at Malevich.

Vic stood, his ears still ringing from the noise. "How the *hell* did that happen? I thought the area was locked down." He glared at the officer.

"It was, sir, but we think there were six drones that must have come in at high speed. We don't know where from. We spotted them late and shot down five that came low across the lake from the north. But there was one that came from south of the dam. That was the one that hit the office building. We never saw it until too late."

"You saw it late? Why was that?" Vic asked. Now he could feel adrenaline beginning to run through his system once again. "What kind of drones were they?"

"Quadcopters carrying RPGs, not so big," the officer said.

"They wouldn't register on radar, because they were so low and small. And our patrol choppers never saw them either." He pointed to the two helicopters that were still hovering high above the dam.

"The drones were carrying RPGs?" Malevich asked.

Like Vic, Malevich was clearly in disbelief that the Russians would dare to attack a meeting of two heads of state using rocket-propelled grenades attached to drones.

The officer nodded.

"Shit," Vic said. "It's the Russians, or their proxies, the militias."

"Of course. Who else?" the officer said.

Vic looked around. "We need to get off this dam quickly. There could be more to come."

"We see no more incoming right now, sir," the officer said.

Vic rapidly regained his focus. It was obvious that the target was the president and his party, not the turbines or the power plant. That was why the drones had targeted the office building where Ferguson and Doroshenko were standing, unless the targeting was exceptionally poor.

But who had informed them where and when to strike? Briefing materials on the visit had been kept very tight, and few people had been read into the communications surrounding it.

Did the Ukrainians have a mole in their midst?

Or was it someone on the US side? That was unlikely, and Vic could hardly contemplate the possibility.

Vic glanced at his watch. They did need to get off the dam, but he needed to call Langley as quickly as possible. He also realized that Jayne was probably about to begin her SDR before the meeting with Suslova. She had to ask Suslova about this—who was passing Moscow secrets that had come close to taking out the US president? Critically, had they chosen to do this deliberately while holding the president's son, knowing that Ferguson was therefore unlikely to want to launch a major retaliation?

It added a new impetus to the operation to get Ferguson's son back. And it added weight to Vic's view that Ferguson was doing his son no favors by insisting that the operation to rescue him be conducted in secrecy. It just wasn't working.

Vic considered who to call first. Jayne was the first priority, under the circumstances.

He reached for his phone, logged on to his secure messaging service, and typed a message to her.

He had only just finished his first sentence when Marchenko appeared in front of him. He looked up.

"Vic, you okay?" Marchenko asked.

"Not really. I banged my knee, but it'll be okay."

Marchenko grimaced. "I've just had a call from our office. They've had a communication, supposedly from the pro-Russian groups in the Donbas area, but we think more likely originating from the Kremlin. It arrived just as the attack was taking place, it seems. They say they knew about the Ferguson-Doroshenko meeting. Well, that's obvious, I guess. But the email condemned the meeting and warned about further consequences if the North Crimean Canal is not unblocked immediately. They're accusing both countries of genocide—trying to deprive Crimean residents of water. And they're also saying Ferguson is interfering illegally by arming and helping the Ukrainians. They're demanding he announces immediately that he will pull all US intelligence and military people out of Ukraine—and they're setting a deadline of three weeks for the withdrawal to be completed. If not, there will be further consequences."

"*Three weeks?* That's ridiculous."

"Yes."

Vic exhaled. His first thought was that this was a joke, given Russia's hostility toward Ukraine. Did Moscow think the US would just abandon Ukraine to its fate? His second, unspoken thought was of Aidan Scarpa. Did the threats imply he was in danger? Surely they wouldn't dare.

"Well, there's nothing much new to what they're saying," Vic said. "Moscow's been complaining about all of those things for some time. What consequences are they threatening in three weeks if we don't pull out—beyond trying to blow Ferguson and Doroshenko to pieces?"

"They didn't say," Marchenko said. He shrugged and grimaced again.

"All right, thanks," Vic said. "We'll need to find out."

Marchenko nodded and walked away, tapping on his phone.

"Vic, we need to get out of here," Malevich said, a note of anxiety in his voice. He began walking toward the CIA's BMW.

"Just give me a minute," Vic said.

He returned to his message to Jayne. He summarized what Marchenko had just told him and instructed Jayne to try to find out from Suslova what the possible "further consequences" might be.

High priority, Vic wrote. *What consequences? In ref. The GRAY WOLF warning? Something different? And a Scarpa connection?*

He tapped on the screen and sent the message.

Only then did he follow Malevich to their car, limping a little as he went.

CHAPTER TWENTY

Friday, June 23, 2017
Athens

The black Mercedes nosed its way past the angular white concrete buildings of the Russian embassy and the guard on duty at the gate and pulled out onto Nikiforou Litra street.

Kira Suslova sank back into the leather seats in the rear of the car as it accelerated past the blue bus stop outside the embassy, where a short line of people was waiting.

"Drop me near the Acropolis Museum," Suslova told her driver, one of several chauffeurs based at the embassy. "I am meeting someone for dinner near there."

"Of course, madam," the driver said.

Suslova stared out the window at the opulent houses of the upmarket Psychiko suburb north of the city, where the embassy was located.

As the car continued southward toward the city, Suslova adjusted her reversible lightweight linen jacket, the hidden inside pocket of which contained her Makarov and silencer.

She could turn the jacket inside out to change its color from beige to dark brown, if required.

Given her status, Suslova had the right to use an embassy car and chauffeur. However, she only wanted to make use of the car for the first part of her schedule today, to take her for dinner at Strofi, her favorite restaurant in the city, with the president of the Greek Chess Federation, Theo Markopoulos.

She certainly didn't want the driver to see where she was headed after dinner, and in any case, she didn't want to take the risk of using a car. Drivers in Athens, in Suslova's experience, were among the worst she had come across in the world. The last thing she wanted while running a tight SDR was to get involved in a traffic accident that might delay her irrevocably, doing interviews with police and being bogged down in legal process.

So her plan after dinner was to walk, and to use buses, the metro, and trains, where she could melt into the background and switch routes hopefully without detection.

Not that she was expecting any tail or coverage today. She had informed anyone who would listen that she had a dinner meeting planned with Markopoulos, which was the reason for her visit to Athens. She'd had a similar meeting with him only three months earlier, so this would be seen as entirely plausible. Everyone knew she was running for the FIDE presidency and needed votes from chess federations worldwide to achieve that. Regular contact with the heads of the various national chess federations whose votes she needed was essential.

Around half an hour after leaving the embassy, her car pulled to a halt outside the Acropolis Museum, as requested. From there, she had only a five-minute walk to the Strofi.

But Suslova had walked only fifty meters when her phone vibrated in her pocket. It was Igor Ivanov, calling on their secure line.

Dermo. Shit. She would have to answer it.

Suslova sat on a concrete bench at the side of the street, entered her private pin to access the call, and answered, glancing around as she did so to check for any sign of a tail. There seemed to be none.

"Where are you?" Ivanov began.

"Athens. I have a FIDE lobbying meeting now," Suslova said. "Is this important, Igor?"

"Yes, very. First, you need to know our militias made a drone strike on the hydroelectric dam in Kyiv earlier, while the US and Ukraine presidents were visiting it."

A shiver went through Suslova. "You mean you've taken them both out? When was this?"

Her first thought was that Robinson and her CIA paymasters would now immediately blame her for not informing them about the Kyiv strike ahead of time. They might not believe she didn't know about it in advance, given her position, thus making it highly unlikely she would ever get her $2 billion back. The drone strike must be the reason why Ivanov had suddenly headed off to Crimea for operational reasons and canceled the update meeting at the Kremlin.

"About an hour ago," Ivanov said. "The presidents were not injured, we understand, but we made our point. The reason I'm telling you is that you may face questions about this while you are traveling. You just need to say it has nothing to do with Russia. The president wants us to deny all knowledge and blame it on pro-Russian militants within Ukraine over whom we have no control. He is planning to argue it is symptomatic of the wider desire by Ukrainians for the country to become part of Russia once again, where it belongs."

"Understood," Suslova said. "A good line to take."

Again, she carefully surveyed the surrounding area. Still, there was nobody within listening range.

"And we have another issue," Ivanov continued. "It's about the asset in Germany I briefed you about, being run by Anke Leonova."

"Right. What about him?"

There was a pause.

"He's the son of the US president," Ivanov said. "Name is Aidan Scarpa. But—"

"Are you serious?" Suslova interrupted, keeping her voice low. She felt the hairs on the back of her neck prickle.

"*Da*. Yes. I'm serious."

"And Anke has him?"

"That's what I mean. But Ferguson and the son haven't had a relationship since Ferguson and the mother divorced many years ago. They don't speak."

Suslova remained silent for a second or two as she digested the news. She had felt frustrated that Ivanov had previously kept the asset's identity a secret. Now it was obvious why.

"Anke and Gavrill Rezanov were moving the guy out of Germany, right?" she asked.

"Yes."

"Why hasn't this hit the US media? Surely it's a massive story?" Suslova asked.

"We think the president's embarrassed about it, so he's trying to deal with it quietly, under the radar. He's got that operative Jayne Robinson involved—which is why I asked you about her before. She's deniable as far as Ferguson's concerned because she's not CIA. Leonova and Rezanov tried to take her out in Vienna, but we don't think it worked. Local papers reported an explosion, but mentioned no bodies found. I might need you to get involved again to deal with Robinson—I will let you know, if so."

Another spike of anxiety ran through Suslova.

"What the hell are you going to do with Scarpa now,

then?" she asked, trying to switch the subject away from Jayne Robinson. "Where is he?"

"Leonova and Rezanov have driven him to Romania. They are at Galati, but not for long."

"What do you mean, not for long? What's the plan?"

Ivanov explained the plan while Suslova listened in mounting astonishment.

Several minutes later, after finishing the call, she continued her walk to Strofi, still finding it hard to believe what she had heard.

One thing was certain. Jayne Robinson would not like what Ivanov had just told her.

CHAPTER TWENTY-ONE

Friday, June 23, 2017
  Athens

Jayne emerged into the evening sunshine outside the Faliro metro station, in front of the Olympiacos soccer stadium in the Piraeus district of Athens. After spending the previous hour traveling up and down various parts of the underground, she was planning to take a walk to the nearby seafront and grab a coffee in the latest stage of her SDR before returning to the metro and heading north again.

Her left shin felt less sore—the wound was slowly healing and walking caused her no discomfort. She descended an escalator from the metro entrance and was standing on a small plaza, waiting to cross the street, when her phone beeped.

Jayne read the secure message from Vic with some amazement.

Had the Russians really used drones armed with RPGs to attack a meeting of two presidents? It seemed an astonishing provocation—one that would inevitably have serious repercussions for relations between the United States and Russia.

She'd had no internet access while underground riding the metro, but now she quickly logged on to some of her usual news channels to find blanket coverage of the incident.

The attack must have been ordered by the Russian president. Nobody would have carried it out without his authorization. Already some commentators were arguing this was a monumental blunder by Putin that would result in retaliatory actions by Ukraine with strengthened covert backing from the US.

Jayne reread Vic's entire message with growing disbelief.

So, the Russians had set a three-week deadline for the United States to pull all its people out of Ukraine and halt assistance to the country, and for Ukraine to unblock the North Crimean Canal, or suffer further unspecified consequences.

Jayne mentally added the item to the list of points she needed to discuss with Suslova, in line with Vic's request. Who had leaked details of Ferguson's Kyiv visit to the Russians?

A sinking feeling in her gut told her that the consequences mentioned must somehow involve Aidan Scarpa. News reporters and commentators so far still knew nothing about his kidnapping, although Jayne was certain that wouldn't remain the case for very long.

Before leaving the plaza, Jayne took out a pack of local Papastratos American Blend cigarettes she had bought during her SDR and lit one. She virtually never smoked, but the act of lighting up and appearing to do so gave her plenty of opportunity to scan her surroundings for any sign of surveillance. She sometimes used a mock phone call for the same purpose. But always, she was looking for faces she had seen before, people who looked out of place, anyone who inadvertently caught her eye, someone ducking into a shop or café when she looked in their direction. Anything that seemed like an anomaly.

But there was nothing.

She continued on, found herself a table at the Street 22 café overlooking the busy marina in Piraeus, drank another coffee, and after carefully surveying the other customers, checked her news websites again.

The attack on the dam in Kyiv had drawn widespread condemnation from international leaders and commentators. A short statement from the Kremlin denied responsibility and said it was entirely due to the actions of pro-Russian separatists inside Ukraine, who opposed the government there and the support being given to the regime by other countries, particularly the United States and the United Kingdom. That was very predictable.

She tapped out a short update on her encrypted app and dispatched it to Neal.

I'm clean. In Piraeus. Heading for meeting soon.

A short response came back a minute later.

Ready to go. Let me know when heading into meeting.

An hour later, after another long, watchful ride on the metro, Jayne emerged from Victoria metro station, six kilometers to the northeast of Piraeus and close to BROWN SITE 3 in the Vathi neighborhood.

The sun had gone down. Night was closing in.

She was now on the final stretch of her SDR, which was always the most nerve-wracking, especially when there was a lot at stake.

* * *

Friday, June 23, 2017
    Athens

. . .

It was now certain, as far as Sidorenko was concerned, that Kira Suslova was up to no good in Athens.

Initially, he thought he was wasting his time. She had gone for dinner at Strofi restaurant with the president of the Greek Chess Federation, where she had conducted a seemingly friendly conversation.

Sidorenko knew that because he had found a good vantage point at a café across the street and watched her through a window.

That dinner seemed perfectly normal. Indeed, Sidorenko had found out that she had met the same man at the same restaurant only a few months earlier. It was in line with her remit to win his vote in the ballot for the FIDE presidency.

After the meal, though, rather than calling for her embassy driver to collect her or taking a taxi back to her SVR-run apartment, she had begun a clear attempt to flush out any tail.

Just after leaving the restaurant, she had turned her usual Kremlin-issued phone off. Sidorenko knew that because he had requested a discreet trace on it from one of his former colleagues within the SVR whose job it was to carry out such monitoring.

Sidorenko's problem was that he didn't dare get too close to Suslova.

He knew her record on the street during her time as a KGB operative.

She was good.

He had therefore hung back considerably farther than he would with other targets. As a result, he had lost her twice, first when she'd moved at some speed through a market and taken an unexpected exit, and again in a park, when she left via a side gate that was hidden behind some bushes. On both occasions, he had been fortunate to have caught up with her again.

By then, he was certain she was on a surveillance detection run.

His suspicions were confirmed when, on three occasions, Suslova changed her appearance. She had emerged from a metro station bathroom with a curly brown wig concealing her usual straight black hair.

Not long after, while visiting a bookshop, she had donned a pair of tortoiseshell glasses, and later she switched from a beige jacket to a dark brown one, although Sidorenko didn't actually witness the change.

Now it was late into the evening, 11:20 p.m., and Suslova had remained in the same area, west of the Field of Ares park, for the past twenty minutes.

Sidorenko knew for certain she was preparing for a rendezvous in this part of the city. Although he was virtually certain that Suslova hadn't seen him, he couldn't afford for that to happen. But equally, it would be a disaster if he were to lose her now after all this effort.

Sidorenko aimed to get photographic evidence of her meeting with whoever it was she was rendezvousing with and to upload the pictures to his secure server in Moscow. He had an app on his phone that would carry out the upload automatically.

Only then would he decide whether to approach and challenge Suslova or leave the confrontation until they were both back in Moscow.

It was always a difficult decision, because the longer a traitor spent with his or her handler, the more likely it was that damaging information would change hands. Yet challenging someone in a foreign country made it far less likely they would return voluntarily to Moscow and receive the justice they deserved.

There was a third alternative, of course.

And that was to eliminate the traitor on the spot—and possibly their handler, too.

Instant justice was sometimes the only option. It was a choice Sidorenko had made many times before. He had never met with objections from anyone inside the Kremlin, from the president downward, when it had been necessary.

CHAPTER TWENTY-TWO

Friday, June 23, 2017
  Athens

Three of the four streetlights on the pedestrianized part of Smirnis street were not working as Jayne turned the corner and made her way past a heap of black garbage bags piled outside a doorway.

But even in the semidarkness it was impossible not to notice the poor state of the buildings in this part of Athens. Most walls were plastered with multicolored graffiti that had been sprayed or painted in some detail. The concrete rendering on several building walls was old and crumbling. A few buildings had been demolished altogether, and the sites were fenced off, awaiting renovation.

This was a rough, densely populated part of town.

That suited Jayne. It was an area where people talking on street corners was the norm. There were still a few locals loitering: girls laughing, two men chatting about sports, a couple kissing in a recessed doorway. Jayne hadn't seen a single policeman in the past half hour.

Nobody gave her a second glance as she made her way past a four-story apartment building, a baby wailing loudly somewhere inside, and stepped carefully around a smashed drain cover that looked like a mantrap for passersby. Two men who were talking on a bench got up and walked off as she went by.

Jayne glanced at her watch. It was now 11:49 p.m. Two minutes to go until the arranged rendezvous with Suslova.

She checked her German burner phone. There were no messages on Signal, nothing from Suslova, which she took as a positive sign.

Quickly, Jayne tapped out a short message on her usual phone and dispatched it to Neal, who was waiting in the Fiat a block away on Acharnon street.

All ok. Going into meeting now. Will message when done and heading your way.

Jayne had removed her blonde wig half an hour earlier and was now her natural dark color once again, although she had left her glasses in place.

She continued toward the corner at the end of the pedestrianized section where the arranged rendezvous was to take place. When she got there, she leaned against a crumbling cement wall, took out her pack of Papastratos, and lit one.

From her vantage point at the crossroads, she glanced down Filis street, lined on both sides with cars that were parked half on the sidewalks, leaving just enough space down the center for vehicles to pass. On the other side of the street, outside a building site, stood a dumpster half-full of old bricks and rubble.

There was no sign of Suslova, and the locals now seemed to have melted away.

Neither was there anyone on Smirnis, where the upper-floor balconies of the apartment blocks on both sides of the street jutted out so far Jayne could imagine the occupants almost being able to reach out and shake hands with those opposite.

She looked around again.

Then, from behind a builder's truck parked halfway down Filis street, a shadowy figure appeared, moving at a steady pace.

A woman wearing a headscarf.

Jayne threw her cigarette to the ground and crushed it beneath her foot.

Instinctively, she touched her Walther in its hiding place in her jacket pocket. Now she could feel her adrenaline level rising, her peripheral vision suddenly clearer.

As the woman drew near, now within twenty meters, Jayne could see it was Suslova. Even in the gloom, she recognized the body shape, the gait, even though she now had curly brown hair instead of her usual straight black style.

"Good evening," Suslova said in English as she closed the gap. Jayne could see her glancing up and down the intersecting Smirnis street, checking carefully.

"Hello," Jayne said. "How was your journey here?"

"Tiring. A long time since I last did such a surveillance detection run."

Jayne was at least glad to hear there had been an extended SDR. She indicated toward the pedestrianized part of Smirnis. "There is an empty bench up there. We can sit and talk."

Suslova nodded, and they walked through the gloom past a broadband street cabinet next to the shell of a building that was being prepared for renovation. It was fenced off with wire mesh to prevent intruders, although the temporary wooden entrance gate for construction workers had been left unlocked.

"I nearly aborted this meeting," Suslova said, her voice

now very low. "Maybe it is my age, but I was not getting a good vibe on the street some of the time."

A slight tremor went through Jayne. "Did you see anyone, anything?"

"No. I was careful. But maybe it's because I don't want to be here. I was just getting a feeling."

That was understandable, Jayne thought. She was certain that a back street in Athens, meeting someone working for the CIA who held a $2 billion blackmail position over her, was the very last place on earth that Suslova wanted to be.

The Russian paused as they sat on the bench. Again she glanced right, then left.

"Anyway," Suslova said, "we have only a small amount of time. I have a lot to tell you. But I need a commitment that you will return my money."

Jayne resisted giving a snort. Now was not the time to antagonize the woman. "You'll get your money when the time is right. Let's see what you have to tell me first."

"Time is running out for me. Our president and counter-intelligence will soon realize that money is missing. I have been lucky, very lucky, that so far it has not been detected. As soon as it is, I will be history, and your source, me, will be no more."

"But you'll not be my source anymore if I give you the money back, will you?" Jayne said.

Suslova stared straight ahead. "I have a couple of things I would like to share with you. High level, not detail, relating to Ukraine and its dams."

"Tell me."

"There is an operation being run out of the Kremlin, Operation Noi, which—"

Jayne did her best to conceal her surprise. "Operation Noi?" she interrupted, trying to keep her voice level. She didn't want to give away what she already knew.

"Yes."

Suslova turned her head slowly and scrutinized Jayne for a second. "Do you already know about that?" she asked.

Despite her efforts, the Russian had picked up the vibe straightaway.

"Very little," Jayne said. "More information would be helpful."

"Unfortunately, I also know little," Suslova murmured. "I mention it now as a heads-up. Is that how you say it? A warning? But the detail will need to come when I can get it. I believe it is an operation to attack Ukraine's dams, but which one, I don't know, and—"

"Yes, I know it's an attack on a dam, or dams," Jayne interrupted, a little impatiently. "But there are seven hydroelectric dams along the Dnipro. We need to know which one. Kakhovka? Dnipro dam? Kremenchuk? Kyiv?"

Suslova shook her head. "I have been taking risks beyond what I should have done to find out. So far, I have had no luck."

Jayne cursed inwardly. On the one hand, she felt impressed that Suslova had voluntarily mentioned Operation Noi, even if she herself knew about it already. It showed a willingness to cooperate that she had not expected. But on the other hand, if Suslova was being left out of the loop on the details of such a seemingly major operation, did that mean her position at the Kremlin had been weakened? It wasn't a good sign.

"Who's running the operation?" Jayne asked.

Suslova placed her hands together in front of her. "At the top level, it is Igor Ivanov at the Kremlin. However, there is also an operational head. I do have a code name: the Khranitel Plotiny, the—"

"The DAM KEEPER."

Again, Suslova's head swiveled. "You know that too?"

"Yes, but not the actual identity of the person. That's what I need. Do you know who it is?"

Again, Suslova shook her head. "This is something I am also trying to find out."

Jayne had to resist rolling her eyes.

Was Suslova bullshitting her? There seemed a distinct possibility.

"So, what can you tell me?" Jayne asked, now feeling distinctly irritated. "You wanted to meet me, just as I wanted to meet you. I assumed there was some solid information you wanted to pass on. For instance, what about the attack on the US and Ukrainian presidents at the Kyiv hydroelectric dam today?"

"That was carried out by pro-Russian militias in Ukraine on the orders of our president," Suslova said. "It was not intended to destroy the dam, not at this stage."

"But it was intended to take out the two presidents? And you didn't warn me?"

Suslova said nothing.

"And the plan could be to destroy the dam in the future?" Jayne asked. "Is that what you're saying? Is that Operation Noi?"

Suslova shrugged again. "It may well be, but I don't know."

Jayne looked right, toward the junction with Filis street. Nobody was there. She looked left. Also clear.

Already they were more than halfway through the six minutes she had mentally allocated for the meeting.

"There is something else I need to ask you about," Jayne said.

"The army engineer from Wiesbaden currently being held by the GRU?" Suslova asked.

Jayne gave a half smile. "Exactly. We are worried about him."

"Because he is the son of President Ferguson?"

So Suslova was not being kept entirely out of the loop, then. This must be very tightly held information at the Kremlin; otherwise it would be all over the Russian media by now.

"Of course, although they are not close," Jayne said. "We need to know what is happening to him. I understand he has been taken from Vienna, where one of your GRU operatives nearly managed to blow me to pieces, to Galati in Romania. We want him back. Where is he now?"

Suslova looked at her and didn't speak for a second. "Unfortunately, the news of the president's son is not good." She checked her watch. "They have taken him down the Danube to the Black Sea—it's an old Cold War exfiltration route, EAST SNAKE TWO. As we speak, he is probably just arriving by boat at the cape."

"At the cape?" *Shit.*

Jayne had a feeling she knew what Suslova was telling her, but wasn't sure. "What do you mean?"

"The cape," Suslova said. "Cape Idokopas on the Black Sea. Putin's Palace. It's near Sochi."

Surely not. Unbelievable.

Cape Idokopas was something Jayne was well aware of. It was the notorious palace that the Russian president had built for 100 billion rubles, about $1 billion, on the eastern side of the Black Sea.

"You can't be serious? Putin has taken Ferguson's son to his palace?"

Suslova nodded. "It's a fortress."

"Why the hell have they done this?" Jayne asked.

Suslova inclined her head. "Apparently, he heard too much. Operational details. But I don't know what."

"And Putin's driving this?"

"Putin and Ivanov."

"How do you know? Are you certain?" Jayne asked.

"Ivanov himself told me."

"Bastards." This was the worst news. Jayne looked at her watch. There was little time left. Presumably the same GRU honey-trap specialist who recruited Aidan was still holding him.

"I know that one of your GRU operatives, Anke Leonova, was holding Aidan," Jayne said. "Is she the one who took him to the cape?"

Suslova nodded. "Her and a Spetsnaz officer, Gavrill Rezanov. They're both dangerous killers."

Jayne stared in disbelief at Suslova. "How the hell are we going to get him out? Because you're getting no money back unless we do, I'm telling you now."

"*Suka*. You bitch. Wait a moment. That's nothing to do with me. I'm trying to help you and—"

"Thanks for the help. I appreciate it," Jayne interrupted, a note of sarcasm in her voice. "But you're getting no money back until Aidan Scarpa is safely out of Russia. So you'd better start thinking hard."

There was a short pause. Suslova exhaled.

"Listen, there is nothing I can think of right now," the Russian said. "I will try to find something that can help you, but—"

Right then, Suslova stopped talking.

Instead, she stared at the broadband street cabinet they had walked past on the way to the bench, about ten meters away.

The next thing Jayne knew, Suslova had thrown herself to her left, off the bench, just as there was a bright flash, followed almost immediately by two deafening gunshots. Splinters flew from the bench as the rounds smashed into the wooden struts.

"What the hell?" Jayne said involuntarily.

Reacting instinctively to what Suslova had done, she rolled to her right off the bench and onto the ground, pulling her Walther from her pocket and, with the ease of long practice, flicking off the safety.

As she did so, she caught a glimpse out of the corner of her eye of Suslova wriggling on the ground on the other side of the bench.

Had she been hit?

Jayne flattened herself to the ground in a shooting position and racked the slide on her gun.

From her left came the dull *thwack, thwack* of suppressed semiautomatic gunfire, this time from Suslova's position. The shots were followed instantly by metallic thuds as the rounds struck the broadband cabinet. Almost immediately there came the deafening crack of two more unsuppressed gunshots in reply from behind the metal structure, followed by the whine as the rounds ricocheted off somewhere.

Jayne had no time to think.

The ambush could mean only one thing.

Someone had followed them.

She caught a glimpse of a reflection of light on something metallic just above the white cabinet. Assuming it was a gun and that Suslova or herself was the target, Jayne reflexively took aim at it and fired.

There was a muffled, distinctly male yelp of pain from behind the box, followed by the clatter of something heavy skidding across the concrete sidewalk.

Jayne's first reaction was that she had hit the gunman's hand or arm as he prepared to fire again, forcing him to drop his weapon.

That seemed to be Suslova's instinct too, because the next thing Jayne knew, Suslova had jumped to her feet and was running toward the broadband cabinet, her gun raised.

"Wait," Jayne yelled.

But she was too late.

Suslova ran straight over to the cabinet and came to a halt.

"Sidorenko," she heard her say. "*Ublyudok*."

There came a stream of rapid, almost unintelligible Russian from a man who Jayne assumed must be on the ground behind the box.

It was brought to a cursory halt by the double *thwack, thwack* of two more suppressed gunshots as Suslova opened fire at short range.

Shit.

This was all going rapidly south.

Suslova turned around. "Come here," she hissed.

Jayne got up and ran over. Behind the cabinet, a man was lying on the ground, dead, with one bullet hole in the middle of his forehead, another below his right eye. His right hand was a bloody mess where the round that Jayne had fired had ripped through it. There was a large silver watch on his wrist, which might have been what Jayne had seen glinting in the gloom.

In his left hand was a phone.

"Gennady Sidorenko," Suslova said. "Counterintelligence chief in the president's office. He's a snake. The bastard was taking photos of us as well as trying to kill us." She pointed to the phone he was holding.

The name rang a bell in Jayne's mind, but that was the least of her concerns right now.

"Bloody hell, we've got to get out of here," she said. "We'll have police here in no time."

Suslova immediately kneeled next to Sidorenko. First, she removed his watch and a ring from his bloodied right hand and looked up at Jayne. "Good shot, that one."

Then she took the phone from his hand, which she immediately switched off, and from his pockets removed a wallet, some keys, a passport, a packet of cigarettes, a driver's license, and a few sheets of folded paper.

"Pick his gun up," Suslova said, pointing to a pistol on the ground a few meters away.

Jayne hurried over, took out a handkerchief, and used it to pick up the gun, a Makarov. She engaged the safety and shoved the weapon into her jacket pocket.

"Help me," Suslova said. "We'll put him in the dumpster around the corner."

Jayne exhaled. That would involve carrying Sidorenko's body at least fifty meters down the pedestrianized part of the street and onto Filis street. And the dumpster would be in view of anyone passing by.

"No. Too far," Jayne said. "We'll be spotted."

This was absolutely the last thing Jayne wanted to get involved in, but she forced herself to look around for alternatives.

Remarkably, despite the gunfire, nobody had emerged onto the street to challenge them, and she could see nobody looking out of windows from the apartment building farther up the street. Perhaps the locals were used to gunshots in this neighborhood of Athens, or perhaps they were too scared to get involved.

"Put him in the building site there." Jayne pointed to the unlocked wooden door to the construction site, which was slightly ajar. "It's Friday. Maybe they won't find him until the workers come back on Monday."

"*Da*. Okay." Suslova nodded.

She grabbed Sidorenko beneath his armpits while Jayne picked up his feet. The counterintelligence chief was heavily built, over 200 pounds, Jayne guessed. It required all their strength to carry him the short distance to the construction site entrance. There Jayne kicked the door open, and they lifted the body inside.

"Put him in there," Suslova said, pointing to a wide trench at least thigh deep over to their left.

Jayne didn't argue. She could see no better alternative, and there was no time to debate it.

They dropped Sidorenko in the trench.

"Throw those over him," Jayne said. She pointed to a pile of old planks that had been stripped from the shell of the building and were awaiting disposal.

They covered Sidorenko with the wood, a camouflage that wouldn't survive an inspection but would keep him out of view of anyone who took a cursory look around the site over the weekend.

"Let's get out of here now," Jayne said. She headed for the door, Suslova following close behind.

Once outside, Suslova grabbed two handfuls of soil from the base of the tree next to the broadband cabinet and threw it over the bloodstains where Sidorenko had been lying. She quickly used the sole of her shoe to rub it in, trying to hide the marks, and then used the flashlight on her phone to check that there were no red stains remaining.

Then they both strode rapidly down the street westward along Smirnis.

Jayne dispatched a quick message to Neal.

Heading to you now. Complications here.

Once they got to the corner of Acharnon street, Jayne stopped. She could see the Fiat waiting near the cell phone shop, as arranged.

"I'm going that way," Jayne said, pointing down the street to the south. "I have a car waiting. I need to know how we're going to get Scarpa out of that bloody Black Sea palace, and I'll expect answers quickly."

"There are a couple of possibilities," Suslova said. It was obvious from the speed with which she spoke that she was anxious. "I know the palace site very well. I've been there a lot. There are always many visitors doing work, carrying out services. I'm involved in one project—it's to provide a high-specification giant chess set for Putin's indoor swimming pool. Specially sculpted chess pieces, no expense spared. You might need to become a sculptor or chess set expert. Leave it with me. I will see if anything is possible and let you know how we might proceed."

"You're serious?" Jayne asked.

"I can think of no other options right now. And that's if they don't pin Sidorenko's disappearance on me—which they will if he was working here with other people against me. My only hope is if he was working alone—and that's possible, because he knew the president has been screwing me, so he would want to keep quiet until he had evidence. I'm heading back to Moscow early in the morning, so we will soon find out. If you don't hear from me again, you'll know what's happened."

Suslova then walked away without another word.

Jayne strode down the street, got into the Fiat's front passenger seat, and let out a lengthy sigh of relief as Neal set off.

"Well?" he asked. "What were the complications?"

"It was bloody messy," Jayne said. "But I'll tell you about that in a minute. Look, I don't know if I'm being played by Suslova or whether I've got a good lead. And if I'm not being played, we have a mission impossible on our hands, I can tell you that."

PART THREE

CHAPTER TWENTY-THREE

Saturday, June 24, 2017
    Cape Idokopas, Russia

Aidan Scarpa called out in his sleep, kicked his legs unconsciously beneath the blanket, and jerked awake.

Then he lay still, his heart pumping, staring at the white ceiling of the cell in which he was incarcerated, clutching the blanket to his chest.

It was the same recurring dream he'd had for the past three nights, sometimes twice a night, ever since he had arrived in Russia.

The dream comprised a replay of the long boat journey he had suffered to get there. Every time the boat hit a wave, it bucked and threw Aidan back hard against the thin rubber mattress on the cabin floor to which he had been secured.

But the bald guard, who Aidan had learned was named Gavrill Rezanov, had tied his wrists and ankles to heavy gym kettlebells for most of the trip, apart from meals and bathroom breaks. It meant that he couldn't use his legs or arms to help adjust to the boat's movement or get into a comfortable position and had no choice but to ride with it.

Now, three days after the voyage, Aidan's lower back, his ass, and his shoulders remained heavily bruised, and his wrists and ankles were chafed from the ropes. His clothes still stank of vomit from where he had been sick three times during the journey.

The two Russians really had it in for him. The journey down the Danube by boat to Vienna, and then in the back of a Toyota 4x4 deep into Romania, had been bad enough. But the sea voyage had been easily the worst part.

He knew the trip had started at Galati, Romania, because he had seen the signs at the marina where the Toyota had arrived and from where they had set off. He quickly worked out that from there, they had taken him down the remaining relatively short distance to the mouth of the Danube and then across the Black Sea to Russia.

Anke, who not long ago had been his lover, was now treating him like a pile of crap. And he knew for sure now that Anke *was* her name, not Irina. He had overheard Rezanov call her that at least twice. They probably thought they didn't need to pretend any longer. And he had discovered Rezanov's name after overhearing him say it to someone on a radio call.

During the entire voyage, Anke had refused to answer questions or give him any information about where they were headed. She told him that if he persisted in trying to ask, she would gag him again. All she said was that it was his fault for eavesdropping in Frankfurt and that he would have to bear the consequences.

He now wished with every fiber of his body that he hadn't stood on the table in that warehouse in Frankfurt and listened to the conversation through the ventilation grille. Or, better still, that he had never met Anke at all.

The vessel on which they had traveled had been functional rather than luxurious. From what he had seen before boarding, it looked like some kind of patrol boat, although it had no military hardware as far as he could see. Certainly, there were no visible guns.

Going by sunrises and sunsets, he calculated they were on board for roughly a day and a half. But there were blinds over the windows, and all he could see was whether it was light or dark outside.

Eventually, the boat slowed to a crawl, bumped against something, then stopped. There came shouts from outside in voices that were unmistakably speaking Russian. That confirmed his suspicions.

Aidan's body had been so stiff that he initially struggled to walk, but after being untied, he followed Anke out of the cabin, along the gangway, and out onto the deck. Rezanov walked behind him, occasionally prodding him in the back with the barrel of his pistol.

There, after hours stuck in the semidarkness, he found himself somewhat dazzled by the combination of the bright sunshine and the white concrete structure to which the boat was moored. It was an enclosed harbor, maybe a hundred yards across, that looked newly built. Two larger luxury yachts stood at the quay next to the boat Aidan had been on.

Behind the harbor, a stony scree slope stretched up to a belt of trees. Aidan noticed the roofs of buildings poking up above the tree line. Below the tree line, just to the left of the harbor, was an odd-looking bunker-like concrete structure. There were other buildings to the right. Several black vehicles, most of them 4x4s and all clearly new, stood on the quayside.

At various points around the small harbor, there were guards in black uniforms who carried assault rifles and pistols in holsters on their hips. Aidan counted at least ten of them.

Aidan assumed he was now somewhere on Russia's Black Sea coast, or possibly the Sea of Azov, north of the Black Sea and east of the Crimean Peninsula.

Anke and Rezanov had taken him along a gangway onto the harbor, where armed guards asked Anke a few questions, took photographs of Aidan, and waved them on.

They had then walked past another checkpoint and through a tiled, well-decorated, and well-lit tunnel that stretched upward through the hillside to the building he was now in.

It was a property on which no expense had been spared. Aidan guessed it must belong to one of Russia's famous oligarchs, maybe even the president. Before being locked in his current cell, Aidan had walked along an exquisitely furnished corridor, with a patterned marble floor, what looked like gold light fittings, and chandeliers that, judging by their sparkle, were made from top-quality crystal. Oil paintings, both landscapes and portraits, hung on the walls.

His cell, by contrast, was along a plain white corridor with a concrete floor and had none of the luxury fittings of the main part of the property. An armed guard was waiting outside when he arrived.

The white-painted room had a red-tiled floor, no windows, and a single plain wooden bed in one corner on which he was now lying. It also had a shower, a toilet, a sink in another corner, and a large circular drain in the center of the room that stank of disinfectant. The floor sloped slightly from each corner of the room to the drain. Next to the drain was a heavy chair made of solid metal and which had hooks and loops welded to the arms, legs, and back, clearly for securing someone to it. Standing against the wall near the door was a stainless-steel trolley of the type used in hospital operating rooms, also equipped with several metal hooks and loops.

There was little doubt in Aidan's mind that the chair and trolley were used as instruments of torture, if required, allowing a prisoner to be strapped down and immobilized. There could be no other explanation. As for the drain, he dreaded to think about why that was needed.

The nightmare that Aidan had just experienced always ended with him eyeing the chair, trolley, and drain, fear mounting inside him and calling out in his sleep, jerking himself awake.

"Shit. What is this?"

When he had first arrived in the room, Aidan felt his bowels twist inside him and had to clench his butt muscles tight to avoid an outcome he certainly didn't want. He had glanced at Anke, who stood facing him, her arms folded tight across her chest.

"Why am I here?" he'd asked. "What the hell are you doing?"

Anke had tilted her head as she looked at him. "I told you. You know too much. That's why you're here."

CHAPTER TWENTY-FOUR

Monday, June 26, 2017
   Moscow

"We have a problem," Maksim Kruglov said as he swept his pig-like eyes around the meeting table in President Putin's private office. "A serious problem. Gennady Sidorenko has disappeared in Athens."

Suslova swore silently to herself and folded her arms.

She had been hoping it might take a little longer before Sidorenko's absence was noticed at the Kremlin. After all, Sidorenko was often away conducting his own investigations without regularly checking in with others.

Suslova glanced across at the president, who sat stone-faced, a file closed on the desk in front of him, listening carefully. He must have been briefed by Kruglov prior to the meeting, judging by his lack of reaction.

"Disappeared?" Igor Ivanov asked. "What do you mean?"

The folds of flesh wobbled around Kruglov's hairy neck as the SVR director leaned forward. "We have not yet been able to find out what happened to him. But I assure you, he has disappeared. He was at the *rezidentura* in Athens on Friday, then went into the city alone on Friday night—we know not why. And he has not returned. Neither the pilot of the Cessna he took from Vnukovo nor his assistant have seen him since."

Kruglov's gaze settled on Suslova, who made an effort to look unblinkingly back at him. She decided it would be better to react proactively to avoid finding herself on the defensive, because Kruglov must know she had also been in Athens.

"I was in Athens on Friday," Suslova said. "I had a dinner meeting with the Greek chess president, and I was at the embassy earlier in the day. Nobody told me about this. What was Sidorenko doing in Athens?"

Kruglov raised his eyebrows, eyeing her for a second before replying. "We don't know. That's the odd thing. He appears to have told nobody about his plans." He paused and continued to scrutinize Suslova. "Do you have any insight into what he was doing there or what happened to him?"

Dermo. Shit. Was this a bluff, or did Kruglov really know nothing about why Sidorenko had gone to Athens? Evidently Sidorenko's body had not been found, or if it had, then it had not yet been identified by the Greek authorities; otherwise Kruglov would presumably have mentioned that. That was good news.

"I have no idea what he was doing there," Suslova said. "And I didn't see him at the embassy."

That was her story, and she was going to stick to it. The meeting, which was the usual scheduled leadership gathering in Putin's second-floor office, also involved Ivanov, as well as the GRU director Colonel General Sergey Pliskin, and FSB director Nikolai Sheymov, who were sitting opposite her.

Sidorenko's deputy in the DX counterintelligence unit, Tikhon Safonov, had not attended the meeting in his boss's absence. Safonov was not part of Putin's Kremlin elite team, and Suslova guessed that although the president knew him, he might take his time before deciding to involve him in these high-level meetings. That suited her, as Safonov was cut from a similar mold to his boss: a highly skilled operator, but also deeply unlikable, suspicious, dangerous, and impossible to trust.

Putin leaned forward and, as was often his habit, eyeballed everyone around the table before speaking. "I want to know what happened to Gennady," he said, his gaze settling on Kruglov. "Do whatever is needed to find out. Get Safonov to investigate. It will be a good test for him."

"I will get that done, sir," Kruglov said.

The president then leaned back in his chair and turned his gaze to Ivanov. "Tell me what is happening to our guest at Cape Idokopas, the American."

Ivanov pursed his lips. "We have him safely in custody there. The EAST SNAKE TWO exfiltration protocols went to schedule. We will keep him there until Operation Noi is complete. Holding him was not our first choice, but he may be useful as a bargaining chip. I'm going to the cape on Friday —I'll look forward to meeting him."

Suslova felt a spike of irritation at yet another reference by Ivanov to Operation Noi, of which she still did not know the details.

Putin nodded and flicked a glance around the table. "Now that you've got him, use him. He will be another lever we can pull following the attack at the Kyiv dam, which didn't quite work as planned but was a good warning shot to the Americans. We want Crimea's water supply back—the dam on the North Crimean Canal must be removed immediately. We want the Americans completely out of Ukraine. It's obvious that President Ferguson doesn't want to go public about this secret son who he never sees. So let's make use of him, alongside Noi."

"How should we make use of him?" asked Ivanov.

"Send the president a private communiqué that makes our position clear," Putin said, a faint grin spreading across his face. "And tell him if he doesn't comply, the private communiqué will become a very public one."

"Yes, sir," Ivanov said.

After a further short discussion about ongoing military and financial support for President Assad of Syria, Putin picked up his file to signify that the meeting was finished.

"Anything else?" he asked.

There were shakes of heads around the table.

Putin turned to Suslova. "On more mundane issues—my swimming pool chess set. What is happening with that?"

"It is moving ahead, sir. The team supplying the set will visit the cape soon to make a detailed installation plan and to design the pieces."

Putin gave her a curt nod. "I'm pleased you are finally making headway."

Suslova had, in fact, thought of little else but the chess set project since returning to Moscow on Saturday morning following the high-octane and near fatal conclusion to her meeting with Jayne Robinson late the previous night.

As she left the president's office, she mentally reviewed her options. It seemed evident to her that the visit by Nikolas Kamov's team to Cape Idokopas was the only possibility for the foreseeable future to get an outsider into the otherwise impregnable fortress at the palace on the cape, and for that person to exfiltrate Aidan Scarpa.

Precisely how that could be done was another issue. But time was rapidly running out. She needed to have another in-depth conversation with Kamov, a trusted friend who disliked Putin but loved making money in equal measure, and to come up with a plan. The big advantage lay in that she would need to be present at the palace to work with Kamov's people on the chess sculpture project.

But it was equally clear to Suslova that in her efforts to secure back her $2 billion and thereby escape her fate in a modern gulag, she was being gradually forced into an increasingly high-stakes game of risk, in which the penalty for failure for her would almost certainly be death—not just for her, but for her nemesis, Jayne Robinson, as well.

They had gotten away with it once in the backstreets of Athens, but to do so again would require extremely careful planning and a good slice of luck.

Monday, June 26, 2017
Berlin

President Ferguson screwed the piece of paper into a ball and threw it across the meeting room table, where it landed in front of Jayne.

"I'm not giving in to that asshole in the Kremlin, I can tell you that," Ferguson said. His icy tone left everyone in the room in no doubt that he meant what he said. "I'm not surrendering to kidnappers and blackmailers, no matter who they're holding captive. I want a different solution, and I need it now."

Ferguson leaned back and fixed his gaze on Vic Walter, who was sitting next to Jayne in the CIA station on the top floor of the American embassy, just a stone's throw from the Brandenburg Gate in central Berlin.

The president had just read the printed demand delivered to him via a back channel, a former US ambassador to Russia who had built a relationship of sorts with the sender, Igor Ivanov, during his time in Moscow. These days, the former ambassador was acting as a part-time adviser to the White House.

Jayne had already seen the demand, which Ferguson's personal assistant Charles Deacon had shown to her and Vic before the meeting. It was short and to the point and reiterated the demands in the email sent after the drone attack at the dam: that the North Crimean Canal be immediately unblocked and that the United States and its allies, including the United Kingdom, withdraw all assistance to Ukraine.

The final paragraph of the missive left little doubt about what might happen if its contents were ignored.

We look forward to full cooperation from the governments of the United States and Ukraine in achieving these objectives. If these demands are not met, there will be material consequences for one particular person and for water supply security generally.

It didn't name Aidan Scarpa by name, but it didn't need to.

Jayne and Neal, who was sitting next to her, had flown to Berlin that morning from Athens on Vic's instructions, using the CIA's Gulfstream V jet, which he had continued to make available to them.

She felt grateful that after she had reported back to Vic following her meeting with Suslova in Athens, it had been him, and not her, who briefed President Ferguson first thing on Saturday morning on what had happened to his son and precisely where he had been taken.

Vic leaned forward and looked at Ferguson. "I think that given the very personal situation you are in, sir, I would not like to advise you on this one. You need to think it through very carefully."

Ferguson's face was now a deep crimson. "I have thought it through. And my answer is the same. I need a different solution. We need to get my son out of whatever hellhole he's in at Putin's Palace. And Ukraine needs to raise security levels on its dams—the Russians are going to target them, and in a much more devastating way than the drones they used on me and Doroshenko. That much is clear."

There was a silence that lasted for several seconds.

Following the drone attack on the Kyiv hydroelectric dam, Ferguson had been whisked out of Ukraine to Poland under cover of darkness using the same train he had arrived on. He had then been flown to Berlin, where he had a meeting scheduled with the new German chancellor.

Jayne stared out the window. She could see the usual hordes of tourists milling around on Pariser Platz, the square onto which the embassy faced at the end of Unter den Linden. Many of the visitors were having their photographs taken in front of the Brandenburg Gate.

"Of course we need to get Aidan out," Vic said. "But we can't exactly send in a bunch of SEALs or land a Black Hawk like we did in bin Laden's compound, so we—"

"Don't patronize me, Vic," Ferguson snapped. "I'm obviously not talking about that kind of solution. Can't you use the tools you've got? What about the woman you hooked last year when we dethroned the German chancellor? Use her again."

"Kira Suslova," Vic said. Out of the corner of her eye, Jayne saw him glancing at her. "We are already working on her. Jayne has a plan, but we don't yet know whether it will be workable."

"Okay," Ferguson said, holding up a hand in front of him. "That's all I need to know. Don't tell me the details for now. It's better I don't know. All I'm interested in is the outcome. Just get it done, whatever it is. And keep it below the radar."

"We'll do that, sir," Jayne said.

She had been about to mention the flight she and Neal had scheduled to Tbilisi for the following morning, after a message received from Suslova's burner phone just two hours earlier. But she decided to keep quiet, and Vic said nothing either. Nor did he say anything about the meeting they had hurriedly scheduled for an hour later with the defense secretary, Philip Monterey, who was in the embassy, having flown to Berlin immediately after hearing news of the attack on Ferguson and Doroshenko.

Now Ferguson was wagging his finger in Jayne's direction.

"Just one thing, Jayne," the president said. "You've done a lot of good work on my behalf over the past few years, and for that, I'm grateful." He hesitated a moment. "I know you've put your neck on the line a few times for me. If this operation you're planning does that yet again, then please be careful. And good luck."

"Thank you, sir," Jayne said. "We may need it."

CHAPTER TWENTY-FIVE

Monday, June 26, 2017
  Berlin

The six-foot frame, graying temples, metal-rimmed glasses, and long-standing pretense of being a little work-shy might easily give the impression to outsiders that Vic Walter was a low-energy, unambitious type. But Jayne had to hand it to him. When there was an urgent task at hand that required action, Vic got it done.

Immediately after leaving the meeting with President Ferguson, Vic arranged a meeting with the Berlin CIA station's disguise expert, who promised some props to match the new false identity that the Office of Technical Services at Langley had already provided for Jayne: German national Elisabeth Voss. She was of similar height and build to Jayne's five feet nine inches, with curly, shoulder-length blonde hair and rimless glasses.

The OTS had sent a false German passport and a visa for

Russia in a diplomatic bag to the embassy in Voss's name. No visa was required for Georgia.

The department had done likewise with one of Neal's false identities, also a German national, that of Hans Maron, who had a shaven head and thick black-framed glasses. It was fortunate that Neal was just as fluent in both German and Russian as Jayne was. The OTS packages also included German driver's licenses and working credit cards.

Now, Jayne was sitting in another room in the Berlin CIA station with Vic and Neal, who had discarded his head bandage as his wound was healing nicely. Opposite her was the defense secretary, Philip Monterey.

Also at the table was another person whom Jayne knew from way back: Jerry Spann, a craggy-faced man in his late forties who was head of the CIA's Special Activities Center. Spann, originally a Delta Force operative, had earned his reputation during the War on Terror, hunting down al-Qaeda leaders in Afghanistan and running the Pakistan drone program. Most recently, he had been managing operations against President Assad in Syria.

Spann was a black ops specialist who knew the Russian Black Sea region intimately. Vic, who held him in very high regard, had already sent him details of the requirement to exfiltrate Aidan Scarpa out of Cape Idokopas.

Now Spann listened, occasionally asking penetrating questions, as Vic and Jayne described the task facing them.

"What are your thoughts?" Vic asked Spann after they finished.

Spann pursed his lips. "Difficult," he said. "Your entry strategy looks doable, with the Tbilisi chess piece sculpture team. I like it. But assuming this Suslova woman can help you sufficiently to get Aidan Scarpa out of the building, that's where your problems might start—extracting Scarpa and yourselves out of there."

"Well, that's why we've asked you in here, Jerry," Vic said.

Spann inclined his head and studied Jayne and Neal from beneath a set of spiky black eyebrows. "Forget any seaborne exfil operation. The sea-facing defenses are too strong—they have radar, submarine nets, torpedoes, you name it. It's bristling with firepower. You'd expect that at Putin's residence. There's also a no-go zone for boats along that section of coast, under the pretext of an oyster and mussel fishing farm license. And there's a reef, hazardous for boats."

"I'm assuming there's no chance of getting a chopper in and out?" Jayne asked.

"No chance." Spann shook his head. "The area around the palace site is designated as prohibited special use airspace—a no-fly zone. Any aircraft going into or even near Russian airspace would get shot down immediately."

"Then what?" Neal said. "Don't tell me it's got to be a land-based op?"

"That's not quite what I have in mind."

Spann picked up his laptop. He flipped open the lid and tapped in a couple of security codes.

"Take a look at this," he said. He turned the laptop so Jayne and Neal could see the screen. There was an image of what looked like a large drone with eight horizontal rotor blades mounted on their own individual arms, spaced around a small cabin in the center, with two front seats and one at the rear. The entire structure was painted black and stood on a pair of broad parallel skids, one either side of the cabin. It looked like a much bigger version of one of the quadcopter drones sold commercially.

"What the hell's that?" Jayne asked. It reminded her of a huge tarantula.

"It's code-named HUNTSMAN—after the world's biggest spider, arguably," Spann said. "It's an eight-engine passenger drone. I'm a drone specialist. I've been working on these things for several years. We've used it a few times already in operations."

"Successfully?" Neal asked, a sharp note of skepticism in his voice.

"Of course. It can take three people as long as they're not too heavy," he said. "Maximum of 550 pounds. Battery powered, range of 170 miles, can do more than 60 miles an hour, and it's virtually silent. We have two of them—HUNTSMAN ONE and HUNTSMAN TWO—on board one of our boats in the Black Sea. It's a battered old Turkish trawler which we occasionally use for low-key operations in that area to avoid attention. Jayne can easily fit on one drone with Scarpa, with Neal on the other, or vice versa."

"Do we fly the drones?" Jayne asked.

Spann shook his head. "We pilot them remotely using an encrypted satellite comms link. There's a command-and-control software system on board the ship that uses algorithms to take them to the target and back. There is a manual control too, a bit like a video games joystick, built into a small dashboard. We'll show you how to use it alongside the GPS on board, but you won't need it. All you'll need to do is press the green button to let us know you're ready to fly when you're on board and strapped in."

"But you said you can't get a chopper in and out. So how do you do it with a drone?" Neal asked.

"We'll launch them off the trawler from outside Russian territorial waters," Spann said. "Then we'll take them over the coast farther south, away from the Cape Idokopas air defenses and special radar systems. They're small, only about five and a half yards across, and a couple of yards high. That includes the arms and rotors—the cabin footprint is much smaller than that, of course. They can fly low, a hundred feet or less, and normal radar is highly unlikely to pick them up, even across the sea. Also, they're coated in stealth paint to further reduce the likelihood of radar pickup—similar stuff to that on the F-117 Nighthawk and the Black Hawk choppers we used for the bin Laden raid. It's made of carbonyl iron balls in epoxy paint, to use simplistic language. It would be a nighttime operation, and of course we'd need good weather."

Jayne leaned back in her seat. There was something in Spann's manner, his confidence, that was gradually melting away the initial dismissiveness that she had been feeling.

"You say radar's unlikely to pick them up," Jayne said. "How unlikely?"

Spann shrugged. "Unlikely, especially if they're flying low, which they will be."

"So what about once they're over Russian territory?" Jayne asked.

"After crossing the coast, we'll fly them over land and have them hover low near the palace," Spann said. "Because it's hilly around that complex, radar will find it even harder to pick them up, especially since they're programmed to hug the ground at a fixed height. The radars are mostly looking out to sea in front of the palace, not over land behind it."

"Can you run a decoy or something out at sea to distract the Russians' attention the other way?" Neal asked.

"I was coming to that," Spann said. "One of our navy destroyers is currently in the Black Sea, the USS Carney. We can run it into that area, just outside Russian waters, which will almost inevitably get them focused in the wrong direction."

Jayne exchanged glances with Neal. She could tell that he too was thinking the approach outlined by Spann might have possibilities.

"What about a pickup location for the drones?" Vic asked. "Presumably you can't do it from the palace site or the grounds that surround it?"

That was another good question, Jayne thought. She knew the palace was on a heavily fortified 180-acre site.

An apologetic look crossed Spann's face. "Unfortunately not. Too risky. That's the potentially tricky bit. You'd need to get Aidan out of the complex to a prearranged point. We've got one in mind nearby. There's a village, Praskoveevka, on the highway just north of the turnoff that leads into the private estate where the palace is built, leading away from the beach. Part of the way through the village, there's a truck stop hidden behind a bus stop and some trees."

On his laptop, Spann clicked to a military maps app that showed a red dot superimposed on a large-scale satellite image of Praskoveevka village.

"That's the pickup point," he said. He toggled again, and a photograph appeared of the bus stop and the highway. "Here's your landmark, the bus stop. Look out for that, then head behind it to find the truck stop."

He toggled again to an image of a large gravel area sandwiched between two banks of trees. "Here's the truck stop. That's where we'll land the drones."

"Got it," Jayne said, committing the images to memory.

"Good. The pickup point is flat and should be easy to access for a car as well as the drones. We'll give you a small infrared transmitter—it's built into a wristwatch. When you get to the pickup site, turn it on and the drones will come. If they don't get a signal, they will wait a kilometer away and won't land, and will eventually turn around and head back to the mother ship. Hopefully that won't happen."

"That's where we'll rely on Suslova," Jayne said. "She'll need to ship us out of the palace to the pickup point."

"And if that doesn't prove possible?" Vic asked. "Or if she decides to knife you in the back?"

Jayne shrugged. "That's the $2 billion gamble we're all taking."

Spann folded his arms on the desk and leaned forward, scrutinizing first Neal, then Jayne. "So, are you on board with my exfil plan?" he asked. "It's the only option I've got. I'm calling it Operation Buzzard."

Jayne caught Neal's eye. He gave a faint nod.

"We're in. We have no choice," she said, turning back to Vic. "One thing—you do realize, don't you, that this Operation Buzzard may also involve exfilling Suslova if she does what we want of her and if she wants out of Russia. Otherwise, we're likely giving her a death sentence. They're bound to figure out what she's done—including killing Sidorenko."

Vic pressed his lips together. "Suslova has spent the last three decades trying to give most of us in the West a death sentence. She's recruited some of the most destructive spies Russia has ever had. Do you really feel compelled to come to her rescue?"

"I feel compelled to do the right thing," Jayne said. "The human thing. If I possibly can."

It was an urge she was familiar with—the guilty need to somehow try and offset the damage done by using other people in order to try to do some good in the world. Putting others at risk for the greater good was an occupational hazard that had caused Jayne an almost constant moral dilemma throughout her career.

Vic leaned forward and wagged a finger in Jayne's direction. "Do what you need to do. But if you bring her out, just don't expect me to hand her back that $2 billion. I'm not retiring on my shitty CIA pension while she vacations on yachts in the Bahamas. We'll find something better to do with it. And do nothing to help her at your own expense— nothing that puts you at risk. Got it?"

Nothing that puts me at risk. Hilarious.

"Got it, Vic."

CHAPTER TWENTY-SIX

Tuesday, June 27, 2017
  Tbilisi, Georgia

Just around the corner from Tbilisi's famous leaning Clock
Tower in Chakhrukhadze Street, with its wrought-iron over-
hanging balconies and quirky buildings, was a workshop set
back from the street behind a tall brick wall and a heavy
wooden gate. It was certainly individualistic, like most buildings in this quarter of the Georgian capital.

Jayne, with Neal close behind her, followed the tall,
heavily built figure of the workshop owner, Nikolas Kamov,
through the gate and up a wooden exterior staircase with
peeling yellow paint to a first-floor verandah.

She was already wearing a shoulder-length blonde wig and
rimless glasses to match the photograph in her Elisabeth Voss
passport, while Neal had shaved his hair to a short stubble
and donned heavy black glasses, like Hans Maron's passport
photograph. Jayne had already provided the false names to

Suslova, so that she could arrange accreditation, and Suslova had given them to Kamov.

Kamov, wearing a white linen long-sleeve shirt over his large belly, opened a door and led the way into a dusty workshop where three men were stationed behind workbenches. All were chipping away carefully with hammers and chisels, making chess pieces out of blocks of white marble. Other finished chess pieces, all about three feet high, stood on the floor.

"Come this way," Kamov said in fluent but accented English. He strode across the workshop floor and through a set of wooden swing doors into an office piled high with papers, files, catalogs, and two dusty computers.

He poured three cups of coffee from a steaming pot and indicated to Jayne and Neal to sit in chairs in front of his desk.

"I have spoken to Kira Suslova," Kamov began. "She asked me to do her a big favor and include you both on my team for the visit to Cape Idokopas." He picked up a file from the desk and waved it. "I have to tell you that despite knowing Kira for a long time, from when I lived in Moscow, I refused outright. I have no love for Putin, but I don't need to be on his shit list either. Whatever you're trying to do in that palace, I can't imagine he would be happy about it. There is also the huge effort required. Kira said I would need to drive, not fly, because if we flew, we would have to go via Moscow's airports, and she didn't want you to do that. Well, it's a thousand-kilometer drive from Tbilisi, probably fifteen hours on the road, and the same coming back. I could do without the drive, and certainly without the extra hassle and responsibility of having other people coming along. Especially people who put me at risk."

Kamov eyeballed Jayne, then Neal, and brushed a hand through his mane of black hair.

There was a silence that lasted several seconds.

Was this mission over before it had begun? Jayne wondered. It looked like it.

"You refused?" Jayne asked, eventually. "So, are we still going?"

Kamov shrugged. "Kira then made me a very large offer, and so reluctantly, I said yes, I'd drive. She's sent accreditation for both of you to be used with security at the palace site and to help deal with any issues at the border crossing into Russia. I don't know why you need to go, and I didn't ask. But she wants me to create authentic roles for you so you appear convincing as team members."

Neal nodded. "Thank you. That's very helpful."

"You can both be design specialists who create the concepts for my sculptors," Kamov said. "But I think it is a crazy idea. I'm only doing it for the money and as a favor to Kira."

He stared at them both again.

"We have excellent reasons for going there," Jayne said. "And we really appreciate what you are doing. We don't want to put you or your team in any trouble."

Kamov huffed and held up his hand. "Trouble? You can stop right there," he said. "I'll be out of there as fast as I can, which will be as soon as I've got my measurements and design ideas fixed for this damn chess set. I don't know how long you need there, or why you're going, but you'll have to find your own way back. There are two pickup trucks in the garage at the back of the workshop. We'll take both. My colleague Oleg and I will be in one, and you two will be in the other, so I hope you've got driver's licenses. I've agreed with Kira that she'll pay for any losses or costs if I don't get the truck back or if I lose the chess piece contract."

Jayne nodded. It would actually be very helpful to have a second vehicle on site that she and Neal might use to get

Aidan to the drone pickup point or for any other purpose, she thought.

"That suits us, and also to find our own way back," Jayne said. "We don't want to interfere with your business trip, and I apologize in advance for any disruption caused."

She paused. "We could also do with some advice on how to appear convincing as design specialists," Jayne said.

They spent the next half hour listening as Kamov took them into his workshop and gave them some very basic advice on how to behave and what to say, although he doubted there would be anyone at Putin's palace with sufficient knowledge to challenge them.

As he concluded his session, Jayne couldn't help feeling a slight sense of guilt. The last thing she wanted was for Kamov, an innocent helper in all this, to get trapped by Putin's security people and accused of collaborating with a CIA exfil operation. The consequences for him could be messy, to say the least, especially if it emerged he had immigrated to Georgia because he disliked the Russian regime.

But that was, unfortunately, the business they were in, and Jayne's mandate from President Ferguson was clear: they needed to get Aidan Scarpa out. There was no time to rip up plans on humanitarian grounds this time.

It was encouraging that Suslova had been prepared to make Kamov a large financial offer to ensure she and Neal got to Putin's Palace, Jayne figured. She must be desperate to ensure this plan worked, probably because she had no other option for clawing back her $2 billion.

Also encouraging from a security point of view was that Suslova had clearly told Kamov very little about why she and Neal needed to go there.

Neither Jayne nor Neal mentioned the drone exfiltration plan and the fact that the second pickup truck would definitely end up being abandoned in Russia. That was for Suslova to make right with Kamov.

"We leave first thing tomorrow morning," Kamov said. "We'll get over the border, stay in a motel near Armavir tomorrow night, which is nine hours from here, then complete the journey on Thursday. Will you be traveling under your real names?"

Jayne nodded. It was best to let Kamov believe that Voss and Maron were their actual names.

"Will you need to be disguised?"

Jayne shook her head. Again, there was no point in telling him the truth.

"And I'm assuming you've not got any weapons with you?" Kamov asked.

Both Jayne and Neal had brought handguns and spare magazines with them on the CIA Gulfstream from Berlin.

"We do," she said. "A handgun each. Only as a precaution."

Kamov shook his head vigorously. "No way. You can't take them across the border. Checkpoint Lars is notorious. They search everything at the crossing. Very thorough, very serious guards on the Russian side. If we have guns, pah. No chance."

Jayne knew from a briefing by Ed Grewall, the CIA's Moscow chief of station, about Checkpoint Lars, the only Georgia-Russia border crossing on the Georgian Military Highway near the town of Kazbegi. It was a remote location high in the mountains of northern Georgia. It was indeed known for its tough search procedures, according to Grewall, although Jayne was very confident they could successfully smuggle through two handguns hidden in a pickup truck, given their expertise.

"I was going to discuss this with you," Neal said. "Can't we hide the handguns on the pickup somewhere? I know how to do that. We can put them—"

"I said no," Kamov interrupted. "I'm not going to end up in a Russian prison or lose my vehicles because of you before we've even gotten into the country. You'll have to leave your guns behind. Anyway, if they don't find them at the border, they will at the entrance to the palace. Forget it."

Jayne swore under her breath.

This operation was already not going as she wanted.

CHAPTER TWENTY-SEVEN

Thursday, June 29, 2017
    Cape Idokopas, Russia

The entrance to the Russian president's expansive estate and palace on Cape Idokopas forked off the blacktop highway that wound its way through the village of Praskoveevka to the beach a couple of kilometers farther south.

Jayne peered out of the passenger window as Neal, at the wheel of their black Toyota Hilux twin-cab pickup, followed a somewhat newer Volkswagen Amarok in which Nikolas Kamov and one of his sculptors, Oleg Uglov, were traveling.

The entrance area was shielded by impenetrable heavy gray steel fencing that was over three meters high and ran alongside the highway. The fence itself was further protected by freeway-style crash barriers.

The road into the complex was blocked by a set of heavy steel booms. Kamov's Volkswagen pulled to a halt in front of the booms, and a security guard in a black uniform walked at a purposeful pace toward them from one of several buildings beyond.

Jayne watched as Kamov lowered his window and held a lengthy conversation with the guard, showing him papers and passes.

Eventually, the guard, an unsmiling, heavily built man wearing a peaked cap, walked to Neal's window, which he had already lowered.

"Your identity documents and your accreditation, please," he said in Russian.

Neal passed him the forged German passports and the accreditation that Suslova had sent to Kamov.

The guard studied the papers, then looked at Neal and bent down so he could properly see Jayne in the passenger seat.

"You are both German?" the guard asked.

"*Da*. Yes, both of us," Neal said in Russian.

"Who are you here to see? What are you here for?" This time, the guard turned his gaze to Jayne.

"As it says on the paperwork, we are designers of chess pieces," Jayne said, also in fluent Russian. "We are guests of Kira Suslova, and we are working on a project to build a large chess set to stand next to a swimming pool on this site. We are here to develop the designs. Then the sculptors will make the pieces."

The guard nodded, removed a walkie-talkie radio from his belt, and stepped away from the pickup. He clicked a button on the radio and began to speak in a low tone.

The passports had stood up to scrutiny at the Checkpoint Lars border crossing into Russia, as Jayne had expected they would. Therefore, it seemed highly likely that they would pass inspection here too. The Office of Technical Services at Langley, which had forged them, was a top-class unit and had never yet let her down.

Eventually, the guard returned to Kamov's pickup, said something through the window, and pointed through the barrier, which rose to allow the truck through. The guard then strode to Neal's window and instructed him to follow Kamov to the vehicle search area beyond the barrier.

It emerged that Kamov was correct about the handguns. They likely would have been found, because the vehicle inspections included a giant airport-style X-ray scanner, sniffer dogs, and a manual search team. Jayne and Neal stood with Kamov and Uglov, a plump man with a gray mustache and hair, next to the two pickups while the searches were carried out.

"We will escort you to your private dachas—you have two allocated to share," the guard said to Kamov when the searches were complete. "We will then take you to meet Ms. Suslova. She is also staying in one of the private dachas."

Jayne had not tried to contact Suslova's burner phone again. It hadn't been necessary and was too risky, certainly once Suslova was on the Cape Idokopas complex. Nor had Jayne received any messages. They would have to rely on face-to-face meetings initially to discuss the chess set, after which they would have a plausible business reason for contacting each other.

Two blue security cars with flashing orange lights on the roofs, one driving in front of their vehicles, one behind, escorted them down a winding blacktop road, which Jayne could see had been carved out of the hillside by excavating an enormous quantity of rock.

They passed the entrance to what looked like a small quarry tucked behind some trees. After about four kilometers, they turned right down a side road where there was a well-spaced group of twelve two-story stone houses built among the pine trees. All were designed with a similar Italianate Renaissance-style architecture.

The guards directed Jayne and Neal to park on the semi-circular driveway that served one house, while Kamov and Uglov were pointed to the one next door.

One of the guards handed Jayne and Neal electronic entry cards, similar to hotel key cards, to operate the security sensor pad outside the front door.

"Ms. Suslova wants to meet you both, and Mr. Kamov and Mr. Uglov, in the main house," the guard said, surveying them through impenetrable black eyes. "I will return in twenty minutes to collect you. Please do not leave this dacha until then. There are security cameras that monitor the area outside the building. You can use your cell phones, but be aware that all communications are monitored."

Jayne nodded and exchanged glances with Neal. This site was even more of a prison than she had expected. How could security monitor encrypted calls? Or was that just a warning shot?

"Why is security so imposing here?" she asked.

"It always is this way here," the guard said. "But we are particularly rigid at the moment because the president is in residence. He likes all precautions to be taken."

Shit.

That was not what Jayne had been expecting, and Suslova had not warned her. Perhaps she didn't know her boss's movements in advance. Putin didn't visit Cape Idokopas often, according to the intelligence she had been given by the team working for Ed Grewall at the US embassy in Moscow.

After the guard had gone, Jayne and Neal dropped their bags in two of the four bedrooms within the dacha and had a quick look around. The entire house was equipped and decorated to an inordinate level of luxury. Even the control knobs for the enormous gas stove in the kitchen were gold-plated, as were the shower controls in the bathrooms.

Jayne couldn't help wondering which Russian government

department's budget had been plundered to pay for all this. Maybe schools, hospitals, or both, and probably a few others too.

* * *

Half an hour later the guard drove Jayne, Neal, Kamov, and Uglov a short distance from their dachas to the palace, past a gas station with two pumps where a chauffeur was refueling a long, black Aurus Senat limousine. Was that Putin's car, Jayne wondered?

They continued down a ramp to a drop-off zone at ground-floor level on the eastern side of the building, which was in a similar ornate Italianate style to their dacha, albeit on a far larger and grander scale.

From there, beneath a covered canopy, they walked to the right of a glass-fronted security office and through a set of double doors into a lavish reception hallway with marble floors, chandeliers, and high ceilings with frescoes and gilded arches.

There, waiting next to an enormous fireplace and three equally large beige leather sofas, was Kira Suslova, wearing a scarlet dress with a plunging neckline.

She stepped toward Kamov and, unsmilingly, greeted him and shook his hand, initially ignoring Jayne and Neal, as Jayne had expected. Suslova was a trained intelligence operative, and the palace was undoubtedly bristling with hidden cameras and microphones that fed into not just the palace's security office but the FSB as well. Intelligence obtained by the CIA's Moscow station was that there were no facial recognition systems in place at the palace, so far. Jayne just hoped that was accurate.

"Nikolas, thank you for coming," Suslova said in Russian. "You and your colleagues have had a long journey. I appreciate it. We have a lot of work to do, and no time to waste. Please, introduce me to the others, and we can get started."

Kamov did so, introducing first Uglov, then Neal as Hans Maron, and Jayne as Elisabeth Voss.

Suslova gave no sign of recognition when she looked at Jayne.

"Good to meet you all," Suslova said. "I'd like to start by showing you the swimming pool where the chess set will be placed. It's on this floor."

She led the way down a long corridor with arched windows offering views over a rectangular interior courtyard, complete with a fountain. Then she passed through a door that took them onto a patio at the side of a three-lane twenty-five-meter indoor swimming pool. The reflections from the gold and eggshell blue decor, and similarly colored high ceiling, gave the water a golden blue hue. The floor-to-ceiling pillars lining each side of the pool lent the entire facility a very Roman feel.

Suslova pointed to one end of the pool, where there was a large open space occupied only by four sun loungers.

"That is where the chess set will go," Suslova said. She turned to Jayne. "Elisabeth, I understand you are the design expert. Now is the time to come up with ideas. The president wants a large-scale board and pieces that will fit with the mood, decor, and ambience of the pool. The pieces need to be elegant and of intricate design, but also light enough for players to lift easily and move them. Can you do that?"

"Of course," Jayne said. "We have a few options for light-weight but malleable materials we could use. Aluminum is probably the favorite, as it won't rust and is light. But I'd like to take a thorough tour of this pool facility first, to get a proper feel for it. Could we start with the changing rooms? I need to use the bathroom, in any case."

Jayne caught Suslova's eye and held it. Hopefully, the

Russian would take the hint. She figured this was a good opportunity to spend a short period alone with Suslova in a place where even the Russian leader would not have had cameras installed, Jayne assumed.

"Of course," Suslova said. "Come this way. I'm afraid I can't take the gentlemen in there."

Jayne followed her toward a door marked with a female symbol. Inside was an opulent marble-floored room with mirrors on three sides and elegant wooden cabinets on the other. There was an oak massage table and showers with gold-plated controls.

Suslova shut the door, put a finger to her lips, and pointed to the door that was marked TOILETS. "That is the toilet, Elisabeth," she said. "I'll wait for you here."

"Thanks." Jayne nodded and walked toward the door. She had a good idea of what Suslova was about to do.

Sure enough, Suslova followed Jayne as she walked through into a large cubicle, three meters square, with fittings just as extravagant as all the others, including a silver toilet seat.

Without speaking, Suslova locked the door behind them, walked to a sink with gold-plated taps, turned the hot and cold full on, and beckoned Jayne to her.

Instantly Jayne had a vision in her mind of Suslova, working for the KGB in East Germany during the 1980s Cold War, behaving similarly with a spy she was handling. The sound of running water was a good precaution against any hidden microphones designed to capture their conversation.

Suslova put her face very close to Jayne's left ear and murmured in English. "Some mixed news for you. Aidan Scarpa is being held on this floor in this building in a secure room, a cell, near here, next to the security office," she said. "There is an armed guard permanently outside the room. There are no windows."

"What about those GRU operatives who brought him here?" Jayne whispered back. "Are they here too?"

Suslova nodded. "Both of them, Leonova and Rezanov. They are spending some time with him and managing the guards. As I told you before, they are formidable. Sharp and thorough." She paused. "If it proves possible to get him out of the room, do you have a plan to extract him off the palace estate and out of Russia?"

Jayne hesitated. Her instinct was not to trust Suslova, but she had no option. She had to gamble that Suslova's desperation to have the $2 billion returned to her would ensure she provided the necessary assistance.

"We have an exfil plan. It means getting Aidan out of the palace complex to a rendezvous meeting place not too far away. For that, we will need your help. We have a pickup truck, but I need you to ensure it won't be detained."

Suslova's eyes widened a little. "You're using a helicopter? Surely not?"

Jayne shook her head. She was only going to give what detail was absolutely necessary. "Don't worry about that. Just help us get him out of here. We'll need a distraction, a diversion, to take attention away from the cell. Can you do that?"

Suslova inclined her head. "There is a possibility. I have been coming here a long time, right through the construction phase. I know the construction director. He has built this place, and it never stops. He's always making changes, improvements. There is a storage building, away from the palace, where construction equipment is stored, and—"

"Explosives?" Jayne interrupted. Her first thought was that a small amount of plastic explosive could be used to blow open the cell door. Maybe a larger amount could be used to create a diversion. Her guess was that with work still underway on the palace site, some of it requiring large volumes of rock to be moved, explosives must be necessary.

Suslova exhaled and paused for a beat. "First, I want to know that I will get my money back. This is a massive risk for me to help you like this. Already, I have done things that will put me in a gulag, or worse—likely a bullet in the back of my head—if they discover me. You have no idea."

There was no doubt what Suslova said was true. The woman appeared stressed. But Jayne had to ignore that. She found that trying to be ruthless in these situations to achieve a critical objective was mentally the hardest part of her job. It always had been.

She did what she had always done and tried to compartmentalize her thoughts.

"You get Aidan, me, and Neal out of Russia safely, and you get your money back. I guarantee it. So, answer my question. Are there any explosives in that store room? Ideally plastic explosive, with remote-controlled detonators and fuses?"

There came a sharp nod from Suslova.

"Can you get it?" Jayne asked.

Suslova closed her eyes briefly. "I can try."

"Second thing, I'll need two handguns and spare magazines," Jayne said. She assumed that someone in Suslova's position would almost certainly be able to source a couple of guns. She probably had them already for her own use.

Suslova rolled her eyes slightly. "I have those, of course. Makarovs."

"Good. We need to move fast, though. I want to get out of here tomorrow night as soon as it's dark. Maybe nine thirty in the evening, or ten. I will need to get everything set up by then. Can you do it?"

There was a pause.

"Driving off the site is not so much of a problem as driving in—normally," Suslova said. "But . . ."

"But what?"

"There is a complication. The president knows your

group is here, the sculpture group under Nikolas. He has taken a close interest in this project, which is why he put me in charge of it. He wants you all to meet him for cocktails tomorrow evening at seven o'clock. Unfortunately, it will not be easy to avoid without alerting him to the fact that something is wrong and putting me in a difficult situation."

Jayne felt her stomach turn over. "You are not serious?"

"I am serious."

"Bloody hell," Jayne muttered. "Why is he so interested in it?"

She felt an immediate suspicion that this was some kind of setup.

Had Suslova engineered this deliberately?

Suslova held up her hands. "He's not much of a chess player, but he wants the chess set to impress high-level visitors, heads of state. Maybe he wants to convey how important the project is to the designers and sculptors. He often has cocktails with visitors, so that's nothing out of the ordinary. He's not really working much here, so maybe he thinks it would be a diversion, a way to relax. It's probably not something to worry about."

Really?

Jayne folded her arms tight.

This was a screwup.

She doubted whether she and Neal could pull off a personal encounter over cocktails with the Russian president without giving away that they were imposters. Whatever one might think of him, he was no fool.

"Where will we meet for the cocktails?" Jayne asked.

"There's a lounge upstairs, on the ground floor, next to the cinema," Suslova said.

"Can't we get out of it? Make an excuse?"

"Difficult. Saying no to the president is not a recipe for longevity around here."

"Saying yes might not be a recipe for longevity either, this time," Jayne said. "Who else will be there? Will there be others to make conversation so we can stay in the background?"

"I will be there, of course, as will other visitors to the palace, and other senior people, perhaps the director of the palace."

"Ivanov? Is he here?"

Suslova shook her head. "He will arrive here by helicopter from Moscow during the evening, ready for a meeting with the president the following day. But he will be too late for the cocktails, I am told. So no."

"Leonova and Rezanov?"

"I doubt very much they will be there. Listen, the focus will be on Kamov, and on Uglov. They are the sculptors. So I will try to direct the conversation to them. But the president may have questions for you as designers."

"And you seriously think we can be convincing?" Jayne asked. "Because I'm far from sure."

"Can you bullshit about the chess set designs?" Suslova asked.

With Kamov's help, Jayne had prepared a fake list of other chess-related projects she had worked on, including for other large houses and palaces in various parts of the world. None could be easily verified. She could talk about those, and since Putin wanted the chess pieces to be figures of famous Soviet and Russian military and wartime leaders, she had also drawn up a short list of those whom Putin was known to admire. They included Josef Stalin, Czar Peter the Great, and Czar Nicholas I. But she certainly hadn't envisaged having to deploy her research in front of the president.

"I can bullshit, of course," Jayne said.

Suslova glanced at her watch. "We've been in here too long. We must go back out. I can come to your dacha later on the pretense of having another discussion about the chess set."

Jayne nodded, and after Suslova had turned off the taps and flushed the toilet, they both returned to the group by the poolside. There, Kamov, Neal, and Uglov were engaged in an animated conversation about the outdoor aquadisco area, a kind of shallow, water-filled dance floor visible through the folding doors that separated it from the indoor pool.

Presumably that was where the president kept his younger guests entertained.

Jayne started questioning Kamov about his ideas for the chessboard design and whether marble or granite tiles would be better for the sixty-four squares required.

She was going to need all the ideas she could get before the encounter with Putin. That much was obvious.

Twenty minutes later she, Kamov, Neal, and Uglov were in the security car being driven back to the dacha.

As they passed the gas station, behind which were two large white cylindrical gasoline and diesel tanks, Jayne watched as a Porsche was being refueled.

That was what gave her an idea.

CHAPTER TWENTY-EIGHT

Thursday, June 29, 2017
Cape Idokopas

Anke Leonova nodded at the guard standing outside Aidan's cell door and unlocked it with her left hand, her Makarov held firmly in her right, its safety off and a round in the chamber. She pushed the door handle down and kicked it open, her eyes sweeping the room ahead of her.

Then she relaxed. Aidan Scarpa was lying on his bed in the corner of the room, his head propped up on a pillow, hands placed behind his head as he scrutinized his visitor.

In her experience, it was always best to avoid risk, and opening a door without being completely certain what was behind it was something she rarely did, even if a guard was standing nearby to assist if needed.

Anke stepped through the door, closed it behind her, and walked slowly over to her prisoner, who didn't move. She had to admit, Aidan looked exhausted, thin and gray in the face, and deeply stressed, although that was probably not surprising given his experience since leaving Frankfurt.

A half-eaten plate of plain pasta, without sauce, lay on the floor next to his bed, along with a plastic beaker of water.

Aidan was still wearing the same clothes he had on when they had left Frankfurt, despite being given a clean pair of jeans, a couple of T-shirts, and a sweatshirt to use. The unmistakable odor of stale sweat hung heavy in the air.

She almost felt sorry for him. Almost.

He was simply a tool that enabled her to get her job done, earn her salary, and enable her to gain sufficient kudos with Igor Ivanov to see her through another few years. The screwup in Frankfurt, when Aidan had overheard her conversation with Ivanov, hadn't exactly helped, and she couldn't afford for anything else to go wrong with this operation.

"How much longer do I have to stay in this shithole?" Aidan asked in a flat tone before she could speak. His voice sounded faint and weary.

"I am hoping not too long," Anke said. "We have things to complete before that can happen, however."

"I'm sure you do," Aidan said, his voice heavy with sarcasm. "So how long, you bitch?"

Anke ignored the insult. There was no point in letting him irritate her.

She shrugged. "I don't know."

That much was true. She didn't know. But the quicker Operation Noi was completed, the better.

In the meantime, Anke's greatest concern was the security around Aidan and ensuring that nobody got close to him. She wasn't worried about him escaping of his own volition, as the chances of that were remote. He wasn't a trained military type who could pull that off.

The risks were rather that someone would infiltrate the palace complex and extract him, or that someone already permitted on site was corrupted and would do it. That CIA operative, Jayne Robinson, was still out there after the attempt to terminate her in Budapest failed, and although it was extremely unlikely she would get onto the Cape Idokopas site herself, the CIA was very resourceful and might try other avenues.

Another potential problem was that someone on the site, maybe a loose-tongued security officer or other member of staff, might somehow leak the fact that they had the son of the United States president incarcerated at the palace.

The last thing Anke wanted was for this to be leaked to the Russian media. They would find it an irresistible story, and then, of course, it would go viral globally.

She could see the likely headlines.

PUTIN HOLDS US PRESIDENT'S SON CAPTIVE AT PALACE

RUSSIA KIDNAPS FERGUSON'S SON

If that happened, Anke knew that the international outcry would be enormous. At present, all the signs were that the US president wanted to keep quiet about his son's disappearance to avoid embarrassment. Presumably, he didn't know where Aidan was, even.

But if the story went public, it would be highly likely that the international pressure on Putin to release Aidan would be massive. Few, probably not even Russia's allies such as China, would view the US president's son as a fair target.

And if Scarpa did escape or was extracted or released at some point, then he would without doubt let the cat out of the bag, and Russia's entire strategy, in the shape of Operation Noi, would be blown.

That would mean Anke's career would almost certainly be over, as would Igor Ivanov's.

Therefore, Anke found herself obsessed with ensuring that security around Aidan remained as tight as it could be.

So far all seemed well, but she decided to head to the neighboring security office and check in with the site security director, Postnik Maly, to ensure he was covering all bases.

The banks of monitor screens and the electronic control desk in front of them made the place look more like a television production room than a security office, Anke thought as she entered the room.

Sitting at a desk in the center of the office was the director of security for the entire Cape Idokopas site, Postnik Maly, a swarthy man with a double chin. Anke had been having regular meetings with him since their arrival at the palace with Aidan Scarpa.

Despite Maly's overt grumpiness, Anke had been impressed by his thorough approach, particularly so while the president had been in residence over the past twenty-four hours. He was one of the longest-serving members of staff at the palace and known to be close to the president.

Maly turned as she approached, his face unsmiling.

"Good morning, Postnik," Anke began. "How are things going?"

"All under control," Maly said. He paused. "How is your accommodation?"

Anke felt a slight sense of surprise. It was the first time Maly had ever inquired about her situation.

"Very good," Anke said. Indeed, the four-bedroom apartment in a building half a kilometer from the main palace, which she and Rezanov had been allocated for their stay, was extremely luxurious.

But she didn't want to go into detail about that with Maly. She flipped her curly dark hair back over her right shoulder and got straight down to business. "Is there anything we need to be worried about?"

Maly folded his arms. "We have been extremely busy monitoring all the many new people on site over the past two days, most of them linked to the president. But the team has carried out thorough vetting and security checks on all of them, and there appear to be no concerns at present."

Behind him, the two officers who were monitoring the bank of CCTV outputs from various parts of the site were busy flicking from one screen to another. It was an endless cycle that Anke could see required significant concentration.

From the start, Maly had seemed to grasp the seriousness with which she was taking Aidan's security, although of course she could not explain to him exactly why, and he didn't need to know.

"How many people have come into the site?" Anke asked.

"About eighty-five over the past day or so," Maly said. "Of those, about fifty are newcomers, never been here before."

"Do you have a list?" Anke asked.

Maly removed a printed sheet of paper from the folder in front of him and pushed it across to Anke. "That's the current list."

Anke carefully scanned down the page. The list included each person's full name, role, and the organization they represented.

"How many of these are non-Russians?" Anke asked. "There are a lot of Western names on here."

"I think forty-seven are foreigners," Maly said, adjusting his black-rimmed glasses. "Most are Europeans. Bankers, accountants, property people, political advisers, a few trades people. They're all involved in the president's assets either here or overseas. Most are either German, British, French, or Italian."

Anke studied the list again. "Are these people cleared to enter the main palace building?"

"They will all be coming in for meetings, so yes, they're all cleared."

"And how many will personally meet with the president?" Anke asked.

"Very few. Most will just meet his staff."

Anke's finger stopped halfway down the page.

"There are sandal and shoe designers from Prague listed here. Who are these people?"

"The president is changing his supplier," Maly said. "He is being fitted for new shoe samples."

Again, Anke prodded the paper with a forefinger.

"And what about these? Sculptors and chess set designers from Tbilisi and Germany?" She looked up at Maly. "What's that all about?"

"The president wants a large chess set to be installed next to the swimming pool," he said. "They are here for that. Kira Suslova is supervising them. She provided the security clearances."

Anke nodded. If Suslova had responsibility for them, that was reassuring, but it was wise to take nothing for granted.

"Are you carrying out the usual vehicle and baggage searches on site entry with these people?"

"Of course." Maly looked offended.

"Interviews with all of them?" Anke asked.

"We have interviewed several, but not all." Now Maly sounded a little defensive.

Anke knew she probably sounded a little paranoid, but the only reason she was here was because she had wrongly assumed Rezanov was competent enough not to make amateur mistakes. Ivanov would not forgive a second such error.

"Can you step it up and interview all of them?" she said.

"And carry out random checks on visitors during the day too, just to make sure they're doing what they're meant to be here to do."

"If you think it's necessary," Maly said stiffly.

"I do," Anke said, a note of finality in her voice. "And so does Ivanov. So get it done."

Maly inclined his head. "Very well. I will get my teams working on it."

"Make sure you start with the foreigners," Anke said.

Maly nodded, a look of irritation crossing his face. "Don't worry. We'll take care of it."

CHAPTER TWENTY-NINE

Thursday, June 29, 2017
Cape Idokopas

Starting in 2008, when the president first took her to Cape Idokopas, Suslova had played quite a hand in the design and construction of the enormous palace that now stood on the site.

At times she had visited almost every month, staying for a week or so if the president wanted her, always for reasons entirely related to his sexual appetite.

She consulted closely with the construction team to communicate the president's ideas on the overall shape of the project and the finer details of the facilities and luxuries that were built into it.

As a result, Suslova had built a good friendship with the palace construction director, Vitas Ushakov, who viewed her as a reliable conduit for the president's views and opinions.

It was vital for Ushakov to incorporate the president's design whims, as far as was physically feasible. Yet on such a large project, that was difficult to achieve. Indeed, on several occasions, entire rooms, or even buildings, had to be ripped up and started again because the result wasn't quite to Putin's satisfaction.

The outdoor amphitheater had proved particularly problematic because the acoustics were not as Putin wanted. The facility had therefore already been rebuilt three times, with a fourth incarnation still ongoing.

Suslova had turned into something of a shoulder for Ushakov to cry on, and she also acted as a buffer between him and the president. She frequently absorbed the latter's anger when mistakes were made and undoubtedly saved Ushakov from being fired on at least three occasions.

The bottom line was that Ushakov was deeply in debt to her, not least because he had a wife and five children to support.

There was no sign of construction work ending either. Work on several new projects within the complex was underway, while there was continuous tinkering with others, such as the underground ice rink built into the hillside next to the two helipads. The president had demanded an exceptionally high level of workmanship for the rink, where he played ice hockey. Suslova also took advantage of it, as she enjoyed skating to her favorite music.

Suslova had already had a couple of brief conversations with Ushakov when she bumped into him inside the palace. He was still working the same fourteen-hour days he had always done.

Now she needed to see him again, this time because he was her only option to obtain what Jayne Robinson had requested: plastic explosive and detonators. She knew Ushakov had a plentiful supply of both in a large storage unit next to the telecoms tower, where the palace's satellite communications and cell phone antennae were located.

The explosive was used to blast away the solid rock that lay beneath a thin layer of topsoil on which the complex stood. Construction of the palace building itself, with its deep basements, and the ice rink had required weeks of almost continuous explosions until Ushakov's men had shifted the thousands of tons of rock required. Likewise with the tunnel from the palace down to the harbor.

Suslova walked from the palace up through the arboretum to Ushakov's office in the administration block not far from his storage unit. Unlike visitors to the palace site, she wasn't going to be questioned by security staff. She had been there far longer than most of them.

She found him poring over a fresh set of plans for a new winery, which the president wanted built on a large tract of land running parallel to the coast three kilometers away.

After his secretary had made them both a cappuccino, they sat outside on chairs beneath a pergola. Now they were at least fifty meters away from the office building, well out of anyone's earshot.

"Is this winery going to be difficult to build?" Suslova asked.

Ushakov exhaled. "It's not the winery itself that's the problem, it's the dacha to be built alongside it, plus the helipad, and the twenty-five-meter heated outdoor swimming pool."

"Why does he want all that when he's got the palace here?"

Ushakov shrugged. "You tell me. My guess is he wants it as a private holiday home for the young gymnast, you know, his mistress. It's more than eight years now, so he probably thinks she needs a permanent home within range of the palace."

Suslova shook her head. The president had indeed been conducting a long-term affair with a former Russian Olympic gymnast, thirty years younger than him. One result of that had been that the president's demands for Suslova's services in the bedroom were now almost nonexistent, for which she was extremely grateful.

Suslova sipped her cappuccino. "Listen, Vitas, I need a favor from you for once."

"Anything I can do, just tell me."

Suslova lowered her voice to little more than a murmur. "I've got a problem with someone, and I need to create a diversion."

"A diversion?"

"Yes. And I need something that's going to create some fireworks to achieve that."

Realization dawned over Ushakov's face. "You're not trying to tell me you want some of my explosives?"

She nodded. "Plastic explosive, the C4 stuff you use, and some of those wireless controlled detonators you've got. I can't think of anywhere else where I could get the stuff."

Suslova had watched Ushakov and his team preparing for enough controlled explosions to know exactly what type of equipment he would have in his storage unit.

Ushakov stared at her. "Where are you going to use this explosive?" he asked.

"It won't be me who uses it."

"Who, then?"

"Can't tell you who," Suslova said.

"Where will they use it?" Ushakov said, eyeballing her.

"Can't tell you that either."

"The answer is no, then. You get nothing from me."

Suslova took a long sip from her coffee. "I've done you a lot of favors over the years. In fact, you have no idea how many I've done that have saved your job. But I will tell you one thing: those favors are easily unwound. At the click of my fingers."

She raised her left hand and clicked her finger and thumb together for effect.

"This is the first time I've asked for a payback," Suslova continued.

Ushakov placed his hands behind his head and studied her with a somewhat quizzical expression on his face. "This is how you operate, isn't it?"

"What do you mean?"

"You spend years putting yourself in positions of power over people, maneuvering, manipulating. Then you cash it all in when you need to, with no regard for those people. They're just tools to be used."

Suslova said nothing. There was a lot of truth in what he was saying. It was how she and many in her business survived and got what they needed to stay afloat and alive in shark-infested waters. After all, the only reason she was here manipulating Ushakov was because she was being similarly manipulated by Jayne Robinson.

"Do you know what you're doing?" Ushakov asked.

"I know how to use C4 and detonators, yes." Now was no time to be getting into a philosophical discussion.

"That's not what I mean, and you know it. I mean, do you know what you're doing?"

Suslova pursed her lips. The honest answer to his question was probably no—she didn't quite know what she was doing, for once. The consequences if she were found out would be extreme. But she could see little alternative because the consequences of the president finding out she'd lost $2 billion of his money would be no different.

So she just nodded. "I know."

"How much do you need?" Ushakov asked.

"Give me four M112 demolition blocks," Suslova said. "I assume you have them?"

An M112 block was a rectangular chunk of the plastic

explosive, roughly twenty-eight centimeters long, five centimeters across, and about four centimeters deep. It weighed about half a kilogram.

"We have hundreds," Ushakov said.

"And I also want two much smaller charges, this size." She held her fingers to demonstrate a shape about an inch and a half across. "And six detonators and control units."

Ushakov nodded and drained his coffee. "I've got some in the back of my Land Cruiser." He waved toward the parking lot behind them. "I'll drop them round to your dacha later. Just be careful what you do with them, Kira."

Suslova leaned back in her seat. Ushakov always gave her pause, and he had just done so once again.

She knew that she still had a choice, of sorts.

Yes, she could just go ahead, grit her teeth, and help Jayne Robinson, hard as it was to do.

Or she could still go to Putin or, more likely, Ivanov and explain everything, hoping for mercy.

Suslova placed her hands behind her head and closed her eyes momentarily. Deep down, she knew there was no going back.

If she went to Ivanov or Putin, there would be no mercy, only pain. And blackness. And death.

The only way now was to get out of there as fast as possible.

CHAPTER THIRTY

Friday, June 30, 2017
Cape Idokopas

The beige marble floor, inset with a square of white marble at the center of which was an ornate circular cocktail bar, stretched at least twenty meters to a floor-to-ceiling window. The hum of conversation and laughter was punctuated with the occasional chink of glasses. A man in a tuxedo at a grand piano in one corner was playing a Grieg concerto.

Jayne glanced at Neal next to her. She straightened her midnight-blue dress, bought from the palace visitors' boutique, and stood in the double doorway for a few seconds, taking in the scene.

Four barmen, all dressed in black bow ties and waistcoats, were working away inside the circular bar, making cocktails that were being ferried to groups of guests by a band of waitresses in green costumes.

At least fifty people were congregated in the room in

groups of varying sizes. A few were seated on leather sofas, but most were standing.

On the left, an open double doorway led into what appeared to be a private cinema, complete with plush red seating.

"Come this way," Suslova said as she led Jayne, Neal, Kamov, and Uglov across the floor to a position near the window. "The president will come through the door. I don't want you to be his first port of call. I'll need to join him when he arrives, though."

Immediately, a waitress approached and handed out cards on which a cocktail menu was printed. "Please, tell me what you would like to drink."

Jayne ordered a Black Sea Margarita, made with black salt, and checked out the other guests. Most appeared to be in their forties or fifties. All were elegantly dressed, the men in dinner jackets and bow ties, the women in high-end evening party dresses.

There was nobody she recognized and no sign of the GRU operative Anke Leonova or her colleague.

Behind the guests, through the windows, the sun was setting over the Black Sea, sending a shimmering strip of gold across the water from the horizon to the coast.

Soon after the drinks arrived, a man in a white tuxedo jacket walked into the room and called out. "Please, ladies and gentlemen, may I introduce the president of the Russian Federation, Vladimir Putin."

Two bodyguards walked into the room, both with pistols in holsters mounted at their hips, followed by Putin. Another two bodyguards, also armed, waited at the door.

Suslova immediately left their group, walked over to the president, and kissed him three times on alternating cheeks. Unlike all the other men, he was wearing a dark business suit and a maroon tie.

Jayne watched as Suslova and the president spoke briefly and then moved to a group of six guests standing next to the bar. Suslova introduced the president to the group and appeared to coordinate the conversation. The two body-guards stood nearby, one on either side of the group, and remained visibly alert for any sign of trouble.

Clearly, the president was going to work his way around the room, moving from group to group, with Suslova as his chaperone.

Jayne was not looking forward to this, and judging by their facial expressions and the somewhat stilted conversation, neither were the others.

"Let's hope this is over quickly," Neal murmured.

Suslova had driven them herself, in her black Porsche Cayenne, from their dacha to the basement drop-off point at the palace building.

But when Suslova had arrived at the dacha to collect them, she had carried her briefcase into the building and taken it with her into the downstairs bathroom, off the entrance hallway.

On exiting the bathroom, she had beckoned Jayne to the kitchen and quietly informed her that the items she had requested were now in a cupboard in the bathroom, where she was certain there were no cameras.

When Jayne went there a few minutes later, she found four sticks of C4 explosive and two much smaller one-inch-square pieces of C4, together with a reel of sticky tape and a pair of scissors. There were also six small remote-controlled detonators, roughly the size of matchboxes, and six wireless remote-control units, similar in size to cigarette packs, that could be swiftly programmed to trigger the detonators, using three-digit code numbers. Jayne had worked with similar devices before, so she was familiar with how they functioned.

Finally, there were two Makarov pistols, with four spare magazines.

After showing Neal what Suslova had brought, Jayne had left all the equipment in the bathroom cupboard. It would be essential for later.

Jayne made small talk with the others about the decor of the cocktail lounge while waiting for the president to work his way around the room to them. That seemed unlikely to take very long, as to Jayne's relief, he was spending no more than a few minutes with each group.

Uncharacteristically, Jayne felt butterflies begin to flutter in her stomach as Suslova turned and led the president in their direction.

"I would like to introduce you all to the president," Suslova began in Russian. "He is very much looking forward to discussing the large-scale chess set with you all." She waved a hand toward the group and introduced each of them by name, getting the false identities correct for both Jayne and Neal, to Jayne's relief.

Suslova then stepped to one side to allow Putin to address them. The two bodyguards positioned themselves at opposite sides of the group, as they had with the other guests—one behind Jayne, another behind Kamov.

Putin nodded at each of them in turn, scrutinizing each of them with a pair of icy blue eyes and an air of complete emotional detachment. Jayne was immediately struck by the taut smoothness of the skin across his cheeks for a man in his mid-sixties. He had obviously had some work done.

"Welcome to Cape Idokopas," he began, looking first at Kamov. "I believe that Kira has explained the importance I attach to the chess set project and what I would like to achieve."

He then turned his gaze on Jayne, whom he looked up and down slowly, quite blatantly scrutinizing her body shape.

Just as well he wasn't looking too hard at her wristwatch, provided by the CIA's Special Activities Center, with its infrared transmitter capability, Jayne thought to herself. It looked like a standard sports-style GPS watch but could guide an incoming drone with pinpoint accuracy.

"I believe you and Mr. Maron are the designers for this project," Putin said. "And you are both from Germany. Very interesting. Tell me, what are your ideas?"

"We like your proposals for chess figures that reflect Russian heroes, sir," Jayne said, also in Russian. "Our sculptor colleagues here are looking forward to producing pieces that highlight this country's great military history and the huge importance that chess has in Russia. And we have in mind a board made from black-and-white marble squares. Simple but timeless."

Neal nodded. "Around it, we are proposing a border of gold, sapphire, and silver, in line with the current color scheme in the swimming pool room."

Putin regarded Jayne without blinking. She could see him scanning all corners of her face.

"You speak Russian with an interesting accent," he said slowly. "Is that German or something else?"

"I apologize," she said. "My Russian is not very good."

"It sounds fine to me," the president said. "It's the accent. I lived in Germany for a few years and knew many people who spoke Russian, but with a different accent from yours. Have you been to Russia before?"

What the hell?

Why was he fixating on her accent? She knew her Russian accent was neutral, because she'd put it through a lot of analysis while working at MI6, and she had worked hard on her pronunciation to ensure her English background wasn't evident.

Did he know something and was just trying to unnerve

her now? Had Suslova briefed him and stabbed them in the back? Or was it just the president's manner to be suspicious?

"I have been to Russia a couple of times, on vacation," Jayne said. "Moscow and St. Petersburg. I'd like to revisit and explore more of the country once we have finished the chess project."

Putin gave a thin smile. "I'm sure you would. Well, the accent apart, you speak Russian very well for someone who has only been here twice. Interesting. Anyway, your proposal for the chessboard sounds good in principle. I look forward to seeing a detailed plan with a 3D digital mockup of what it will look like before I approve it, though. Enjoy your stay here."

He gave a quick nod to all four of them, then moved on to the next group. Suslova, who hadn't spoken during their interaction with Putin, went with him without a word.

Jayne glanced at Neal, who gave a slight shrug.

Suslova walked respectfully a half pace behind the president as he made his way out of the cocktail lounge, his two bodyguards following close behind them.

The entire process of introducing Putin to the guests, group by group, and initiating a brief conversation with each, had taken no more than twenty minutes. Suslova had carried out that function many times before and never enjoyed it. Today, it had been particularly nerve-wracking.

At the door, the other two bodyguards were waiting along with Postnik Maly, the head of security.

The president paused and turned to Suslova. "Thank you for handling that, Kira," he said. "Tell me . . . the chess sculpture group. I was a little intrigued by the German pair. The woman, Ms. Voss, spoke Russian with a certain accent. She said it was German. You tell me she's German. In my opinion, it wasn't German, and I'm struggling to place it. I have a good ear for accents."

He raised an eyebrow and looked Suslova in the eye. "How much due diligence did you do on that group?"

Suslova felt her scalp tighten. She had thought that Jayne Robinson's performance had been excellent, and she could detect no real accent in the way she spoke Russian. It seemed quite neutral, as she would have expected from someone who had a long and successful career as an intelligence operative.

So what did the president mean? Had he learned of their plan? That was extremely unlikely; otherwise he would never have come to meet "Voss" and "Maron" in the first place and would have had them summarily dealt with, as well as Suslova herself.

Suslova knew very well that Putin had always been a para- noid and suspicious character, ever since she had first gotten to know him in East Germany in the late 1980s. Back then, he was a product of his upbringing, his training, and the envi- ronment in which he worked. Now, as president, he'd grown even more wary.

As far as Suslova could see, there were no grounds for the president to be any more suspicious of Jayne Robinson and Neal Scales than anyone else currently at the palace. Checks on all guests were carried out rigorously by the FSB unless the president's lieutenants, such as Suslova and Igor Ivanov, invited people to the site. In that case, he trusted them to ensure those checks were carried out thoroughly and to involve the relevant intelligence agencies: the FSB, SVR, or GRU.

"The Germans are employed by the Tbilisi company on contract," Suslova said. "But of course, I've had their back- grounds checked thoroughly."

It was partially true, as thorough checks had indeed been

carried out on her orders by the FSB earlier in the year on both Kamov and Uglov. "They all came back green."

The president furrowed an eyebrow. "Maybe you have," he said. "Still, I want our own security team to run further spot checks on them, their accommodation here, and their vehicles. I want it done immediately when they arrive back at their dacha from these cocktails. Don't do anything here in front of all the other guests. I don't want to create the wrong impression."

"Of course, sir, I'll get it done," she said, facing Maly. "Let's—"

But before Suslova could say any more, the president turned, beckoned Maly over, and began to give him instructions.

CHAPTER THIRTY-ONE

Friday, June 30, 2017
   Cape Idokopas

Suslova took a shortcut as she drove Jayne and the others back to the dacha in her Porsche, taking a right just after leaving the palace and bypassing the gas station. She said nothing during the brief journey, but after parking in the driveway as Kamov and Uglov headed toward the house, Suslova took Jayne and Neal to one side after they got out of the car.

By now, the sun was long gone and night had settled in. The streetlight outside the dacha threw all of their shadows across the driveway.

"Some bad news," Suslova said, her voice low. "Jayne, as you might have guessed from his questions, the president decided there was something not quite right about your Russian accent. He told me you didn't sound like other Russian-speaking Germans he knew and asked what security checks I'd made on you all. He's now ordered his head of security to make further checks at this dacha."

"Oh, bloody hell," Jayne said. Her eyes narrowed. "You haven't told him who we are?"

"Are you mad?" Suslova asked. "Do you think I'd write my own death warrant? No. He just suddenly got suspicious of his own accord. He doesn't know anything; otherwise you'd have been in handcuffs before you left the cocktail lounge. But he's making checks. He's always been paranoid. That's why he's survived so long."

Suslova looked at her watch. "Look, you're going to have to bring your plans forward. You need to get going right now. And you're going to have to take me out of here with you. They're about to uncover what I've been doing—I know it."

Jayne looked at Neal. This mess had been quite predictable. The president had somehow been spooked, though there seemed no obvious reason why. And he had then spooked Suslova, who now wanted out, just as Jayne had warned Vic.

Suslova was right. They needed to go now.

"I'll send Vic a message to tell him to activate Operation Buzzard," Neal said. "I suggest we go get those pistols and the explosives immediately, then get out."

"Agreed." Jayne nodded.

Neal took out his phone and tapped away as the three of them hurried into the house.

As Jayne shut the door, she saw a set of headlights turn the corner a hundred meters away at the end of the street that led to the dacha. They began to head in their direction.

Shit. Were they coming already?

She and Neal went straight to the bathroom off the hallway, where she removed the two handguns, the spare magazines, the C4 blocks, and other equipment from the cupboard. She handed one of the Makarovs to Neal and swiftly checked the other. The magazine was full and the gun looked well maintained. She pushed the gun and the other items into a plastic carrier bag.

Right then, the doorbell chimed loudly.

Jayne emerged from the bathroom into the hallway, Neal just behind her.

As she did so, the front door swung open and a uniformed security guard stepped through, holding a pistol. He must have let himself in using some kind of master key card.

Behind him was another uniformed guard, also holding a handgun.

"What are you doing?" Jayne asked in Russian. "We are staying here as guests. I don't expect to find security guards coming into our dacha uninvited."

To her right, Kamov and Uglov appeared through the door that led from the kitchen, presumably having heard the doorbell.

The first security man's head swiveled in their direction.

"We need to carry out some checks here," the guard said. "I will need to see your passports and papers and I will need to search the dacha and ask a few questions."

As he finished speaking, there came two successive whip-crack gunshots from the far end of the hallway, and the security man's body catapulted backward into the other man standing behind. He then slumped to the floor and lay motionless, blood pumping from one bullet wound in his neck, another between his eyes.

"What the hell!" Kamov shouted.

Suslova, who Jayne realized had fired the shots, emerged from the living room door and moved fast across the hallway, holding her gun in front of her, pointing directly at the remaining guard.

Bloody hell. This woman Suslova was something else.

Jayne caught movement out of the corner of her eye as the guard began to jerk his gun upward.

But instantly there came another deafening gunshot from next to Jayne. The guard's head flew back in a plume of red, and he collapsed to the floor.

Neal.

Jayne glanced sideways to see her colleague lowering the Makarov she had given him.

"We need to hide these two," Neal said as he stepped forward. He stuffed his gun into his pocket, grabbed the first guard beneath the armpits, and dragged his body into the bathroom. Jayne did the same with the second guard, while Suslova used some paper towels to clean up as much of the blood from the floor as she could.

Once that was done, Suslova shut the bathroom door. "Let's get out of here." She pointed to the bag containing the C4 sticks. "Have you decided where to use those charges?"

It was obvious Suslova, having decided she needed to get out of Russia with Jayne and the others, now regarded herself as an integral part of the operational team.

"I'll use one charge at the gas station," Jayne said. "Those big white gasoline tanks. It looked like a self-serve station to me. No staff on duty as far as I could see."

"Good thinking," Suslova said.

"Can we put another on the helicopter landing pads or the refueling tanks there?"

Suslova shook her head. "It's guarded around the clock. You won't get near the tanks."

"Where, then?"

Suslova pursed her lips. "I'd suggest the cell phone tower. There are no guards there, normally. Use the same trigger unit for that and the gas station so they go off simultaneously. That will knock out a lot of the communications and draw in most of the security staff from the palace building. Trigger the charges just as you drive down to the basement drop-off area. Then, when the chaos starts, walk past security and blow Scarpa out of his cell."

"Good in theory," Jayne said. She felt a little skeptical.

"It'll be your only chance."

Well, she was probably correct in that assumption.

"Where's his cell?" Neal asked.

"Take the corridor through the door immediately to the left of the security office at the drop-off area—not the main doors to the right. The cell is the second door on the right," Suslova said.

"All right. Then we'll need a charge at the main entrance gate," Jayne said. "Otherwise we're not getting out. They'll stop us." She gave Suslova a meaningful look.

"You're asking me to do that?" Suslova said. "I don't think I—"

"You'll have to," Jayne interrupted. "We don't have another option. I can't take care of Aidan Scarpa and the main gate at the same time." She eyeballed Suslova.

Suslova exhaled. "*Bozhe*. God," she muttered. "All right. I can place a charge at the main entrance security office to clear the exit route. I'll program it to a separate remote."

"How are you going to plant the charge?"

Suslova thought for a moment. "I'll head there now and speak to the duty officers before the other sticks are triggered. I'll say I have an urgent parcel that's being collected by a courier imminently, and I'll leave it with them. I've done that before, so they won't think anything of it. They are a bit dozy at night."

"And the parcel will have the charge in it?" Jayne asked.

"Correct. They'll keep it on a shelf in the office ready for collection—that's where they all sit at night. After I've left the parcel, I'll then meet you at the quarry entrance on the road heading to the exit—the road that goes past your dacha, not the one past the helipad and telecoms tower."

Jayne had already worked out that there were two roads leading from the palace to the exit gate. She certainly didn't want to try driving past the telecoms tower if they had just blown it up, so what Suslova was saying made sense. She had spotted the quarry entrance on the way into the complex.

"I saw courier bags, boxes, and labels in the utility room," Neal said. "I'll go get some." He disappeared through the door to the kitchen.

"Assuming all goes well, we can trigger the entrance gate stick as we get near it," Suslova said. "We can also use one of the small charges if we need to remove the booms at the exit."

"Good," Jayne said. Suslova had evidently accepted the reality that she had no choice but to help, and her knowledge of the site was extremely useful.

It was indeed hard to argue with Suslova's plan, despite the speed with which it had been devised. Jayne simply didn't have enough knowledge of the palace complex to come up with an alternative.

For it to come off would obviously require things to go their way, though.

Jayne turned to Kamov and Uglov, who were still standing in the doorway from the kitchen.

"This is madness," Kamov said. "I want to play no part in this. There are two dead bodies in that bathroom."

"You also have no choice, unfortunately," Jayne said. "You will both need to come with us—right now. I suggest you go with Kira in her car. That is a safer option than with us, frankly."

"I agree," Suslova said.

"But the plan was for me and him to leave first and get

back to Tbilisi by road," Kamov said, indicating toward Uglov. "How are we going to leave now?"

"Passenger drone," Jayne said.

"A drone? A *drone?*"

"Yes. There's no alternative. You're coming," Jayne said.

Kamov threw up his hands and swore long and hard.

Jayne removed one of the C4 sticks, a detonator, and a control unit from the bag. She inserted a short cable from the detonator into a socket on the control unit, then tapped in a three-digit code, 789, to pair them together. It meant only that specific control unit could trigger the detonator, provided the code was used correctly.

She showed Suslova the code.

Suslova nodded. "Got it."

Jayne unplugged the detonator and pushed the twin metal pins at the rear of the unit into the soft C4 explosive, ensuring that it was properly molded around them.

Then she handed the primed C4 and the control unit to Suslova. "Good luck."

Neal returned, clutching a gray self-sealing plastic courier bag, an old shoebox, a pen, and some sticky labels, which he handed to Suslova. She immediately got to work putting the explosive stick inside the box and wrapping it in the plastic bag.

Jayne rushed to her bedroom to change out of her blue dress. She just had to hope that reinforcements from security were not on their way to the dacha, that they could plant the C4 explosives as planned, that they could reach and open the cell where Suslova said Aidan Scarpa was being held, and that he was still there.

Not too much to ask, she thought to herself as they headed out the door a few minutes later.

CHAPTER THIRTY-TWO

Friday, June 30, 2017
    Cape Idokopas

The clattering of helicopter engines, initially faint and distant, grew rapidly louder as the Toyota Hilux, with Jayne in the passenger seat and Neal at the wheel, headed toward the palace along the blacktop.

Surely the palace security team wasn't already chasing them with choppers? Jayne mentally ruled out that possibility. They couldn't know, not yet.

Instead of turning left to the palace building, Neal turned right, in line with Suslova's directions, toward the telecommunications tower.

As Neal drove, Jayne turned her attention to pairing two detonators with one of the remote trigger units, using a three-digit code as she had done previously. That meant that when she activated the remote trigger, both detonators would be set off simultaneously. Then she pushed the two detonators into two of the remaining sticks of C4 and placed them on the floor at her feet, now ready for use.

Next, she did the same with the much smaller square piece of C4, inserting the detonator and pairing it with another remote trigger unit. That would be used to blow open Aidan Scarpa's cell door. If anything, the charge was a little larger than required to blow open a door, but better to be safe, Jayne thought.

As they headed up the hill, the helicopter engines grew louder. Then, as they rounded a corner, beyond the tree line to their right, they saw a chopper at a height of only about thirty feet, clearly illuminated by bright floodlights on the ground.

The aircraft, which looked to her like a Mil Mi-8, descended slowly to a large, oval-shaped double landing pad and settled on the white concrete surface at the side farthest away from them. A similar helicopter was stationary and silent on the landing pad nearest to the road.

Neal slowed down a little. "I don't like this."

"Keep going. We can't stop now," Jayne said. She pointed to a black limousine and a security car with an orange roof light waiting at the far end of the landing pad. "It's likely Ivanov arriving. Suslova told me he was coming from Moscow this evening."

Neal drove straight past the landing pad and continued along the road, which curved round through the trees. To Jayne's relief, there were no sirens behind them, no sign of the security car in pursuit.

After seven hundred meters, they rounded another sharp bend through the trees and emerged into a cleared area past a concrete wall. Jayne saw the telecoms tower looming above them, its red safety lights blinking gently in the dark to warn helicopters and aircraft to keep their distance.

"Pull in there." Jayne pointed to a graveled area off the

road to their right, near the base of the tower. She could see a path that ran a short distance between the wall and the trees to the tower.

Neal braked to a halt, and Jayne grabbed one of the C4 sticks and jumped out of the Toyota.

Without hesitating, she jogged along the path until she came to the nearest corner of the steel tower, which was mounted on a large concrete base, perhaps twenty meters square. High up on the structure above were what looked like several cell phone base stations and two satellite dishes.

Jayne kneeled and nestled the C4 stick and its detonator up against the inner side of the heavy steel beam that formed the leg of the tower, then stood back. In the gloom, it was almost invisible.

That would do. She knew the charge would slice through the steel beam like a knife through butter, bringing the entire structure to the ground.

Jayne jogged back to the Toyota and jumped back into the passenger seat.

"Next stop the gas station," she said. "Let's go."

Neal turned the car and headed back down the hill, through the trees, and past the helicopter landing pad. The newly arrived chopper, like the other one, was now stationary and silent, and the two cars that had been there were gone. The floodlights were still on, however, and Jayne could see a few men working near the choppers.

They continued past the turnoff that led to their dacha and toward the palace building. The gas station came into view on the left as they rounded a bend. Thankfully, it was deserted.

"Pull in next to the pumps, as if we're filling up," Jayne said.

Neal did so, and Jayne picked up the second C4 stick and detonator and climbed out of the car. At the rear of the gas station, nestling between some bushes, were the two long cylindrical fuel tanks she had spotted previously. One had a large red sign on it marked GASOLINE, the other DIESEL.

Jayne strode over to the gasoline tank, which was set on a base constructed of brick and cinder blocks. She squatted and placed the explosive as far beneath the tank as she could reach, up against the base. It was now resting only a foot below the tank.

Now for the final and likely most risky and difficult task facing them: liberating Aidan Scarpa and escaping the palace complex intact.

Jayne hurried back to the Toyota. "Let's keep moving," she said. "I'll trigger it when we're out of the danger zone."

The palace building was only another half kilometer south of the gas station. Jayne could see the lights glinting through the trees and reflecting against the low cloud that now hung above the site.

As they headed to the palace along the road through the trees, two security cars came toward them at speed, head-lights blazing on full beam and dazzling both Jayne and Neal.

But Neal kept going and continued toward the helipad.

Jayne knew from experience that they were now safely out of the blast radius of the explosives she had planted. The palace building was less than 150 meters away now.

She picked up the remote trigger unit and switched it on.

"Now?" she asked Neal.

Neal braked to a crawl, then nodded. "Do it."

Jayne pressed the button on top of the trigger unit and turned around to watch the outcome through the rear window of the pickup cab.

The first explosion, at the communications tower, was farther in the distance and lit up the night sky at the top of the hill like a New Year's Eve fireworks show. That was the tower, although from here it was impossible to see whether it had destroyed the steel structure.

Almost immediately, the second device erupted like a volcano. The boom physically rocked their pickup truck and sent an enormous sheet of orange flame soaring into the sky as the gasoline tank exploded. Within a few moments, there came a second, equally loud explosion and eye-searingly bright flash as the neighboring diesel tank also went up.

The overall effect was as if a series of bombs had landed on the palace complex.

Within seconds, there came the piercing sound of a klaxon and sirens, presumably as emergency alarms were activated across the site. A security car shot up the ramp from the palace drop-off zone, its orange light flashing and a siren blaring. It was swiftly followed by another.

"Time to go down to the drop-off," Neal said. "They must be panicking down there already."

He accelerated gently down the ramp, just as two more security cars raced up it at high speed in the opposite direction.

Now Jayne could see a small group of security guards gathered around a man who was giving them directions, pointing up the ramp and gesticulating with his hands.

For a few seconds, Jayne worried they might draw attention by driving into the drop-off zone now, but the attention of everyone down there was now focused elsewhere.

Neal brought the pickup to a halt in one of the parking bays opposite the canopied area in front of the entrance and the security office, just as a minibus appeared from the direction of the harbor. It braked to a halt outside the security office, and most of the officers congregated there climbed on. The bus then headed up the ramp and out of sight.

"Now's our chance," Jayne said. "Let's go."

"Agreed," Neal said.

Jayne picked up the small square of C4, including the detonator, and pushed it into a plastic bag, together with the remote detonator unit.

Carrying the plastic bag in her left hand, she then climbed out of the pickup, as did Neal, and without hesitating, looking straight ahead, they both headed across the block-paved drop-off area toward a door just to the left of the security office. To their right, the officer who had earlier been instructing the others was now in an animated conversation with three other men.

There was nobody visible inside the glass-fronted security office as Jayne strode past. She opened the door to the left and walked through, Neal right behind her.

Sure enough, they found themselves in a corridor with doors leading off to the right.

But outside the second door, where Suslova had told them Aidan Scarpa was being held, stood a young blonde-haired uniformed guard, a pistol in a holster at his right hip. He glanced up as they approached, looked surprised, and reached for his gun.

But Jayne was quicker. She whipped her Makarov out from its holster and pointed it at him. "Open the door," she said in Russian.

The guard's eyes widened, and he reflexively raised his hands. "Who are you? I don't have the key. I'm under strict instructions to leave this guy locked up."

Jayne waggled the pistol a little. "Open the door," she repeated in a level tone.

"Honestly, I can't." He shook his head, his voice rising. "I don't have the key. I promise you."

Neal stepped forward to Jayne's right and tried the door handle. It was locked.

Jayne's snap judgment was that the guard was telling the

truth. They were going to have to use the explosive she was carrying.

Before she could speak, Neal stepped forward and, in what seemed like a blur, swung his pistol hard at the guard, whacking him in the temple with the butt before he could move his hand to defend himself.

The guard dropped to the floor like a sack of potatoes.

Jayne stepped forward and quickly went through the guard's pockets, searching for keys. She found nothing.

Neal tried the handle of the room next door, which swung open. It was an office with a desk and a table and chairs, but little else. Nobody was in there.

"I'll put him in here," Neal said as he grabbed the guard beneath the arms and began to drag him in. "Set up the explosive, quick."

Jayne didn't hesitate. She removed the small C4 charge and detonator from the bag, placed it on top of the heavy metal door handle and pushed down a little to ensure it wouldn't slide off.

Neal emerged from the adjoining room and closed the door.

"Let's get out of the way and trigger this," Jayne said.

She knocked on the door, which was made from heavy metal, and called out in English, "Stand back from the door. I'm blowing it open."

There was no response, so she repeated the call. Still no response.

"We'll have to just get on with it," Neal muttered.

They both hurried down the corridor to where it ended in a T-junction, turned around the corner to the right, and went another few steps along.

"Okay?" Neal asked.

Jayne nodded, took the remote control unit from the bag, turned it on and pressed the button.

There came a deafening bang from around the corner and a dense cloud of dust and debris flew down the corridor as far as the T-junction.

They waited a few seconds, then made their way back to the cell, both of them spluttering a little because of the dust.

The door, now hanging open, was bent and twisted and almost off its hinges. Most of the door frame was lying in fragments on the floor, as were large chunks of the plaster from around the door.

Jayne stepped over the debris and peered through the cloud of dust that was still hanging heavy in the room.

"Oh shit," she said involuntarily. "Shit, shit, *shit*."

There, lying on the red-tiled floor, face up in the center of the room, was the figure of Aidan Scarpa, his eyes shut. He was lying next to a large circular drain, near a bed. Jayne noticed a shower, a toilet, and a sink in the opposite corner of the room and what looked like a metal torture chair. There was an overpowering smell of disinfectant.

Jayne kneeled next to Aidan and grabbed his wrist to check his pulse.

It took her only a few seconds to realize that he was alive but was out for the count.

Jayne turned to Neal. "Completely unconscious. We'll just have to carry him out to the car."

Neal nodded. "Let's do it."

He stepped over and grabbed Neal beneath the armpits, while Jayne lifted his feet.

Between them, they lifted him out into the corridor and carried him to the door, Jayne at the front, Neal at the back.

There, she placed his feet on the floor in order to open the door.

As she opened it, a security car flew past, its orange light flashing. She glanced around and saw another idling security car with a driver waiting inside. The driver was looking out his window at another security man—the one who had earlier seemed in charge and was giving the instructions.

The man in charge stood twenty meters away with his back to the car and to Jayne and Neal, shouting into his phone and gesticulating with his hand as he did so.

Jayne swore inwardly.

There was no way they could lug Aidan to their car without bringing attention to themselves. As it was, she was surprised the guards didn't hear the explosion outside Aidan's cell; the sirens and chaos outside must have covered the sound.

Jayne started thinking furiously about another solution. Shooting the guards would be a last resort, but they might have to.

Right then, the guard in charge spun around and walked to the passenger side of the car, opened the door, and ducked into the front seat, still yelling into his phone. He pulled the door shut and the car then sped off up the ramp, leaving the area completely empty.

"Thank God," Jayne said. "Get him to the car."

She lifted Aidan's feet once again, and moving as fast as they could, they headed to the pickup.

Jayne opened the rear door of the Toyota with one hand while holding Aidan's feet with the other, and between them, they bundled him onto the rear seat so he was out of sight.

"This is a nightmare," Jayne muttered as she climbed into the passenger seat.

Neal started the engine, reversed out of the parking bay, and set off up the ramp.

Farther up the road, the sky was a bright orange color from the blazing fuel tanks at the gas station. It lit up the sky so brightly that Jayne could see clouds of black smoke billowing upward.

"Take the shortcut," Jayne said. She pointed to a narrow

road that cut off to the right through the trees, where Suslova had taken them after the cocktails reception. "We'll bypass the gas station."

Jayne knew the gas station would be crawling with security, and she was keen to avoid it.

Sure enough, they encountered no other vehicles as Neal navigated the way back to the main road that led to the exit.

Five minutes later, they pulled into the entrance to the quarry. Jayne spotted Suslova's Porsche tucked behind some trees, its lights off. She parked next to it and lowered the window, as did Suslova. Kamov was in the passenger seat and Uglov was in the back.

"Do you have him?" Suslova asked.

"We do. But he's unconscious," Jayne said, glancing over her shoulder. Aidan was still lying on the back seat, completely out of it. "Don't know if it was the blast that did it or what."

"But he's alive?"

"He is," Jayne said. "I hope he'll be okay. Did you place the charge at the security gate?"

Suslova nodded. "It's done."

"Trigger it now," Jayne said. "Then follow us out the gate to the exfil site. If we need to blow up the boom at the exit, we'll do it when we get there. We need to move fast."

The main gate was only a kilometer and a half from where they were.

Suslova nodded, reached down to her feet, and picked up the remote-control device, which she immediately activated.

A second later, there came an enormous blast from the other side of the trees to the northeast, and another mushroom of orange fire soared skyward.

"Let's go," Jayne said.

Neal set off, turned right out of the quarry entrance, and continued down the road toward the main entrance. Jayne glanced over her shoulder and was reassured by the sight of Suslova's Porsche following them close behind.

They rounded a hairpin bend and as they drew nearer to the exit, she saw in front of them a scene of utter devastation.

The security office at the main gate had disappeared almost completely. All four walls were mostly gone, apart from a few segments of brick, and the roof was lying to one side at an angle of forty-five degrees. Debris lay everywhere, and the remains of the building were burning fiercely.

Jayne could see immediately there was no need to destroy the booms adjoining the office. They were lying on the ground, bent and twisted, about ten meters away.

The only issue was the amount of debris littering the road out of the complex.

"Can you drive across that?" Jayne asked.

"We can do it," Neal said. He steered around a large piece of brick wall, crunched across some wood and glass, and then over a steel beam to which broken plasterboard was still attached.

"Good thing we have the four-wheel drive," Neal said as he wrenched the steering wheel first one way, then the other, to maneuver around or over the obstacles.

Jayne looked over her shoulder again. Aidan was bouncing around on the back seat as the Toyota ran over the debris, so she leaned over and put a hand on his chest to hold him in position. Suslova was still trailing them. Her Porsche, also all-wheel drive, appeared to be navigating through the rubble quite capably.

To the right of the road behind them, opposite the ruined security building, she caught sight of a security guard running after them, perhaps forty meters behind Suslova's car, his phone clamped to his ear.

Shit.

The blast hadn't killed all of them, then.

"We've been spotted," Jayne said. "Keep going."

Neal nodded.

Finally, they were over the debris and out through the remains of what had been the barriers.

Neal turned right onto the highway that led through the village of Praskoveevka.

Again, Jayne looked over her shoulder. Suslova's car was even closer behind. The guard she had seen was now standing near the site entrance, gesticulating frantically and still speaking into his phone.

"Go," Jayne said. "I just hope those bloody drones turn up to schedule."

Neal accelerated hard up the road with a screech of tires as Jayne clicked the button on her infrared beacon watch, getting it ready to activate as soon as they reached the pickup point.

Jayne, recalling the images of the drone pickup point that the CIA's Special Activities Center head Jerry Spann had shown her, now looked out for the bus stop landmark that she needed.

No more than two minutes later, she saw it on the right side of the highway.

"There," she pointed. "Turn off."

Neal braked hard and swung off the highway, continuing along a stretch of concrete road past the bus stop and a bank of young conifer trees until he came to a large gravel area on the left. There, he came to a halt and parked. A few seconds later, Suslova's Porsche pulled up next to the Toyota.

As Spann had indicated, it appeared to be a good choice of landing point. It was hidden from the highway, but it was flat and had plenty of room for an incoming drone to land without any risk from tall trees or overhead electricity cables.

Jayne clicked the button on her watch, which beeped

twice, activating the infrared beacon that was intended to guide the drones to them.

"Kira, you'll need to go in one drone with Nikolas and Oleg," Neal said. "Jayne and I will go in the other with Aidan. We'll need to look after him."

Jayne kept her eyes glued to the tree line to the east, where she assumed the two drones would come from. They just had to hope the technology worked as intended.

Sure enough, a couple of minutes later, they heard a whirring. In the gloom, helped by a faint glow from the streetlights on the nearby highway, Jayne could just about make out two black, somewhat futuristic-looking devices as they appeared at little more than fifty feet over the trees. They hovered for a few seconds above the gravel, then one of them slowly descended and landed on a pair of long skids beneath its central cabin. A short while later, the other did the same, landing about thirty meters away from the first.

They were identical to the images that Spann had shown Jayne and the description he had given, perhaps five-and-a-half meters across including the arms and rotor blades. The cabin in the center seemed not much larger than a motor-cycle sidecar.

Suslova thought likewise. "You want us to go in those?" she asked. "They look like toys."

"We have to," Jayne said, a note of irritation in her voice. "There's no alternative. If you want to stay and face the consequences, you can."

She looked at Neal. "We'd best get Aidan into the rear seat. We'll sit in the front."

Jayne quickly checked Aidan's pulse again. It was fast, but still reasonably steady. She and Neal lifted him, still completely unconscious, out of the back seat of the truck and carried him to the drone nearest to them. He felt like a dead weight, and Jayne just hoped that they weren't doing him some irreparable damage by moving him in this way. She was certain that doctors would advise them not to do so while he was unconscious.

Jayne opened the small side door of the drone, folded the front seat forward, and, with difficulty, they maneuvered Aidan into the cramped rear seat. Jayne folded the three-point seatbelt across him and clicked the buckle into place.

She glanced at the small dashboard in the front, which was as Spann had shown her, with a gaming-style console and the green button she needed to press to signal they were ready for takeoff.

Jayne then went over to the other drone, where Uglov was already strapped into the rear seat, Kamov and Suslova in the front. She showed Suslova the green button.

"Good luck," Jayne said. "I suggest you wait for us to take off to make sure the damn thing works properly, then immediately press the button."

She then returned to her own drone, where Neal was also now ready.

Jayne climbed in, fastened her seat belt, and shut the door.

"Let's get out of here," she said. She pressed the green button.

The eight engines immediately began to whir. The drone lifted smoothly off the ground.

Jayne gave a thumbs-up signal through the window to Suslova, away to her left.

The drone reached just above treetop level, then moved sharply eastward. Jayne looked left again and watched as the other drone followed.

Operation Buzzard was off the ground.

"Bloody hell," she said. "The damn things actually work."

CHAPTER THIRTY-THREE

Friday, June 30, 2017
   Cape Idokopas

"What do you mean Kira Suslova's just driven out of the site?" Igor Ivanov snapped.

The president's special adviser had arrived at Cape Idokopas by helicopter from Moscow, only to find himself literally in the middle of a firestorm within a few minutes. The gas station and communications tower had both been blown up, and now he had just been told by the head of security, Postnik Maly, that there had been a third massive explosion at the entrance gate security office.

President Putin had already called Ivanov in a state of genuine panic after the first two explosions, having initially thought there was some kind of coup attempt underway. Thankfully, that did not appear to be the case.

"One of my guards watched Suslova drive her Porsche out of the main gate," Maly said, completely out of breath after running up two flights of stairs and down a long corridor to the room Ivanov was using. "She had two other people in her car and was following one of the pickup trucks, a Toyota, that the group from Tbilisi was using. The guard said he saw two people in that one. Both cars drove right through all the wreckage, then northward through the village at high speed. We think they caused the explosions and that they have the American president's son with them—he's gone from his cell."

"*What?*" Ivanov said, his voice rising sharply. "Gone?"

"Yes, sir. He's gone. The guard outside his cell was knocked unconscious. And the door to the cell was blown open with a small explosive charge, likely after the big detonations outside. It wrecked the doorway and corridor. We're now certain they blew up the gas station and comms tower as a diversion to get him out."

"*Sukin syn.* Son of a bitch," Ivanov muttered. "Why are you so sure it was the chess team? How did this happen?"

Maly looked at the floor. "The president asked me earlier to get them checked out, so I did that immediately. Two guards went straight to their dacha, but we've just found them shot dead."

"*Dermo*," Ivanov said.

"Also, sir, I earlier sent high-resolution photos from our CCTV and the chess team's details to the FSB. They've just come back to me. They say according to their face recognition system, the woman on the team, supposedly a German designer, is actually a British operative, Jayne Robinson, who works for the CIA. Obviously using false ID and disguise while here. And one of the men, supposedly German as well, is also CIA, Neal Scales. It's them who have orchestrated the whole thing. We think Suslova must have helped them. No idea why."

There was silence for a couple of seconds as Ivanov digested what he had just been told.

"Right, we need to get after them," Ivanov finally said, a grim edge to his voice. "I want them in custody. They can't get far. We've got two armed choppers on the helipad. Efim brought me here—get him back up to the landing pad, brief him, and tell him to get in the air."

Efim Manin was the hugely experienced military helicopter pilot assigned to Ivanov and who had flown him from Moscow in a Mil Mi-8 attack helicopter.

"Will do, sir."

"And tell Efim he's got my authority to do whatever's needed to stop them. If it means casualties, so be it. Shoot up the bastards' cars. And get pursuit vehicles on the highway at the same time."

"I'll do it now, sir. We also have CCTV cameras along the highway at three-hundred meter intervals. We are checking output from those right now."

"You said they headed north, away from the beach?" Ivanov asked.

"That's what the guard saw, yes."

Ivanov frowned. "They can't be thinking of getting out of Russia by road—that's just not going to happen. And if they're not going by sea, they must have a chopper or plane coming in for them. Put the radar people on full alert—make sure they miss nothing."

"Yes, sir."

Maly grabbed his walkie-talkie from the holster on his belt, rapidly tapped in a number, then issued instructions.

* * *

Friday, June 30, 2017
Cape Idokopas

. . .

Efim Manin, a forty-year-old now in his third year as chief helicopter pilot for Igor Ivanov and other senior Kremlin leaders, settled himself into his seat.

He glanced at his copilot, Kuzma Dubasov, in the seat to his right. "You did the weapons checks before we left Moscow, right?"

Dubasov nodded. "All loaded, including the cannons."

Manin nodded, then immediately opened the throttle, causing the engine whine to rise sharply. When the throttle was fully open, he pulled up steadily on the collective control lever to his left and simultaneously began to press down on his left foot pedal.

Slowly, the fearsome-looking Mil Mi-8 attack helicopter left the landing pad and rose vertically.

When the chopper was well above tree level, Manin nudged the cyclic lever directly in front of him slowly forward. The aircraft's nose tilted down a little, and it began to move forward.

"Right, let's get after them," he said.

It was dark now, but Manin knew where the highway was, and headed directly for it.

He had just reached the highway when his radio crackled. It was the deputy head of the radar unit, based in his control room near the now-destroyed communications tower. Thankfully, the blast had not impacted radar operations.

"Efim, we are picking up something southeast of the palace," the radar officer said. "We're trying to establish what it is. It appeared momentarily, then disappeared again. We suspect whatever it is must be flying very low, and it's a few kilometers inland. Mr. Ivanov is instructing you to head there."

"But I was told that Suslova and the others left the palace by road," Efim said. "I was told to locate and destroy their cars. That's what I'm about to do."

"Security located their cars using CCTV. Abandoned in a truck stop in Praskoveevka just to the north. No sign of the occupants. Security thinks they may have been picked up from there."

"By helicopter?" Manin asked.

"That's what we think is on the radar, most likely. A small one. It has no authority to fly, which is why Mr. Ivanov wants you to head there. Same instructions apply. Find and destroy it. There are no other aircraft or choppers authorized to be in that airspace."

"Coordinates?" Manin asked.

"Here's what we have for last contact."

The officer rattled off the coordinates, which Dubasov tapped into his navigational computer as Manin swung the chopper around and accelerated fast in a southeasterly direction.

The helicopter carried a fearsome array of armaments. At the front, there were two forward-firing UPK-23-250 pods equipped with rapid-fire GSh-23L twin-barrel 23mm cannon. The starboard- and port-side stub wings each carried two BV820-A launchers for S-8 80mm unguided rockets.

All the weapons were fired using buttons on the pilot's or copilot's central cyclic control sticks.

Within a few minutes, Manin had the Mil Mi-8 heading southeast on a beeline toward the target coordinates at a speed of more than 230 kilometers an hour and an altitude of six hundred feet. They were now flying well below the low-lying cloud.

As they drew near, the radio crackled again.

"Reporting another blip, we believe same helicopter," the same radar operator said. "Further southeast than previously, estimated speed of travel around sixty kilometers an hour. Another very brief blip. Definitely flying extremely low. We lost it immediately. It's quite hilly there."

The operator read out the revised coordinates, which Duabsov again entered into his computer.

Manin took the chopper down farther, to three hundred feet.

Less than two minutes later, Manin had the Mil Mi-8 at the point given, which was roughly forty kilometers southeast of the palace.

"I'm seeing no navigation lights," Dubasov said.

"Me neither. Put the searchlights on."

Dubasov reached up to the bank of controls above his head and switched on the twin searchlights positioned at the front of the helicopter, the direction of which was controlled by two small joysticks mounted just beneath his dashboard.

Manin pushed his collective control down a little, taking the chopper down a little more, to around 275 feet. This was somewhat dangerous, he knew, given the hilly terrain, but if his target was flying even lower and probably without lights, there was little alternative if he was going to locate it using the searchlights.

"There," Dubasov said, jerking up in his seat and pointing to the starboard side of the helicopter. "What's that?"

Manin peered in the direction his copilot was indicating. Nothing.

Then, as Dubasov adjusted the searchlight, he caught a glimpse of something in the beam.

"I saw it," Manin said, pointing. "Over there."

He adjusted course a little. "Keep the light on it."

Dubasov fiddled with his joystick, swearing as he struggled to keep the searchlight level. "I see it. That's not a chopper."

"What, then?" Manin was unable to watch the target continuously, mindful of a hillside rising no more than half a kilometer ahead of him.

"Don't know. Looks like some kind of drone. Get closer."

Manin did as asked, pushing the chopper closer over to starboard. As he did so, he got a better view.

"It *is* a drone," Manin said. "A huge one. What the hell? A passenger drone. Got a cabin in the center. It's like the GRU's project. Painted black as a coal mine."

Manin had seen a similar passenger drone device under development at the GRU's headquarters in Moscow and had been invited to carry out a test flight in it, which he had so far been unable to do.

"We have to take it down," Manin said. "That's the one the radar guys picked up, for sure."

He turned the chopper's nose until it was pointing directly at the drone as Dubasov reached for his cyclic control and placed his thumb on the trigger button for the 23mm cannon.

Dubasov applied his right eye to the optical gunsight mounted above his seat and turned up the brightness a little to compensate for the blackness of the target. Manin tried to get the drone dead ahead for him.

Then came the loud chatter of machine gun fire, which lasted for the next several seconds as Dubasov continued shooting. Then came a short pause, as he stopped firing.

"Got him?" Manin asked.

"No."

There came another burst of 23mm gunfire, again lasting several seconds.

Then Manin saw a bright white flash directly ahead, followed by an orange glow.

"Got him," Dubasov said. "Got the bastard."

Sure enough, the orange glow grew brighter. Then there was an audible boom, an explosion, as the drone blew apart, scattering burning debris across the night sky. It fell swiftly down to earth, leaving trails of orange and red behind.

"Good night, CIA," Manin said as he punched the air.

"I thought Postnik told you there were five or six people who ran from the palace," Dubasov said. "Would they all fit on one drone?"

Manin paused. "Good point. I don't know, but not if it's the same size as the GRU's. Maybe there's another, then. Let's keep on searching."

* * *

Friday, June 30, 2017
Berlin

"Shit, he says we've lost one of the drones," Jerry Spann muttered, glancing up at Vic Walter, his phone clamped to his ear.

Vic, sitting at the table in the Berlin CIA station's top-floor meeting room, jerked forward in his seat, spilling his coffee a little. "Lost one?" He felt his stomach turn over.

Spann's phone call was via a secure internet link with Kris Arnold, his officer who was running the drone exfiltration operation from the Turkish trawler that was being used as the mother ship in the Black Sea.

Spann, who was hunched over his laptop, lowered his head again and scrutinized the screen, listening to his officer.

Vic put his cup down and strode around to the other side of the table so he could see the screen.

"He says both drones were showing on the monitor until a few minutes ago," Spann said, glancing up again. "Now there's just one. The other just disappeared."

Vic stared at the screen, which showed a satellite map view of the Russian Black Sea coast running southeast from Cape Idokopas. It was a duplicate of the monitor inside the operations room on the trawler, which was just outside Russian territorial waters, twenty-three kilometers offshore.

On the map was a blue dot, slightly inland from the coast, moving slowly southeast. That was the drone. Out at sea, just a little farther southeast, was a red dot, representing the trawler.

"Which drone has gone?" Vic asked.

"HUNTSMAN TWO."

"So what happened? Shot down? Engine failure? Comms failure?" Vic asked, his voice now sounding croaky.

"They don't know," Spann said, still with his phone locked to his ear.

Vic's heart sank. "But who was on which drone?" he asked, knowing there was no way of telling.

"They have no idea," Spann said.

Vic swore and threw up his hands. "Jayne? Neal? The president's boy?"

Spann just shook his head.

CHAPTER THIRTY-FOUR

Friday, June 30, 2017
   Black Sea

The drone dropped a little more until the moonlit waves that were rushing by below, decorated by flickers of silver, were almost touchable.

It was now heading out to sea at a height of only a hundred feet and traveling faster than it had while moving over land. The low cloud had cleared as soon as they crossed the coast, and the moonlight meant that at last it was possible to see a little of where they were going.

Following the high-octane adrenaline rush caused by their escape from the palace complex and the uncertain scariness of the initial phase of the drone flight, Jayne's mood had flipped to quite the opposite.

Now she felt sick to her stomach.

The sight of the other drone being blown apart in a cloud of orange and white flame a few hundred meters away from theirs was seared into the back of her mind. She kept replaying it over and over, like a video clip on repeat.

Then came the feeling of utter, scalp-tingling fear as she watched the Russian helicopter, its twin searchlights sweeping the skies behind them, as it searched for its second victim.

For more than twenty minutes, the chopper had continued crisscrossing the area, its searchlights blazing. But always, thankfully, its lights never touched their drone.

Eventually, the Russian helicopter crew had given up.

Quite how the chopper had so quickly found the drone containing Suslova, Kamov, and Uglov, Jayne didn't know. Her understanding was that the drone was highly unlikely to be picked up on radar, given its low altitude, small size, and stealth paint coating. But the helicopter crew hadn't found them by accident.

However, she knew that the destroyed drone had been the slower of the two. It had gradually lost ground so that by the time it was shot down, it was some distance behind, maybe four hundred meters or more.

Jayne guessed that the weight of its three occupants might have been a factor in their drone's slower rate of progress. Both Kamov and Uglov were quite fleshy and significantly heavier than the others.

She glanced behind her at the figure of Aidan Scarpa.

He was still unconscious and had now been so for a worrying amount of time. She leaned across and checked his pulse yet again.

"How does it feel?" Neal asked. He had asked every time she checked.

"Still quite strong," Jayne said. "But I would say more irregular. Feels jerky."

"Oh God." Neal looked down at the floor of the drone's cockpit and folded his arms across his chest. "Ferguson will kill us if he doesn't make it. And so will Vic—there's no other way of knowing what Operation Noi is."

He checked his watch. "Can't be too long to go now."

Jayne agreed with his assessment. "Maybe another ten minutes, perhaps fifteen."

The drone seemed to be moving more quickly now, and the trawler where they were due to touch down was only about twenty-three kilometers offshore.

She, too, hoped that Scarpa would be all right and that the necessary medical attention he needed could be given once they reached the ship.

Jayne looked first to the starboard side of the drone, then to port. There was no sign of any pursuing helicopters, no Russian patrol boats below about to open fire on them, as far as she could see.

Then, ahead of them, she saw a black speck through the gloom, just about visible against the silver moonlight reflecting on the tops of the waves. Rapidly, it grew larger.

"Is that ours?" Jayne asked. "Better be."

Neal leaned forward in his seat, stretching as far as the seat belt would permit as he peered ahead. "Don't know."

For several anxious seconds she watched and waited, half fearing that she would see a flash, then feel the terminal impact of a Russian rocket.

But nothing came.

Soon, the drone slowed sharply to a crawl and edged toward the boat, which was now only a little ahead of them.

Then it descended, again at a very slow rate. Now Jayne could see the deck and a host of men scurrying around, clearing what looked like boxes and fishing nets away.

The drone hovered without moving for a short time, then descended again, and finally there came a bump as it landed on its skids, lurching from one side to another, causing Jayne to also whiplash from left to right.

The engines cut out, and a group of men moved smartly to the drone, securing the sleds with ropes. Another group tugged a tarpaulin toward it. Clearly, and sensibly, it wasn't going to remain open to view from roving satellites or surveillance aircraft.

Someone opened the door at Jayne's side and put their head in.

"You made it. Jayne Robinson? Neal Scales? I'm Kris Arnold."

"That's us," Jayne said. She had been briefed by Vic that Arnold was running the operation from the ship. "We had a difficult flight."

"We saw on the scanner that something happened," Arnold said.

"The Russians blew the second drone to pieces," Neal said. "Helicopter shot it up. We were lucky—"

"Where's Aidan Scarpa?" Arnold interrupted, a note of anxiety in his voice. "Don't tell me he was on that drone?"

"He's here, unconscious," Jayne said, gesticulating behind her. "We need a doctor for him. Urgently. He's been out cold since we left the palace. Pulse is irregular. I'm really worried about him. I hope you've got a doc on board."

"We have. I'll get him."

Arnold turned and called to someone behind him, while Jayne unclipped her seatbelt and climbed out of the drone, Neal close behind.

As they did so, the trawler's engines, which had been idling, roared into life. The ship did a ninety-degree turn to port and headed southwest toward Istanbul, leaving a broad V-shaped white wake behind it that glistened in the moonlight. Jayne knew the journey of almost five hundred nautical miles would take probably twenty-two hours, at least.

Two men came running, pushing a gurney. One of them,

wearing a white jacket, folded the drone's front seat forward, leaned behind, and checked Aidan Scarpa's pulse.

"Any idea how this happened?" he asked, turning his head.

Jayne paused for a second. "We, um, had to blow open his cell door to get him out. With explosive. I'm not sure if that's what did it."

"I see. It is beating a little bumpy," he said. "We'll get him inside and check him out properly. His color looks a bit gray."

Carefully, the two men eased Scarpa out of the drone and onto the stretcher. Then they pushed him across the deck and through a door into the cabin. Jayne, Neal, and Arnold followed close behind.

In contrast to the worn, aging exterior appearance of the trawler, complete with peeling paint, deteriorating fishing nets, and rusty equipment, the interior of the boat was quite the opposite. The cabin, fitted out in a modern stainless steel and glass style with one-way windows, was divided into sleeping and bathroom quarters, a well-equipped ops room with satellite communications, a galley, dining and lounge area, and a medical room. It was to the latter that Scarpa was taken by the doctor and his assistant.

While the doctor went to work on Scarpa, Jayne and Neal joined Arnold in the ops room for a secure debriefing video call with Vic Walter and Jerry Spann at the Berlin CIA station.

Vic was visibly relieved to see Jayne and Neal but became quite somber as Jayne described as succinctly as she could what had happened.

"So you're one hundred percent sure we've lost Suslova?" Vic asked. The video showed him hunched over the table in the meeting room, his arms folded, forehead creased, peering over the top of his glasses.

"No doubt about it," Neal said. "No chance of surviving that. All three of them, gone."

Vic looked down at the table. "I'm sorry to hear that. I'm also sorry, from a professional point of view, that we've once again lost a top asset inside Russia. I'm wondering if we should have managed the situation better."

Was he criticizing her? Jayne wondered.

"It was always going to be high risk," Neal said. "We knew that. But given they had Aidan, we had little choice. I don't know how the hell they found the drone."

"Radar?" Vic asked.

Jayne shrugged. "I thought Jerry said we'd be too low and too small for that, and the drones have the stealth coating."

"I did," Spann said. "But I did say it doesn't make them completely invisible. Just highly unlikely to be spotted. Maybe you were unlucky."

"Suslova and the two Tbilisi guys were some way behind us," Jayne said. "They got caught. We didn't, luckily. I suspect they were slower because the two guys were big and heavy."

"It may have slowed them down," Spann said.

"Vic, have you briefed the president on Operation Buzzard?" Jayne asked.

Vic shook his head. "I'm holding off on that. Hopefully, I can give him some positive news rather than telling him that Aidan's unconscious and we don't know what the prognosis is. I'm also hoping Aidan can tell us more about why the Russians took him in the first place—if they revive him. *When* they revive him, I should say."

"When." A voice came from behind Jayne. "Not if."

She turned to see the doctor standing there.

"You'll be pleased to know Aidan is back with us," the doctor said. "He was severely concussed, he's still groggy, as you might expect, and we will need to keep very careful watch over him. But my feeling is he will be okay."

Jayne stood, swaying a little as the ship lurched to one side in the sea swell. "Can we speak to him?"

The doctor nodded. "He has said a few words. You can try."

Jayne and Neal walked with the doctor through to the medical room, where Aidan was lying on a hospital-style bed, propped up against pillows, his eyes open.

"Aidan, I'm Jayne Robinson," she began. "This is Neal, my colleague. We brought you out of Russia on your father's instructions while you were still unconscious. We work for the CIA. How are you feeling?"

Slowly, Aidan's eyes focused on Jayne. "I remember nothing," he said. "Only an explosion, a bang."

"Well, I'm glad you're back with us and talking," Jayne said. "We were worried about you. The explosion was our fault. Trying to get you out of that cell. You must be feeling fairly groggy?"

Aidan gave a faint smile. "You could say that. But you got me out. Thank you."

"We were pleased we found you," Jayne said. "Your father has been very concerned about you."

She paused, trying to keep her voice as low and casual as she could. "But if you don't mind me asking a few questions, why did they take you in the first place?"

Aidan's eyelids fell and remained down, like shutters over a window.

Has he gone again?

"Aidan?" she said, her voice soft. "Are you okay?"

Silence.

Aidan's mouth slowly opened. "They took me because I overheard what they were saying," he murmured, his voice almost too low for Jayne to decipher.

"About what?" she asked.

"Operation Noi."

"Operation Noi?" Jayne asked. "We're aware of its existence, but we don't know what it is, exactly. Who did you overhear, and what did they say?"

"I heard Anke Leonova," Aidan said, opening his eyes again. "She was talking to a man called Igor on a conference call. I heard it when they thought I couldn't hear."

"Igor? Igor Ivanov?" Jayne asked.

"I don't know. Just Igor."

Jayne felt butterflies in her stomach. "And Operation Noi? Do you know what Operation Noi is?"

"Uh-huh," Aidan grunted. "They are going to activate it. They discussed the details."

"So what is Operation Noi?" Jayne asked, trying to remain patient and keep her voice slow, although she could feel adrenaline running through her like rocket fuel. Aidan wasn't quite with it yet.

"It is a plan to blow up a dam, to destroy it. I heard what they were planning."

"But did you hear which one?" Jayne asked. "Because there are seven along the Dnipro River. That's what we need to know."

Aidan gently shook his head. "No, not on the Dnipro River. Not in Ukraine."

Jayne paused, feeling slightly confused. "Not in Ukraine? Are you sure?"

"Yes. It's not in Ukraine."

"Where, then?" Jayne asked.

There was a short pause, and Aidan's eyelids fell again. Then he lifted them and looked Jayne in the eye.

"It's in the United States," he said.

Jayne felt as though a bolt of electricity had just run through her. She exhaled vigorously and looked up at Neal, whose eyes had widened.

"Bloody hell," she said, turning her attention back to Aidan. "The Russians are planning to blow up a dam in the

United States? Are you sure about this? You couldn't have misheard or made a mistake?"

"No mistake," Aidan said. "I understand Russian very well. I am fluent."

"Did you hear which dam?" Jayne asked.

"No," Aidan said. "Only that it sounds like a big one."

"The Hoover?" Neal asked. "Grand Coulee? Glen Canyon?"

Aidan's eyes wandered to Neal. "They didn't say which dam. They just referred to it as Operation Noi. But they have someone who is running the operation, who is in charge. I heard that."

"Who?" Jayne asked. She grabbed a handrail along the side of Aidan's bed to keep her balance as the ship lurched to port.

"Someone code-named the DAM KEEPER. *Khranitel Plotiny* in Russian. They spoke about the DAM KEEPER," Aidan said.

"We also heard about this DAM KEEPER," Jayne said. This corroborated what GRAY WOLF had told them prior to his demise. "But did you find out any more?"

"They said that Igor had known him longest. I remember that."

"Him? So it's a man. What's the actual name?"

"I don't know a name. They didn't say."

Jayne grimaced.

This was priceless information.

No wonder the Russians had grabbed Aidan.

Jayne's first thought was that Operation Noi must be part of the much wider ongoing Russian initiative, codenamed Operation Pandora, to undermine the United States over a long period. The existence of Pandora had been uncovered by Jayne and Joe Johnson three years earlier during another investigation in the Black Sea region. Targeting a US dam would fit right into that strategy.

"I'm sorry," Aidan whispered. "I was stupid. I fell for a honey trap. So foolish."

Jayne already assumed that, having seen the Himmel Bar videos, but Aidan had confirmed it.

"Was that with Anke?" she asked.

Aidan nodded. "She told me her name was Irina."

Jayne was dying to ask how he had overheard all the information he had just given but decided that could wait. They just needed to keep the questioning to the real essentials.

But she could see that filling in the blanks was going to be problematic.

"Do you know anything else about this DAM KEEPER?" she asked.

"He works for the US government. I got that bit. He is high level."

Jayne again caught Neal's eye. His eyes were wide in disbelief.

"Which part of the government?" Jayne asked.

There came a slight shake of Aidan's head. "I don't know. But I heard them talking about using ammonium nitrate explosive. And I know what that is."

"Did you hear when this is going to happen?" Neal asked.

"Soon," Aidan said, his eyes now closed again. "They were organizing it when I overheard the conversation in Frankfurt. It must be soon."

Aidan's head sank into his pillow.

Soon?

Jayne's mind immediately went back to the warning that Valentin Marchenko's SZR office in Kyiv had received a week earlier, warning of consequences if the North Crimean Canal was not unblocked immediately and if the United States did not pull all its intelligence and military people out of Ukraine within three weeks.

But she and everyone else had been certain those threatened consequences would come inside Ukraine—not the United States.

And if there was a three-week countdown to that happening, it meant there were now only two weeks to go.

"I think you need to let him rest for a while," the doctor said. "You can speak to him again later."

Jayne turned to Neal. "This is unbelievable. We'd better get back and brief Vic."

PART FOUR

CHAPTER THIRTY-FIVE

Saturday, July 1, 2017
    Cape Idokopas

Within less than twenty-four hours, Igor Ivanov's worst fears had been confirmed.

The brief report on the desk in front of him, from the palace head of security Postnik Maly, stated that only three bodies had been found in or around the wreckage of the drone shot down in thick forest southeast of Cape Idokopas the previous night.

One was Kira Suslova, and the others were the two chess piece sculptors from Tbilisi, Nikolas Kamov and Oleg Uglov. The identities of all had been confirmed.

Ivanov looked out the window of the office he was using on the ground floor of the palace building, along the corridor from the president's office suite. The sky was a cloudless azure blue, and the sun was blazing across the Black Sea— weather that could not be less reflective of the foul mood he was in.

The scenario he had suspected to be true was now inescapably correct.

Aidan Scarpa had been liberated from his cell by intelligence operatives Jayne Robinson and Neal Scales amid the chaos following the explosions on the palace site. The three of them had then fled the cape and out of Russia aboard a second drone.

The bodies of the two palace security guards who had been sent to check the dacha being used by Robinson and Scales had been retrieved from the bathroom where they were found. Both had fatal bullet wounds.

Meanwhile, Anke Leonova and Gavrill Rezanov had remained at their apartment away from the main palace building and knew little of what had happened.

"*Svoloch*. Bastards," Ivanov said, almost spitting out the word.

Initially, he had failed to understand how Scarpa, Robinson, and Scales had avoided detection on their drone. Efim Manin and his helicopter co-pilot had found no trace of it in the darkness of the previous night. Apart from the initial blips on radar that had enabled Manin to find the first drone, there had been no further sightings.

But as more information emerged from the crash site, the difficulty in locating the second drone became less surprising. They were small, had been flying very low, and had some kind of anti-radar stealth coating that would have further reduced their detectability. The truth was, the radar team had been lucky to get any kind of reading.

This deployment of passenger drones was a new development by Western intelligence that Ivanov had not seen previously, although he knew the GRU had a similar project in the pipeline.

The implications of what had happened had been clear to Ivanov over the weekend, but despite that, he had been hoping that when the wreckage and bodies were recovered, they would include Aidan Scarpa and Jayne Robinson.

That was not to be.

Robinson and Scales had somehow pulled off a maneuver that they were no doubt now toasting with fine champagne somewhere in the West.

It was also now very clear to Ivanov that Kira Suslova had been a traitor of the highest order to the Motherland.

Quite unbelievable.

Suka. The bitch must have been working with Robinson and Scales all along. There was no other way they could have engineered their way into Russia and the palace. Their accreditation documents were signed by Suslova.

Quite how she had been recruited was far from clear. But Ivanov was determined to get to the bottom of it. Suslova, to him, seemed the most unlikely candidate for recruitment. She was a patriot. So he suspected there must have been some huge blackmail or other leverage involved. He knew that President Putin would demand answers, too.

His mind flashed back to when he thought he'd seen Suslova eyeing his Operation Noi file in a meeting in President Putin's office after he accidentally left it in sight. Had that been a key moment?

One thing was certain: Ivanov was not looking forward to breaking news of Suslova's betrayal to the president.

But that wasn't his immediate priority.

His focus now needed to be firmly on delivering Operation Noi, which was of huge strategic importance in persuading the United States to get out of Ukraine and getting the North Crimean Canal unblocked.

Operation Noi was also a key component of a much larger, long-running and wide-ranging strategic umbrella plan, code-named Operation Pandora, which was a close-guarded secret within the Kremlin. It was designed to undermine

Russia's biggest and oldest enemy, the United States, over a long period.

The aim was to destabilize the US politically, economically, and socially and to disrupt and disorient the leadership and the ordinary population. In particular, an objective was to destroy the faith US citizens had in their president, their leadership, and their long-standing institutions, particularly the judiciary and the military. Operation Pandora had so far resulted in some successes, but also some failures. Nonetheless, the agenda remained, and Ivanov expected that President Putin would continue to push it hard.

Aidan Scarpa was now the biggest threat to Noi, and thereby to Pandora. But Ivanov had devised a plan that he believed would resolve that, and he knew who he would order to implement it.

Ivanov picked up his phone, called Anke Leonova, and asked her to come to his office.

Less than ten minutes later, Leonova walked in, looking a little pale and with bags under her eyes, but an angry look on her face. Her curly dark hair looked dank and unwashed. Like him, it seemed she hadn't slept well last night.

Ivanov knew she was furious about the extraordinary fiasco that had taken place, but was also worried about being blamed. However, he was putting the responsibility for that firmly elsewhere—with Kira Suslova, who helpfully for him, could no longer defend herself.

He indicated to the chair in front of his desk, and she sat down.

"Anke, we can't just let Operation Noi unwind or else the president will have us all thrown to the fire," Ivanov said. "You have successfully carried out operations in the United States before."

Anke nodded.

Before she could speak, Ivanov continued. "I need you to do another."

"Aidan Scarpa?" she asked, her forehead creased. "No chance. We won't get near him again."

Ivanov shook his head. "Not Scarpa. You're right, we won't get near him. But although Scarpa knows the DAM KEEPER's code name, he doesn't know his real name, right?"

Anke nodded. "The conversation he overheard, we didn't use his real name, correct."

"So that's where the CIA will focus. Trying to figure out who he is. And although Scarpa knows we're targeting a US dam, he doesn't know which one."

"Also correct," Anke said. "They'll be trying to find that out, too."

Ivanov paused. "There's one other factor they don't know. And which neither you nor Scarpa know."

Anke folded her arms, pulling her thin black sweater tight against her chest. "The illegal who's going to blow up the dam, I assume," she said.

Ivanov nodded. "Right again. And what I want to do is eliminate any chance of Robinson, Scales, or any of the CIA half-wits figuring out who that is. There's only one person who can lead them there, and that's—"

"The DAM KEEPER."

"Yes. If the CIA figures out who the DAM KEEPER is, it's almost inevitable they'll force him to reveal the illegal's name."

Anke's eyes narrowed a little. "Are you trying to tell me you want me to eliminate the DAM KEEPER?"

"Precisely. We have no option. If he's gone, he can't talk. But first, you need to make sure he instructs the illegal to implement Operation Noi immediately. Force him to do that, if necessary. Then get rid of him."

"Understood," Anke said.

Ivanov stood and walked to the window. "There is something else."

"Jayne Robinson?"

"Indeed. Jayne Robinson," Ivanov said. "I need you to eliminate her, too. She not only appears to be leading the operational side of this CIA initiative, but she's done incredible damage to us over recent years. I want to go to the president and tell him she won't be doing anymore."

"After what she's done, it will be a pleasure," Anke said, her mouth set in a hard line.

"I'd also like to know how the hell she got involved in handling or recruiting Suslova," Ivanov said. "But let me take care of that."

Anke nodded. "I might need some help to nail Robinson. She moves fast."

"Well, you'll need to be faster. I'll brief Director Kruglov and Director Pliskin, and we'll get their people to help you as much as possible."

Ivanov knew he would need to draw on the resources of Kruglov's SVR and Pliskin's GRU for his plan to work. There was no way that Leonova could complete the task he wanted from her without a great deal of support.

Anke inclined her head. "*Da*. All right. I'm sure I can get into the US again, no problem. I have two identities I can use, and there's someone in Mexico who's gotten me across the US border before."

Ivanov nodded, walked back to his desk, and sat down.

"When do you want me to go?" Anke asked.

"Yesterday, ideally."

Anke tossed her hair back over her shoulder and gave a faint smile. "I'm a quick worker."

"So I hear."

CHAPTER THIRTY-SIX

Monday, July 3, 2017
Washington, DC

It was only when Jayne sat down at the White House
Situation Room conference table that she became aware,
through her sleep-deprived brain fog, that the jacket she had
hung over the back of her chair and her trousers still carried
the smell of sea salt.

She wrinkled her nose in embarrassment. But since
arriving back in DC that morning on the overnight flight
from Istanbul, she had only changed her underwear and her
blouse and certainly hadn't had the chance to wash anything.

Thankfully, she was several yards down the wooden
conference table from President Ferguson, who had just
walked in. He was sitting, as usual, at the head of the table
beneath the presidential seal that was mounted on a plinth on
the wall behind him.

"I would like to thank you, Jayne and Neal, for getting
Aidan out of that Russian hellhole," President Ferguson

began. "And I will thank you properly, in due course. But the job is only half done, and we have a crisis on our hands, with little time to fix it."

Aidan was still in the hospital in Istanbul, receiving round-the-clock care and undergoing a series of tests before being given clearance to fly back to the United States. His concussion had been severe, so no risks were being taken.

The president folded his arms and scanned the faces around the table. "So, after a weekend trying to work out which dam Operation Noi is going to hit, and who the hell the DAM KEEPER is, we don't seem to be any further forward."

He raised his thick eyebrows in a characteristically challenging fashion.

President Ferguson, his aide, Charles Deacon, Vic, and the rest of the entourage who had been in Berlin had traveled back to the US capital on Sunday following a briefing from Vic and a series of intense discussions that occupied all of Saturday.

Meanwhile, in DC, the CIA's director, Arthur Veltman, and his FBI counterpart, Robert Bonfield, had liaised with Vic and had begun a counterintelligence operation aimed at discovering the identity of the DAM KEEPER and which dam was the target.

Both men were now sitting opposite Jayne, who was next to Neal and Vic.

Bonfield, who along with his FBI team was taking prime responsibility for the operation given that it was now focused on US soil, leaned forward. "Mr. President, we are working on a list of people who might match the profile of this so-called DAM KEEPER, using the information provided by Aidan. Someone senior in the government machine who has a link to dams. There are a lot of possibilities, unfortunately. But we are working around the clock to narrow them down as rapidly as we can. Iain is taking the lead."

He indicated to the wiry man with cropped gray hair sitting next to him, Iain Shepard, who was the FBI's executive assistant director in charge of the counterintelligence division, known internally as CD.

Ferguson nodded. "I think we should continue running this operation below the radar. I want nothing in the media about Aidan. The question is, will the Russians continue with Operation Noi now that Aidan has been extracted from Cape Idokopas, given what they must know he has passed on to us?"

The president, as was often the case, had cut directly to the critical question.

"Unfortunately, we have lost our most important source inside the Kremlin," Vic said. "Kira Suslova was the only one who might have been able to help. But my gut instinct, given the speed and aggression with which they are acting toward Ukraine, is that the Russians will accelerate their plans, not cancel them. A week ago, they issued a three-week ultimatum. My instinct is that they will want to continue and use Operation Noi as a tool to tilt public opinion in the US toward our withdrawal from Ukraine. The destruction of a huge hydroelectric dam, critical to power supplies, and a massive flood in a populated area, causing widespread deaths and damage, might just do that. People might just say, enough is enough."

There was a short silence around the table.

"I agree with you, Vic," Ferguson said.

There were nods from the others.

"So, given the time constraints," Vic continued, "we are reliant on tackling this at our end. I agree we should continue below the radar for the time being—there is no sense in causing a mass panic in towns and cities around every dam in the country. We don't know which is being targeted yet—there are at least eighty of them above three hundred feet tall, and hundreds of others that are still quite large. But we need to be prepared to move fast when we find out more. Tens of thousands of people may need to be evacuated."

"Agreed," Bonfield said. "And a media storm now would either cause the DAM KEEPER and his team to implement Operation Noi immediately, when we haven't had time to run him down, or force him underground to resurface another day, maybe a year down the line. We might never find him then."

The president placed his palms flat on the table and scrutinized those present one by one. "So who has ideas on what we can do to accelerate this process? Vic? Jayne? Neal?"

Something had been nagging at Jayne since the initial conversation she'd had with Aidan on the trawler. It stemmed from what he had said about the man named Igor, who had to be Igor Ivanov, the Russian president's key adviser—the man known as the Black Bishop of the Kremlin.

However, she wanted to pursue her idea through her own channels.

Now was not the time to mention it to the president, when she wasn't sure whether her idea had legs or not.

She folded her arms on the table. "Mr. President, I'm sure we all have ideas we will be pursuing once we can think them through in more detail. Neal and I are glad we could bring your son out of Russia. He's given us some great leads, and I hope he recovers quickly. I can assure you we'll be doing everything we can to make his ordeal, and ours, pay dividends and stop this Operation Noi."

The president pushed his chair back. "Thank you, Jayne. I'll look forward to that. Do whatever you need to do to make that happen."

He stood and left the room.

As Jayne, Vic, and Neal also made their way out of the Situation Room, collecting their phones from the lead-lined security box in the reception area as they went, Vic gave Jayne a look.

"You've got something in mind, haven't you?" he asked, as they climbed the stairs that led from the basement up to West Executive Avenue, the street that led between the West Wing and the old executive building. "I can read you like a book."

"Maybe," she said. "What I've got most in mind right now is flying up to Portland this afternoon to see Joe. I haven't seen him in ages. We've got some catching up to do." She winked at Vic.

He gave a half smile. "You know what I mean. And it's not what you'll be doing with Joe behind closed doors."

Jayne paused for a second at the west basement entrance. "I may be completely on the wrong track, which is why I didn't want to talk about it earlier, especially in front of the president."

"Tell me anyway."

"It's to do with Igor Ivanov. Aidan said that he overheard the Russians saying that Igor had known the DAM KEEPER longest. Assuming the DAM KEEPER is a Westerner, to me, that's the key to this. How, when, and where did Igor Ivanov get to know the DAM KEEPER in the first place? That's where we need to focus."

"Should be easy enough, given we don't know the DAM KEEPER's identity and therefore can't track his movements." There was a sarcastic tone to Vic's voice.

"We know Igor Ivanov's identity," Jayne countered.

"But we're going to struggle to track his past movements."

Jayne inclined her head. "I'll discuss it with Joe. He's good at that sort of thing."

CHAPTER THIRTY-SEVEN

Monday, July 3, 2017
Portland, Maine

Cocoa, Joe's chocolate Labrador, stood next to the bed, rested his head on the mattress, and gazed up at Jayne with unblinking brown eyes.

"You been wondering where I was, boy?" she asked as she stroked his ears. "I think you have."

Cocoa gave a slight whine in response and licked her hand.

"That'll be a yes," she said.

"We shouldn't have him in the bedroom," Joe said. "He's not used to seeing us like this. Might give him a fright."

He glanced sideways at Jayne, who was lying naked and feeling good in the kind of way she always did after they had finished making love.

"We're done," she said, grinning. "So it's okay. No action to watch."

"Are we done? Completely?"

"Temporarily done. At least for another hour or so."

Joe laughed and stretched out his six-foot one-inch frame on the bed. He reached out a hand and slowly ran it across her abs, which were still pleasingly taut for someone who was nearing her fifty-sixth birthday. The sensation felt good, and Jayne relaxed even more. His muscle tone, too, was pretty good for someone a couple of years older than her, she couldn't help thinking.

"I'm glad to have you back again," Joe said. "I've been missing this. But it sounds like you did a great job at Putin's Palace."

"I'm telling you, that building is unbelievable," Jayne said. "I wish I could have actually enjoyed being there. But we've still got a long way to go."

She had arrived home an hour ago at Joe's house in Portland, where she had been based for the past three years, having made the move across the Atlantic from her apartment in London. It had taken her a while to adjust to life in the US, not least because she had become a kind of stand-in mother to Joe's two children, Carrie, now aged twenty, and Peter, who had recently turned nineteen. Joe's wife, Kathy, had died back in 2005 from cancer.

Jayne had already updated Joe on the outcome of the operation in Russia, the need to track down the DAM KEEPER, and his links to Igor Ivanov. Although Joe was not part of the operation, she and Vic had worked with him for decades and both trusted him implicitly. Besides which, he very often had insights and perspectives that helped her investigations.

They just lay on the bed for a while, the warm early evening breeze blowing in through the window. The two-story Cape Cod–style house on Parsons Road was only just along the street from Back Cove, an inlet off Casco Bay, and there was a definite whiff of sea salt in the air.

Cocoa eventually wandered out of the room. Joe's two children were out visiting friends. The house was silent.

"So, Ivanov and this DAM KEEPER," Joe said, running a hand across the short-cropped semicircle of gray hair that ran around his extensive bald patch.

"They're the key," Jayne said. "Identifying who this DAM KEEPER is lies in finding out how and where they got together. Ivanov might well have recruited him personally— but how and when? We're fairly certain Ivanov has never spent time in the US, but Aidan said he overheard the Russians saying Ivanov had known the DAM KEEPER the longest. From where? With Suslova gone, we're a little stuck. Vic's team's working on it, but it's going to be difficult."

Joe lay thinking for a short time.

"I had some dealings a few years ago with a guy, Don Nichols, who helped me with some open-source research," he said. "A grumpy guy, but he got hold of some intel that was vital for one of my war crimes investigations. It came from publicly available sources, but not obvious ones. He's very good on the tech side. He knew where to look and how to get it. Databases available on the dark web, social media, you name it. Don is top-class. Works freelance now, like us. Got sources everywhere. Russia, Iran, China."

"That name rings a bell."

"Worked for the Defense Intelligence Agency for thirty years."

"Ah, yes. DIA. Someone mentioned him to me when I was at MI6, but I never met him. Highly rated, wasn't he?"

"I've kept in touch with him. He rose through the ranks to be deputy chief of their clandestine service, an ops guy— he's been into Russia and elsewhere undercover when needed. Vic knows him well because the DIA and CIA collaborate a lot—despite the rivalry between them. Something happened and he took early retirement recently. He still does some work for the DIA's clandestine guys under the radar. But he's set up his own company now, Open Intel Group, and works with an assistant who helps him with stuff on the web."

"Hope he likes a challenge," Jayne said. "We'd need him to pin down Ivanov's movements going back years. Can we call him?"

Joe sat up on the bed. "We can have an initial chat, but he won't discuss much over the phone or email. We'll have to see him."

Jayne exhaled. "Well, time is short. Don't tell me. He lives in Costa Rica or Spain or somewhere?"

Joe shook his head. "Actually, not too far from here. In Boston. I'll have a shower, get dressed, and then we can get on a call to Don. If he thinks he can help, we could drive down to see him."

CHAPTER THIRTY-EIGHT

Tuesday, July 4, 2017
  Boston

The enormous four-story redbrick corner house on Fairfield Street in the heart of Boston's upmarket Back Bay neighborhood told Jayne all she needed to know about how well its owner, Don Nichols, was doing.

Following an encouraging phone call the previous evening, it had taken her and Joe almost three hours to drive down from Portland to Boston early that morning, thanks to heavy Fourth of July traffic.

Within ten minutes of entering his home, it was fairly clear that the confidence Joe had in Nichols was well-founded.

A large room on the third floor of the house had been set up as a kind of operations hub, with two giant TVs on the wall, a meeting table, and a long desk in one corner with three computer monitor screens. On another wall was a map of the world. On the roof, Nichols had installed a giant satellite dish, cleverly hidden from view to anyone passing in the street below.

"I took out two bedrooms to make this ops room," Nichols said as he poured coffee at the meeting table. "Worth it, though. I decided after leaving the DIA that I would run my own show, and I was going to do it properly. Sometimes I'm out of the country on operations, sometimes I'm based here directing others. And if I'm here, I need to have a proper setup."

Nichols, a muscled fifty-year-old with a full head of salt-and-pepper hair, a deeply tanned face, and quick eyes, sat at the table facing Jayne and Joe, his shirt sleeves rolled up. "Now, what do you need?"

Jayne told him about Igor Ivanov, giving as much detail as she thought appropriate at this stage. "We need to know when and how and where he could have built this relationship with the DAM KEEPER," she said. "It didn't happen in the US, we're fairly sure."

"Tricky," Nichols said. "I've heard of this guy, Ivanov. He's on most intelligence agencies' radars, I'd guess, and if he's professional, he will have tried to cover his tracks when going out of Russia."

"Let's hope he didn't see the need," Jayne said. "It most likely would have happened in a place where both of them were located for a while, so they had the opportunity to get to know each other. I doubt this stemmed from a one-off meeting."

Nichols sipped his coffee. "I'd agree. I can get hold of travel details for individuals from Russian databases that I buy from black market sellers on the dark web. Russian data protection measures are as porous as a sponge. A few quick transfers of cryptocurrency, maybe a thousand dollars' worth, and I can get what I need. Sometimes I don't need to pay, because the databases are already on torrent networks. But it's a long and difficult process to narrow it down to what I need."

"How do you narrow it down?" Joe asked.

"Passport numbers, usually," Nichols said. "Nearly all flights, train bookings, whatever, are linked to passport numbers. Sometimes they are their own genuine passports, but often, in the case of Russian operatives or anyone working undercover, they use false documents."

"Right," Jayne said. "But how do you get the passport numbers?"

Nichols gave a half laugh. "A Telegram bot. Or I could try a data seller on an online forum. There are lots of them. The black market for data in Russia is large. Corruption is massive. I can get dates of birth, passport numbers, car license plates, driver license numbers, cell phone numbers. You name it."

Jayne knew what he was referring to. The encrypted Telegram messaging service that was popular in Russia and other former Soviet countries was used widely by intelligence officers and senior officials because it was supposedly secure. But well-designed computer bots could get around that and extract any information that had been sent or received using the service.

Similarly, corrupt officials in government departments, ranging from passports to police to courts, often supplied large volumes of data in exchange for cash.

"What about flight details?" Joe asked.

"Airline flight manifests, the passenger lists, are sold by corrupt airline officials," Nichols said. "No problem with that. But we need the numbers of the passport or passports they're using first so we can pin down the person we need."

"How long do you need?" Jayne asked.

Nichols shrugged. "Impossible to say. You'll have to leave it with me." He eyed Jayne. "How urgent is this?"

"Very."

She wasn't going to tell Nichols about the threat to blow up a dam. He didn't need to know that. But if he had worked at such a high level inside the Defense Intelligence Agency's clandestine service, he would grasp the need for speed.

"All right," Nichols said as he drained his cup. "Give me a few hours, then come back. Go for a walk along the river. Get some lunch."

The house, which Jayne guessed must be worth about $10 million, was only two blocks away from the Charles River, with its waterfront esplanades and parks.

Nichols ushered them down the stairs and out the wide, black front door.

"I'll call you if I find something helpful," he said. "But these searches can get complicated. I can't guarantee anything."

CHAPTER THIRTY-NINE

Tuesday, July 4, 2017
Boston

Jayne and Joe returned to Don Nichols's house just after 2:00 p.m. following lunch at a New Orleans–style restaurant, Buttermilk and Bourbon, on Commonwealth Avenue, the long tree-lined boulevard that ran through several neighborhoods south of the Charles River.

The former Defense Intelligence Agency officer had sent a message to Joe telling them to head back when convenient.

But as soon as Nichols opened the door, Jayne could tell from his slightly downbeat manner that he had not made the progress he had hoped for.

"It's been difficult," Nichols said, leading them back up the stairs to his ops room. "Ivanov seems to cover his tracks well when he travels out of Russia."

"So, nothing?" Jayne asked, as she sat opposite Nichols, who had a laptop open at his meeting table.

"Not quite nothing," Nichols said, tapping at his

computer. "I pulled in several airline passenger list databases, some of which show him traveling under his real name. For instance, since 2014 he's been to Crimea many times—usually flying from Moscow to Simferopol Airport."

Simferopol, Crimea's second largest city after Sevastopol, had become the effective administrative center of the region since the 2014 Russian annexation.

"Doubtless he's going to Crimea so much because he's using it as a base to run undercover operations in Ukraine," Joe said.

Nichols nodded. "Since Russia annexed Crimea, it's been a launchpad to prepare attacks on Ukraine. And as Russia considers Crimea part of Russia, he probably thinks it's fine to travel under his real name."

"But there's nothing under his real name for other foreign trips?" Jayne asked.

"No," Nichols said. "Not under his real name. But he has been overseas under a false name. Look at this."

Nichols turned his laptop around and pointed to the screen. "This is the passenger list, the manifest, for an Aeroflot flight from Moscow to Helsinki in March last year. I bought it along with all the historical Aeroflot manifests for the past fifteen years. A very useful investment. I get an updated version every couple of weeks."

On the screen there was a list of seat numbers with corresponding passenger names next to them.

"This is the business-class cabin list for March 10 last year," Nichols said. "There's a woman, Kristina Ivanova, who is sitting next to a man, Nicolai Khrenov, on that flight. I know that Kristina Ivanova is the wife of Igor Ivanov, which is why I searched for her as well as for Igor. Always sensible to search for close relatives of the person you're interested in, because the Russians rarely go to the trouble of creating false identities for operatives' relatives."

"Why?" Jayne asked.

"Too much hassle and cost. Maybe they're lazy. And it's definitely her, because her passport, which I got from another database, matches the one listed on the manifest. So it looks at first glance that Igor's wife has traveled by herself to Helsinki, yes?"

He looked up at Jayne, then Joe, who nodded.

"But then here's another flight manifest, this time Aeroflot business class from Moscow to Cyprus, July 2013," Nichols said, toggling to another screen, which also showed a passenger list. "Again, we see Kristina Ivanova has a seat next to Nicolai Khrenov. A coincidence, you might think. Until you see this from December 2012."

Again Nichols toggled to another screen. This time it showed Kristina Ivanova on a flight from Moscow to Istanbul in May 2011, also sitting next to Nicolai Khrenov. He then showed another similar journey, from December 2008, to Caracas, the Venezuelan capital.

"There are lots more journeys like that," Nichols continued. "I did some further research, using a database for driver's licenses, and found a listing for Nicolai Khrenov there too. But here's the thing: this Nicolai Khrenov's address, linked to the driver's license, is listed as the same one as none other than Igor Ivanov, in Moscow."

"Khrenov is Igor Ivanov," Joe said.

Nichols nodded. "He uses that identity for his foreign trips. And he's done so for a long time."

"But are any of those trips frequently repeated to the same destinations, or for long durations, so he might have the opportunity to forge a relationship with our DAM KEEPER?" Jayne asked. "Or are they just one-offs?"

"They look like one-offs for a day, a few days, never much longer," Nichols said.

"That's understandable. He's a high-level government

operator," Joe said, a quizzical expression on his face. "He likely wouldn't spend a long time anywhere. Is it useful for us to know that?"

"Probably not," Nichols said. "But when I searched for flights within Russia, something odd caught my eye. Look at this."

Nichols again toggled his screen and showed Jayne and Joe another passenger manifest. "This one is an internal Russian flight on Aeroflot, from Moscow to Vladikavkaz, down in the south, near the border with Georgia. There he is again. Our friend Nicolai Khrenov."

He looked alternately at Jayne, then Joe. "The odd thing is, Ivanov traveled under his false identity—by himself. There's no Kristina with him. And he repeated that journey to Vladikavkaz countless times from 2004 to 2010. I've seen at least sixty identical journeys, but there might be more."

"Really?" Jayne said. "So he traveled under a false identity on all those flights within Russia? Why would he do that?"

Nichols shrugged. "That's what I wondered. Seems unusual."

"Did he have a mistress or something in Vladikavkaz?" Jayne asked.

"I wondered that too. But I've messaged a senior Russian military source of mine, inside GRU headquarters in Moscow, who knows all of these people. He told me that Ivanov has had a mistress or two, but they are in Moscow. He tells me that at that time, Ivanov was masterminding a top-secret GRU operation, preparing for the Russian invasion of Georgia in 2008, and got involved in a lot of activity around the border to facilitate that, including heavy corruption of local officials to turn a blind eye to what was going on. And get this: he said the local officials included an American who was in charge of a border-crossing construction team. It sounds very messy."

"An *American*?" Jayne asked. "In Georgia?"

There was a scraping sound next to Jayne as Joe pushed his chair back, stood, and began to pace across the room. "Wait a minute," Joe said. "Ivanov was working on the Georgia invasion? I spent a long time doing some consultancy work with the International Criminal Court on war crimes allegations against Russians for atrocities against ethnic Georgians during that conflict. I was at Kazbegi, the town near the Checkpoint Lars border crossing, to interview locals."

Jayne's mind immediately flashed back to her long journey with Kamov and Uglov from Tbilisi to Cape Idokopas. After passing through Kazbegi and Checkpoint Lars into Russia, they had gone past Vladikavkaz, only sixty kilometers farther on.

"Vladikavkaz is only an hour's drive from that Checkpoint Lars crossing," Jayne said.

"I know," Joe said. "Anyway, there were indeed a lot of seriously corrupt people around there—they let the Russians take a ton of weaponry across the border to kill the local Georgians during the five-day war in 2008 and never said a word or raised the alarm. It was horrific. About twenty thousand ethnic Georgians were murdered. Most of the fighting was farther west in South Ossetia, but some of the Russian troops marched straight down that highway where Checkpoint Lars was being built. Someone let them do it. And what Don is saying is right in line with what I was told."

Jayne looked at him, waiting.

"I was told by locals that among those taking bribes from the Russians was at least one senior American," Joe said. "There were a lot of Americans there over a five-year period, up until 2009, working with the Georgia government to build Checkpoint Lars. They all lived a few kilometers away in Kazbegi. I could never prove anything. Nobody was prepared to stand up and give evidence for fear of Russian reprisals. So despite the later prosecutions in the European Court of Human Rights in Strasbourg, nobody from Checkpoint Lars was included in that. But I was told things by locals who saw what was happening. They turned a blind eye to what the Russians were doing."

There was silence for a couple of seconds.

Jayne swiftly grasped the implications of what Nichols and Joe had said.

"So it could have been that Igor Ivanov, during the long period he was working at Vladikavkaz, bribed this American to let him run operations against the Georgians and take Russian troops through there without any interference?" Jayne asked.

Joe nodded.

"Which Americans were building Checkpoint Lars then?" Nichols asked. "How come they were involved?"

"It was the US Army Corps of Engineers," Joe said as he returned to his seat.

Jayne felt herself go cold.

"It was a big project, two or three million dollars," Joe said. "The USACE's paymasters at the Department of Defense wanted to try to build good relations with Georgia, and they also wanted to reduce the risk of weapons of mass destruction, explosives, warheads, and so on being moved south from Russia through the Caucasus region to places like Iran. So the US offered to help Georgia, along with many other similar projects. Of course, the Russians didn't like it."

Jayne sat up in her chair. "Who was that senior American? Who was in charge of that project?"

Joe shrugged. "I'm just trying to remember. It was a long time ago."

"That could be who we're looking for," Jayne said, urgently. "Come on, Joe, think."

Joe rocked back in his chair. "It was a guy named Merriden. Yes, that was him. Frank Merriden. He moved on to become commander of the USACE's Europe operations soon after. I spoke to him in Kazbegi, but I remember he wasn't very helpful."

"Frank Merriden?" Jayne said, her voice rising. Now her mind was racing like the wheels on a slot machine. "He's the commander of the entire Corps of Engineers now. Reports to Philip Monterey. I met him only four weeks ago in Vic's office. You have to be joking?"

Joe shook his head. "I'm not joking."

Jayne stared at Joe as realization dawned. "He could be the DAM KEEPER, then," she said. "Maybe once Ivanov had him on the hook in Kazbegi, he wouldn't let him off—and he's still on the Kremlin's payroll."

"Could be," Joe said. "Except we have no proof. Just as I had no proof of the corruption in Kazbegi."

Jayne slapped both palms down on the table. "We'll just have to bloody well go and get it, in that case."

CHAPTER FORTY

Tuesday, July 4, 2017
    Portland

"Good work, but the slight problem is you don't have a shred
of proof," Vic said. The video monitor screen in Joe's study
showed the CIA deputy director of operations sitting with
his arms folded on the desk in front of him.

"Not yet," Jayne said. "But I'm certain there's no smoke
without plenty of fire." She glanced at Joe and was pleased to
see him nod in agreement. She felt somewhat irritated that
Vic was stating the obvious.

The monitor showed Vic in his office on the seventh floor
of the CIA's Original Headquarters Building. Sitting next to
him was Neal, who had remained at Langley after Jayne flew
back to Portland.

She and Joe had just explained to Vic and Neal what they
had found out from Don Nichols about Igor Ivanov, and Joe's
recollections about Frank Merriden.

"I can't call Bonfield and ask him to send his boys around

to Frank's place without some kind of justification," Vic said. "Especially not with someone that senior. I'd get my ass kicked from here to LA if it was wrong."

Jayne remained silent. She knew Vic was correct in what he said.

True, what they had on Merriden was purely speculative, although both she and Joe were convinced there could be no other logical conclusion.

Merriden had the inside information on Aidan Scarpa and his role in Frankfurt with the US Army Corps of Engineers. That knowledge would have enabled Ivanov's operative Anke Leonova to target Scarpa, who could be used to source information while leaving Merriden seemingly guiltless.

The demise of GRAY WOLF—and almost of Jayne and Neal—must have stemmed from information provided by Scarpa.

Also, Merriden had been one of very few people in the loop on the details of President Ferguson's visit to Kyiv. That information would have facilitated the drone attack on the hydroelectric dam.

The problem, at least as far as Vic was concerned, now lay in the murky, shark-infested waters of Washington politics. She couldn't afford to put Vic, or Robert Bonfield for that matter, in a situation that could leave them seriously embarrassed. She needed Vic's support especially, but also Bonfield's to a lesser degree, if she was to continue operating effectively in the kind of role she was currently fulfilling.

She would have to find another way forward. And she already had a good idea of what that would need to be.

"All right, Vic," Jayne said. "I've already thought how we resolve this—and quickly."

"We need to move fast," Neal said. "Got to stop the bastards. We've only done half the job, getting Aidan out of Russia."

Vic nodded. "Of course. So as soon as we're done, I'll go next door and consult with Veltman about the best way forward."

Director Veltman's office was right next to Vic's and even had a connecting door.

"Good," Jayne said. "You go and consult. But in the meantime, I'd like to get moving. Do you know where Merriden lives? Presumably somewhere within commuting range of the Pentagon."

There was a brief silence on Vic's end of the call. Jayne could see him staring directly into the webcam on his desk.

"Do I know where Frank lives?" Vic said. "Is this connected to the thinking you've been doing?"

"Possibly."

"Well, yes, I do know," Vic said. "I went there once for a dinner a couple of years ago."

"Sounds nice," Jayne said. "Where is it?"

Vic gave a short laugh. "Funnily enough, it's only a mile and a half from where I'm sitting right now. In McLean. An easy commute to the Pentagon."

"I thought we might pay him a visit," Jayne said. "I'd like to get on a plane back to DC as fast as we can." She glanced over at Joe. Again, she received a slight nod of approval in return.

"Pay him a visit, or pay his house a visit?" Vic asked as he tapped on his phone screen. "I know what you're like, Jayne. And you, Joe."

He didn't wait for an answer but instead held his phone up and read out an address on Ballantrae Farm Drive. "Very upmarket area of McLean, big houses and gardens. You didn't get that address from me."

"Of course not," Jayne said.

"You both going?" Vic asked.

"He'll probably remember me from Kazbegi in 2009," Joe

said. "So yes. It'll probably rattle his cage a little, might help loosen his tongue."

Vic inclined his head, a look of resignation on his face. "Maybe. I'm struggling to think of a better option right now. Listen, I know what Ferguson said in the Situation Room yesterday. Something like Operation Noi must be stopped, and you need to do whatever you need to do to make that happen. I don't think there'll be any flak flying from his direction if you push the boundaries. But the problem will be with local police and the feds if you do something you shouldn't. I don't want stories all over the media and questions being asked in the Senate accusing the Agency of taking the law into its own hands and going beyond its authority. This is not our territory, not our job to do this kind of thing."

Jayne tried to avoid rolling her eyes. "Vic, we've been here before many times. This is why you employ me."

Vic looked down at his desk and raised both hands. "Okay, okay. You're on it. Just don't involve me, that's all."

"Let me know what you need, Jayne," Neal said, looking into the camera. He turned to Vic. "I won't involve you either."

"You know what we need, Neal," Jayne said. "The usual, please. Walther for me, Beretta for Joe. A drone with a camera might help. There are a few other things."

Jayne started to reel off a list of items.

CHAPTER FORTY-ONE

Wednesday, July 5, 2017
  McLean, Virginia

It was dark when Anke Leonova's somewhat battered silver Honda Accord sedan turned off Interstate 66 and headed north toward McLean.

It had taken her more than a day, several gas refills, a few naps, and a lot of coffee to make her way up from Texas, where she had finally arrived from Sochi via Athens, Mexico City, and the border crossing into the United States at Nuevo Laredo.

Despite her tiredness, her adrenaline began to flow as she followed the satnav on her phone. The device was running on a SIM card obtained from the same dealer in Houston who had supplied her with the car, a Makarov handgun, and ammunition and who was a long-standing contractor to the GRU. Indeed, she had used him on her previous operation inside the US.

As with that operation, her Maltese passport, in the name

of Rebecca Olivari, had functioned perfectly at both Mexican and US passport control. A shoulder-length blonde wig was all she needed to match her appearance to the photograph in the document.

The SVR and the GRU were continuing to advise their operatives to use Maltese passports, which allowed their owners to enter the US without a visa under the Visa Waiver Program that applied to about forty European countries.

They didn't even need to produce forgeries. Malta's policy of offering citizenship to anyone willing to inject $1.1 million into investment projects in the tiny Mediterranean island country made it very easy.

Not just intelligence operatives and illegals but oligarchs too were taking advantage of the scheme if they needed to get into the US. Anke had long ago added a Malta driver's license, bank account, and working credit cards, which combined gave her an entire false identity that could be used almost anywhere.

Now she just had to hope that Frank Merriden was at home, and that he didn't have visitors. She knew from the traces the GRU had done on the family's phones that Merriden's wife, Viva, was in Ireland visiting relatives. The couple's two adult children lived in Chicago and LA.

Most likely, he would be alone.

Anke munched yet another caffeine chew as she turned right off Dolley Madison Boulevard, a divided highway, and beneath the trees that stood on either side of the entrance to Ballantrae Farm Drive, where Merriden lived. She needed to be as alert as possible, despite her lack of sleep.

She was very aware that this neighborhood, the leafiest, greenest, and among the most exclusive of suburbs, was only a short distance from the CIA's headquarters at Langley. But despite them having somehow extricated Aidan Scarpa from Cape Idokopas, she was very confident they would know nothing that could link Merriden to Operation Noi, or enable them to link his code name, the DAM KEEPER, to the man himself.

Nevertheless, she needed to be careful.

Anke followed the road as it curved around to the left, then the right, past some enormous and ornate properties, mostly built on plots that were forty or fifty meters wide.

Then, on the right, she saw the house, which she recognized from the photographs she had been sent by Ivanov's office. It had two flags mounted on the gateposts that marked the entrance to the driveway, one American, the other Irish, reflecting Merriden's wife's family background.

The house, built from red brick, had three stories, one of them built into the red-tiled roof space, and a large U-shaped driveway. There was a triple garage on the left side of the property, joined to the house.

As she drove past, to her relief, she noted that there were no cars parked in the driveway. It seemed unlikely that Merriden had visitors. There were lights on in two of the downstairs windows. He was presumably still up and awake.

Anke continued to the end of the street, then slowly turned around and stopped at the side of the street. The digital clock on the dashboard read 9:48 p.m.

As usual, before launching herself into an unknown situation, Anke hesitated. But she knew she couldn't afford to delay. The job needed to be done, and quickly.

Anke took out the Makarov from a bag in the front passenger's side footwell, put on a light jacket, and pushed the gun into the right pocket. Then she took out her phone, tapped out an encrypted message to Igor Ivanov, and sent it.

Here. Going in.

Then she drove back up the street, turned into the semi-circular driveway, killed the lights, and rolled the Honda to a halt near the front door.

There she turned off the engine, climbed out, walked up to the front door, and rang the bell.

Several seconds later, the door clicked partly open. The security chain rattled, preventing it from opening fully.

Through the gap, Anke could see a tall man with a well-sculpted head of silver hair and a military bearing. She knew from the photographs she had seen that this was Frank Merriden.

"Hello, how can I help you?" he asked.

"I'm sorry to disturb you late in the evening," Anke said, keeping her voice low. "I've been sent here by Igor Ivanov. We need to talk, urgently."

There was a momentary silence, and she saw Merriden recoil a little in surprise. She could see him eyeing her up, a distinctly suspicious expression on his face.

"Who is Igor Ivanov?" Merriden asked, lowering his tone to match hers.

"I don't have time to play games," Anke said. "You know very well who he is. I have a codeword to use to prove I'm genuine. DAM KEEPER."

Merriden blinked, but didn't move. "What's your name? Have you got any ID? Why are you here without notifying me? I was always told that nobody would come here unless it was an absolute emergency and that there would be a warning if that was going to happen."

Anke could feel her level of irritation rising. Time was too short. She clicked on her phone screen and showed Merriden a scan of her GRU identity pass, which she had downloaded after entering the US.

"There. My GRU credentials," Anke said. "We couldn't take the risk of communicating electronically. This is an emergency, as you can imagine. And I don't want to stand outside your house talking. It's too risky. We don't know who's watching. Can you let me in, please?"

Merriden studied Anke's phone screen. "This photo is of a dark-haired woman," he said, glancing up at her.

"Wig," said Anke, tugging briefly at the corner of her hairpiece, near the temple. "I'm not exactly going to travel into the United States under my real identity, am I?"

Merriden swore softly.

"It seems I have no choice," he said.

"Is there anyone else in the house?" Anke asked.

Merriden shook his head.

"Good."

"Damn it. You'd better come in." There was another rattle as Merriden undid the security chain and swung the door open.

CHAPTER FORTY-TWO

Wednesday, July 5, 2017
  McLean, Virginia

It was almost ten o'clock when the black Toyota Camry drew to a halt in the shadows at the back of the deserted parking lot of the large Methodist church off Dolley Madison Boulevard.

Jayne looked around. The darkness, the trees that shielded the parking lot from the highway, and the cover provided by the church buildings meant that here, right in the southeastern corner of the lot, they were out of sight of anyone driving past.

"This'll do," Jayne said.

Following careful study of a large-scale CIA map and satellite photographs supplied by Neal, she and Joe had decided to approach Frank Merriden's house in Ballantrae Farm Drive from the rear, via a long private lane serving other properties that abutted it.

Jayne's thinking was to sneak into the house and take

Merriden by surprise. That ruled out parking the car in the driveway and ringing the bell or approaching the house from the front at all. Even at night, they might easily be spotted from the house itself and potentially from neighbors' properties.

Because the houses in this neighborhood were built on such large plots among heavy tree cover, it seemed feasible to approach via a more surreptitious route, especially under cover of darkness.

Neal, who was driving the car, had procured the handguns that Jayne and Joe had requested, together with spare magazines and other items, including a lightweight rope ladder that would enable them to scale fences or walls if needed. He also had a small drone equipped with an infrared night-vision camera linked to his phone, on which he could view the images.

All three of them were wearing black long-sleeved jackets, shirts, and trousers and black balaclavas that covered everything apart from mouths and eyes.

Both Jayne and Joe also wore identical GPS watches with an inbuilt emergency alarm. If the relevant button was pressed for more than three seconds, the watch would send an alert to Neal's phone to tell him they were in trouble, together with their precise location.

"Let's get moving," Joe said. "We don't want to get this guy out of bed."

"Any sign of trouble, just call me in," Neal said. "I'm in the mood to beat the shit out of anyone Russia-related."

He was joking, but Jayne didn't smile. "Keep your cool, Neal. I don't want a firefight in there."

"Don't worry. I'll stick to my drone. Will message you with an update when I've checked out the house."

Jayne and Joe climbed out of the Toyota and walked to the eastern edge of the parking lot, where a tall wooden fence marked the boundary between the church property and the private lane off Dolley Madison Boulevard.

Jayne stood on her toes and peered over the fence to check nobody was there. Then she threw the rope ladder over the top, securing it by putting one of the steps over a fence post. They both swiftly climbed over onto the private lane, which was wide enough for only one car.

Jayne pulled the rope ladder over and tucked it beneath her arm. Although there were three other houses off the lane on the left, the deep darkness beneath the trees lining the lane made them virtually invisible.

As they passed one house on the left, a dog barked three times from somewhere inside. Jayne jumped and stopped, half expecting the animal to appear and chase after them.

But the dog went silent once again, and they continued.

At the end of the lane, past the third house, the way ahead was blocked by another fence, behind which Jayne knew was Merriden's property.

"Over we go," she murmured.

She was about to throw the ladder over the fence when from behind them came a bright flash of headlights and the growl of a diesel engine.

"Quick, behind the tree," Joe said.

He dived for the shadow behind a large oak tree on the right side of the lane, and Jayne followed.

They pressed themselves into the space between the tree trunk and the hedge behind it as the car drew nearer. By now, the entire width of the fence they had been about to scale was bathed in bright white halogen light.

Jayne could feel her stomach flip over as she heard the vehicle slow.

Police?

But then the lights swiveled away from the fence as the

car turned into the driveway of the house they had just passed.

A few seconds later, the engine stopped, the lights went off, and there was a click followed by a dull clunk as a car door opened and closed. Then came footsteps and the faint sound of a key in a door.

Then silence once again.

"Wait a few minutes," Joe whispered in Jayne's ear.

Eventually, they reemerged from behind the tree. Jayne threw the rope ladder over the fence of Merriden's garden and they scaled it quickly, landing in thick rhododendron bushes.

Jayne pulled the rope ladder over and placed it at the foot of the fence, covering it with scattered brush. They wouldn't need it again until they exited the site.

Slowly they edged forward, taking extreme care to minimize any noise, until, through the foliage, Jayne could make out the gleam of light from two downstairs windows of Merriden's home. Another few steps and she could make out the outline of the house against the night sky, about forty yards away. It was a large property, with three stories and tall chimneys on both sides.

As she studied the house, her phone vibrated in her pocket. Covering the screen with her hand to prevent the light from showing, she checked it. It was a short message from Neal, updating on the output from his drone camera.

Old silver Honda Accord on front drive. Light in two downstairs windows and hall. Nobody outdoors. Triple garage closed.

Well, Merriden either drove an old Honda or he had a late evening visitor. Given the affluence of the neighborhood and Merriden's high-level job, Jayne guessed the latter. He likely owned a smarter car than an old Honda. That was interesting.

She murmured the news to Joe, who grunted in response. It wasn't going to change anything, even if he did have a friend or colleague visiting. They would have to adapt. They couldn't abort.

Jayne eyed the property again through the leaves. The garage, adjoining the house on the right as they looked at it, would have a connecting door into the house. There was also a white pedestrian door at the rear of the garage, leading onto a patio that separated the rear of the house from the lawn.

She pressed her mouth to Joe's ear. "Small garage door. That's our way in."

Again, Joe grunted his assent. "Can try."

The bushes that formed a semicircle around the lawn at the rear of the house extended to within a few yards of the garage doorway. Jayne and Joe made their way through the foliage until they were close to the garage door. Here they were well out of view of the house windows.

In Jayne's back pocket was a small but extremely useful set of tools she usually brought with her on this type of operation, including a set of pick rakes and a tension wrench. Acquired during her time with MI6, they usually enabled her to pick most locks fairly quickly. She took the kit out of her pocket.

"I'll give it a go first," Jayne murmured. "You keep a lookout."

Joe was equally adept at picking locks, a skill he had picked up many years ago during his time with the CIA in the late 1980s.

Listening and watching carefully, she edged out of the bushes to the white door and bent over the lock. Joe followed and stood nearby.

Without hesitating, she inserted the tension wrench, an L-shaped tool, into the base of the keyhole. Then the rake, a three-pin Bogota, went into the top of the lock. As she turned the wrench clockwise a little, she simultaneously worked the rake in and out. Gradually, all the pins in the lock were prevented from dropping, and the lock clicked open.

Joe stepped over and tapped her on the shoulder in appreciation.

There were two cars in the garage, a Mercedes station wagon and an Audi Q7 SUV, both new. In front of them, against the rear wall, was a long workbench with an array of tools.

On the far side, behind the Audi, was another door, which was closed. Jayne and Joe made their way past the cars and stood next to the door.

There was a keyhole, so Jayne bent down and looked through it. All she could see was a washing machine. A utility room. She then pressed her ear to the keyhole and could hear the faintest sound of distant voices, one of which sounded like a woman, but it was impossible to pick up what was being said.

Jayne carefully tried the door, which proved to be unlocked, but there was no way of knowing what was on the other side.

They would just have to take a risk.

Jayne turned and looked at Joe, who just nodded, indicating she should open it. He had removed his Beretta from his pocket and now clicked off the safety and gently racked the slide, loading the chamber.

Jayne took her Walther from her jacket pocket and did likewise.

Then, with her gun in her right hand, she slowly pushed down on the door handle with her left and pulled it toward her, praying that it didn't squeak or rattle. Thankfully, it didn't.

She opened it six inches, then stood silently, listening and looking. The utility room was long and narrow, with the washing machine, a tumble drier, a stainless-steel sink, a chest freezer, and a tall fridge lining the opposite wall. At the far end was another door, which was open a couple of inches.

The sound of voices that she had picked up through the keyhole was now slightly more distinct. But they were coming from somewhere much deeper within the house, and there was no way of making out the actual conversation. One thing seemed clear, though: there was one woman and one man, unless there were others who were remaining silent. The woman was presumably the owner of the Honda parked outside.

Jayne looked at Joe, who pointed through the door, indicating that she should continue.

She opened the door fully and stepped softly through to the other door, holding her Walther ready.

Through the slightly open door, Jayne could see a large, square kitchen with an enormous gas oven and stove and a central granite-topped island on which stood three bottles of red wine. In the far corner was another door, fully open. Through the door was a carpeted corridor with paintings visible on the wall.

Now the voices could be heard much more distinctly. They seemed to be coming from a room adjoining the kitchen.

" . . . make the call now, give the code name," the woman said. "Then tell him Operation Noi must be implemented immediately. You understand?"

She spoke fluent English but with a distinct accent, which Jayne realized was either Russian or from one of the former Soviet satellite states. That, and the reference to Operation Noi, sent Jayne's alert system into high gear and she glanced at Joe, who raised both eyebrows.

There was a pause before the man replied in a deep bass voice. "Sure, I will make the call. But I still don't understand why the need to send you from Moscow to tell me this. Why not use the usual communication channel? Surely that is far quicker and less risky. This doesn't make any sense."

There was a distinctly anxious note to the voice, which Jayne recognized from the Langley meeting a few weeks earlier as Merriden's.

"Just get the phone," the woman said.

There came the sound of footsteps on floorboards, the squeak of a drawer or cupboard being opened, a rattle, and then more footsteps.

"Is it charged?" the woman asked.

"I always keep it charged."

"Does he pick the messages up immediately?" the woman asked.

"No," Merriden said. "But I usually message his burner."

"Then call his normal phone. "

"That's not—"

"Just do it," the woman interrupted.

There came a series of faint beeps, presumably as Merriden started to dial.

Jayne turned to Joe and leaned in close to his ear. "We have to stop this," she said.

As Joe nodded, Merriden's voice came again. The call must have been answered immediately.

"This is DAM KEEPER, repeat, this is DAM KEEPER."

After a momentary pause, he spoke again, his voice rising a few tones.

"Activate Operation Noi. Repeat, activate Operation Noi now. Immediately."

There was a slight pause.

Jayne pushed the kitchen door open and strode toward the far door.

"Yes, I said *now*," Merriden said. "Do it right *now*. Understood?" A pause. "Good."

There was another beep. Jayne assumed he had terminated the call.

Merriden spoke again. "Okay, it's done. Now you can get out. And tell Ivanov I don't appreciate the in-person visit. Use the damn phone next time."

"Ivanov has no interest in talking to you anymore," the woman replied, her voice level.

There was a click, and the distinct sound of a pistol's slide being racked.

"No!" the man's voice rose to a squeal. "No, no, no! What the hell are you doing?"

Shit.

Jayne's stomach tightened like a vise. She didn't hesitate. She accelerated into a sprint out of the kitchen and ran out the door into the hallway, holding her gun in firing position.

As she turned right toward the voices, she heard the man yell. "No, please, no! Don't do it!"

Only a few feet along the corridor was another open door. Jayne realized instantly they had to be in that room. There was no other option.

She skidded to a halt outside the door, gun raised in front of her, just as there came two earsplitting gunshots in rapid succession.

Jayne didn't stop to think.

She saw a blonde woman, side on to Jayne, right arm outstretched, holding a gun.

The woman must have seen Jayne in her peripheral vision. In a split second, she turned on her heel, swiveled her gun, and fired in Jayne's direction.

Jayne, acting on instinct, ducked sharply down to her left as the round whined past her.

As she moved, Jayne kept her focus on the woman's upper body and fired twice, just as the woman pulled her trigger again.

The woman's round smashed into the wall behind Jayne but in the same split second, she screamed as Jayne's rounds struck her.

She fell backward and sideways, her left arm jerking reactively upward. Her gun clattered to the floor from her right hand and skittered across the floorboards into the wall.

The woman fell hard, banging her head on the floor, moaned loudly, then lay still.

Next to the wall a few feet away to the right, the mustachioed figure of Frank Merriden was also lying flat on his back, motionless, his arms and legs splayed at odd angles. Blood was pulsing from one gunshot wound in his forehead and another in his left chest.

CHAPTER FORTY-THREE

Wednesday, July 5, 2017
  McLean, Virginia

Jayne crouched over the unconscious blonde woman lying on the living room floor. Her right arm had been shattered by the two rounds Jayne had fired, one of which had hit her in the bicep, the other a little lower, near the elbow. Blood was pulsing from both wounds.

But Jayne then noticed the woman's hairline. Dark hairs were protruding out from beneath the blonde, and Jayne realized she was wearing a wig.

Jayne grabbed the woman's left wrist and checked her pulse, which was a little fast but seemed strong.

She turned to Joe. "Better call the paramedics," she said. "She's going to fade fast, losing blood at this rate."

Joe nodded. "I'll use the house phone, not my cell." He walked toward a landline telephone that stood on a coffee table next to one of the sofas.

As Joe took out a handkerchief and used it to pick up the

phone, Jayne stood and walked back into the hallway. On a row of coat hooks was a silk scarf. Jayne took it and returned to the living room, where she wound it tightly around the woman's upper arm, pulled it tight, and knotted it. That was the closest she could get to a tourniquet. It should save her from bleeding out until the paramedics arrived.

There was no point checking Merriden. The bullet wound in his forehead told its own story.

Joe came off the line to the emergency medical services operator. "They're coming. They'll be ten minutes. We'll leave the front door open for them and get out of here fast; otherwise the cops will hold us up for hours, days even. We can't afford that."

"Agreed," Jayne said. "Vic can deal with the red tape later."

While Joe hurried off down the hallway to open the front door, Jayne tugged at the woman's wig, which eventually came free. Sure enough, beneath it was a mop of curly black hair.

Leonova.

Jayne now recognized her from the CCTV images she had seen from the Himmel Bar.

"Bloody hell," she said as Joe returned. "It's Anke Leonova, the GRU woman who honey-trapped Aidan Scarpa."

Joe stared at her. "Can't be."

"It bloody well is. She's the one who tried to blow me up on the boat in Vienna. Her and her GRU friend."

Only then did Jayne glance at the cell phone that was lying on the floor next to Merriden's body. She walked over and picked up the device, which was still switched on. It was a basic Samsung, presumably a burner. She bent down and went through Merriden's pockets, which contained a new iPhone. The Samsung was certainly not the general's main device.

Jayne tapped on the Samsung's screen and checked the list

of recently dialed numbers. Then she used her own phone to take a photo of the list. The top one must have been the call Merriden had made under duress from Leonova to activate Operation Noi.

For a second, Jayne thought of calling the number, but then decided against it. Doing so would likely drive the person to ground and make them impossible to trace. Anyway, dealing with a Russian sleeper terrorist on US soil was a job for the FBI or Homeland Security.

She placed both of Merriden's phones in her pocket. They could be scoured for more information and evidence later.

There was no doubting the urgency that Merriden had injected into his instructions.

And it meant that Jayne now needed to respond in kind.

She toggled over to the secure encrypted communications app on her own phone, then tapped on Vic's number.

Vic was still in his office only a mile or two away from Merriden's house and had just come off a call to Charles Deacon at the White House.

"Listen, Vic, things have moved fast," Jayne said, phone clamped to her ear as she followed Joe out of the house the way they had come in. As she walked, she gave a swift account of what had happened.

"Bastards. Unbelievable," Vic said.

"I should've moved faster," Jayne said. "I'll take the blame for that."

"Not your fault," Vic said. "Great job done."

"One thing's certain," Jayne said. "The GRU sent Leonova to force Merriden to activate Operation Noi, then kill him to cover their tracks. And we've confirmed he was the DAM KEEPER. We need to trace whoever Merriden was talking to —fast. I got the number from his phone—I decided against calling it. Let me give it to you."

Jayne read out the phone number she had taken from Merriden's burner.

"Thanks," Vic said. When he initially answered Jayne's call, he had sounded somewhat weary, but her news had injected a new energy into his voice. "I'll get Alex to track this down—I'll get him out of bed. They should be able to pinpoint where the phone was last used and trace its position live if it's still switched on."

Following a promotion, Alex Goode was the director of the NSA's signals intelligence directorate at the agency's Fort Meade headquarters in Maryland. He was now running the agency's global operations for collection of data, including hacks and tracing of phones, emails, computer systems, and radar and weapons systems.

"We'll need a jet or a chopper on standby for when we get a location, then," Jayne said as she exited the garage.

"We'll do that," Vic said. "I'll need to get back to Bonfield and get the feds involved too now. They'll need to come and clean up everything at Merriden's house. And they'll need to take charge of Leonova in the hospital. We can't let the police have her."

"Good," Jayne said.

"You and Joe get out of there right now and get yourselves back to my office—quick as you can," Vic said. "You've done your job. I'll fix things with Bonfield."

"We're leaving now," Jayne said as she followed Joe through the rhododendrons. She ended the call.

A few minutes later, just as Neal drove them out of the church parking lot, an ambulance with siren blaring flew past them in the opposite direction and turned sharply right into Ballantrae Farm Drive.

CHAPTER FORTY-FOUR

Wednesday, July 5, 2017
  Arizona

The tall, dark-haired man, whose US passport said he was named Jakub Volker, leaned over the safety barrier, folded his arms, and stood still for a moment. Then he tilted his head forward and stared down the 726-foot wall of concrete that stretched below him—the Hoover Dam, which had blocked the mighty Colorado River in its tracks since the 1930s.

A short time earlier, he'd received the call from the DAM KEEPER. He'd known it would happen at some point. Normally, the guy messaged his burner phone, which he kept hidden at his house. He had certainly never called his work phone before. That was a first.

This was undoubtedly urgent.

It was time to kick Operation Noi into action and do his bit for the Rodina, the Motherland.

The DAM KEEPER's voice had sounded different from the previous times they had spoken. It was distinctly strained and tense. Volker assumed that was likely because the operation he was now finally setting in motion was such a major one, with consequences that would certainly be devastating.

Volker, a dam maintenance deputy, gazed down at the base of the huge structure, where the Colorado resumed its long flow southward toward Mexico and the Gulf of California. Behind him, at the back of the dam, the second tallest in the United States, was Lake Mead, the country's largest reservoir, 112 miles long.

He could see the enormous twin concrete turbine halls that stood on each side of the river far below. They formed the heart of the hydroelectric power plant that had been built as an integral part of the dam. There were seventeen turbines altogether, eight in the hall on the Nevada, or western, side of the river, nine on the Arizona side.

Each of the turbines was driven by a fast-flowing stream of water that arrived through thirteen-foot diameter concrete pipes from Lake Mead. Together, the turbines could provide enough electricity to power 1.7 million homes across the region, while the reservoir supplied drinking water to about twenty million people.

At this time of year, Lake Mead and the Colorado River were packed with tourists, sailing and motorboat users, fishermen, and campers. More than a million people a year visited the dam, most of them during the summer months.

But Volker tried not to think about them; they would be an unavoidable casualty.

Instead, he walked to the elevator, took the long ride down in the ornate car, with its elegant marble and brass fittings, and returned to the control room near the base of the dam.

Four men were sitting at computer terminals at an island in the middle of the room. Beyond them, red lights winked on a monitoring panel that covered almost all of one wall.

The team was controlling the amount of power output generated by the turbines. The computerized control system automatically calculated and implemented the volume of water required for the turbines to deliver that specific output. The resultant electricity was then distributed via high-voltage power lines across the states of Nevada, Arizona, and California.

"I'm done here," Volker said. "I'm on my way, guys. Good to catch up with you all. See you soon." It was his usual farewell. He needed to keep everything appearing normal.

There were grunts and nods from the night-duty team, two hours into their shift. Volker had been there for his usual catch-up with the team leader, Archie Davies.

Davies stood and walked over to shake his hand. "Good to see you, too. Take it easy," he said. "When will we see you next?"

"Not sure," Volker said. "But I'll be in touch in the next day or two."

"You staying with your lady in Vegas tonight?" Archie asked.

"I think I'll drive home, actually," Volker said. "Got a lot to do in the morning."

"You're going to drive all the way home? That's a long way, buddy, and it's late. You sure?"

"I'll be okay. There'll be no traffic on the highway," Volker said.

"Drive carefully, then."

"Of course. Will do."

Davies looked at him and paused for a second. "Are you okay?"

"Yes, all good."

"You sure?"

Volker nodded. "Absolutely."

He turned and headed out the door. He had spent most of

the past decade working for the Bureau of Reclamation, the federal government agency that was part of the Department of the Interior and that owned about 340 dams across the country, of which the Hoover was the largest. There were fifteen dams in total up and down the Colorado River.

However, despite being well-liked by colleagues, none of them knew Volker's true identity or background story.

Volker wasn't his real name. It was Oleg Spassky.

And when colleagues asked about his accent, which most people did, he told them all he was born in Prague, in the Czech Republic. That wasn't true either, because he originated from St. Petersburg, in Russia. Pretty much the only factual part of his backstory was his age, forty-one, and the girlfriend he had acquired a few years earlier who worked as a casino manager in Las Vegas, thirty miles away to the northwest. He had lied to her about everything, too.

In fact, Volker was an illegal, an undeclared operative for the GRU, the Russian foreign military intelligence service.

Because of his previous engineering experience with dams in Russia and parts of Eastern Europe, he had been recruited very deliberately by the GRU's Department 5, which ran the so-called illegals program. They had originally sent him to the United States using a false Maltese passport, which they told him was a well proven method. It had certainly worked.

He had then been planted in a dams maintenance role with the Bureau of Reclamation. From then on, Volker had been controlled from a distance by the man who had just called him, whom he knew only as the DAM KEEPER. He had no idea what his real name or job or address was.

Volker swiftly proved himself to be highly capable and had been promoted several times, which involved moving up and down the Colorado River to work at various dams. After five years in the US, he applied for and was granted residency.

He tugged at his goatee. He now had some work to do.

Thankfully, he had done almost all the preparation for this day long in advance. In practical terms, he had to take only a few relatively straightforward steps to set the wheels in motion.

But that couldn't happen for several hours, probably close to sunrise the following morning.

Volker got into the elevator car again. As it took him up to the top of the dam, where he had left his Ford Ranger pickup in the employee parking lot on the Nevada side of Lake Mead, he took out his phone. Instinctively, he didn't like the fact that the DAM KEEPER had called his work cell phone. Although he knew the guy was using a disposable burner, which he would most likely get rid of, he nevertheless felt a little concerned. Maybe it would be best to turn his own phone off while he was traveling and until the deed was done. He didn't want to run any risk of being traced. Volker pressed firmly on the power button until the screen went black.

The elevator doors opened, and Volker stepped out into the fresh air. He now faced a long drive through the night, followed by another, even longer drive.

The DAM KEEPER had told him he always needed to be ready to move fast if required. Well, tonight he was going to have to move far as well as fast.

In the morning, the dominoes would start to fall. He had done his research very carefully, so he knew.

It was going to be spectacular, that was for sure.

The Kremlin would love it.

* * *

Wednesday, July 5, 2017
Washington, DC

. . .

When Jayne arrived with Neal and Joe outside Vic's office on the seventh floor of the CIA's Original Headquarters Building, his executive assistant, Helen Lake, stood and greeted them.

Like most employees at Langley, Helen accepted the long hours required without objection. As usual, she had a mug of steaming black coffee on her desk.

"Go in," Helen said. "He's on a conference call with Alex Goode about that phone number."

"Thanks, Helen," Jayne said.

Helen pushed her long red hair over her shoulder, opened the door to Vic's office, and ushered them through.

Sure enough, Goode's slightly geeky-looking face was peering at them from the large secure video monitor on Vic's wall, his sandy hair perennially combed over the top of his balding head in an increasingly vain attempt to hide it.

"Come in," Vic said. "Alex's team has moved fast on the cell phone that Merriden called. Alex, do you want to tell them?"

"Ah, Jayne, Neal, Joe," Goode said. They all knew each other. "I was just telling Vic. The traces on that number put it at the Hoover Dam down in Arizona when Merriden made the call to it. We're now pulling out all the stops trying to find out who it belongs to. Unfortunately, it's been switched off."

Jayne stopped dead. "The Hoover?"

Vic nodded. "Unfortunately, yes. I'm about to call Bonfield. The feds will need to take charge of this, even if so far we've been doing his job for him. I don't want to piss him off any more than he was when I told him about what happened at Merriden's house."

Jayne felt the skin across her scalp prickle. She had been to the Hoover Dam several years earlier as part of a house-boat trip on Lake Mead, so she had an immediate image in her mind of the enormous devastation that would ensue if the dam was destroyed.

"Bloody hell," Jayne said. "Yes, call Bonfield. But we need to get to Arizona immediately."

"You and Neal can go as soon as we've done what we need to do here," Vic said. "There's a Gulfstream on standby at Dulles. I'll stay here and work on this with Joe and the techs."

Jayne removed the two phones she had taken from Frank Merriden from her pocket and placed them on Vic's desk. "You'd better take these. Merriden's burner and main phone. They'll likely be useful."

Vic nodded. "We'll need to hand them over to the feds, but we can download the contents quickly here first. The techs can go through everything on them while you're flying."

"I agree I should stay here," Joe said. "If the techs pull anything on Merriden's Russian contacts, I may be able to help with the background on them."

Vic stepped over to the door and asked Helen to call the technical team's night manager to come up from his ground-floor office immediately and collect both devices for analysis.

On the monitor, Goode could be seen tapping at his desktop PC. He then peered at the screen, reading something.

"Guys, I've just had a message from the team," he said, still looking at his screen rather than into his camera. "The phone belongs to someone named Jakub Volker. Works for the Bureau of Reclamation."

"Must be an employee at the Hoover," Neal said.

"I'll call Bonfield now," Vic said, picking up his phone from his desk. "He can get the dam security people at Hoover to grab him."

CHAPTER FORTY-FIVE

Thursday, July 6, 2017
  Arizona

More than three hours after leaving Washington's Dulles International, the CIA's Gulfstream G200 had begun its descent toward Boulder City, the nearest airport to the Hoover Dam, when the satellite phone on the table in front of Jayne rang.

She had finally started dozing, and the beeping made her jump.

Neal, who was sitting on the opposite side of the four-seater table, picked up the receiver and, on hearing who the caller was, switched it to loudspeaker mode so Jayne could hear. "It's Vic," he said.

"One of my team has located a night shift control room manager at Hoover Dam," Vic said. "We've got him on the other line. Archie Davies is his name. Stand by. They're going to patch him into this call so we can all talk to him. He appears to have had last contact with Jakub Volker a few hours ago."

There was a pause, a couple of clicks, then a long beep.

"Hello, Mr. Davies," Vic said. He briefly introduced himself and did likewise for Neal and Jayne, explaining they were in midair en route to Boulder.

"I know my colleagues haven't been able to explain to you exactly why we need to talk to you," Vic continued. "But it is very important. Can you just tell us about Jakub Volker? I understand you were the last one to speak with him at Hoover?"

"Yes, sir," Davies said, his voice sounding remote and tinny. "He left after meeting with me and the rest of the team. Listen, what is this about? I don't usually get calls from the CIA, and the FBI has also been calling my boss here. Do you mind telling me why you're asking about Jakub?"

"It's a national security issue," Vic said. "I can't say too much right now. What frame of mind was Volker in?"

Davies cleared his throat. "Well, I did think he seemed distracted. I even asked him if he was okay. And the odd thing was, despite finishing late here, he said he was going to drive home. Normally he just goes to his girlfriend's place in Vegas if he's working here. It's nearby."

"*If* he's working there?" Jayne asked. "Doesn't he normally do so?"

"No."

"Where is he based, then?" Jayne asked.

"He's normally based at one of the other dams. Glen Canyon," Davies said. "He just comes here for occasional meetings. Like I sometimes go to Glen Canyon and other dams. We brainstorm ideas, help each other."

Jayne tried to visualize a map of Arizona and the region around the Colorado River, but Neal beat her to it.

"Glen Canyon must be several hundred miles from Hoover, though," Neal said. "You're telling me he lives there? And decided to drive home through the night?"

"Correct. That was what I thought odd," Davies said. "It's three hundred miles to his place in Page, right near the dam. He wouldn't get there until four in the morning. That's why I wondered if he was okay."

Jayne didn't like the sound of that. "Did he say why?" she asked.

"No. Just said he had a lot to do in the morning."

Jayne caught Neal's eye. His forehead was creased, and he was fingering his chin.

"Can you please tell me what this is about?" Davies said. "Is this a terrorism situation or something?"

There was a pause. Jayne decided to let Vic answer that question. She could see he was going to have to explain more to get answers.

"It could well be," Vic said. "I'll be frank with you. We have reason to believe he's planning to blow up a dam. We thought it was Hoover. But maybe we were wrong about that."

"Holy shit!" Davies said. "Blow it up? You've got to be kidding me. No, I can tell you're not kidding."

"Unfortunately not," Vic said.

"How the hell do you know that?" Davies said. "Why think that? I've worked with him for years. He's good. He can't be a terrorist. He's a foreigner, of course. Czech, I believe. But not a terrorist."

"Never mind how we know," Vic said. "We just do. And we need to alert your security people at Glen Canyon —immediately."

"If it's true, then you need to do a whole lot more than that," Davies said, a note of panic in his voice. "If he blows up

Glen Canyon he's basically blowing up Hoover too—and all the other dams downriver from it. And their hydro power plants. Knock one over and the others will go. All of them. And the lights could go out across the region—that'd be a lot of power generation destroyed."

"Really?" Vic asked. "Would that actually happen?"

"Of course it would," Davies snapped. "The volume of water behind Glen Canyon, in Lake Powell—it'd knock everything over, I'm telling you. It would be the biggest disaster you could imagine."

There was silence for a second.

"You're sure about this?" Jayne asked.

"Listen, ma'am," Davies said. "That's a seven-hundred-foot dam you're talking about. Eight and a half trillion gallons of water are stacked up behind it. It'd go down the Colorado —boom—like a tidal wave, a tsunami. It'd destroy everything in its path, then straight over the top of Hoover and take that dam with it, together with its power plant. Then you've got double the amount of water barreling down the river."

"Then presumably the next dam would also go?" Neal asked.

"Of course. The next one downriver from the Hoover is Davis Dam. That would be gone, then Parker would go, and the others downstream. You'd have tens of thousands of people dead. Towns destroyed. I'm telling you that's what would happen. I know."

"How could he destroy a dam that size?" Jayne asked. "Would explosive even do the job?" She was no engineer, but it was obvious that to destroy a concrete structure of that enormous scale would be difficult.

"Explosive, yes, if there's enough and if it's put in the right place," Davies said. "There's ten million tons of concrete in that dam. But all you need is a small hole, maybe five inches across. After that, water pressure does the rest. Inside a few minutes it would become a ten-inch hole, then fifty inches, then fifty feet. Then the whole thing would go down. It would have to be done by someone who knew where to put the explosive. And someone who had the access to bring it in."

"And you think Jakub Volker would know where to put it?" Neal asked. "And he would have the access?"

"He's the maintenance expert at the dam," Davies said. "He's good. A very bright engineer. He'd know. And of course he would have the access. He works in the bowels of these dams every day of his life—like I do."

Jayne leaned back in her seat.

Davies clearly did know what he was talking about.

And what he was saying made complete logical sense.

The destruction of Glen Canyon Dam would have far-reaching and devastating consequences far beyond just the local area around it. It could be the single most deadly disaster in US history.

"Alternatively, could he have already planted explosive at Hoover Dam and has just run—to get away before it goes off, or before he triggers it?" Jayne asked.

"Shit, I don't know," Davies said. "My God. I'm not sure if he would have had the opportunity. I don't think he spends enough time here. But now you're making me wonder."

"From what you're saying, he knows Glen Canyon Dam best if he works there?" she asked.

"Yes, correct."

Jayne felt a thin film of sweat forming on her forehead. "We need to decide where we head, Mr. Davies. Hoover or Glen Canyon. Which is his most likely target?"

There was an audible groan from Davies. "I don't know if I can answer that question," he said.

"You're right, Jayne," Vic said. "We have to make a call."

Jayne exhaled and glanced at Neal across the table.

This was impossible. Surely, she told herself, if Volker really was planning to destroy a dam, he would do it where he had most opportunity to prepare and execute such an operation.

"My gut tells me Glen Canyon," she said. "He knows that best. He works there. Let's tell the pilot to take us to Glen Canyon instead of Hoover. Which airport is it up there? I can't think."

"Page Municipal," Davies said. "Ten minutes from the dam."

"I agree," Neal said. "Vic?"

"Think that's the right call," Vic said.

"I'll tell the pilot," Neal said. He stood, walked toward the front of the plane, and opened the door that led to the cockpit.

"Vic, can you get Bonfield's guys to Glen Canyon from Page, and to Hoover from Vegas?" Jayne asked. "If we go to Glen Canyon, we need to be sure Hoover's being searched and made secure and safe."

There was a short silence.

"Vegas, yes, there's an FBI field office there," Vic said. "I'm certain Bonfield's already sending his people to Hoover. But there's no FBI office in Page, or anywhere near Glen Canyon, as far as I know. Phoenix is the main Arizona office. There are a few satellite offices. Nothing in Page, I don't think. It'll have to be the local police."

"Bloody hell," Jayne muttered. "If there's no FBI in Page, it's even more important we fly there instead and leave Hoover to the feds."

The chances of getting a fast, quality response from the Page police department in the middle of the night were likely not great, she guessed. But there was no alternative.

"I agree with you," Vic said. "I'll double-check the feds are covering Hoover. And we'll get a police car lined up in Page to take you to the dam when you land."

Jayne's mind was whirring now, going through a mental checklist. "Mr. Davies," she said. "Can we have your cell number so we can reach you quickly if needed?"

Davies read out a number, which Jayne tapped into her phone. She assumed Vic had done likewise.

"Also, do you have a photograph of Volker you can send us?" Jayne asked. "We'll need to know what he looks like. And also his car details."

"There is a photo and vehicle details on the system," Davies said. "I will send it all to you."

"Thanks," Jayne said. She read out her cell phone number.

"You've been very helpful, Mr. Davies," Vic said. "We'll be in touch again soon." There was a click as he cut Davies out of the call.

"I've a feeling this guy Volker, or whatever his name really is, must have something well planned out," Jayne said. "He must have, if he's driven through the night to get back to Glen Canyon."

"I fear you're right," Vic said, his tone grim. "But we're going to have to make sure the bastard doesn't succeed. I'll notify security at Glen Canyon."

As he spoke, the Gulfstream banked a little to port.

Jayne reached down and took her Walther from her bag on the floor. She had refilled the magazine following the gunfight at Merriden's house, and now, more out of habit than anything, double-checked to ensure the chamber was empty and the safety was on.

Neal reappeared through the cockpit door.

"It's going to take around half an hour, maybe forty minutes to Page, according to the pilot," he said.

Jayne winced. "Shit."

Neal looked at her. "What if Volker has something else planned—not Hoover Dam, not Glen Canyon Dam, but something we've not considered?"

Jayne shook her head. "I don't know, Neal. I just don't know."

CHAPTER FORTY-SIX

Thursday, July 6, 2017
Glen Canyon Dam, Arizona

It was still dark, although there was a faint glow in the sky to the east, as Jakub Volker steered his Ford Ranger along Highway 89 over the Glen Canyon Dam Bridge. He glanced to his left over the floodlit dam, nearly three hundred yards north of the bridge, its sheer vertical white concrete face stretching down hundreds of feet to the Colorado River below.

At the foot of the dam, running two hundred yards across the full width of the canyon, stood the power generation plant, housing eight enormous turbines driven by water flowing through pipes from Lake Powell.

Somehow, it was hard to believe this day had come. Volker had been planning it for so long.

But there were still hurdles to overcome. The timing of the call from the DAM KEEPER had been a very long way from ideal, coming at a time when he was several hours' drive away, at the Hoover Dam.

Volker drove off the bridge and turned immediately left onto the access road on the east side of the dam for employees and contract workers. The visitor center and parking lot were on the west side.

Now, despite his lack of sleep, Volker felt wide awake, his senses working in top gear, and he felt a surge of adrenaline rush through him.

The several cans of energy drink he had consumed, combined with strong caffeine tablets, had helped keep him awake during the long drive through the night. Interstate 15, and then Highway 89, which had been largely deserted as he made his way east.

Normally, he made the journey during the day and enjoyed the dry, rocky scenery, with its stark and barren features. At night, it was much harder to concentrate, with only white painted lines on the blacktop to focus on.

Volker's headlights picked out the DO NOT ENTER signs and concrete barriers ahead of him. He slowly steered around them, lowered his driver's side window, and came to a halt next to the security building in front of the closed electric steel gate that barred entry into the site.

A uniformed guard, David O'Hara, whom he knew well, emerged from the security building and came toward his window.

Volker was already on edge. But there was something about the way O'Hara was walking, a brisk stride rather than his usual saunter, that set an alarm bell ringing inside his head.

A second later, the alarm bell doubled in volume when he spotted another security guard come out of the building and follow O'Hara. Never, in the whole time Volker had worked at the dam, had two guards come out to his pickup before, especially at this hour.

There was something wrong here. Volker knew that instinctively.

Had these guards been tipped off somehow?

"Jakub, you're very early," O'Hara said. His voice sounded different, strained.

"Morning, David," Volker said, deciding to stick to the script he had prepared. "Way too early, you're right. But I've got a team of guys coming in first thing to do some repair work down in the plant. I need to get the portable generators down there for them. It'll take me a couple of hours, at least."

It was very unusual for Volker to arrive so early, although he had done so before on a handful of occasions when his work schedule demanded it.

"No rest for the wicked," O'Hara said. He made a note on a timesheet fastened to his clipboard, which was used to log all incoming vehicles.

"Can I go through?" Volker asked.

"I'm going to have to ask you to wait here for a minute. We need to check something."

Wait here a minute? Shit.

That had never happened before, either. Normally, O'Hara waved him straight through.

"Why? What's going on, David?" Volker said, trying to keep his voice as level as he could. Behind O'Hara, he could see the other guard, who had taken a few steps backward, tapping on the keypad of his walkie-talkie.

What to do?

"A few things are happening on top of the dam. Don't worry," O'Hara said. He turned around and looked at his colleague, his back now to Volker.

Volker reached down unobtrusively with his left hand to the storage compartment at the bottom of the door, where he had placed his Glock 19 pistol, a round loaded in its chamber, which was how he always left it in the car, just in case.

He could see the other guard still tapping on his walkie-talkie. There was absolutely no doubt that within seconds, he would be telling someone that Volker had arrived.

This was not a time to hesitate.

There was too much at stake.

Volker picked up the Glock, transferred it to his right hand, and then without pausing, raised it and fired two shots in rapid succession at O'Hara, one of which smashed into the back of his head, the other into his upper torso.

O'Hara fell forward, arms spreadeagled, and hit the floor face-first, just as his colleague turned around to look, walkie-talkie still in hand.

Without pausing, Volker fired two more shots at the other guard, both of which struck him in the center of his chest, throwing him backward onto the concrete, where he lay still, his head twisted at an odd angle.

Volker got out of the Ranger, leaving the engine running, walked quickly over to O'Hara, and unclipped the remote control for the security gate from his belt. He had seen the guard use it on many occasions.

He pressed the top button, and to Volker's relief, the huge steel gate began to slide slowly open.

While the gate was opening, Volker grabbed O'Hara beneath his armpits and dragged him through the open door of the security office, leaving a trail of blood on the floor. He dropped the guard's body behind the long front counter, out of sight. He then repeated the exercise with the other security guard's corpse.

After shutting the security office door, Volker got back into the pickup, pushed down on the accelerator, and slowly steered through the gate, then followed the access road around a curve to the left. He drove onto the white concrete surface of the dam itself, which was more than thirty feet wide at the top, and parked next to a row of twelve other vehicles. By eight o'clock, there would be many more cars here.

Somewhat to his surprise and relief, there was nobody in sight, and no sign of police vehicles or officers.

Volker picked up his white hard hat from the rear seat, put it on, and pushed the Glock into his waistband. He then got out of the Ranger, locked it, and walked a few yards to the east elevator shaft, which was built into the front, down-stream face of the dam and stuck up above the top like a square turret.

Unlike the west elevator shaft, used by visitors and tourists, this one was only for employees. Both shafts ran from the top of the dam down 528 feet, almost to the bottom of the 710-foot structure at river level. From the elevator lobby at the bottom, there were tunnels leading out the front of the dam to the power generation plant and the turbines hall.

As he drew near the elevator lobby, another security guard walked out of it and stopped dead, staring at Volker. He was also carrying a walkie-talkie. Volker recognized him but couldn't remember his name.

"What are you doing here?" the guard asked, placing both hands on his hips.

"Got an early start," Volker said. "Big job to do down in the turbine hall." As he spoke, he reached into his waistband and pulled out the Glock.

The guard took a step backward. "No, no, don't do that," he squawked, raising both hands above his head. "No, please."

But Volker fired two shots straight into the guard's face. He collapsed to the ground.

Volker strode over to the guard, lifted him under the armpits, dragged him to the cleaner's closet next to the elevator, and shoved the body inside among buckets, mops, and a vacuum cleaner.

He then shut the closet door, hurried to the elevator doors, and pressed the call button.

The elevator door opened instantly.

After years working at Glen Canyon, Volker had an intimate knowledge of the maze of horizontal tunnels—sometimes called adits—galleries, chambers, rooms, and vertical stairwells and walkways inside the huge concrete structure. All were accessible via a series of stopping points for the two elevators, as well as foundation tunnels that led through the bedrock on either side of the dam.

The internal tunnels, most of them five or six feet wide and seven and a half feet high, were for many purposes, including checks on the dam structure. This included monitoring for water seepage and leaks, the integrity of the concrete, and for movement, using vertical plumb lines inside special wells.

The longest of the horizontal tunnels was the so-called filling line gallery, 235 feet below the top level and slightly nearer to the upstream, or rear, side of the dam than the front. Among its many functions, it gave access to the huge pipes that funneled water from Lake Powell to the hydroelectric generation turbines so they could be checked and repaired if necessary.

Volker was heading to the elevator stop that served that gallery. Very quickly, the elevator car was descending at a pace fast enough to make his stomach feel as though it had been left behind.

The elevator slowed to a halt, the doors opened, and Volker exited. The well-lit lobby area outside the elevator doors led into a short tunnel that took him to the long, curving horizontal gallery that ran almost the full length of the dam. There he turned left, heading toward the western side of the dam.

This was now a can't-fail operation. With three dead guards and doubtless a high-level alert out among the remainder of the security and other staff who were spread out at various places through the dam, he needed to press ahead and somehow ensure he succeeded.

Very soon, the police would also be here, that was for certain.

Quite how the plan had become known to others Volker had no idea, and he didn't intend to waste his energy and thoughts on it right now, as there was nothing he could do about it.

The plan had been in place for a long time. It centered around the amount of maintenance work required within the dam, which was extensive. It was a never-ending task. And so the requirement for portable generators to power all kinds of tools and equipment in areas where there was no power supply was significant.

Volker's team stored the 3.7-kilowatt diesel generators in large, wheeled plastic crates, quite similar to those used to pack belongings when moving to a new house. That way, they were kept free of dust and dirt and, at around 210 pounds in weight, could easily be moved to wherever they were needed.

He kept the crates and generators in a chamber just a short distance along the filling line gallery from the tunnel to the elevator.

Over the last couple of years, Volker had gradually brought additional wheeled crates down to the chamber and stowed them out of sight in a second storage room at the rear, which he kept locked. Now there were fourteen of them in the room.

However, these crates did not contain portable generators.

ANDREW TURPIN

Rather, they were all filled with small pale gray granules that had no smell but were extremely deadly when prepared in the correct way.

It was ammonium nitrate, much like the dry agricultural fertilizer used by farmers to feed their crops.

Ammonium nitrate became extremely combustible when mixed with diesel fuel, or fuel oil, which was the magic, really explosive, ingredient in his bomb. The granules of ammonium nitrate were actually more of an accelerant.

When combined, the two elements—ammonium nitrate and fuel oil—provided an astonishingly highly powered explosive known as ANFO.

Sourcing and storing the ammonium nitrate granules had been the most difficult part of Volker's plan. The material had been obtained by some other contact of the DAM KEEPER's, who stole it from farms in various parts of the United States. It had arrived at his home piecemeal in plastic sacks, and he had brought it into the dam in small quantities over several months.

Sourcing the diesel fuel wasn't a problem at all, because it was needed to power the portable generators. There were more than twenty plastic one-gallon containers of diesel standing on a shelf next to the generators, and Volker intended to simply use those.

Volker opened the door of the chamber, went inside, and closed the door behind him. He then wheeled three of the crates containing the generators over to the door. If anyone happened to come in, which was extremely unlikely, especially at this time of the morning, he had a ready-made explanation for his presence there.

At this level inside the dam, the concrete structure was roughly 147 feet thick in total, thicker than the crest, at 35 feet, but much thinner than the base, which widened out to about 300 feet thick.

The tunnel and the chamber he was in were much closer to the rear of the dam than the front. From here, there was about 104 feet of concrete to the front, but only about 43 feet to the rear, lake side.

Volker had picked this part of the dam knowing that, from his careful calculations, an explosion using the volume of ammonium nitrate he had put together would blow a significant hole through the lake side, allowing the water in. But it would also puncture the front side of the dam, as well as allowing water to pour into the lift shaft and other internal tunnels and galleries.

Once the water was flowing through, the enormous pressure created by the volume and depth of Lake Powell would do the rest.

It would rip the dam to pieces within a couple of hours.

Then, several hours later, the tidal wave of water hammering down the Colorado River would tear down the Hoover Dam too. And so on, and so on. That was how the dams would fall, one by one. Volker could picture each one in his mind.

CHAPTER FORTY-SEVEN

Thursday, July 6, 2017
    Glen Canyon Dam, Arizona

The sun had just poked its head above the horizon to the east
when the CIA's Gulfstream landed at Page Municipal
Airport. All around, the rocky orange and gray landscape of
the Great Basin Desert stretched as far as Jayne could see.

Her phone began to beep as a series of messages arrived.
Two were from Archie Davies, one with a photograph of
Jakub Volker, the other with details of his car, a black Ford
Ranger pickup, including the license plate.

Another, to both her and Neal, arrived from Vic, telling
them that a Page police car should be waiting for them at the
airport on arrival, ready to whisk them to Glen Canyon Dam.

Jayne pushed her Walther into her waistband and a spare
magazine into her pocket. Neal did likewise with his Beretta.

Sure enough, as they made their way down the aircraft
steps a few minutes later, a police cruiser with blue lights
flashing and headlights on screeched to a halt on the tarmac.

Both officers inside got out and walked over, each in dark blue long-sleeve uniforms, looking in their forties.

"Mr. Scales? Ms. Robinson?" one of them asked.

"That's us," Jayne said.

"Sergeant Alpenstein. This is Sergeant Gibbs." He indicated to his colleague. "We've just had instructions to take you to Glen Canyon Dam."

"Good," Neal said. "How long?"

"Ten minutes. Get in. We've sent another two cars to the dam already."

Alpenstein, a burly man with short, dark hair, took the wheel, with Gibbs in the passenger seat and Jayne and Neal in the back. After a short journey through the low-level, mainly single-story housing and industrial areas of central Page, the cruiser pulled up at the security building next to the employee entrance on the eastern side of the dam. Another police cruiser was parked next to the building, its lights flashing and the driver's door open.

Alpenstein waited a couple of seconds.

"Where the hell is the guard?" he muttered. "Where's our officer?"

Gibbs leaned forward. "And why is the gate open?" He pointed at a large steel security gate.

Just then, a uniformed police officer emerged from the building and ran over to Alpenstein's car window, clearly agitated.

"There's two dead security guards in there," he said, his voice rising. "Both of them shot. One is David O'Hara. I know him."

"*What?*" Alpenstein said, shooting up in his seat.

"Two dead guards."

"Holy crap, it's Volker," Jayne said. She felt her stomach turn over. "He's shot the guards, and he'll be in the dam planting his bomb right now."

She looked across toward the security office. There were what looked like blood trails visible on the gray concrete.

"Shit, let's get around to the dam," Alpenstein said. "You stay here, Alex," he told the officer.

"The other car went straight around there," Alex said. "Left us here to check the security guys."

"Okay." Alpenstein pushed his foot down hard on the accelerator and the car shot through the gate and around the access road.

"My guess is he'll put it on a timed fuse," Neal said. "Then he'll go. Unless he's on a suicide mission, which I doubt."

Jayne nodded. "We need to get in there and find him."

"Agreed," Alpenstein said. "Problem is, if it is a bomb on a timer, it's freaking dangerous."

"Any other dam officials here yet?" Jayne said. "Have they been alerted?"

"They've been alerted," Alpenstein said. "I understand the deputy facility manager has been in charge overnight. He's now on top of the dam, near the elevator shaft. Vernon Williams. Gray shirt, I'm told. White hard hat. We need to speak to him."

Jayne nodded.

Alpenstein drove around to the top of the dam and parked at the end of the access road rather than with the other vehicles parked on the top of the dam itself. A police car was stationary next to them, roof lights also flashing.

"I'm not putting my car on that dam if there's a bomb underneath it," he said.

Jayne ignored him. "Where's the elevator?" she asked.

Alpenstein pointed to a square turret that was sticking up high above the moon-shaped dam's parapet, next to the roadway. "That's the east elevator shaft. The western one is on the far side."

Indeed, there was another identical turret about 170 yards away on the far side of the dam.

Jayne spotted a black Ford Ranger parked near the eastern elevator shaft entrance. "That must be Volker's truck," she said.

She and Neal got out and ran over to the elevator, followed by Alpenstein. Another policeman was there with a man wearing a white hard hat and a gray long-sleeve shirt, who was standing next to the parapet. The man spun around as they approached.

Before he could speak, Jayne said, "Mr. Williams, I'm Jayne Robinson, CIA. I think you know we're looking for Jakub Volker. There are two dead security guards at the front gate, who he's shot. We believe—"

"Two dead guards?" the policeman with Williams said.

"Yes," Alpenstein said to his colleague. "Alex is round there, and—"

"We believe Volker's in the dam, planting a bomb," Jayne interrupted, looking at Williams. "It'll likely be on a timer. We need to find it. There's very little time. Where's the most likely place if he wants to do maximum damage?"

Williams nodded, his brow deeply creased. "There are a lot of tunnels below us. But he would need to blast through the back of the dam, where the water is, as first priority. So somewhere close to the back. There's a utility gallery tunnel across the full width of the dam, but it's too high, I think. Water pressure would be too low up there. There are the tunnels at the bottom, serving the power plant, which you can see down there."

He pointed down. Jayne glanced over the parapet to see a long, white rectangular concrete building stretching across the full width of the base of the curved dam, hundreds of feet below them. To the left of it was a parking area with two cars and a truck.

"But the dam's too wide to blow up there," Williams said. "It's three hundred feet thick."

"So where, then?" Jayne said. She was feeling exasperated at this game of elimination, though she realized Williams was simply thinking it through as he spoke.

"I think the filling line gallery tunnel," Williams said. "It also runs across the full width of the dam, about a third of the way down. The concrete's about a hundred and forty, hundred and fifty feet thick there. The tunnel, the gallery, is closer to the back of the dam. But it's very long and has many, many chambers and sub-tunnels off it. It'll still be like trying to find a needle in a haystack."

"Shit," Jayne said. She knew what she was going to do. She took out her phone and tapped on the number she had stored for Archie Davies at Hoover Dam.

Thankfully, Davies answered within a few seconds.

"Archie, Jayne Robinson here. We're at Glen Canyon. Volker is here inside the dam, but we don't know where. Any clues about where he might put a bomb? Vernon Williams here thinks the filling line gallery is the most likely place."

There was a brief pause.

Come on.

"Well," Davies said. "My last visit there, I helped Volker take several portable generators from a storage chamber on the filling line gallery. He had a load of them stored there, and a lot of diesel to fuel them. I remember it stank of diesel. He seemed to know that part of the dam very well. And Vernon is correct in that the filling line gallery level is far less thick than farther down the dam, so it would be easier to breach with explosive."

"Where is this storage room?" Jayne rapped out.

"Near the east elevator somewhere. Can't remember exactly where."

"Anything else you recall?" Jayne asked. "Anything unusual there?"

"All normal, I think," Davies said. "Why do—"

"That's all I need to know," Jayne interrupted. "Stand by your phone. I'll call you if I need anything more."

"By the way, the FBI is here," Davies said. "Big team. They're all over the dam. We've been helping them search. Found nothing so far."

"Okay, thanks."

She ended the call and turned to Williams. "Filling line gallery—just like you said. Can we get there right now?"

Williams nodded, strode over to the elevator door, and pressed the down button.

The elevator was already at the top, and the doors opened immediately. Jayne and Neal got in, followed by Sergeant Alpenstein and Williams, who pressed the button for the filling line gallery.

* * *

Thursday, July 6, 2017
    Glen Canyon Dam

Volker worked as fast as he could down in the filling line gallery storage room.

He removed the lids from all fourteen crates of ammonium nitrate, then poured diesel into each one, spreading it around and stirring the mixture with a wooden stick so as many as possible of the granules were soaked.

Then he wheeled the first crate out of the storage room, through the chamber, and out the door and pushed it a short distance along the filling line gallery tunnel.

When he reached another short, narrower tunnel that led

at right angles off the main tunnel, he flicked a switch on the wall, which turned on the roof lights. He then pushed the crate along it until he reached the end, where there was a spiral metal staircase that descended to a chamber used to check the penstocks, or huge water pipes, that led from Lake Powell to the generation turbines.

Volker shoved the crate into a large recess to the left of the staircase, where it would be well out of sight of anyone passing along the main filling line gallery tunnel.

This was the ideal place to trigger his explosive. The explosion would take place not only as near to the lake side of the dam as he could get, but also in a short tunnel that would channel its full force toward that rear-facing wall of the dam. He knew that explosions always took the path of least resistance, and the tunnel would help with that.

Then he hurried back to the storage room and began, one by one, to wheel all the other crates to the same place, where he pushed them next to each other in a cluster.

When he had moved all the crates, he unlocked a small chest he had left in the storage room and removed fourteen small detonators and cables that could be used to connect them together. He also took out fourteen lengths of Tovex, a water-gel explosive contained in cigar-shaped plastic sleeves, a booster that would ensure the ANFO exploded as intended with maximum impact. Finally, Volker took a box containing a fully charged car battery to power the detonators, a set of jump leads with alligator clips, and a timer.

Volker carried all the equipment to the boxes of ammonium nitrate, placed one detonator alongside a length of Tovex in each crate of ANFO, wired them all together, and connected the car battery and timer using the jump leads.

Volker then set the timer to twenty minutes, pressed the start button, and checked that the digital countdown reader on the timer was ticking down.

Then he exited the small tunnel, turned off the light, and returned to the chamber and storage room, where he checked he had left nothing.

Volker realized that having shot the security guards, he would now run far too much of a risk to try exiting the dam in his own pickup truck the way he had come in.

But there was another way out of the dam, one that he had used several times before. Thinking quickly, he calculated he should be able to get away and out of sight before the fireworks began.

He hurried out of the storage chamber and closed the door with a sharp click.

CHAPTER FORTY-EIGHT

Thursday, July 6, 2017
  Glen Canyon Dam

"This is quick," Jayne said, feeling her stomach jump as the elevator descended.

"Twenty seconds, then we're there," Williams said. "Yes, quick."

Jayne checked her watch. Sure enough, after about twenty seconds, the elevator car slowed to a halt and the doors opened.

Williams led the way out into a small lobby area, down a short tunnel, and into a long, well-lit one that stretched right and left. The tunnel curved as it followed the shape of the dam, so the ends could not be seen.

"This is the filling line gallery," Williams said. "But where Volker's generators are, I have no idea."

Jayne looked right, then left. "He kept them in a storage area, according to Archie Davies. I'm thinking that's maybe where we'll find Volker too."

"There's quite a few along here, so—"

But Williams was interrupted by the loud click of a door shutting sharply, then the sound of footsteps away somewhere to the left, toward the western side of the dam.

Jayne turned quickly, just in time to see the flash of something white at the point where the tunnel curved to the left. Then it disappeared again. Was it a cap, a hard hat? It sure looked like it.

"Hello?" she called. "Who's that?"

But the only response was the sharp sound of running footsteps echoing on the concrete tunnel surface—and heading away from them.

Jayne glanced at Neal.

She knew instinctively.

"That's got to be him," Jayne said.

Neal nodded. "Nobody else is going to run." They broke into a sprint, with Williams and Alpenstein following immediately behind.

As they ran, they passed a couple of doors and the entrance to another narrower tunnel, which had no lights on. They had gone no more than thirty or forty yards along the gallery, which reeked of diesel fuel, when Williams called out behind them.

"There's a storage room here," he said.

Jayne, irritated at the intervention, jerked to a halt, as did Neal, and they turned to see Williams opening a door.

"The generators," Williams called as he held the door open. "They're in here. The diesel smell—that's what made me think they might be here."

"Neal, can you look?" Jayne snapped. "I'll chase."

"Okay." He turned to Williams. "Can you help me?"

"Sure," Williams nodded.

"I'll come with you," Alpenstein said, taking two steps toward Jayne. "That guy's very dangerous."

"Thanks," Jayne said.

She turned and resumed running, Alpenstein following just behind. As she did so, she pulled her Walther from her waistband, flicked off the safety, and held it ready in her right hand.

Ahead of her, she could still hear the echo of footsteps as Volker—and it had to be him—continued to run hard. It was at times like this that she was thankful she continued to run for fitness and stayed in good condition.

The tunnel continued to bend around to the left in line with the shape of the dam, which meant Volker remained out of sight.

The clatter of footsteps ahead of her slowed sharply, then restarted, but more faintly.

A few seconds later, Jayne discovered why. She spotted a tunnel off to the left at a right angle to the main one.

Now the footsteps ahead had stopped, but Jayne guessed Volker had taken the offshoot, so she sprinted hard to the junction.

"Careful," Alpenstein called from behind her. "Take a look."

Realizing that was good advice, Jayne stopped and peeked warily around the corner.

As soon as she showed herself, there came two deafening gunshots that echoed down the tunnel. The rounds smashed into the concrete wall behind her, sending fragments of masonry flying and causing her to jump backward.

"Bastard," Alpenstein said. "Wait a second."

A moment later, Jayne heard a loud ping and realized the gunshots had been to buy time while Volker waited for the dam's western elevator car to arrive.

Again she peered slowly around the corner, this time without a resultant hail of bullets. At the end of a short tunnel, she could see a lobby area and a pair of steel elevator doors that were closing.

Shit.

Jayne sprinted toward the elevator, which looked identical to the eastern one they had descended in, and caught a quick glimpse of someone inside as the doors sealed shut.

She reached the elevator and smacked her palm against the closed door in frustration.

Volker had got himself into a car and away.

Jayne turned to Alpenstein. "Can you radio to your guys on the top? Tell them to grab him when the elevator gets there."

Alpenstein shook his head. "No radio signal in here."

It was only then that Jayne noticed the illuminated directional arrows on the control panel, showing the car was heading down.

Down?

Slightly confused, having expected Volker to head upward in an attempt to get back to his pickup and off the dam, she turned to Alpenstein, who, now breathing heavily, came to a halt beside her.

"He's gone down," she said.

Alpenstein threw up his hands. "We'll just have to wait until he gets out and the elevator comes back."

He was right. There was no alternative.

Jayne checked her watch.

Come on.

* * *

Thursday, July 6, 2017
    Glen Canyon Dam

. . .

Volker, holding his Glock 19 in his right hand, willed the car to descend faster, although in truth, it was already traveling at a rapid rate toward the bottom of Glen Canyon Dam's western elevator shaft.

There had been no doubt about what he had heard and seen in the filling line gallery tunnel a minute earlier—something that had caused his stomach to flip over in a moment of panic.

As he came out of the storage chamber, he had caught a glimpse of the dam's deputy facility manager, Vernon Williams, accompanied by a woman and, behind them, a uniformed policeman.

Volker knew Williams well and also knew he was running the graveyard overnight shift at the site that day.

He had heard what Williams said, his voice echoing clearly along the tunnel.

"*. . . where Volker's generators are, I have no idea.*"

Then there had been the woman's voice.

"*He kept them in a storage area, according to Archie Davies. I'm thinking that's maybe where we'll find Volker too.*"

They were after him, which was hardly surprising, given what he'd done to the security guards. Nevertheless, the police had arrived on site more quickly than he had anticipated.

And it sounded like Archie Davies had directed them to the filling line gallery storage room.

This was not unfolding at all the way that Volker had originally planned or envisaged. He had now been left with no choice but to run.

The question now was, could he move fast enough to get away from the dam to avoid being caught? And would his explosives be detonated before they were discovered?

His instinctive decision to fire a couple of shots down the

tunnel at his pursuers to give himself time to get into the elevator had worked.

Now he needed to get off the dam site using his alternative route out.

His escape plan had always been to drive north, away from the Colorado River through the national parks and forests to Salt Lake City, where he could disappear. Although he no longer could use his own truck, he had a spare key at home for another one belonging to his elderly neighbor in Page. That's where he would now head.

Finally, the elevator car slowed sharply, bumped almost imperceptibly, then stopped.

The steel doors opened in front of him. Volker jumped out into the elevator lobby area, then ran to the left along a brightly lit tunnel neatly lined with ceramic tiles. He then went left again toward the power plant at the foot of the downstream side of the dam.

There he paused momentarily, took a GPS alert beacon from his pocket that the DAM KEEPER had sent him, and pressed the red button twice, as he had been directed.

The DAM KEEPER's instructions were to activate the small beacon device once the timer on the explosive inside Glen Canyon had begun its countdown. He assumed that it was to send an alert to someone in Moscow.

Then he resumed running.

CHAPTER FORTY-NINE

Thursday, July 6, 2017
Glen Canyon Dam

Finally, after a seemingly interminable wait of about a minute and a half, there was a loud ping from the elevator as the car returned to the filling line gallery level.

As soon as the doors opened, Jayne and Alpenstein jumped inside.

"Bottom level?" she asked. "He won't want to get trapped inside the dam."

It seemed unlikely Volker would stop at another level halfway down the dam, where it might be difficult to get away from the site. She didn't know the layout at the bottom but had seen vehicles down there so assumed there must be another access road of some kind.

"Yes, bottom," Alpenstein said.

Jayne pressed the button for the lowest level, the power plant.

She just hoped she was correct.

The car seemed to take an eternity to complete its trip to the bottom, although in reality it was no more than about forty seconds.

They emerged into a modern, tiled lobby that from the signage looked as though it was designed more for dam visitors than workers.

Now where?

"Left," Alpenstein said. "No other option."

Indeed, the only way was left. They ran to another left turn, which was again the only option, as the way ahead was barred by a steel gate. Jayne then sprinted to the end of another tiled tunnel, where there was a set of swing doors. Alpenstein's heavy footsteps clattered behind her.

Jayne burst through the doors and found herself outdoors on an elevated walkway at the foot of the dam, with an area of grass to her left. Ahead of her was the long rectangular power plant building she had seen from the parapet at the top.

The walkway continued for a short distance to another set of swing doors into the power plant.

There was no other way to go, so she ran along the walkway and through the doors. Now Alpenstein was several yards behind.

There was, predictably, no sign of Volker, given the head start he'd had.

Now she was in a viewing gallery area that overlooked a massive hallway, maybe eighty feet high, with eight giant generation turbines, painted yellow, red, and gray, standing in a line across its full length.

There was pipework, walkways, and stairs everywhere, typical of other power stations that Jayne had been to.

Then, at the far end of a raised walkway that ran horizontally along the right side of the turbine hall, at least 150 yards away, she glimpsed someone in a white hard hat running away from her.

The figure immediately turned right and disappeared.

Was that Volker?

It had to be.

Jayne ran across the viewing area, through another set of double doors, and onto the walkway down the right side of the turbine hall.

Her footsteps clanged metallically and rhythmically on the steel floor as she sprinted.

By now, Alpenstein was a good distance behind and struggling to keep up.

When Jayne finally reached the end of the turbine hall, she turned right through the only set of doors there. She found herself on a raised platform at the end of what looked like some kind of service or maintenance building, with cranes, winches, tools, and equipment everywhere.

At the end of the building, maybe sixty or seventy yards away, a big metal rolling garage door was open, leading out onto a parking area. Jayne spotted the truck and two cars she had seen from the dam's crest earlier.

She paused. Would Volker be hiding somewhere in the maze of equipment below, or would he have dashed for the door?

Unless he had a death wish, Jayne knew he would want to get off the dam site as quickly as possible. Hiding would be no help to him.

A set of steel stairs descended to ground level, so Jayne clattered down them as fast as she could, still holding her Walther ready in her right hand. She hit the ground at the bottom of the steps and resumed running toward the vehicle door. To her right was a pedestrian door that she guessed also led outside.

As Jayne drew near the garage door, she heard the throaty

roar of a diesel engine starting up outside, somewhere to the right. Two seconds later, a large forklift appeared from the right and sped across the yard in front of her, a cloud of exhaust smoke billowing behind it.

Hunched over the steering wheel was a man in a white hard hat.

Jakub Volker.

The forklift, a large orange-and-gray Toyota model with chunky black tires, accelerated toward the open mouth of a road tunnel at the far end of the parking area.

Without hesitating, Jayne raised her Walther, took aim at the speeding forklift's rear left tire, and fired twice. She then adjusted her aim to the right rear tire and fired twice more.

For a second, she thought she'd either missed or the rounds had just ricocheted off the rubber.

But then came a loud bang, and the forklift veered sharply to the left just as it reached the tunnel. It smashed into the gray concrete entrance arch, where it came to an abrupt halt.

A moment passed. Then Jayne saw Volker jump off the forklift and duck down behind the far side of it. The next thing she knew, there were two gunshots in quick succession. One of the rounds whined as it ricocheted off the floor less than two feet to her right, leaving a scar on the concrete.

Shit.

Where's bloody Alpenstein?

She reactively dived to the floor and rolled to her left, then got herself on her elbows, ready to return fire.

There came two more shots, both of which clanged loudly into something metallic only a short distance to Jayne's right, but the forklift obstructed Jayne's line of sight to Volker and meant she was unable to return fire.

A few seconds later, she saw the silhouette of Volker running behind the forklift, bent double to try to avoid incoming rounds and heading into the tunnel.

But before she could move, there came more gunshots, this time from somewhere outside the building.

Volker's arms flew up vertically in the air, and he was thrown forward to the ground.

Jayne jumped to her feet and sprinted to the vehicle doorway of the building.

Standing a short distance to her right was Alpenstein, holding his pistol, eyes firmly focused on the tunnel.

Jayne followed his gaze to see the slumped silhouette of Volker, now lying on the concrete surface, no more than five yards into the tunnel.

"Got the bastard," Alpenstein said.

"Thanks," Jayne said. She realized that Alpenstein must have exited the maintenance building into the parking area through the side door. "We'd better get to this asshole quickly."

Alpenstein nodded.

They both ran through the parking area, past the crippled forklift, and into the mouth of the tunnel. It was wide enough for two vehicles side by side and was lit by overhead lamps.

As Jayne drew near Volker, her Walther raised just in case, he half turned over and looked at her, groaning loudly. She saw his gun, a Glock, lying a few feet away, and went to pick it up. She then turned back to him.

Blood was bubbling slowly from a gunshot wound in Volker's lower back, staining his blue shirt a dark red.

"Where is the bomb, the explosive?" Alpenstein said loudly, his tone level but urgent as he crouched down next to Jayne, both of them eyeballing Volker. "Where? Tell me."

Volker gave an almost imperceptible shake of his head. "Go screw yourself," he murmured, in a voice that was scarcely audible.

"Come on. You've lost this fight, Volker," Jayne said. "Where is the bloody explosive? What part of the dam?

Where have you hidden it? If it goes off now, you're dead. There's no escape for you, or us. So tell me."

"Bitch. I'll never tell you," he muttered.

"Did you put a bomb at Hoover Dam, too?" Jayne asked.

"Burn in hell."

Then Volker's eyes rolled up. He flopped back onto his stomach and appeared to slip into unconsciousness.

"Shit, has he gone?" Jayne asked.

"Don't know," Alpenstein said. "He's not good. He was obviously planning to escape through the access tunnel."

"Where does it go?" Jayne asked.

"Goes to Page. It's a two-mile tunnel," Alpenstein said. "You stopped the forklift just in time. Good job. I'll call the medics and my colleagues to keep this fool secure."

He took a radio from a holster on his waist, tapped a button on the keypad, and quickly rapped out instructions.

"The bloody bomb is the urgent thing," Jayne said as soon as he'd finished. Her mind was now running at full tilt. "Where is it? We'll get nothing out of Volker. Leave him for the medics. We'd better get back to the storage chamber and help them look."

Jayne glanced at her watch and realized it was now at least ten minutes since they had first disturbed Volker outside the storage area. "Let's run."

"Yep, let's go," Alpenstein said.

They ran back the way they had come, through the maintenance building and the turbine hall, across the covered walkway, and back to the elevator. Alpenstein struggled to keep up, so she forged ahead.

A few minutes later, she was standing back outside the generator storage chamber in the filling line gallery tunnel, two-thirds of the way up the dam.

There was no sign of Neal or Vernon Williams, but the door to the storage chamber containing the generators was still open, as was another door a little farther along the tunnel.

A few seconds later, just as Alpenstein arrived, Neal emerged from the storage room, followed by Williams.

"There you are. What happened to—" Neal began, his voice tense.

"We got him. Where's the bomb?" Jayne interrupted. There was no time to explain what had just happened to Volker.

Neal threw up his hands. "Just generators in crates. And diesel in plastic containers."

"No explosive?"

Neal shook his head. "Nothing. We've checked all the crates," he said. "There's a storage room at the back of the chamber. That's empty. And we searched two other chambers along there, also empty." He pointed toward the other open doors farther along the tunnel.

Jayne put her hands on her hips.

"It doesn't make sense," she said. "He sprinted from this area after we saw him. We heard the door shut—so he was in the generator storage room or another one next to it. And we know he's trying to destroy this bloody dam."

"I know," Neal said. "But I'm telling you, there's no explosive in these rooms."

"But it stinks of diesel here," Jayne said. Indeed, the all-pervading smell of diesel fumes hung heavy in the air, so much so that she could feel her chest closing up a little, making it hard to breathe.

She had a sudden thought. "Aidan told us he overheard the Russians talking about using ammonium nitrate explosive to take down the dam."

"He did," Neal said.

"And what do you need to add to ammonium nitrate to detonate it?" Jayne asked.

"Diesel," Neal said, without hesitating. Like her, he knew the methods terrorists generally used.

"Exactly. So the smell up there makes me think it has to be near there."

Jayne looked at Williams, standing a few yards away. "Vernon, is there anywhere else near these storage chambers where that bastard could have put his explosive? I ran past one or two other doors and a smaller tunnel."

"There's that chamber," Vernon said, pointing to a third door several yards along from the others. "We haven't searched that yet."

Vernon strode over to it, opened the door, and flicked on a light switch.

But the room was also empty.

"Shit," Jayne said.

"And this tunnel," Jayne said, pointing to a narrower unlit tunnel another few yards farther on. "Where does it go?"

"Leads to a penstock inspection chamber," Vernon said. "Via a short spiral staircase."

"Let's take a look," Jayne said.

Vernon ran to the tunnel entrance, with Jayne and Neal close behind, and pressed a switch that turned on several ceiling lights. Now the smell of diesel really was overpowering.

They had gone no more than seven or eight yards when Vernon, ahead of Jayne, stopped dead. "Holy shit."

She drew level with him and stared.

In a large recess to the left, on the floor, were several plastic crates surrounding a metal spiral staircase that went down. All the crates open. They were filled with a brown and gray substance, and each had a device sticking up from its center, joined by wires to a cigarette pack–size box on the floor.

The box had a red digital timer that was flashing numbers. Another cable led to a car battery.

"Fuck!" Jayne yelled.

The digital timer read 1:02 and was counting down by the second as she watched.

1:01, 1:00, 0:59 . . .

"Disconnect the battery," Neal said, his voice rising. He pushed around past Jayne. "Let me do it—I'll pull the jump leads off the battery."

He bent down, grabbed both alligator clips on the battery terminals, squeezed the handles, and carefully removed them.

The red digits on the timer read 0:56.

Then the numbers flickered and died.

Jayne could feel her heart pumping and sweat trickling down her forehead.

"Bloody hell," she said, sinking slowly to her haunches. "Bloody hell."

CHAPTER FIFTY

Thursday, July 6, 2017
    Glen Canyon Dam

Jayne stood on top of the dam as a group of six police officers gingerly carried the final few crates of the ammonium nitrate explosive out of the nearby eastern elevator car. They loaded them onto the flatbed of a waiting police pickup truck, which then drove off extremely slowly along the dam access road and out of sight.

"That's all of it," Sergeant Alpenstein said. "Thank God. We'll dispose of the stuff safely."

It was the third truckload of ammonium nitrate to be removed from the dam within the past twenty minutes.

To their left, an ambulance was waiting, its red and blue roof lights flashing as paramedics carried a stretcher on which lay the dead body of a security guard who had been found in the cleaner's closet, next to the elevator. He was another one of Volker's victims.

Alpenstein stood watching the paramedics, hands on hips.

Eventually, he turned to Jayne, who was with Neal and Vernon Williams. "Thanks for doing what you did, you guys," Alpenstein said. "You did well to pinpoint where that explosive was being kept."

"I had guidance from a guy at Hoover," Jayne said. "He knows the layout here and gave us something to work on. Vernon here was also a great help. Maybe we got lucky too. That amount of ammonium nitrate would have blown this dam into the next state."

Her eye was caught by the flashing roof lights of another ambulance far down below them in the parking area next to the power plant at the base of the dam.

The ambulance, which Jayne knew was carrying Jakub Volker, set off slowly and entered the access tunnel where he had been shot only forty minutes earlier. Ahead of the ambulance and behind it were two police cars, which were detailed to escort it through the tunnel to nearby Page Hospital.

It had taken paramedics some time to stabilize Volker before moving him. However, even if he did pull through, it was obvious he now faced an extremely long stretch in prison for his attempt to destroy the Glen Canyon Dam.

"So you think the Russians were behind this?" Alpenstein asked.

"We know they were," Jayne said. "It was an operation that had been carefully planned for a long time. The Russians went ahead now because they want the States out of Ukraine and to stop assisting the government in Kyiv—they want to invade the country. They also want water supplies restored to the Crimean Peninsula. They were trying to make a big statement to President Ferguson."

"Bastards," Alpenstein said.

By now, the sun was well on its journey up into a sky that was relentlessly blue, and Jayne could already feel the temperature rising. It was likely to reach ninety degrees Fahrenheit today.

Jayne had now gone more than twenty-four hours without sleep, and the adrenaline supply that had kept her going over the past few hours was dwindling rapidly.

She felt as though she'd been hit by a truck.

Jayne walked away from the others and over to the parapet of the dam, facing out over Lake Powell to the rear of it. She urgently needed to call Vic to update him on what had happened, but first she needed to take a moment to get her thoughts in order.

There were ski boats, fishing boats, and other craft out on the water, their owners oblivious to the drama that had just gone on a short distance away.

A bird, it looked like an American coot, dived toward the lake's surface, and nearby several ducks and other birds that she didn't recognize floated on the water. All would likely have been swept away, together with the boating enthusiasts, if the dam had been destroyed and Lake Powell had disappeared.

So, this was Operation Noi—a planned strike on a dam six thousand miles from Ukraine, in the heart of the southwestern United States.

It was certainly not what she or anyone else had expected when they had first heard of the operation from GRAY WOLF in Zaporizhzhia three weeks earlier.

Even GRAY WOLF had assumed it was aimed at one of the Ukrainian dams on the River Dnipro—not one on the Colorado River.

It just showed how vital it was in this game not to jump to conclusions or take things for granted but to keep pushing and pushing until answers were uncovered and the truth revealed.

Aidan Scarpa had paid a price after inadvertently getting

one key part of the puzzle. Thankfully, his price had not been the ultimate one, unlike that of GRAY WOLF, Kira Suslova and—very nearly—Jayne and Neal themselves.

Fifty-six seconds.

It was a number that Jayne kept repeating to herself. The image of the red countdown timer ticking down below the one-minute mark was burned into her mind as vividly and painfully as if it had been branded there.

It was precisely how close she, Neal, and tens of thousands of others had come to losing their lives in what would have been a most calamitous disaster for much of the southwestern United States—and one which the Russian president would have celebrated wildly behind the walls of the Kremlin.

The Russians were relentless in their attempts to attack, undermine, and destroy Western structures and democracy. It took a certain kind of vigilance and determination to ensure they didn't succeed. Jayne felt a sudden surge of pride that she, Neal, and the others involved in this operation against Moscow had come out on top. It was the motivation that kept her going. They weren't going to win.

It was remarkable how they had functioned as a team, Jayne reflected. Each of them had brought certain pieces of the puzzle together in a way that reflected their own abilities and character traits.

Jayne turned again, leaned back against the parapet, and faced Neal, who was now in an animated conversation with Vernon Williams.

Was there anything they had missed?

Had the FBI found anything at Hoover?

That remained her biggest worry, that Volker had planted explosives at that dam too, also on a timer, before he had left the previous evening.

But having seen the volume of explosive he had deployed here at Glen Canyon, packed into fourteen plastic crates, her doubts mounted that he would have been able to assemble a similar bomb at Hoover, which he appeared to visit only intermittently.

But she had to make sure. Jayne took out her phone and called Vic on their secure line. She needed to brief him immediately.

"What's happening?" he said immediately on answering. He, too, had been awake all night, and his voice sounded even more gravelly than normal.

She told him.

"Did the feds find anything at Hoover?" Jayne asked.

"Nothing."

"Thank God."

"They're still there, still searching," Vic said. "What's your gut feeling?"

Jayne paused. "My gut tells me this one at Glen Canyon is the only one." She explained why.

"That makes sense," Vic said. "Let's hope so. I'll inform the White House—my guess is the president will need to see both of us for a debriefing, along with Neal and Veltman."

Jayne sighed. She knew Vic was almost certainly correct. President Ferguson would want a thorough debrief, given the huge national security implications of what had happened, and especially the personal involvement of his estranged son.

"I heard you sigh," Vic continued. "Listen, Jayne, you and Neal can get some sleep on the plane back here. Then have a proper rest tonight. Sorry, but you know how it is here—if the president calls, we jump."

He went on to apologize further, but Jayne was hardly listening.

Instead, her attention was caught by the sight of two Great Blue herons flying over the dam, their enormous wingspans standing out against the azure sky behind them as they slowly flapped their way northward. Little did they know how close their feeding and nesting grounds had come to destruction. Ignorance was bliss, perhaps.

All Jayne knew was that now she was looking forward to flying north again herself, back to Portland, Maine, and some normality for a while at Joe's house near Back Cove. That would have to wait for a day or two.

"No problem, Vic," she said. "We'll get ourselves back to DC and see you later."

* * *

Thursday, July 6, 2017
   Moscow

Igor Ivanov hated the so-called chess table meetings, where President Putin called his subordinates in for one-to-one discussions. He usually sat them down at the square, ornately engraved wooden table that stuck out perpendicularly from the center of his main desk.

It meant he had to face the president, eye to eye, in a very confrontational style. Except the confrontation was always coming from one side of the table only, and it wasn't Ivanov's.

He knew there would be no escaping the scrutiny or the verbal judgments that were to come, especially today, given that the news and updates that Ivanov had to disclose to the president were entirely negative.

"You may enter now," Putin's aide said as he emerged from the twin sets of double wooden doors that formed the entrance to the president's second-floor office in the Kremlin's Senate Palace building.

Ivanov rose from his chair in the anteroom outside the office and walked through the doors and across the parquet floor, which was mostly covered by intricately woven pale gray Bokhara carpets.

The president was already seated in the beige leather seat to the left of the highly polished chess table, leaving the chair on the right free for Ivanov.

Putin didn't bother to get up, or shake Ivanov's hand, or offer any kind of greeting, for that matter.

Rather, the president rocked back in his chair and folded his arms, waiting. To his left, behind his main desk, a Russian flag hung limp on a short pole that stood next to the wooden wall paneling. Behind the other side of the desk hung another flag bearing the presidential standard.

Ivanov sat down.

"So, Operation Noi has failed, it seems," Putin began, his voice dead level, devoid of any emotion, as usual. It was a statement, not a question. He glanced at his watch. "It is now several hours past when you said that dam would be destroyed. It clearly will not happen. That is a major blow to our overarching strategy and to Operation Pandora."

The president leaned forward and folded his arms on the table. "The chain of failures means that we have been forced to dispose of our once valuable asset, the Khranitel Plotiny, the DAM KEEPER—whom you recruited and were responsible for. My instructions were to ensure that he at least implemented Operation Noi before that happened. But not even this has been done."

"Sir, we believe that the DAM KEEPER did what was required of him," Ivanov said. "Anke Leonova did force him to implement Noi, and she did then dispose of him. However, it appears that Leonova ran into difficulties and is currently in the hospital with serious gunshot wounds. We believe she may have been interrupted by US intelligence after Noi had been activated."

"Why do you think that?" Putin said as he leaned forward.

"Noi has not been activated. It has failed. There has been no explosion at the Glen Canyon Dam, no flood, no power outage, no national disaster, no huge outpouring of hostility against President Ferguson and his cabinet for their incompetence. None of the things you promised have happened."

"Sir, we received an alert from the beacon carried by our operative at Glen Canyon to confirm that the timer on the detonator had been activated. We believe that US intelligence operatives may have interrupted the scheduled explosion at Glen Canyon. However, we have no confirmation."

Now Ivanov could feel beads of sweat running down his forehead and wet patches forming beneath his arms. Putin's office was warm, and yet he felt obliged to keep his jacket on because the president always did so.

"How?" asked Putin.

It was always the one-word questions that were the most menacing.

Ivanov felt his stomach turn over.

The truth was, Ivanov felt very uncertain about how so many elements of the plans he had so carefully put in place had gone wrong over the past few weeks. The enemy always seemed to have been one step ahead, and he was currently at a loss to work out how.

But there was one inescapable truth: the betrayal of Russia by Kira Suslova had been an important element in what had happened.

Ivanov couldn't bring himself to utter her name, fearful of the president's reaction.

"Sir, that is what we need to find out," he said instead.

"So let's sum up," Putin said. "In the space of a week, you have presided over several failures, each of which has effectively led to the next. First, failing to ensure the asset we recruited in Frankfurt, Aidan Scarpa, was separated from highly sensitive intelligence about Operation Noi, which he somehow overheard. Then, failing to ringfence Scarpa, to prevent him passing on that intelligence to the CIA— because he was exfiltrated from Cape Idokopas from under your nose at the cost of several Russian lives."

"And," Putin continued in a voice that dropped a couple of tones, "we also have what appears to be the seeming recruitment of Kira Suslova by CIA agents—how that happened, I would really like to know. And, furthermore, despite the identity of the DAM KEEPER not being known to Western intelligence, Operation Noi has failed. A remarkable list of disasters, capped by the disappearance in Athens of Sidorenko, and the apparent injury to and capture of Leonova, as well as the sleeper agent at the Glen Canyon Dam. Well done. A triumph all round."

Ivanov looked down at the floor. There was nothing he could really say in mitigation. It wasn't all his fault, but there was no point in saying that right now. It was, admittedly, a list of disasters, as the president had said. A key objective of recruiting Aidan Scarpa had been to use him as a conduit for information from the DAM KEEPER, Frank Merriden. The thinking was that this would greatly reduce the need for high-risk direct communications between Ivanov and Merriden, who had rightly been paranoid about being caught and therefore didn't pass on anywhere near as much information as he potentially could have.

But now, both assets were gone anyway, Anke was in US custody, and Operation Noi, so long in the planning, had indeed failed. It was the lowest of low points for Ivanov.

"Sir, I believe we have on this occasion been outmaneuvered," Ivanov said.

"By whom?"

Ivanov suspected that Putin, himself a former KGB operative who remained very close to all of Russia's intelligence services, knew exactly who had outmaneuvered him. He just wanted to maximize the embarrassment involved in the admission.

"Go on, tell me by whom," Putin repeated.

"We believe it is the former British Secret Intelligence Service operative, Jayne Robinson, who has been working for the CIA," Ivanov said. "She works with other very capable people. They have been difficult to squash, I have to admit."

"Difficult?" Putin said, his voice still unnervingly level. "Or is it your incompetence that is making them appear difficult? It's far from the first time that this Robinson woman has embarrassed Russia, is it not?"

Ivanov again lowered his gaze to the floor and said nothing.

"Should I assume that it was also Robinson who carried out the recruitment of Kira Suslova?" the president asked.

Ivanov bowed his head. "It seems likely, sir."

There was a short silence as the president stared straight ahead of him.

"And next, you're going to confirm for me that Robinson was the woman in that chess piece sculpture team whom I met at the cocktail party, pretending to be a German?" Putin continued. "Aren't you?"

"Unfortunately, yes, sir," Ivanov said. "It was Suslova who signed off their credentials and security papers."

Putin eyeballed him. "It's a pity that I'm no longer an operative. My immediate instinct at that reception was that something was wrong with those designers and sculptors. The accents. Why do your people and the FSB not pick up on the signals? It's quite extraordinary. So obvious. So incompetent. So amateur. A disgrace to the Motherland."

Ivanov said nothing. He hadn't been there for the cocktails, but there was nothing he could say in his defense. Putin must know that once Suslova had signed off on the papers, his intelligence services were far less likely to interfere.

"This is a double blow," Putin said. "We will not back off, but it is going to force us down another route—one that I cannot predict right now."

It was obvious to Ivanov that the failures would force Putin to rethink his strategy to push the US away from supporting Ukraine and to turn American public opinion against more support for the Kyiv regime, as well as how to restore water supplies to the Crimean Peninsula. He certainly wouldn't throw in the towel.

"I will also need to rethink what role you will play—if at all," Putin continued.

The president's tone was flat, but the underlying threat was unmistakable.

"I can only apologize for the failures, sir," Ivanov said.

"Apologies count for nothing," Putin said. "It is delivery that I am interested in. And the next delivery I need is a report on Kira Suslova that will tell me how, precisely, she was recruited by Robinson."

"I will find out, sir."

"You will," Putin said. "Robinson must have got leverage over her somehow. Check her finances. You might start with the $2 billion that I had transferred to her Cyprus bank account last year to fund her campaign for the FIDE presidency. What's happened to that money? Does she still have it? I want it back safely into my Kremlin account."

"Sir, do you believe something has happened to that—"

"I don't know," Putin interrupted. "But I have a gut feeling that there is a financial reason behind what happened. Suslova was a patriot. Find out. Also, I want a replacement candidate for the FIDE presidency role—I don't want to see that job go to one of Russia's enemies. Get me a list of possibles, quickly."

"Yes, sir, I'll do that," Ivanov said.

"And Gennady Sidorenko? Any update on his situation?" the president asked.

Ivanov had not been looking forward to this question, but he knew it was coming after the president referenced Sidorenko earlier in the meeting.

"Unfortunately, there is an update, sir, and it is not good news," Ivanov said, lowering his tone. "We have heard from a source within Athens police that a body was found on a construction site in the Vathi neighborhood. It appears to have two fatal gunshot wounds to the head, and another to the right hand, and fits the description of Sidorenko. It was found the day after Suslova and Robinson were in Athens— but we have only just been notified, and we have not yet been able to identify the body. We know the two of them were holding a meeting, because photographs of them sitting together on a bench near that location, taken on Sidorenko's phone, were automatically uploaded to the server here. Sidorenko's deputy, Safonov, located the images as part of his investigation into the disappearance. I saw them a few hours ago."

President Putin leaned back in his chair and pressed his palms together, as if praying, his face impassive. "This just about makes my day complete, hearing this news. Do you assume Robinson or Suslova shot him?"

"I'm sorry, sir. We assume it was one of them. My guess is Suslova, but I'm not certain about that. We also don't know who fired first, but Sidorenko had a track record in that area."

Putin exhaled slowly. "Let's move on. I will expect from you a clear strategy to extract retribution on Robinson and her colleagues. I also expect a plan to get Anke Leonova back. The illegal I am not so bothered about."

"Of course, sir. I will bring a team together to begin work on that," Ivanov said. "Gavrill Rezanov and others."

"Go, get out of here," the president said. "You will discover your fate when I send for you next."

The president pointed toward the door.

Ivanov rose, nodded to the president, and extended his hand, knowing almost for certain that Putin would spurn the gesture, which sure enough he did. Instead of shaking hands, the president just eyeballed him without blinking.

Ivanov turned, walked to the door, and let himself out, knowing it could well be the last time he did so.

CHAPTER FIFTY-ONE

Thursday, July 6, 2017
Washington, DC

Jayne had expected to be ushered down to the basement of the White House's West Wing and into the Situation Room, as was usually the case when she needed to accompany Vic and his colleagues for a briefing with President Ferguson.

But when she and Neal arrived at the West Wing's entrance lobby direct from Dulles International Airport, they were greeted by Charles Deacon, who instead took them along the ground-floor corridor past the vice president's and chief of staff's offices and around the corner to the Oval Office.

There, sitting on one of the twin sand-colored sofas, were Vic and his boss, Arthur Veltman. On the other sofa, facing them, was the figure of another man whom Jayne had not expected to see so quickly: Aidan Scarpa. The defense secretary, Philip Monterey, was seated on a chair to Scarpa's right.

Ferguson, who was sitting behind his carved wooden desk made from timbers taken from the nineteenth-century British frigate *HMS Resolute,* rose and greeted them.

"Take a seat," Ferguson said, indicating toward two armchairs near the white marble fireplace at the northern end of his office. "I wanted to meet you both here so we could have a smaller discussion—and so we could include my son in a more private setting. He only arrived back in the United States last night after doctors in Istanbul gave him the all-clear to fly."

Jayne had slept for about three hours on the CIA Gulfstream during the flight back to Dulles from Page Municipal Airport but still didn't feel much better than she had before boarding. Her head felt as though it was being squeezed in a vise, and she was struggling to remember precisely what had happened and when. She hoped the president wouldn't question her in too much detail.

Her phone had been buzzing with messages since the Gulfstream landed, including from both Valentin Marchenko, at the SZR's headquarters in Kyiv, and Abram Malevich, the CIA's Kyiv chief of station. Both wanted to know how she was doing and to congratulate her. She would get back to them all, but that would have to wait for now.

Jayne and Neal sat in the armchairs, while Ferguson sat on the sofa next to Aidan, who looked a little ill at ease. Jayne wondered if it was his first visit to the White House. Deacon perched on another chair next to the *Resolute* desk, near Monterey.

"First, I would like to thank you both for the incredible job you have done over the past few weeks," Ferguson said. "The demands have been huge, the stakes have been extremely high, and the time frame short. And yet you have delivered and done so with great skill. On behalf of myself and Aidan, I would like to express my gratitude." He clapped his son on the shoulder.

"It's been very much a team effort, sir," Neal said. "But thank you, I appreciate it."

The president glanced first at Jayne, then Neal. "I understand you stopped this Operation Noi with very little time to spare. Your timing was impeccable. Not bad for a Brit."

He gave a broad grin in Jayne's direction.

"Thank you, Mr. President," Jayne said. "You're correct. There was less than a minute to spare—the Russians came extremely close. They have some very dangerous people. Igor Ivanov, in particular, is a serious threat to this country, but the lower-level operatives are also tough, as we've all found to our cost."

"I would like to add my congratulations to those of the president," Monterey said. "Jayne, Neal, you have both saved me much embarrassment, given that Merriden was my direct report." The defense secretary looked across at Vic. "You too, Vic. I will remember this. I owe you one. Thank you."

"We've all played a part," Vic said. "But thanks."

"What is the latest update on Anke Leonova?" Aidan asked, his lips pressed together.

Jayne could understand his interest.

"Still under police guard in the hospital," Vic said. "She'll be inside prison as soon as she's fit to stand trial."

Aidan nodded. "Let's hope so." He paused and looked alternately at Jayne and Neal. "I would also like to thank you both. I'd probably still be locked up in Cape Idokopas and the entire Colorado River basin would by now have been destroyed if you hadn't got me out."

He paused for a second, glanced sideways at his father, then added, "There are, of course, other positives to come out of this too."

Ferguson winked at him.

The unspoken message seemed to be that Aidan and President Ferguson had made a start with rebuilding their relationship. Jayne wasn't going to ask about that. It was their private business. But she was glad they seemed to be heading in the right direction after such a long time apart. She assumed that Ferguson's team would be doing all they could to keep Aidan's involvement with the Russians out of the media. So far, they appeared to have succeeded, although Jayne felt that at some point it would all come out. Somebody would leak it. They always did.

"And the illegal at Glen Canyon Dam, Volker?" the president asked. He glanced at Vic. "What do we know about him?"

"The FBI is doing a deep dive into his background, Mr. President," Vic said. "They have already determined that Jakub Volker is not his real name—it's Oleg Spassky. And he's not Czech, he's Russian, as you might expect. He's been in the US for a long time. I suspect that he was probably hand-picked by the GRU to come to the US and take a job at the dam many years ago with this exact operation in mind—probably because he speaks good English. He has likely been a sleeper ever since, biding his time and waiting for instructions."

The president pressed his lips together. "And how many more of those do we have inside this country? That's what I'd like to know." He leaned forward and eyed Jayne. "However, we have turned the tables on them this time. I understand that the entire operation to extricate Aidan was founded on you continuing to exploit this Suslova woman."

"Yes, Kira Suslova," Jayne said. "We were fortunate that we were well positioned to persuade her to help, so to speak. A pity, therefore, that we lost her en route out of Russia, along with two others. She might have been a useful asset to us in the future."

"*Persuade?*" the president asked. His eyebrows rose and the faintest of smiles crossed his face. "From what I understand, there are other words you could use than persuade, Jayne. But I agree it is a shame."

Jayne was glad he didn't directly mention the $2 billion that had been coerced out of Suslova several months earlier, and which was still sitting in a CIA offshore account. She had already expressed a wish to Vic that the money be used for humanitarian purposes to help the people of Ukraine in the event of a Russian invasion, which seemed increasingly likely. Vic, in turn, had discussions planned with Veltman and Deacon to work out whether and how that might be done, if needed.

Ferguson paused. "When we have finished here, I will go to the press briefing room and give a live television statement about the attempted attack on the dam. Given the volume of media coverage from Glen Canyon and the shooting of Frank Merriden, I can hardly avoid doing so. I will, of course, claim the credit for thwarting the Russian operation."

"Of course, sir," Jayne said. She fought hard to hold back a grin. It was only to be expected that Ferguson would make political capital out of the success, especially as he had only recently been reelected president.

There had indeed been a wall of media coverage that had rapidly built as the day went on, driven initially by TV and online journalists in Arizona who had picked up on events at Glen Canyon from their police contacts. Within hours, it had become a national and international story. Similarly, there had been leaks in Washington, DC, about the killing of Frank Merriden by an unknown assailant. The identity of Anke Leonova, who remained in the hospital under police guard, had not yet worked its way into the media, but that, and the linkage between Merriden and Glen Canyon, would inevitably emerge.

Ferguson folded his arms. "I will need to apologize to the nation for the behavior of Merriden and for our failure to pick up on his relationship with Ivanov," he said, with a glance at Monterey. "I think we will accept collective responsibility for that. Obviously, I won't be able to name or thank you, Jayne and Neal, during my statement, much as I would like to."

Jayne and Neal both nodded in acknowledgment. Being thanked on live television was the very last thing she wanted. She looked at Vic, Veltman, and Monterey, who all appeared somewhat relieved for not being blamed by the president for failing to detect Merriden's treachery. She wondered, though, if the defense secretary might later find his position under threat as a result of what had happened.

Ferguson directed his gaze to Veltman and Vic, sitting opposite him. "We will all need to discuss how this affects our approach to Ukraine."

Veltman nodded. "Let's do that separately. But at the high level, it is clear to me that Russia, more than ever, is intent on invading Ukraine sometime sooner rather than later. Their demands and threats to us to end our support for Ukraine, and to restore water supplies to Crimea, underline that. They clearly want to use Crimea as a launching pad for an invasion. And their so-called Operation Pandora to undermine the US is also being used to try to destroy our public support for Ukraine. They want our people to view the potential price paid for supporting Russia's enemies as being just too high."

"Well, that's one thing we'll never allow to happen," Ferguson said, waving a hand toward his desk. "I didn't choose a desk made from the *Resolute*'s timber for nothing."

Deacon caught the president's eye and tapped his watch.

Ferguson nodded and looked at his guests in turn. "I need to go and make my television address now. Thank you again for what you've done. You've enabled me to send a clear message to those bastards in Moscow: mess with us if you want, but you'll pay heavily. And that'll be the underlying tone of what I say on camera."

With that, Ferguson stood and followed Deacon out the door.

EPILOGUE

Friday, July 7, 2017
    Portland, Maine

The shower water hit Jayne full in the chest as Joe turned it on swiftly and mercilessly. She squealed at the ice-cold shock until the hot began to flow a few seconds later.

"That'll teach you," Joe said.

"Teach me for what?"

"For exhausting me relentlessly," Joe said, a half grin on his face.

It was past three o'clock in the afternoon and they had just gotten up after what was initially intended to be a post-lunch siesta, but had almost inevitably turned into a long session of love-making.

For the first time in weeks, Jayne felt utterly relaxed, full of hormones and postcoital chemicals. The shower was her happy place, especially when she had Joe to share it with.

She squirted some shower gel into her hand and began to rub the soap into Joe's chest, gradually working her way downward. Predictably, he started to become aroused again, and she giggled.

"Sorry, I know you're hopeful, but I can't take any more," she said. "You'll have to wash yourself."

"You're a dealer in disappointment," Joe said. He laughed.

Twenty minutes later, they were sitting on the deck in Joe's garden, soaking up the afternoon sunshine with a glass of sauvignon blanc from the Napa Valley, a part of California that they had both visited several times.

"So, you've proved yourself damn useful this week," Joe said.

Jayne caught his eye. It was the third "dam" joke he'd delivered in the past few minutes, but in her current mood she couldn't help laughing.

"I wouldn't have been damn anything without your help in getting that intel from Don Nichols," Jayne said. "It was critical."

She meant what she said. Uncovering the link that was established between Igor Ivanov and the DAM KEEPER, Frank Merriden, a decade earlier had been the key to unlocking the investigation. As was often the case, Joe's encyclopedic knowledge of all things Russian had proved decisive.

Often, over the recent operations that Jayne had been involved in, she found herself missing working full time alongside Joe. But, as a parent, he had decided to take much more of a back seat for the time being, even though his kids were now old enough to take care of themselves. She knew he still felt a heavy responsibility toward them. For that reason, she had deliberately tried to only involve him in a more peripheral way, where she knew he could really add value. She knew him well enough to be certain that when he was ready to do more, he would say so. She didn't question him too much about it.

"Don's a very useful operator," Joe said. "Worth keeping in

touch with. We need to send him several bottles of something decent—more expensive than that." He pointed to the Napa Valley bottle that stood on the oak garden table.

Jayne glanced at Joe. "He's definitely someone to keep on board."

There was a loud bark from somewhere indoors, and Cocoa, Joe's chocolate Lab, wandered out through the folding doors that led onto the deck. Cocoa took one look at the table, saw there was nothing edible there, and lay down in the shade.

After the White House briefing with President Ferguson the previous evening, Jayne had caught up on some sleep at a hotel near to Dulles Airport before taking a morning flight to Portland, where Joe had met her, having returned from DC the previous day.

It was good to be back home.

Jayne took a sip from her wine glass.

"Is there any update on the woman who killed Merriden, and the illegal at Glen Canyon?" Joe asked.

"They're both under police or FBI guard in the hospital," Jayne said. As always, she had mixed feelings, including guilty ones, after being put in a situation where she had to pull the trigger on someone. Over the years, she had come to terms with it and saw it as simply part of the job, but she still always found the aftermath the hardest part.

"They'll recover, though?" Joe asked.

"They'll be okay. I assume they'll be charged as soon as possible and will face trial. I'm not so worried about the illegal, Volker, or Spassky, whatever his name is. It's the woman I hit, Leonova, who bothers me more. She's a serious professional. I'd like to see her in prison for a long time. I mean, never mind what you think of Merriden—the fact is she's murdered a US citizen in cold blood in his own home. And she tried, and failed, to take me down multiple times. But my worry is that when she's recovered, the US ends up sending her back to Russia in some kind of prisoner swap. She's going to be like a wounded bull looking for revenge if that happens."

Joe shrugged. "That's likely to be some time down the line, if it happens at all. I wouldn't worry about that."

Jayne inclined her head. "We'll see. I hope you're right. Something tells me it won't be long before we see the next Russian operation against Ukraine and the West. They're upping the ante each time. Not sure where it's going to end."

She leaned back in her chair, closed her eyes for a few moments, and tried to think of family rather than Russia, and to bring herself back to the present.

Joe's children, Carrie and Peter, were back home for summer vacation from their studies at Boston University, which was also their father's old college. Jayne knew that Joe secretly took pride in the fact they had both made that choice, although he often teased them about it.

Both of his kids were out working their vacation jobs this afternoon, but Jayne found herself looking forward to seeing them later when they returned home. They were always full of amusing stories, in Carrie's case about the eccentric customers she served at the coffee shop, and in Peter's about some of the clients at the gym where he helped out.

"It's the contrast between operational life and the cooldown afterward that always hits me," Jayne said. "One minute pumped full of adrenaline, working on the edge, knowing that one wrong move could be my last. Then this, sitting in the sun with wine in hand."

She raised her near-empty glass toward Joe, who gave a slightly wry smile in response.

"Tell me about it," he said. "It's the same every time, and hard to decide which is the normal. But you're right, it's the contrast that always gets you. The trick is not to get addicted to the adrenaline."

He picked up the bottle from the table.

Jayne grinned. "Well, that wine is definitely helping to dilute it."

She held out her glass for a refill.

"You've still got it, haven't you?" Joe said as he poured. He looked up at her and winked. "You really have."

"Just about still got it, yes. Though sometimes I do wonder quite how."

They both laughed.

* * *

THE NEXT BOOK

If you're a member of my **Readers Group** I will email and inform you as soon the next book in the Jayne Robinson series, book six, is ready for pre-order. To join the group, just use the link below and you'll get a free ebook copy of *The Afghan*, the prequel to the Jayne Robinson and Joe Johnson series. (If you've already read it or don't want the ebook, just ignore the email you'll receive containing the book file).

https://bookhip.com/RJGFPAW

If you like **paperbacks or hardcovers**, you can buy copies of all of my books at my website shop. They make good gifts! I can deliver to anywhere in the US and UK, although not currently other countries. That may change in the future. You will find generous discounts if you are buying multiple books or series bundles, which makes them significantly cheaper than using Amazon. Buying your paperbacks this way also means I do not have to give Amazon their usual large portion of the sale price—so it helps me as well as you. Go to:

https://www.andrewturpin.com/shop/

* * *

ANDREW'S READERS GROUP

If you enjoyed this book, I would like to keep in touch. This is not always easy, as I usually only publish a couple of books a year and there are many authors and books out there. So the best way is for you to be on my Readers Group email list. I can then send you updates on the next book, plus occasional special offers. There's no spam and you can unsubscribe at any time.

If you would like to join my Readers Group and receive the email updates, I will send you, **FREE**, the ebook version of another thriller, *The Afghan*, which forms a prequel to both the **Jayne Robinson** series and my **Joe Johnson** series and normally sells at $4.99/£3.99 (paperback $11.99/£9.99).

The Afghan is set in 1988 when Jayne was with Britain's Secret Intelligence Service and Joe Johnson was with the CIA —both of them based in Pakistan and Afghanistan. Most of the action takes place in Afghanistan, then occupied by the Soviet Union, and in Washington, DC. Some of the characters and story lines that emerge in my other books have their roots in this period. I think you will enjoy it!

The Afghan can be downloaded **FREE** from the following link:

https://bookhip.com/RJGFPAW

The **Jayne Robinson** thriller series so far comprises the following:

1. The Kremlin's Vote
2. The Dark Shah
3. The Confessor
4. The Queen's Pawn
5. The Dam Keeper

If you have enjoyed the Robinson series, you will probably also like the **Joe Johnson series**, if you haven't read them yet. In order, they are as follows:

Prequel: *The Afghan*
1. The Last Nazi
2. The Old Bridge
3. Bandit Country
4. Stalin's Final Sting
5. The Nazi's Son
6. The Black Sea

To find my books on Amazon just type "Andrew Turpin" in the search box at the top of the Amazon page — you can't miss them!

* * *

IF YOU ENJOYED THIS BOOK PLEASE WRITE A REVIEW

I find that honest reviews of my books are the most powerful way for me to bring them to the attention of other potential readers.

Therefore, if you enjoyed reading this novel, then I would very much appreciate it if you would spend five minutes and leave a review—which can be as short as you like.

You can find the book on the Amazon website by typing "Andrew Turpin The Queen's Pawn" in the search box.

Once you have clicked on the page, scroll down to "Customer Reviews," then click on "Leave a Review."

Reviews are also a great encouragement to me to write more!

Many thanks.

THANKS AND ACKNOWLEDGEMENTS

I would like to thank everyone who reads my books. You are the reason I began to write in the first place, and I hope I can provide you with entertainment and interest for a long time into the future.

Every time I get an encouraging email from a reader, or a positive comment on my Facebook page, or a nice review on Amazon, it spurs me on to press ahead with my research and writing for the next book. So keep them coming!

Specifically with regard to **The Dam Keeper**, there are several people who have helped me during the long process of research, writing, and editing.

In particular, I have two editors who consistently provide helpful advice, food for thought, great ideas, and constructive criticism, and between them have enabled me to considerably improve the initial draft. Jaime Brockway, of Refine Editing (and also owner of Pristine Editing), gave me a lot of valuable feedback at the structural and line levels, and Jon Ford, as ever, helped me to maintain the authenticity of the story in many areas through his great eye for detail. I would like to thank both of them—the responsibility for any remaining mistakes lies solely with me.

As always, my brother, Adrian Turpin, was a very helpful reader of my early drafts and highlighted areas where I need to improve. I also had very valuable input from my small but dedicated Advance Readers Group team, who went through the final version prior to proofreading and also highlighted a number of issues that required changes and improvements—a big thank-you to them all.

I would also like to thank the team at Damonza for what I think is another great cover design.

AUTHOR'S NOTE

Dams, and the immense volume and power of the water they hold back, the electricity their associated hydro generation plant can produce, and the rivers they block, have long captured the imagination of film and documentary makers and writers everywhere—partly because of the potential for disaster, too.

Dams have certainly been very much in the news over the last few years, notably in Ukraine, where in June 2023 Russia destroyed the Kakhovka Dam on the Dnipro River, with the loss of at least fifty lives, as part of its on-going occupation of and war with Ukraine. There was also the devastating Derna dam collapses in September 2023 in Libya, with an estimated 18,000 deaths.

It was the speculation that Russia might attack Ukraine's dams, and then the actual attack on the Kakhovka Dam, that partly inspired my plot in **The Dam Keeper**. There are seven large hydroelectric dams on the legendary Dnipro River, which winds its way through Ukraine to the Black Sea. Most of them have been actual or potential targets for Russian troops, saboteurs, and missile attacks since Russia invaded Ukraine in February 2022, and this gave me the germ of an idea.

Incidentally, I have throughout my book chosen to use the term "Dnipro River," which is the Ukrainian form of the name. Prior to the Russian invasion, the term "Dnicper River" was more widely used, which is the Russian variant. The river actually rises near Smolensk, Russia, and flows about 1,400 miles through Belarus en route to Ukraine.

But I remember being fascinated by dams long before the Ukraine-Russia conflict. As a youngster growing up in Grantham, Lincolnshire, here in the UK, the story of the

Dambusters was the stuff of local legend. The Dambusters was the nickname given to Royal Air Force's 617 Squadron, a bomber unit. During World War II, 617 Squadron, based at RAF Scampton in Lincolnshire, succeeded in destroying the Möhne and Edersee dams in Germany, and damaging the Sorpe. Their aircraft of choice was the famous Lancaster bomber.

Operation Chastise, the codename given to the Dambusters mission, was based out of St Vincent's Hall, a mansion house in Grantham. We used to drive very near to it every day en route to and from school. My father had a copy of a book by Paul Brickhill, entitled The Dambusters (published in 1951), which told the story of those raids and which I read as a teenager. I still have the book at home, together with a copy of the film that was based on the book.

So I knew that my idea for a spy thriller based around the theme of dams, and the potential threats to them, had good potential. It set me off down my usual creative road—the "What if?" highway.

I hope that you have enjoyed the end result.

I should point out that, although built around a factual backdrop, my plot and the characters within it are purely fictional. Any resemblance to real-life events and people is entirely coincidental. On the occasions where I have described real life places and organizations, I have done so in an entirely fictional manner. This includes the depiction of the Russian president, whose character and actions as portrayed in this book stem from my imagination.

In particular, there is no suggestion that there is actually a corrupt commander of the US Army Corps of Engineers, and certainly not one codenamed the DAM KEEPER by the Russians, as far as I am aware. Similarly, to be the best of my knowledge, members of the USACE, based in Wiesbaden, near Frankfurt, are not leaking information about their activities in Ukraine to Moscow. Nor did USACE employees, as far as I am aware, take bribes from Russian intelligence officers to allow Russian troops and weaponry through to attack ethnic Georgians during the conflict in 2008—that was purely a fictional device to accommodate my plot.

Regular visitors to Frankfurt who frequent a certain cocktail bar in Elbestrasse, named the Kinly Bar, might recognize some of my descriptions of the "Himmel Bar" which I have placed in the same street. However, I would not like to suggest it is a hunting ground for Russian femme fatales who are looking for victims to fall into their honeytraps. Equally, I have no idea whether they have surveillance cameras on the premises or not.

I would like to apologize to the owners of the Marina Wien, the marina in Vienna, for "blowing up" a river cruiser on their property. I'm certain that under normal circumstances, it is a very safe location for boat owners to moor their craft.

The properties in Ballantrae Farm Drive, McLean, Virginia, are mostly upmarket and well-appointed. If my fictional house in that street, belonging to Frank Merriden, bears any resemblance to the real ones, that is purely coincidental and accidental. Hopefully there will be no deadly, heavily armed GRU operatives visiting the actual properties and the owners can sleep safely at night.

Also, I am certain that security measures in place at the enormous landmark dams in the United States, such as the Hoover and Glen Canyon, are such that any terrorist would have very little chance of actually blowing one up—although in theory, it could happen. I let my imagination run, somewhat, in describing how Jakub Volker was able to place his ammonium nitrate explosive in the network of tunnels that run through Glen Canyon, although the tunnels very much do exist. Apologies to the Bureau of Reclamation, the federal government agency which is part of the Department of the Interior and which owns Glen Canyon and the Hoover dams among about 340 dams across the country.

For details of further reading relating to the plot of **The Dam Keeper**, see the next section, which covers some of the sources I used during my research prior to and during the writing of this book.

Finally, the production of this book during 2023 has been a particular challenge given that I very sadly and very unexpectedly lost my wife, Jacqui, during December 2022. It has been a difficult year indeed for me and our two adult children. The research, plotting, and writing of a thriller of this complexity is tough enough at the best of times, so I am proud that I managed to complete it on time. I hope you enjoy the end result.

All the best,

Andrew

St Albans, November 2023

RESEARCH AND BIBLIOGRAPHY

Within hours of Russia launching its invasion of Ukraine on February 24, 2022, President Putin's troops made an unsuccessful attempt to seize the Kyiv hydroelectric dam on the Dnipro River very near the country's capital.

A couple of days later, Ukraine's air defenses shot down a Russian missile that was targeted at the same dam.

The Kyiv dam, built in 1964 at Vyshhorod, about nine miles upriver from the capital city, created a reservoir 68 miles long and containing 264 billion gallons of water.

If that dam had been breached, it would have sent a tidal wave down the Dnipro River, likely resulting in the destruction of other dams and flooding much of Kyiv itself. There would certainly have been a huge loss of life.

It struck me that here was a potential theme for one of Jayne Robinson's investigations, a train of thought that evolved gradually over the following months. By the final quarter of 2022, when I began to plot out the book, I was increasingly convinced that I could create a story that would hopefully be entertaining, but also perhaps educational.

Although those early Russian assaults on the Kyiv dam were foiled, the speculation about further Russian attacks on the cascade of seven hydroelectric dams along the Ukraine section of the Dnipro continued. It seemed inevitable that at some point, one of them would succeed.

Sure enough, in June 2023, the Kakhovka hydroelectric dam, much farther downstream in Kherson province, was blown up. This hardly came as a surprise: many months earlier, in October 2022, the Ukraine president Volodymyr Zelensky had warned of evidence that Russia had planted mines in the dam and was planning to destroy it at some point.

It was just the latest instance of weaponizing water—a military strategy that has been deployed almost since time began.

Indeed, Ukraine itself has used a similar strategy against Russia following its invasion and occupation of Crimea in 2014. Almost immediately after that invasion Ukraine dammed the North Crimean Canal, cutting off the flow of water from the Dnipro River to Crimea—which previously provided about 85 percent of water for the peninsula's 2.4 million inhabitants. Of course, after the 2022 invasion of Ukraine, Russia immediately removed the dam and restored flows of water along the canal to Crimea. This situation, too, features in *The Dam Keeper*.

There are good accounts of the Ukraine-Russia water wars in several places, and indeed broader articles about how water assets have been systematically targeted as part of a wider strategy during military conflicts.

A good starting point is "Water as weapon, and casualty, in Russia's war on Ukraine," in the Bulletin of the Atomic Scientists in October 2022. You can find it here: https://thebulletin. org/2022/10/water-as-weapon-and-casualty-in-russias-war-on-ukraine/

Politico magazine carries an interesting piece on the same subject, "Russia's war on water in Ukraine," at: https://www. politico.eu/article/russias-war-on-water-in-ukraine/

H2O Global News has an interesting article, "Russia's Hidden Water War in Ukraine," at: https://h2oglobalnews. com/russias-hidden-water-war-in-ukraine/

International Rivers magazine also has a good analysis, "Weaponising water — Ukraine's dams are targets in Putin's war," that can be found at: https://www.internationalrivers. org/news/weaponising-water-ukraines-dams-are-targets-in-putins-war/

I refer in several places in The Dam Keeper to covert

work done by the CIA to help Ukraine's military and intelligence services prepare for a conflict with Russia. There is a good account of some aspects of that program in Yahoo! News, "Secret CIA training program in Ukraine helped Kyiv prepare for Russian invasion,", found at: https://news.yahoo.com/exclusive-secret-cia-training-program-in-ukraine-helped-kyiv-prepare-for-russian-invasion-090052743.html

The US Army and other countries' military have been involved in training, equipping, and otherwise assisting Ukraine's armed forces since 2015. See: https://www.7atc.army.mil/JMTGU/

A key building block of my plot in **The Dam Keeper** is the role played in Ukraine by the United States Army Corps of Engineers (USACE). The USACE's Europe District, based in Wiesbaden, Germany, has indeed carried out substantial work for the Ukraine government, notably on the Dnipro River and its cascade of dams and locks. In 2016, it conducted an assessment of work needed, particularly on the locks, in order for commercial and other river users to be able to continue reliably using the waterway to transport goods and materials.

The report can be found here: https://mtu.gov.ua/files/USACEreport.pdf

There is also a Powerpoint slide presentation on the findings here: https://operations.erdc.dren.mil/nav/17febimts/01%20-%20BEHRENS_%20Improving%20the%20Dnipro%20Waterway.pdf

I thoroughly enjoyed researching President Putin's palace at Cape Idokopas, on Russia's Black Sea coast north of Sochi. It is a remarkable complex, and notable not least for the lengths to which he has gone to try to conceal his ownership of it.

However, opposition figures in Russia, as well as many other journalists, have gone to considerable lengths to uncover the truth. Among them is Kremlin critic Alexei Navalny, currently serving a prison term in Russia for his activities as a dissident. He has produced a report and a film that contains incredible detail about the palace and its contents.

You can find the report here: https://palace.navalny.com/

And the video can be found here on YouTube: https://www.youtube.com/watch?v=ipAnwilMncI

There is another good article about the palace in The Drive, which you can find here: https://www.thedrive.com/the-war-zone/38876/putin-has-created-the-ultimate-bond-villain-lair

Given the prevalence of drones of all shapes and sizes over recent years, it is hardly surprising that much work has been done to develop passenger drones, sometimes known as Unmanned Aerial Vehicles, or UAVs. Clearly, such vehicles have military and espionage uses, and it is these that provided me with the blueprint for the drone that was used to exfiltrate Jayne, Neal, and Aidan Scarpa out of Russia.

Here are details of one passenger drone, in C4ISRNET: https://www.c4isrnet.com/unmanned/2019/08/08/this-flying-taxi-drone-could-inspire-new-technicals/

Here's another article in Forbes magazine which shows six different passenger drone projects across the world: https://www.forbes.com/sites/bernardmarr/2018/03/26/6-amazing-passenger-drone-projects-everyone-should-know-about/?sh=6f22513e4ceb

My depiction of Anke Leonova in The Dam Keeper is largely a product of my imagination. However, "State School 4," at Kazan, where she was trained, did exist, according to some former CIA officers, including Jason Matthews. He subsequently wrote an excellent spy thriller, *Red Sparrow*, which featured a fictional graduate of that school.

Apart from that, there is a long factual history of intelligence services, particularly Russian ones, making use of honeytraps in order to recruit certain individuals and obtain highly classified information. A flavor of these can be found on Wikipedia's "Sexpionage" page at: https://en.wikipedia.org/wiki/Sexpionage

The revelation of the DAM KEEPER's identity as Frank Merriden came about chiefly because of Joe Johnson's fictional involvement with members of a US Army Corps of Engineers project to build a new $2.4 million border crossing station at Kazbegi, on the Georgia border with Russia. The only true part about my storyline is that the USACE actually did build the border crossing station there between 2005-2009. For details see: https://www.army.mil/article/28042/corps_of_engineers_finishes_5_year_project_only_crossing_between_georgia_russia

The chapters about the attempt by Russian "illegal" operative Jakub Volker to blow up Glen Canyon dam required some substantial research. For those interested in the construction and operation of dams, there is a detailed set of original plans, dating back to the 1960s, available at: http://www.riversimulator.org/Resources/USBR/GCDtechnicalData.pdf

The plans show the intricate network of tunnels inside the dam, required for maintenance purposes, along with a massively detailed account of how Glen Canyon was constructed. It is fascinating material.

A more user-friendly option is available in the form of a couple of YouTube videos of an internal tour of Glen Canyon Dam.

The first is available at: https://www.youtube.com/watch?v=qfmBiyO23Cc

And the second is at: https://www.youtube.com/watch?v=iZW71ot-9WM

I hope these sources give you a taste of some of the material I drew on while writing *__The Dam Keeper__*. Half of the fun of piecing the plot together lies in the research and determining whether plot lines are credible in real life or not. I try to make them as credible as I can, albeit with some creative license to allow for the fact that I'm writing fiction, rather than a factual story.

There were, of course, many more sources on which I drew, too numerous to mention. I hope it is helpful—I am quite willing to exchange emails if readers have questions about any others not detailed here or if you spot something that you think should be corrected.

ABOUT THE AUTHOR AND CONTACT DETAILS

I have always had a love of writing and a passion for reading good thrillers. I also had a long-standing dream of writing my own novels, and eventually, I got around to achieving that objective.

The Dam Keeper is the fifth in the **Jayne Robinson** series of thrillers, which follows on from my **Joe Johnson** series (currently comprising six books plus a prequel). These books pull together some of my other interests, particularly history, world news, and travel.

I studied history at Loughborough University and worked for many years as a business and financial journalist before becoming a corporate and financial communications adviser with several large energy companies, specializing in media relations. I am now a full-time writer.

Originally, I came from Grantham, Lincolnshire, and I now live with my family in St. Albans, Hertfordshire, UK.

You can connect with me via these routes:

E-mail: andrew@andrewturpin.com

Website: www.andrewturpin.com.

Facebook: @AndrewTurpinAuthor

Facebook Readers Group: https://www.facebook.com/groups/1202837536552219

Twitter: @AndrewTurpin

Instagram: @andrewturpin.author

Please also follow me on Amazon, then you will automatically get updates from them on when the next book is published.

https://www.amazon.com/Andrew-Turpin/e/B074V87WWL/

Do get in touch with your comments and views on the books, or anything else for that matter. I enjoy hearing from readers and promise to reply.

Made in the USA
Las Vegas, NV
09 December 2023

82342777R00260